Jerilyn,
So nice to
Hope you enjoy
books. God b'
Elaine

Twelve Days 'til Christmas

Ema Jane

PublishAmerica
Baltimore

ISBN: 1-60836-938-2
PUBLISHED BY PUBLISHAMERICA, LLLP
www.publishamerica.com
Baltimore

Printed in the United States of America

For all the lost, missing & exploited children out there—
may God be with you; may you find your way home.

Ema Jane

Dedicated to:
Stella Mae MacArthur-Hartin

In loving memory of:
Auril L. "Bud" Hartin
April 24, 1934—October 7, 2003

Thanks for a *lifetime* of happy memories!
I love you both very, very much!

Miracles:
December 13th—A *smile*
December 14th—*Laughter*
December 15th—*Friendship*
December 16th—*Hope*
December 17th—*Compassion*
December 18th—*Trust*
December 19th—*Wishes* & *wants*
December 20th—*Shining star*
December 21st—*Letting go*
December 22nd—*Love*
December 23rd—*Giving*
December 24th—*Christmas story*

Luke 2: 7 "And she brought forth her firstborn son,
and wrapped him in swaddling clothes, and laid him in a
manger; because there was no room for them in the inn."

Look for Ema Jane's first book in this trilogy…
"Devoted Love Sweet Revenge"
ProteaPublishing.com
Amazon.com

Prologue

December 10th, present day...

MERRY BETH WATERS quickly glanced over her right shoulder, at her five-year-old daughter strapped safely in her car seat in the back seat, and smiled. Hope Bethany was a lovely child with beautiful, soft green eyes and thick, fiery red curls down her back. She generally had her hair in a long braid and today was no exception. She was a Christmas baby and like her father, who'd died before she was born, was warm, softhearted, kind, loving, gentle, quiet and usually smiling and happy.

"Just think baby—next Friday will be the last day of day-care until after the New Year. Then mommy will have two whole weeks off from teaching my class, and tomorrow we're going Christmas shopping and decorating our tree! Are you excited, baby?" Merry Beth asked with a smile, as she turned up the radio as Elvis started to sing "*Blue Christmas.*"

"And I get to put our spe'caall bright star on top, right Mommy? Let's sing "*The Twelve Days of Cris'mas*"—you know it's my fav'rit." Bethany looked at her mother with love and happiness and trust, as any five-year-old would, with huge and excited, happy and trusting glossy eyes.

"The star is *your* job. All right, let's sing, you go first." Merry Beth's hands tightened on the red steering wheel of her father's old '69 Chevy, as the back tires hit a spot of black ice. She glanced at the speedometer, frowned and eased up on the gas accelerator and smiled when she slowed to a safer twenty miles an hour.

Sweat broke out on her forehead and hands, and she frowned as she stared ahead at the thick, falling snow and icy snow-packed roads, thinking... *Easy, take it nice and slow—you've ridden on roads like this your entire life. You can do this. Man, oh man—where did this storm come from so fast? Just breathe—that's it... breathe in, breathe out. You can do this. Dear Lord, give me courage...*

"On the first'deded day of Cris'mas, my true love gave'deded to me—a par'tig in a pear tree," Bethany sang at the top of her voice, swallowing against the giggles in her throat.

Christmas—it was a time for joy, singing, worshiping God's Son who'd come to earth so long ago in a Bethlehem manger, mistletoe and hoped-for world peace, family gatherings, turkey, tinsel, cranberry and pine, decorated tree and giving gifts; a time for singing carols and laugher.

As the car straightened Merry Beth chuckled lightly at her daughter's singing voice before continuing the song; her daughter always left out certain letters and divided most words in two. "On the second day of Christmas, my true love gave to me—two turtle doves, and a partridge in a pear tree!"

Merry Beth and Bethany were true Yankee's, both born and raised in the little town of Winterville, Maine—just south from Eagle Lake, off Route 1 North, about thirty miles to the Canadian border off the Saint John River. The road ahead seemed like endless miles of nothing but white Maine wilderness with this latest winter storm. Even the tall pine and white birch were covered in a thick blanket of white. Again, Merry Beth smiled. She loved Maine and wouldn't ever consider living anywhere else. Maine was home.

To her, Maine was quiet, peaceful and safe—compared to the major cities all across America. She knew she wouldn't ever want to raise her daughter anyplace else. They were on their own now, with both sets of Merry Beth's grandparents dead and gone. Merry Beth's mother had died from breast cancer when she was just Bethany's age, and her father had passed away from a freak boating accident just three months ago on September the third. They missed him terribly.

"I love to hear you sing, baby. You have a beautiful singing voice," Merry Beth said while holding the wheel tighter.

"Mommy, I made'deded you sum'ting real spe'caall in day care today! My t'churr help'deded me. It has gold and silver glitter on it, and I paze'teded a shiny yell'ooo star on it! I fix'deded it so we can hang it on our tree, Mommy." The little girl smiled at her mother as she reached for her book bag with Tweety-bird on the front to find the special tree ornament.

"My t'churr said'deded it was sooooooo pree'ttiee."

Merry Beth loved the snow, the icicles hanging from just about every rooftop, the Chickadees song while searching for food in the cold and snowy tall pine trees. She loved the lights of every color adorning the houses she passed, in the windows and doorways, the sweet-smelling pine wreaths on just about every door decorated with red and green bows and pine cones, the children laughing as they played happily in the snow building angels and snowmen, the stores decorated with holly and pine and mistletoe and blinking lights.

"Mommy! Look! It's snooo-ing! Isn't it pree'ttiee, Mommy?" Bethany giggled with huge watchful eyes as she watched in awe and excitement out her side window.

"Yes, baby—it is." Merry Beth's heart pounded with a slight taste of fear as the back tires started to slide on the icy road once more. "We're almost home, honey. About five more miles to go and then you can help me make some Christmas cookies after supper—how's that sound? Some chocolate chip ones!"

Bethany's eyes lit up with excitement. "Can I sp'inkle the little red dots on top? I'll save one for Lisa, Mommy. She loves cookies!"

"Yes, baby—you can." A snow plow passed her going the other way as Merry Beth reached over and turned up the defroster a few notches thinking, *Come on, Merry Beth—just a few more miles and we'll be safely home. Take it nice and slow. Why hasn't the plow dropped dirt and plowed on my side yet?*

She noticed the huge yellow 'M' ahead and smiled. Traffic was light, yet the parking lot to the fast food restaurant was packed. *McDonald's! Yes! Good idea—let's stop there for supper. We deserve a treat—maybe later the roads will be clearer.*

She kept her eyes ahead at the huge yellow 'M' in the distance across the street from the bank, the IGA, and the Irsing Truck Stop, and smiled despite the thundering in her chest and ears and tight grip on the steering wheel. She knew Maine weather and knew storms could blow right out of nowhere in a matter of minutes. When the weather report called for inches of snow, sometimes you received a foot or more. The weather in Maine could change quicker than a bat of an eyelash.

Holly leaves and beautiful, snowy pine trees were covered with ice as Merry Beth worked her way slowly through the strong and raging winter storm towards home. *Just a few more feet to go—you can make it—nice and slow now…*

Bethany continued with her singing, unaware of slippery roads and dangerous curves in the road ahead. "On the third day of Cris'mas, my true love gave'deded to me—three French hens, two turr'lle doves and a par'tig in a pear tree." She giggled and glanced at her mother and asked, "Mommy—tell'deded me one more time what a par'tig is!"

Merry Beth smiled. Her daughter was the pride of her life. She couldn't imagine her life without her. "It's a small European game bird, baby; another one of God's creatures."

"What kind'deded of game do they play, Mommy? Do they like to play Jacks and Hopscotch?"

"I'm sure they do, baby." Merry Beth frowned with worry and another touch of fear tiptoed up her spine, as her tires started to slide once more. *Pull over, Merry Beth—McDonalds is just ahead. Thank you Ronald McDonald! A Big Mac and hot coffee sounds real good about now!*

"Mommy! Look! There's ic'Don'llds—can we stop, Mommy?" Bethany clapped her hands in excitement.

Merry Beth shook her head yes with another smile across her face as she put on her right blinker. There was a shiny light-blue BMW behind her and she thought he'd followed much too close the last few miles. She hit her brake easily so he'd back off, he did, thankful that her car didn't spin or slide on ice again.

"Yes, lets—I'm starving! You've been such a good girl you can have your favorite ice cream for dessert after your Happy Meal. I wonder what the prize is this week."

"We didn't finish our song, Mommy!"

"We'll finish it later after we eat, baby. On the rest of our way home," Merry Beth lightly promised. *Hopefully by then all the roads will be plowed and sanded and a little safer...*

"O'kay, Mommy."

Just as Merry Beth hit her brake to enter the crowded McDonald's parking lot, a black Ford pickup truck came out of nowhere and broad-sided her driver's side door. It hit her with so much force that her father's cherished car crumpled and cracked, and spun into a complete one-eighty degree turn in front of the huge McDonald's yellow 'M' sign.

Merry Beth screamed as terror bore down on her and her daughter. Everything around her seemed to turn black, black and icy cold. Suddenly, all thoughts of Christmas and singing, shopping and eating out disappeared as the *Death Angel* appeared. His name was George and he was silent and close by Merry Beth's side, but she didn't see him sitting there or feel his touch on her right arm.

The windshield broke and shattered into tiny pieces all over Merry Beth's face and eyes. "Close your eyes baby!" she cried out as deep, penetrating pain sliced silently inside her skull as the left side of her face hit the side window, just before it also shattered. It seemed an eternity before all noise around them stopped and blessed silence hovered over them, but it was only seconds, five earth-shattering seconds that would change Merry Beth's life forever.

The smell of burning brakes mixed and mingled with the strong odor of gasoline in Merry Beth's nostrils, as fluffy white snowflakes fell heavily all around her. White pain, hot as lava, slashed across her chest and left arm. She screamed her daughter's name before blackness snatched her away into the blessed world of unconsciousness, safety and blessed quiet and release.

Tears burned Bethany's eyes. "Mommy, I'm scared!"

Her daughter's sweet voice reached her ears as she drifted slowly away. "Bethany…hold on, baby…don't be scared because Mommy's right here…and I…won't leave…you!"

It seemed that that was easier said than done, as she walked towards the thick white fog, as if in slow motion; it seemed in her mind. Were her feet touching the ground? When she saw the bright light just ahead and heard the beautiful singing in the distance, Merry Beth knew in her pounding heart her life on earth was over, and prayed silently to God to keep her baby girl safe from harm, hurt and pain without her on earth.

On earth, the handsome yet unseen and unheard *Death Angel* lingered near the horrifying, fatal accident scene. He was watching, listening and praying as paramedics carefully lifted Merry Beth's lifeless, unconscious, bruised and bloody body from the snow on to a stretcher, and up into the back of an ambulance fifteen minutes later.

Bethany, frightened beyond what her five-year-old mind could comprehend, sobbed for her mother the entire way to the hospital in a stranger's arms, safe from all harm and the storm that raged out of control around them.

He tried, the very best he could, to calm and soothe away Bethany's childlike fears through his own. But no matter what he said or did, he couldn't seem to allay her fears and tears and cries for her bloody and dying mother.

* * * * *

As Merry Beth continued to slowly walk towards the bright light she said to her daughter, thinking she was right beside her, "Oh, Hope Bethany—look! Look at the pretty bright light. Oh, there's your daddy…and the angels! Oh, look, I think I see Jesus! Is that Him? He's standing by the pretty gate made of Pearl…oh, my goodness—it's so pretty, baby…now, I don't want you to be scared. Everything is going to be all right…"

Merry Beth turned back to reach for her daughter's little hand, and stopped dead in her steps. Her daughter hadn't answered and was nowhere behind her or by her side. She wasn't following her, answering her or looking up at her with those pretty and sweet, trusting eyes like she always did. That was odd—where in the world was she?

Despite the bright and welcoming and soothing light that seemed to be quietly calling out her name to continue her journey towards peace, straight ahead, icy panic set in across her thundering heart. Where was Hope Bethany?

She didn't want to leave her young daughter behind, alone in the world without her, and tears burned her eyes as she cried out with a racing heart, "Hope Bethany—where are you? Come to Mommy, baby. Come to Mommy…*right now!* I mean it, Hope Bethany—where are you? This isn't funny—not one little bit!"

Chapter One

Matthew 1:18-19 "Now the birth of Jesus Christ was on this wise: When as his mother Mary was espoused to Joseph, before they came together, she was found with child of the Holy Ghost. Then Joseph her husband, being a just *man*, and not willing to make her a public example, was minded to put her away privily."

Winterville Regional Hospital E.R.—let the miracles begin...

THERE WERE NO soft words or touches in his life, no more smiles or laughter, cheer or glee. There was only loneliness, constant pain—the anguished and physical kind, and darkness. And after almost three years he doubted any of it would ever go away. They were as constant and as real to him as breathing. This was his life now, since losing his family.

He sensed that God, Christmas and angels were far, far away as well—like a sad, forgotten dream or lost faith, and any past occurrences of golden ringing Christmas bells in his world now remained still and silent. He knew the taste of tears, and wondered if God's grace would ever save him from this constant feeling of slowly drowning.

Baron paced nervously back and forth, back and forth in the little emergency room lobby with a worried frown across his brow, and a troubled, racing heart. He didn't want to be here, and didn't want to be involved with the woman and child in the terrible car accident in front of McDonald's. He wanted to remain safely tucked away in his own world of isolation and quiet aloneness.

He was sure someone had brought him to the very spot where he now stood waiting for word on the injured woman and her scared child. Was it God's hand that led his every step, even though he hadn't prayed in years? He seriously doubted it. God wasn't a part of his life, not since He'd taken his family away.

At this moment in his life, he doubted God would even hear his prayer if he bothered to pray. His mother had often told him it was true when he was a young boy, but he'd lost that childlike faith. For some reason he felt drawn to the injured woman and the child, like a strong current yanking him under the powerful waves.

Were the woman's eyes the same color as the child? Where was her husband; he'd noticed the pretty rings on her left hand. Was her gaze as soft as her skin—like rose petals? He didn't like these questions and didn't even pretend to understand them, and it was hard to resist the strong urge to turn and flee.

He'd been right behind the beautiful, classic red Chevy and had watched in horror as the black truck hit it broadside, hard and fast. He'd been the one to call the accident in on his cellular. His fingers shook violently when he'd made the call. It was hard to swallow the bitter taste of past, dark memories as they flashed across his eyes as he ran towards the crumpled car. He couldn't help but think, at that moment, what a wonderful world it would be if every day could be like Christmas.

He knew the world didn't work that way. Had it ever? The way it used to be, before the accident that had changed *his* life forever, before the accident that had ripped apart *his* very world, before the accident that had torn apart *his* very soul and ripped his family from his arms in less than a heartbeat.

He'd been the first one at the scene earlier, and had pulled the frightened and crying child from the crumpled, twisted wreckage of what remained of the classic red car. He'd quickly placed the child in someone's arms, he didn't know who and, smelling gasoline, had immediately turned back to pull the injured woman from the crumpled mayhem and madness.

Blood, there was too much blood. He'd saved both mother and child, yet he didn't feel like a hero—as just seconds passed before the car literally exploded all around them, when a second car had come from out of nowhere and hit the crumpled red car from behind. He'd shielded the injured woman as best he could with his own body as fiery flames, hot and fierce, and shattering metal and glass exploded all over them, as the force from the explosion threw them face first into the tall snow-bank. Frantic McDonald's employees and other concerned motorists' and citizens came running to help after that.

Someone had placed the crying child back in his strong arms. They actually trembled as he'd held her sobbing body close to his beating chest. Surprisingly, to himself mostly, he'd whispered kind and reassuring soft words to the frightened child, hoping to calm her down. He'd held the child in his arms until the ambulance and police had arrived at the scene.

He'd known the young driver in the black pick-up was dead with just one glance. He hadn't missed the smell of the strong liquor in the chilly air; and the sight of empty beer cans and broken vodka liquor bottle lying shattered in the white snow near the third crumpled car left him feeling sick to his stomach, dizzy and nauseous; as past memories slithered close from the accident years' back.

He'd quickly pushed back the dark and familiar scene in his head from almost three years ago when a drunken driver had snatched away his wife of four years and seven months, along with their infant son, on a long ago Christmas Eve.

In exactly thirteen days it would be three years since that fateful night when his entire world had literally stopped turning. To remember back only brought silent screams inside his head, and black pain to his lonely, broken heart. To remember back only made the bitterness and now coldness in his angry heart and empty life all the more real. It crushed him, and like he was indeed drowning, tried to keep him under in that dark world of nothing but blackness and emptiness. He was alone; he liked alone.

He'd lost his family and there was nothing he could do to ever get them back. He shook his head, clearing his thoughts. There really was no sense to think back on those terrible, darkened, shadowy days after the accident now. Since the funeral he lived his life in limbo and inside a huge dark void—not feeling too much, not caring too much and ignoring the cold truth, trying desperately to find a reason to go on, trying desperately to find a purpose; a meaning for his life without his family.

And there was no way Becky and Baron Jr. would be home for Christmas. Not now, and not ever again. He'd spent every moment since the accident searching for the answer to the simple question, 'Why?' In his heart, did he blame God?

There had been nothing he could do for the pretty, young woman lying on a blanket in the snow in front of the tall, yellow 'M' in front of McDonald's. Where the blanket had come from, he had no clue. She'd been ghostly white and it was clear terribly wounded in the crash. There was blood dripping from her nose, and down her face from cuts and abrasions on her left temple and cheek and forehead. Her left arm hung at a funny angle; clearly it was broken. She'd been out cold, and he couldn't help but fear that the beautiful woman was near death, as someone carefully wiped the glass-chips and dripping blood from her eyes and nose with a handkerchief.

He knew she was married by the pretty gold-and-diamond wedding rings on her left hand. He didn't know her name but knew he wanted to, and that scared him beyond madness. He was a solitary man—a man who lived his life in solitude, seclusion, concealment, complete privacy and aloneness. He didn't *do* reaching out very well, and never planned to again.

He didn't want to be involved with this young woman and child. He'd distanced himself from family and friends since he'd lost his wife and infant son, and he wasn't about to let himself care again. No, to him life was always gray— just gray and empty now. The bright colors were gone, and to care again—well, the risk was too high, too deep. He just couldn't do it.

Green holly and tempting mistletoe didn't mean a thing when facing the Christmas holiday alone. Hot chocolate and Christmas cookies tasted like steel in his dry and scratchy throat when eating and drinking them alone in front of a warm yet chilly, lonely fire. Christmas hymns and carols seemed empty and void, barren and senseless to him when listening to them alone in his now cold, dark, unloved and empty house.

Shiny, blinking Christmas lights aglow of red, green, yellow and blue meant nothing to him without his wife and son's laughter to enjoy the festive, merry sight on houses, rooftops and trees; they only reminded him of how it used to be, and would never be again.

The bright red-and-silver stockings no longer hung in his house from his massive marble fireplace mantle. Even the wonderful Christmas story of baby Jesus' birth in Bethlehem so many years ago seemed to have lost its sparkle of hope and peace in his heart; it was true, he feared—he blamed God for his loss.

The beautiful yet unseen guardian angel that watched over Baron Michael Williams since he'd lost his family, constantly prayed for a miracle. If there was ever a man who needed one, he did; and time was indeed running out for him, he needed help and he needed it now! The light in his eyes was almost out, the sand almost out of his hourglass as well.

Baron glanced quickly up and stopped his nervous pacing when a nurse with pretty brown eyes, and soft shoulder-length brown hair walked towards him carrying the child in her arms. The little girl was asleep and he couldn't help but wince and flinch back as the nurse wearing a nametag that stated, 'LPN Annie Brackett' placed her in his arms with a careful flop and a huge, warm and caring smile.

"Your daughter is fine. She didn't get a scratch from the accident. Poor thing—she's so exhausted from crying for her mother that she cried herself right to sleep in my arms. The pediatrician on call tonight, Doctor Allan Jefferson, X-rayed your little girl to be sure there wasn't any broken or fractured bones; there is no apparent head or neck trauma…other than being exhausted from crying for her mother, she's fine." The pretty nurse smiled up at him as she reached out to gently touch the little girl's freckled right cheek.

He panicked and his rapid beating heart thundered in his ears. His throat felt scratchy and dry and he could barely speak. "No—there's s…some kind of m…mistake. I'm not…"

"You can go in now and sit with your wife. She hasn't opened her eyes yet, but has stabilized. You must be scared out of your mind out here by yourself. Come on, love—I'll show you where we've placed your wife." She lightly touched the sleeve on his black leather jacket on his right elbow, and led him through double knotty-pine sliding doors that simply stated, 'Merry Christmas—a season of hope and miracles!'

"Wait…you don't understand…I'm not…" he stammered.

"Don't be frightened from the tubes and wires and IV's. Your wife is badly bruised, and her clothes are bloody, but she's a very lucky woman. I'll clean her up and change her into a clean hospital gown. Come on, step closer…it's all right."

"Her i…injuries…?" Lord, help him. Was that *his* voice?

"Your wife has suffered a broken left arm and will be in a cast for at least eight weeks; she has a slight concussion—nothing to worry about there, except for keeping a close eye on her for dizziness and such, and she has cuts on her left temple and forehead which required stitches. She has tiny cuts all across her face which will heal nicely and probably not leave any scars. They'll heal in no time. She also has two cracked ribs on the left side, and tiny cuts across her hands. Other than the ribs, there aren't any other internal injuries…"

He sucked in his breath. "Stop, I don't…"

"She also has seatbelt bruising across her chest, but she's going to be fine, sir. I don't understand why you were waiting out there in the lobby. You could have come in here with your wife…" The pretty and experienced nurse seemed to explain all of it to him in one breath. He felt dizzy and slightly sick to his stomach.

Despite his hard-as-steel strength, hysteria was reborn inside his heart in seconds. He couldn't seem to find the right words to explain the sense of panic that waltzed back into his empty life, as the young nurse practically pushed him around the long blue-and-white curtain where the mother of the sleeping child he held in his arms lay unconscious, bloody and still ghostly white.

He wanted to tell the nurse that he wasn't her husband; that the precious child sleeping so soundly in his arms wasn't his daughter; that there had been some kind of terrible mistake, he wanted to scream the truth—the words wouldn't come. He felt like his tongue was trapped in his dry throat.

He stopped dead in his steps as he stared down at the woman lying so still and lifeless against the white hospital sheets. He winced and jerked back from the terrifying sight of cuts, blood and bruises, IV's and wires, monitors beeping and, God help him—he couldn't do this. He started to hyperventilate.

The nurse passed him a gold and diamond wedding ring and a stunning, expensive diamond engagement ring. He stared down at them in the palm of his right hand like they were burning his very skin. Dear God, he couldn't do this! Not again!

"You better take your wife's rings for safe keeping, sir. I took them off because of swelling. With the broken left arm her fingers are pretty swollen and will be for some time. I didn't want her rings to have to be cut off or lost in the shuffle around here." She noticed how he'd paled and hadn't said a word.

She lightly touched his leather jacket left sleeve. "She's really going to be all right, sir…I promise. The abrasions and stitches to her left temple and forehead look bad but…"

The rings felt like they weighed a ton in the palm of his hand. His eyes whirled back to the E.R. bed. The left side of her face looked like she'd been terribly beaten. Her right hand and wrist was bandaged with a thick, white dressing. Her left arm was in a cast. There were scrapes and cuts all across her forehead, cheeks and chin.

She was hooked up to so many tubes, wires, IV's and machines that he felt sick to his stomach from the sight of it; and swallowed against the threatening tears glistening across his dark lashes. Men like him didn't cry, not ever. Not once since the funeral almost three years ago, and he wasn't about to now.

The evidence from the shattered and broken driver's side window and front windshield was scattered all across her pale and bruised face. He closed his eyes against the terrible sight and turned away. To look at her only brought it all back. He couldn't face it again. He needed air. He couldn't breathe!

"Her right wrist is really swollen. It's not broken so…"

He raced from the E.R. room and lobby on legs he couldn't feel—leaving the wounded, bruised and broken woman alone. He couldn't look at her anymore. To do so only brought back the sight of his wife and son lying bloody, broken and dead on stretchers in the very same emergency room unit. They were forgotten to many, but never him. Would the physical pain ever go away so he could live at peace and ever breathe easier? He doubted it. His life was flying at a rapid pace past him, quickly out of his control, unreachable, because of that fact.

It wasn't until he was back outside standing near the huge, festooned, silver and gold decorated pine tree near the hospital sign that he even realized he still held the woman's sleeping child in his arms. He closed his eyes and lifted his face to the darkened night sky. There wasn't a star in sight. The thick snow from earlier on in the day had now turned to fluffy, tiny graceful flakes, just one or two here and there, and he tasted the snow on his tongue as it melted across his warm lips. It did little to ease his thundering, painful heart.

A snowplow passed by at that moment, dropping salt and dirt in its wake on Main Street. He dropped the beautiful rings in his leather jacket pocket, zipped it shut, and held on to the pretty little sleeping child, like she was indeed *his* lifeline. She weighed no less than a light feather in his massive arms. Her hair was orange-red and curly and long, her skin was freckled and soft—like a newborn baby kitten she seemed to purr and sleep in his arms, so trusting.

Why did the sleeping child have to be so beautiful? How old was she…five, six? What color were her eyes again? Blue, violet…oh yes, green—dark, like wet summer grass or sea-green emeralds. And her hair—he buried his left hand in its curly masses. It was as smooth and as soft as melted silk, curly and fiery red, thick like melted butter or whipped cream between his fingers.

To care again! *Oh, God in Heaven—why are you doing this to me?* To open up his broken heart again meant opening up old, unhealed wounds! *You are the One who took away my wife and son—my life!* To touch again! *Why dear God—why? Why my wife and my son on that fateful night? I don't understand it. I can't get past it—this terrible, crushing pain I always feel across the place where my heart used to be every time I see their faces! Help me, dear God—please, I'm begging You!* He didn't know why he cared anymore, but deep down where secrets are kept, he did. Deep inside he knew he wanted to live again!

To him—to smile and laugh again would mean he'd somehow forgotten his dead wife and son, and would betray their memory. It would mean that he'd gone on living without them. He couldn't do it. He hadn't smiled or laughed once in almost three years; he knew he was slowly dying inside because of that fact.

Although weary to the bone, he turned quickly back towards the emergency room entrance with a heavy and burdened heart, knowing he couldn't go on this way. He was drowning and needed help. Would the injured woman and her sleeping child become his lifeguard and pull him up from drowning?

In seconds he stood in front of the long emergency room registration desk and watched as the look of surprise flashed across Nurse Brackett's chocolate eyes from his words.

"This child is *not* my daughter, and that woman in there is *not* my wife!" He placed the sleeping child in her arms, turned and quickly walked away, leaving the nurse staring after him in shock and disbelief. In his heart he wasn't walking away—he was running and running fast. He couldn't breathe!

"But, of course they are! Hey, where are you going? Come back! Everything's going to be all right. You'll see. Please, come back!" Nurse Brackett stared down at the sleeping child in her arms through her own wall of tears and whispered, "Don't worry sweetie—everything's going to be all right. You'll see. Come on love—let's find a quiet place for you to sleep until your mommy wakes up, until your daddy comes back. He's just a little scared right now—shock does that to a person, but he'll be back. I promise. Don't be scared. I'll take care of you."

Two very different worlds had just collided because of one senseless accident. Merry Beth's was safe and happy, secure and strong, sober and diligent; yet lonely at times. Baron's was unsure and sad, questionable and weakened, unsteady and lethargic; lonely all the time. Would the two ultimate strangers be able to reach out to each other and help each other chase the unseen dangers that lingered close away, before it was too late for one, or both, of them?

As he sped from the snow-packed and icy E.R. parking lot in his BMW, Baron reached over and turned up the heater full blast. He doubted that he'd ever be warm again. Not in this lifetime. He took in huge breaths, trying hard to calm the pounding of his heart. Sweat broke out above his lip. His sweaty hands trembled on the wheel. White spots danced wildly in front of his tired eyes. He swallowed against the rising vomit in his dry throat. His entire body trembled from head to toe. Not from fear but from weariness. Merry Beth's pretty gold and diamond rings inside his jacket pocket were heavy, yet soon forgotten.

* * * * *

It was Friday, December the 11ᵗʰ—just short of 7:30 a.m. when Merry Beth slowly walked away from the bright light. She carefully and slowly opened her eyes. She didn't feel any pain, did she? She felt tired though, sore and very much out of sorts and confused. What happened? Where was she—a hospital? Was this Winterville Regional Hospital?

Her heart started to race fast in her chest. Something terrible had happened. What was it again? Where was she and where was her baby? Why did her arms and legs feel like they weighed a hundred pounds each? And why was it so quiet? And why was the room suddenly spinning wildly out of control like a colorful child's toy Top? She shook her head to clear it.

Why is my mind so fuzzy? Where am I? What is this place? Where's my baby? Hope Bethany…where are you, baby? Come to Mommy! Her eyes searched her surroundings and she winced from the terrible sight of tubes, wires, IV's and machines that she was hooked up to.

The hospital—why in the world am I in the hospital? She remembered the accident then, it came back to her like remembering a terrifying nightmare bit by bit, and she tried hard to swallow the sobs of hysteria rising quickly in her dry throat. Bethany—where was Bethany? Surely, she wasn't…dead?

She blinked against the sudden tears across her burning eyes and couldn't control them to hold them back, as they slowly fell down her pale and bruised cheeks; she swallowed the fear and uncertainty as if they were huge lumps in her scratchy throat and cried out, "*Help me…*"

The man who stepped from the shadows in her I.C. Unit closer to her hospital bed was a stranger. He was very tall, with broad shoulders and a *huge* chest. He seemed to be a giant-of-a-man. Who was he, friend or foe? From what she could see his hair was as black as burned coal, and she couldn't help but think he was well over-due for a haircut. His eyes, she couldn't quite see the color because he was too far away, and they and his face were shadowed by the impressive black Stetson he wore.

He was dark and mysterious looking, dressed in black from head to toe. From his silky black shirt and black leather jacket, to black jeans and black cowboy boots, he looked like—death. She winced at the thought and closed her burning eyes for a moment, feeling very much out of her depth and alone.

"My daughter…?" she could barely whisper. "Please…tell me…where is my…d…daughter…?"

"Your daughter is fine. She wasn't hurt in the accident."

Dear God, thank you! Her eyes lifted and met his and she whispered in a raspy voice, "Where—w…where is s…she?"

His voice was deep and husky; was it soothing, or should she be afraid? "She's safe," he answered quietly.

When she moved her head, razor-sharp pain snapped at her left temple like scorpion's claws and she closed her eyes against it, sucking in her breath.

19

Her thoughts made her dizzy. *Goodness—doesn't the man believe in wearing bright, sunny colors? What's with the morbid black? I, on the other hand, prefer bright cheery colors like red, yellow, pink and light blue.* She shook her head to clear away the cobwebs and dizziness. *My baby! Where is Bethany? Dear God, where is Bethany?*

"My daughter—she...is she *really* all right?" Merry Beth whispered before opening her eyes once more.

He slowly stepped closer and she winced. Everything he wore shouted money and mourning. And those eyes! They zeroed in on her like he was the bounty hunter and she was the found prized prey.

"Yes."

"Are you *sure?*"

"Your daughter is fine," he whispered huskily.

She sighed with blessed relief, believing him, and said as the rising panic took control of her senses, "Personally, I *hate* black. Even when my father died I wore a pretty *blue* dress. Why be sad? He's in Heaven with God now. So, what has *you* so rattled and s...sad? You look like s...someone died, or...something."

She cringed. What in the world had made her say these things to a complete stranger? Who was he and what did he want with her? Her heartbeat tripled and she fought hard to catch her breath, as the room began to spin all around her once more.

She heard his quick and sharp intake of breath, and listened to the sounds all around her—the beeping from one of the machines above her to the right, the nurses at the I.C.U. station outside her door laughing with friendly cheer, the ticking of the clock on the wall...she couldn't see a clock, was it above her head? And her beating heart—it wouldn't ease its fearful pounding.

The rest was silence, except for the soft, sweet promising Christmas music playing in the background from somewhere not too far away. The song that played soothed her doubts and fears in moments. She'd always loved this song, from when she was a child Bethany's age. She couldn't help but smile, the panic and hysteria falling away, now a thing of the past.

"Silent Night," she whispered softly, as the tears she fought against slipped through closed lashes.

"Excuse me?" his voice deep and rich and husky again.

"It's always been my husband's favorite Christmas song."

When she sucked in her breath again he asked, "Are you in pain?" He jerked back from the bed, heart racing, thinking, *What a stupid, pathetic question, Williams.*

Of course she's in pain—get a grip, for goodness sakes. Make sure she's going to be all right and then get your butt out of here. Now! And don't get pulled into this situation—just walk away. Let the missing husband come and soothe away her bruises, tears and fears. Let him be the one to comfort her and pull her into his arms. Let him be the one to kiss her bruised brow and tear-stained freckled cheeks!

Despite his thoughts, when the woman sucked in her breath like she was trying not to cry out in pain, Baron stepped even closer to the bed than before and let out a huge sigh of relief. It had been almost twenty-seven hours since the accident and he was relieved to finally hear her soft voice. It sounded like hot melted butter—was that possible, it was comforting—despite her obvious pain and confusion. He didn't understand why her velvety voice had rocked him to his very soul just now. His knees shook from it. He didn't understand what it was that had called him to come back to the I.C.U.—but here he was, like a blubbering idiot, being pulled in to this woman's life.

His shaking knees reminded him that he wanted to turn away and run for his life, run as far and as fast as he could. He despised hospitals and hated the decorations of red-and-green garland and twinkling white lights all around the I.C.U. desk outside her unit at the nurse's station. And that Christmas music—it made him cringe from the inside out. He wanted to scream again! He didn't want to be here and felt closed in again. This wasn't happening. He couldn't do this. He had to get out and stay away!

Despite all that, he asked, "You've been in an accident—do you remember any of it?" His voice was thick, like whipped cream, and Merry Beth couldn't help but to think lacking in emotion and feeling. He seemed quiet, too quiet, and withdrawn, like he was here but a million miles away at the same time. Her heart pounded wildly in her chest and she quickly opened her eyes when memories from the car accident suddenly flashed across her fuzzy memory.

Her entire world shifted, violently. *"Bethany! Please, tell me, where's my baby…where's my daughter? I want to see her—right now!"* When he didn't answer right away panic crashed in her frightened heart quickly—just as the man who'd hit her car had, fast and furious and out of the blue. As she tried to sit up and tear the tubes, wires and IV's from her right arm, she cried out from frustration and sudden fear. And the pain in her right wrist made her cringe then cry out.

Her frightened eyes sought his shadowed ones. "You're not telling me everything. I just know it! *Where's my daughter? Please—tell me she isn't dead!"*

Against all odds Baron reached out to help her. He knew immediately he should have never touched her, as he tried to hold her down on the bed. "I told you, she's fine. Please, take it easy! Don't tear at the tubes and wires like that—*are you crazy?*"

"Why is my right hand and wrist all bandaged up like this? I can't *do* anything! Why is my left arm in a cast? *Where's Bethany? Please*, please tell me where she is!"

"I will…but you have to lie back down and lay still first!" His hands seemed to burn where they held her down.

Tears burned hot and Merry Beth was too weak and too frightened to hold them back or fight against his hold. His hands on her skin seemed to scorch it, yet she shivered and searched for his eyes once more. "Who are you? Are you the man who h…hit my c…car in the accident?" She started to fight against his hold again.

"No…" Baron stepped closer and touched her for the third time since pulling her from the wreckage. He ignored the glistening shock waves and tingling sensations spreading quickly up and down his arms, as he held her down by her shoulders so she'd stop struggling. "Take it easy, I told you—your little girl is safe. She wasn't hurt. There isn't a scratch on her. She's fine. You need to lie still. You've been pretty banged up…there are cuts and bruises, broken bones and cracked ribs…"

"No, I want to see my daughter…right now!" she cried out.

She continued her struggling and he said, "Be careful. You have a broken arm and cracked ribs!" Baron frowned. She was too fragile and he didn't like to touch people. He winced, knowing deep in his heart, *he* was the one who didn't like to be touched. Never again! Touching someone else's life only brought pain. Risk and pain, loss and regret, bitterness and then anger all added up to nothing but *alone* and emptiness.

Merry Beth lifted frightened, tear-filled eyes to stare into his midnight-black eyes for the first time. Her breath caught in her throat. He was very masculine, very handsome and *very* huge and steel-beam-strong. He seemed to tower above her and she couldn't help but wince and flinch back from his caring touch.

There was a terrifying darkness in the depths of his eyes, one she couldn't place or understand. He was too close and too strong and too powerful for her taste, and she couldn't help but whisper, "Please, don't hurt me…"

He didn't miss her frightened eyes or her strong reaction to his words and touch. He immediately dropped his hands from her arms and stepped back away from her hospital bed. He felt like his legs were going to give way and rubbed a shaking hand over his tired eyes to ease his pounding heart.

"I would *never*…hurt you," he whispered softly, barely recognizing his own voice. Air—he needed air again. Suddenly it seemed too hot in here! He felt claustrophobic and closed in, the room swayed and he reached out for the wall to still his unsteadiness.

"Please…where's my baby girl? I need to see her. It's all I ask. Are you *sure* that she's all right? Are you *sure* that she wasn't hurt in *any* way? How long was I out—she must be so scared? I need to see her for myself, to see with my very own eyes that she's okay. She's all I have in this world—she means…everything to me. I couldn't bear it—couldn't survive it if anything happened…happens to her…"

Moving her body brought pain, and she paled and sucked in her breath. His dark eyes—they frightened her. His steel strength—it over-whelmed her and made her feel helpless and small.

All he saw at that exact moment was his dead wife's pale and bloody face. He couldn't find his voice to save his life if he was finally drowning. When he didn't answer and just stared down at Merry Beth, she gave in to the fear as panic set in quick like a raging river again. She cried out, "*Please! Just let me see my daughter!*"

Baron stared at the machines that were now beeping wildly and loudly off the charts above her head. In seconds three I.C.U. nurses were pushing him away from the fragile, soft, beautiful but frightened woman's eyes.

Baron started to explain. "She's asleep in the…"

Merry Beth cried out, "She's dead…*isn't she?*"

"Please sir—you'll have to step back!" one of the nurses ordered firmly, as she prepared to give Merry Beth a shot to calm her down. He cringed at the sight of the needle the nurse quickly placed on Merry Beth's right arm.

Merry Beth pleaded, wincing, "No, don't put me to sleep! I want to see my daughter!"

Baron gladly turned away from those pleading and fearful eyes and fled. But not before he heard the woman ask, "Please, tell me—what's your name? Who…who are you?"

His only thought at that moment was to escape the tears in her fearful eyes. He wanted to run away from the blood and bruises, run fast and furious as far away from this woman as he could. He didn't want to hear her creamy voice, didn't want to see her frightened eyes or tears, didn't want to feel her soft skin under his fingertips—such soft skin, and to touch her—what a grave mistake that had been! He had to get out of the hospital, and get out now! He didn't want to feel anything anymore, ever. Feeling hurt.

He didn't answer her, didn't glance back at her, didn't smile at her, didn't want to be connected to her in any way, didn't want to ever look into her eyes again, didn't want to ever touch her again as he fled. But he knew, in his heart as he walked quickly away, with just one too many touches they were connected. It was too late.

Mrs. Merry Beth Waters and her little girl were already inside his head. The trick was, he thought as he turned the key to his light-blue BMW and spun like a wild man possessed from the parking lot, to not let them get inside his heart.

To do so meant he'd have to rejoin the land of the living again, and he didn't want to. To do so meant he'd have to care and reach out again, and he didn't want to. To do so meant he'd have to open closed doors—doors he'd slammed and locked shut almost three years ago, and he wasn't ready to unlock and open them again.

Doors if unlocked and reopened would bring him more pain. Because that's all that life was now—pain.

He was tired of the pain but welcomed it.

He just wanted to be left alone.

He didn't want to reach out again, feel again, cry again, laugh or enjoy life and living again. He just wanted to die.

Why had he done it? Why had he ever touched her?

Would God help him now? Have mercy!

He doubted it.

What a fine bloody mess!

* * * * *

It was Saturday, December the 12th and Merry Beth was still in I.C.U., frustrated, anxious to go home; still in pain. She wanted out of here and out of here now! It angered her that she'd been hit by a drunk driver. Yet, she was thankful that her daughter wasn't hurt.

"What do you mean—*that* man pulled me and Bethany from dad's car?" Merry Beth held her daughter tightly in the crock of her right arm. She was sound-asleep and thankfully, unscratched and unhurt. "What exactly are you telling me? *He* saved us—the man in black? Are you absolutely *sure?*"

The sound of her baby girl breathing softly in her sleep close to her breast was like warm sunshine hitting her face after a cold, bitter, wind and rainstorm. It brought her relief but not answers. Her heart raced in her bruised but mending chest. She hurt everywhere yet managed to smile through her pain. She'd learned how to do that by watching her father her entire life.

Nurse Annie Brackett smiled and answered, "That's what I've been told, love."

"You mean—*he* actually risked his own life to save us? Who is he? I don't recall ever seeing him around town. How am I going to thank him if I don't even know his name? He pulled us from dad's car before that second car hit us and…" Merry Beth rested her throbbing head back against her pillows and sighed heavily with a worried frown. "…it exploded."

"Maybe he'll come back," the pretty nurse suggested.

"My head is splitting, and it feels like I've split the left side of my skull wide open. My face looks like someone hit me with a baseball bat. I'm all cut and bruised. I went a little crazy when I thought something really terrible had happened to my daughter. Oh, my—what that nice man must think! When am I going to be released so I can go home?" She sighed heavily, out of breath from her many questions and racing heart.

"Not for at least a week, the doctor said."

"I'm fine; really…I just want to go home. I have to. It's almost Christmas—there's still so much to do to get ready!"

"Jeffery—one of the paramedics on the scene—told me, as they wheeled you in, that nice man pulled you and your girl from your wrecked car right before it exploded into flames! That handsome man saved your lives, literally. You probably wouldn't be here now if not for him. The entire E.R. staff is still talking of him—he's a true-blue hero," Nurse Brackett said with a friendly smile.

"I have to find him. I need to thank him for so much. I don't know what I would have done if anything had happened to my daughter while I was unconscious after the wreck…"

"I mistook him for your husband, you know."

Miracles were in the making, but Merry Beth didn't realize that yet. Christmas was indeed a season of joy and miracles. This she did know, and smiled.

"There *has* to be a way I can find out who he is," Merry Beth said with hope in her heart. She wasn't a woman who ever gave up a good fight, and wasn't about to start now.

Nurse Brackett answered, "If he's an honest man, he'll be back. I'm so sorry love, but…I gave him your rings. Like I said, I thought he was your husband."

Merry Beth glanced at her left hand and noticed for the first time her wedding rings were gone. "Oh, no…"

The nurse winced. "I'm so sorry. I'm *sure* he'll be back…he seemed so intense, so serious, so committed."

The young nurse faked a smile as a woman dressed in light pink walked in carrying a breakfast tray. "Hello, Cindy. I *love* your Santa's hat!"

Cindy smiled her thanks as she placed Merry Beth's breakfast tray on her eating table. "Thanks. It's a gift from my husband. The little bell on the end rings every time I take a step and patients can hear me coming all the way down the hallways." She smiled as she turned away. "Eat and enjoy."

"Thanks, Cindy." Nurse Brackett turned back to her patient. "You've been pretty much out of it since the accident. I took it upon myself to fill out your breakfast, lunch and dinner menu card for today. I hope that's okay? And your rings—I feel so bad…but like I said, I have a feeling he'll be back."

Memories from her wedding day flashed before her eyes, and Merry Beth smiled. "I don't want you to worry about my rings. It wasn't your fault. You had no way of knowing. I'm sure he'll be back." *Yes, he'll come back. He has to. I need to thank him!*

The nurse placed the cold steel from her stethoscope on Merry Beth's chest. "Take a deep breath for me—that's good." She listened and smiled. "Your lungs and breathing sound wonderful." She began taking Merry Beth's vitals next.

"With the hit you took on your left side, I'm surprised your injuries aren't worse. You were very lucky."

"No, my daughter and I are blessed." Merry Beth shook her head yes that anything the nurse chose for her to eat was fine, and wiped the tears away from her lashes and smiled as she reached for her tray. "This looks good. I'm starving!"

"I ordered cereal, juice and toast for your little girl, too."

"Thank you—you're an angel."

After she wrote down Merry Beth's vitals on her chart, the caring nurse helped her with the tray. Merry Beth's thoughts flashed back to the mystery man who'd saved her and Bethany. There was something about his dark eyes that haunted her; something wasn't quite right in his world. He was hurting and she wanted to help him. There'd been a deep sense of sadness about his eyes, his speech and his entire manner, though his hands had been caring yet strong when they'd held her down when she'd struggled against his hold.

Nurse Brackett frowned and asked, "Do you want me to call anyone for you? You slept the evening and night away last night and there is no one listed on your hospital records as next of kin to call. Your daughter—she's exhausted. I could bring a small cot in here for her to sleep in by yours, if you want. It's against our I.C.U. policies but I think I can break them this once."

Merry Beth glanced at her sleeping daughter. "She can't stay here—not for an entire week…"

The nurse reached for Merry Beth's chart and wrote down her blood pressure. "Your BP is fine. You'll probably be moved from I.C.U. today into your own room."

"No, there's no one to call…" The only family she had left now was her daughter. Even her late-husband's parents were dead and gone. And his only sister and her husband lived far away in Lynchburg, Virginia. She didn't want to call and worry them. Wait…Debbie! Of course…she'd help.

As Merry Beth added milk to her hot Cream-of-Wheat she said, "Actually, there is someone you can call. Please, think back. Do you know *anything* about that nice man that helped us?"

"Jeffery said he was driving a really fancy, shiny light-blue BMW. You know—the kind that the *rich* and *famous* drive. And it's really strange, but his license plate simply stated 'BMW', weird, eh? He left abruptly sometime Thursday evening, around seven-thirty, I think, but when I came to work yesterday morning he was here. He stood over there in the shadows and watched over you for hours."

"He w…was? He did? Are you sure?"

"Yes. He never approached your bed or even touched you in any way, not once in over ten hours. He stood over there in the dark corner and watched you while waiting for you to open your eyes, I guess. You know the rest, as soon as you woke up—after a few minutes he just…left, and hasn't been heard from or seen since."

"That's really weird. What does it mean?"

Nurse Brackett shook her head and passed her a little piece of paper and a pen. "You and your daughter were very lucky, Mrs. Waters. >From what Jeffery said, it was a pretty bad crash. The young man in the black truck that hit you— he was D.O.A. and…"

Merry Beth wrote her pastor's name and number on the paper and winced. "D.O.A.…?" Her fingers shook and tears blurred her vision. Deep in her heart she knew what it meant. The man who'd hit her car was dead.

"It's hard to do much with this wrist all bandaged like this. I'm right handed." She held her sore wrist to her breast. "But, believe me; I'm thankful my baby and I are all right."

"It means 'dead on arrival'. He was drinking and driving, I'm afraid. I'll never

27

understand why people do that. So many lives gone, snatched away, so quickly, because of people who drive while they are drunk. It's so stupid and senseless, and the young man in the second car that hit you is lying in a comma—his chances aren't good." The young nurse picked up Merry Beth's chart and prepared to leave.

Merry Beth smiled, despite her painful wrist and ribs. "Thank you for all you've done; for both my daughter and I."

"Yep, you were very lucky—*very* lucky, indeed. Now, eat! You need to get your strength back. If you need me just beep for me, okay?" Nurse Brackett smiled down at mother and sleeping daughter. "You want to move her so you can eat?"

Merry Beth smiled. "She's fine, and thank you."

The nurse adjusted several I.V. tubes. "I'll be close by if you need me. I'm sure you'll be transferred to another room out of I.C.U. later, just as soon as the doc comes and gives you clearance."

Merry Beth added pepper to her scrambled eggs. "I've already sent up my prayers to God in thanksgiving. *He* is my strength and my refuge. He keeps my baby girl and me safe with His strong, yet gentle and guiding hand."

Nurse Brackett looked at the little paper Merry Beth had passed her and smiled. "Oh, I know Pastor Todd. His niece, Kristi, is a good friend of my oldest daughter, Elyse. They're in the same classes together at the high school. They're like two peas in a pod—they're never apart if they can help it. I don't think there's a weekend the two of them aren't at my house or Pastor Todd's house for sleepovers. I'll go call him right now for you, love. Don't you worry about a thing, okay?"

"Thank you, Annie." Merry Beth smiled and watched the nurse walk away. There was absolutely no way she could stay here in the hospital for an entire week. It was almost Christmas! There was so much to do. And number one on her 'to do list' was finding the mysterious handsome stranger who'd saved her and Bethany's life. She had to thank him; she couldn't afford to waste one second. Life was too precious and way too short for most.

His eyes—they were so sad, so dark, so far away; so empty, yet filled with so much emotion. She'd get him to smile if it were the last thing she did! She prayed for a miracle before she woke up her daughter to eat her breakfast.

Life was for living, and she was thankful to be alive. For some strange reason, she knew in her heart that the stranger who'd saved her life, wasn't.

* * * * *

Pastor Todd Michael Thomas—Merry Beth's best friend, Debbie's brother-in-law, walked into Merry Beth's hospital room two hours later, and smiled as he reached for her right hand. "I came as soon as I could. I'm so sorry, Merry Beth. Is there anything I can get you? Is there anything I can do for you, anyone you want me to call?"

He reached for the huge orange chair that sat by the hospital bed in the corner and pulled it closer to the bed. "Debbie said to tell you that she is dropping by later this afternoon to see you."

Merry Beth smiled. "I should have called her by now…"

"Debbie's been frantic wondering where you've been. She's called your house a dozen times. The nurses tell me that your left arm is broken—tell me what I can do to ease your pain." Pastor Todd was a big man, but his hands were gentle and caring like his heart. He truly cared for every member of his church on a one on one basis. He'd lost his only brother in a freak boating accident last winter, and watched over Debbie and her three children like they were his own family. Indeed they were, in a way…secretly in his heart.

Merry Beth smiled at her pastor and assured him she was going to be fine. "I'm not in any pain, Pastor Todd—honest! You look as white as a ghost. I'm going to be just fine, you'll see. And there is something you can do for me. Is there any way you think Debbie might take Bethany for me? She's tired beyond belief. She's scared and misses her own bed, and needs a bath and clean clothes and…"

He smiled. "Say no more. You know she'll take her."

"I probably won't be released until sometime tomorrow morning, is that okay? The doctor wants me to stay a week but…I can't. There's too much to do—Christmas is coming!"

"You know how much Bethany loves to play with Lisa, and you should stay in the hospital—you need your rest."

"I know, but—if the doctor will discharge me, I'm going home! The pain medication they have me on is taking away the edge from the pain in my broken arm and sprained wrist. My ribs are really sore with only two cracked, not broken. There's no reason why I can't go home. There's so much to do—*it is almost Christmas!*"

"You really should take it easy for a few days in here, Merry Beth. Get some rest, and make sure you're really okay. You and Debbie have been best friends for years—I'll call her right after I leave here. Is there anything I can get you or her from the apartment? Maybe Debbie and Kristi can stop by later and bring them to you."

Merry Beth pointed to the drawer in the stand by her bed. "Nurse Brackett put my purse inside that drawer—can you pass it to me and I'll get you my apartment key? You'll never know how much this means to me. I really appreciate it. It's wonderful to have a friend like Debbie. I'd be lost without her."

As he turned towards the drawer she explained, "Someone pulled my purse from the wreckage just before dad's car exploded. I swear that I can still smell the gasoline and burning brakes, and hear the vehicles crumbling all around Bethany and I…and I think I always will." She couldn't help but shiver a little.

Pastor Todd opened the little drawer and passed her the black suede purse. "If you write down what Bethany needs I'll give the list to Debbie later."

Merry Beth searched her purse for her house key and a pen. "All her clothes are in her room in the white wicker dresser by the closet—underwear, socks, jeans and sweaters—everything she needs. Her shoes are in the closet and she can tell you which books she likes the best. Do you think Debbie would mind reading her a bedtime story? I always read to her at bedtime and…" Tears glistened across her lashes and she wiped them away with shaking fingers.

"Are you all right…?" her pastor asked softly.

She put out a huge smile. "I'm sorry—the accident—it happened so fast. I can't believe that man who hit us is d…dead, and the second young man is in a comma…near death…"

Pastor Todd reached out to lightly touch her shoulder. "Take it easy, Merry Beth. It's going to be all right."

"I don't know what I would have done if something had happened to my b…baby…" she stammered, close to tears again.

"Try not to worry. Bethany will be just fine. Kids are resilient. They rebound faster than we do. I've already sent news of your accident over the wire and got you started on the prayer chain right away. Is there anything *you* need?"

"Yes. There was this man that helped Bethany and I…" She explained to her pastor about his rescue and asked, "Do you think you could try to find out who he is for me? One of the paramedics told the duty nurse he drove a light-blue BMW and his license plate said simply 'BMW'. I don't know if it's his initials? Do you think you could find out his name and where he lives or phone number? I have to see him—to thank him…"

Pastor Todd smiled as Bethany stirred awake. In seconds she jumped up into his arms, happy and excited to see him, hugging his neck. "I'll do my best…hello, sweet angel."

"Pastor T.! Mommy has boo-boo's on her arm and face."

"Yes, I see. She's going to be just fine, you'll see."

"I need to contact him so I can thank him face to face for saving Bethany and me. If he hadn't pulled us out—we wouldn't be here today. There aren't too many people left in this world who are true heroes—not like that. It's like he was this angel that came from out of the frightening mayhem to save us by pulling us from that wreckage. I wonder who he is."

She shivered against the memory of the accident, yet thankful for it at that same time. Because of the wreck she'd been once more reminded, like when her husband had died, how precious life was and how fast it could all be over.

"God is trying to tell me something, Pastor Todd. I wonder what it is. Life—it's a precious and fragile thing…"

The pastor touched her right arm lightly and squeezed it slightly to reassure her that everything was going to be all right. "I'll do everything I can to find out who he is, okay?" He tickled the child and laughed as she giggled in his strong arms.

"Look at you—you're growing bigger every day."

"Mommy—Pastor T. is tickling me again!"

Merry Beth smiled up at her happy daughter. "Yes, I see—tickle him back, baby. He won't care."

Bethany did and Pastor Todd hugged her tighter. "You just rest and don't worry about a thing. Everything will be just fine, you'll see. You're a child of God and He always takes care of His own."

He turned to leave after leaning way down so Bethany could kiss her mother's cheek. "I'll be back in the morning to see how you're doing."

"Thank you, Pastor Todd," Merry Beth whispered. She explained to her daughter that their pastor was going to take her to Debbie. "Tell Debbie that I really appreciate it. I can always count on her through thick and thin, she's always been there for me. Bethany, baby—you be good for Pastor Todd and also Miss Debbie."

The delightful child smiled down at her mother. "I will, Mommy…I prom miss!"

"You're going to need transportation. I have a car you can use until you get everything squared away with your insurance company. It's an old car—a Toyota that's seen better days, but it runs perfect and could be the transportation you need until you get another car. You're more than welcome to use it, if you'd like to. I'll have your name added to the insurance." He glanced at her bandaged wrist. "Are you going to be able to drive? If not, I could…"

Merry Beth smiled her thanks and said, "I'll manage. Thank you for taking care of my little girl for me. I didn't know whom else to call, and yes, I'd appreciate it if I could use the car until I get everything squared away with All-State. My Agent, Sandy, is a peach and she's promising for everything to be taken care of in about a week or two. I don't know how I'm ever going to thank you, Pastor Todd. You have helped me so much in the last five years…I miss dad, so much…" She was rambling and bit down on her tongue and took huge calming breaths.

"You're one of God's children, and I'm thankful you weren't taken from us. God must be trying to tell you something, Merry Beth. There's some kind of mystical purpose for this accident. God always has a plan, and He can always create something wonderful out of tragedy. When a door gets closed I believe a window will be opened. You wait and see, mark my words, it'll happen. I've seen it time and time again in my own family—especially after my brother died."

The stranger's dark, black, midnight eyes flashed in front of hers at that moment and she frowned with worry. He'd looked so lost, so alone, so distant and so *angry*, but why? Was this the reason for the accident—to meet this man and somehow help him to smile again? "I'm sure God will work it all out in His own time. He always does," Merry Beth whispered. "I live my life in faith; Pastor Todd—it's a part of who I am. I can't imagine being alive without my faith. Life would be so meaningless and very empty."

Before her pastor carried her daughter away she closed her eyes as he prayed, "Dear God, thank you for keeping Bethany and Merry Beth safe in that accident. We pray for that dead young man's family. Please, dear Father—touch Merry Beth with Your healing hands, and if it's Your will—help me find the mysterious stranger that pulled them from that car before it exploded into flames. In Your Name we pray, Amen."

As he turned slowly away he said, "Don't worry, Merry Beth, remember—when God closes one door he always opens a window close by, even if it's a small one."

"Bye, Mommy! I lovededed you!"

Merry Beth blew her daughter a kiss. "I love you, too!"

Merry Beth smiled and relaxed back against her pillows, thankful beyond words to be alive. Her daughter was safe. A new mission was born in her heart—to help the strong and handsome stranger who'd saved her life. To make his ebony and lonely eyes smile again. Could she do it? Christmas was only a few weeks away, the season of hope and giving. Yes, she could!

Who was he; what was his life's story? Was he engaged, married, a father? Was he a stranger passing through town—one she'd never see again? Who had caused the haunted look of sadness she saw in his deep-set, ebony eyes—a girlfriend, a fiancée, a wife, a son or daughter?

What was his name? What did he do for a living? Was he an honest and true-blue kind of man, or a thief or con artist or criminal? She'd seen many things in his dark eyes, but he was indeed an honest man. She just knew it. She also knew he needed her—this was why God had put them in the same path. She *had* to help him; there were so many ways she could.

Merry Beth smiled. The sun was shining through the open hospital room widow. It started to snow lightly and it was very beautiful coming down. She didn't see a bird feeder or see the birds, but she could hear the Chickadee's singing their special tune just outside the window.

It was wonderful to be alive!

* * * * *

It was Sunday, December the 13th, and Baron's boss asked over the phone line, "Does this mean you're back? I'm gonna have to make some calls to get you re-instated."

"I'm back," Baron replied over his home office phone. He hadn't worked a day in almost three years, and now he wanted back in. He wanted his life back; he wanted to live again! Was it because of what he'd gone through with Mrs. Waters and her beautiful freckled-cute-faced daughter?

"Why now? It's been almost three years, Bear. I can't believe it's been that long—how time flies…"

Everyone at the precinct called him 'Bear'. It had grown on him years ago and had stuck with him since his early days as a Maine State Trooper. His reputation on the job of being hard like stone, cold like ice, fierce and strong like a northern grizzly, and unmoving or unbending when it came to arresting and bringing to prosecution criminals—had virtually disappeared since the accident. He rubbed his throbbing left temple hard. What had happened to that man? Was he now a crumbled pile of pathetic nothingness?

"It's time—don't you think?" Baron glanced all around his home office with a frown. So dusty and dark, so gloomy and forlorn, so quiet and empty, this thing called his pathetic life.

"Are you sure?"

"Very."

"Am I gonna be kicking myself in the sorry butt for letting you back in?" his boss and best friend asked. "I'm gonna have to *really* pull some strings to make this happen…"

"No, you won't be sorry. I'm ready to get back to work, Mitch. If I have to spend one more day alone in this pathetic, empty, dark and gloomy house by myself—I'm climbing the walls, man. I *need* to work—for my own sanity."

Christmas—there's always Christmas. Yeah, right—bah-humbug! Never again, just concentrate on the work, get focused, breathe; just breathe. The stone-cold silence over the land line made sweat break out across Baron's pounding forehead.

"You're the one who shut yourself off, Bear."

"I know that. Give me a break, would you?"

"And now you want back in. Imagine that…"

"I need the work, Mitch. What else is there?"

"I don't know, you tell me."

"I witnessed a terrible car accident Thursday evening in front of McDonald's in-town Winterville, Mitch. I guess you could say it was kind of like my…wake-up call." The darkness and shadows and dust in the expansive and homey office made Baron shiver, and he stood to open his curtains and blinds to let the daylight in for the first time in almost three years.

"You're really sure…?"

"Just stop analyzing and asking the why and do it!"

"Come in to my office first thing in the morning and I'll give you back your badge and gun. We've missed you around here, Bear. It's about time you got your sorry butt back to work. I have cases backed up like you wouldn't believe—there's this…one case I'm working on that I could really use your help with, old friend. I'll fill you in, in the morning. I'll tell the guys you're coming back. They'll be thrilled. It's been too quiet around here with you gone. Are you *sure* you're ready?"

Sweat dripped slowly down Baron's left temple and he wiped it away, in frustration, with his left-hand fingertips. He closed his eyes for a few moments against the headache that pounded there, against the light that poured in the open curtains and dirty blind, before he answered truthfully, "Yeah, I'm sure. I'll see you in the morning. Thanks, Mitch."

As Baron hung up the phone he slowly walked to his bedroom closet in search for a shirt that wasn't black. The days of mourning were over. It was time to get back to work, time to live again, time to put the past behind him and move on, time to let go of his lost wife and son. Could he do it? He asked himself that question over and over, as he began the chore of cleaning and airing out his house from top to bottom.

He was determined to, no matter what. As he worked at dusting, vacuuming, doing laundry and cleaning his kitchen and bare floors, his thoughts remained on the pretty Merry Beth Waters and her sweet, little, delightful, freckled-faced daughter. Against all odds, he'd dreamt about Mrs. Waters' eyes the night before, and her soft-as-butter smile and her velvety baby-skin and her tempting perfume and kissable lips...

What did the dream mean?

He didn't know, and didn't want to know!

He loved his wife and son.

Though gone, they'd always be his *only* family!

There would not be another.

Not ever!

* * * * *

Three hours later, exhausted from cleaning his house for the first time in three years, he frowned when his front doorbell rang. Not one single living soul had walked through the front door since the day of the funeral. He frowned, wondering who it could be. His parents were both dead and he had no brothers or sisters, no living relatives within a hundred miles of Maine.

The bell rang again, he winced. "Yeah, yeah, yeah...just a second, stop ringing the bell! *Who is it? Will you please stop ringing the bell?*" he thundered through clenched teeth. "*Is your finger stuck on the doorbell like glue, or what? Whatever you're selling—I'm not interested!*"

He opened his door wide and stared down at the woman and child on his porch. "It's...you."

The little girl was smiling from ear-to-ear up at him—like a beacon of bright light to lead his way through a raging rain storm, holding her little yellow mitten finger on his front doorbell. He winced, thinking, *Oh, man—I don't need this, why me? Dear Lord—just make them go away. It's too soon...much too soon. What now? Please don't do this to me...I'm not ready!*

Merry Beth reached out and pulled her daughter's finger away from the doorbell button. "Hope Bethany...that's enough—stop that!" Her pretty eyes lifted to Baron's, filled with apology.

Man, what a smile! *"What are you two doing here? And how did you find my address?"* Baron thundered, losing his temper.

When Merry Beth and Bethany remained silent yet smiling up at him from ear-to-ear he hissed, "Well, don't just stand there like two frozen frogs on an old pine log—*state your business here, and then be merrily on your happy and smiling way, because I don't do this happy and smiling stuff very well! I don't need this intrusion on my life!*"

Psalm 57: 1 "Be merciful unto me, O God, be merciful unto me: for my soul trusteth in thee: yea, in the shadow of thy wings will I make my refuge, until *these* calamities be overpast."

Chapter Two

Matthew 1:20-21 "But while he thought on these things, behold, the angel of the LORD appeared unto him in a dream, saying, Joseph, thou son of David, fear not to take unto thee Mary thy wife: for that which his conceived in her is of the Holy Ghost. And she shall bring forth a son, and thou shalt call his name JESUS: for he shall save his people from their sins."

Miracle #1, a smile, December 13th, Sunday, 9:45 a.m.
WHEN MERRY BETH and Bethany remained silent yet smiling, he thundered Merry Beth's way, agitated that they were invading his space, "*And why aren't you in the hospital? Do you have a death wish or something? You're covered with bruises and stitches and cuts!*"

Baron crossed his arms over the light-green-and-white flannel shirt that covered his broad chest. He stood in front of the two so they couldn't enter his home, his life. He didn't want them to, did he? His jaw twitched from wanting so hard. No. Of course he didn't!

The bruised yet oh, so beautiful woman's next words made him flinch back and he regretted his loss of temper and heated words. Lord, help him—it was true. Life had moved on after the accident. But why now, why with *this* woman and child?

"It was definitely *truly* a miracle from our special God above that we found you, Mr. Williams. After all, it's almost *Christmas!*" Merry Beth said with a warm, friendly smile.

His dark angry eyes made her wonder if she'd made a terrible mistake in coming here uninvited, and she thought, *Oh, boy—he sounds infuriated and annoyed. Is he going to be friend or foe, predator or prey, angry or nice? Come on, Merry Beth—don't chicken out now. Just thank the man and be on your merry little way before he bites your head off again!*

She winced at his next words, they were low and husky, but she heard. "I don't believe in Christmas…not anymore."

She blew out her breath. "My baby and I wouldn't be here today if not for your act of kindness. We wanted to thank you in person, Mr. Williams. You're our hero!"

Merry Beth continued to stare up into his ebony eyes and couldn't help but flinch back from the look of pure panic across his darkened lashes. He was fighting for control for some reason, and she watched the muscles in his jaw twitch, was it in anger? *Yes, that's what I see in his eyes again—anger—but, why? Why is this man's eyes filled with anger and sadness?*

"My Mommy and me wand'deded to thank you, Mr.—I forgot his name, Mommy!" Bethany glanced up at her mother with questioning emerald eyes.

"His name is Mr. Baron Williams, baby." Merry Beth touched her daughter's nose softly and lightly with her finger. Her right hand was still bandaged and throbbed unmercifully, yet she smiled.

Baron didn't miss how her soft emerald eyes were filled with dancing light and love when she looked at her daughter. Her husky voice was way too soft, way too creamy—like melted marshmallows. Her eyes were too green and too trusting. Her pearly white smile was too tempting and too huge. Her right hand was too bruised yet caring. Her manner was too giving and strong. She was everything he wasn't. *Nice!* They were two worlds apart and he planned on keeping it that way. Caring again, reaching out again—he wanted no part of it and wanted to scream, '*No! Go away, and don't look back!*'

"Believe me, I'm no hero," he said huskily.

Bethany glanced back up, way up, at Baron and smiled. "We wand'deded to thank you, Mr. Bear'ronn Will'amms for saving us!" She stepped a few steps closer to him bravely. "We brought'deded you a present!"

Why in the world would he be so angry? Oh, boy—I can see it was a mistake to come here and barge in on him this way! Merry Beth couldn't help but reach out for her daughter and pulled her back to stand close in front of her on the top step. She placed her right-bandaged hand on Bethany's right shoulder and held her firmly in place. It started to snow gently at that moment, and Bethany jumped up and down with excitement, despite her mother's firm restraint.

"Do you like'deded presents, Mr. Bear'ronn Will'amms?"

"Bethany…be still. Come on, we better go…"

Baron didn't miss Merry Beth jerk from the pain in her bandaged right hand, yet didn't reach out to ease it. He did, on the other hand, manage to whisper to the little girl, "Easy…"

Merry Beth couldn't help but jerk back from the pain that slashed across her bruised and cracked ribs and sprained right wrist, as her daughter jumped up and down with excitement because of the snow. "Easy, baby—Mommy's still a little sore…"

"Mommy—look! It's snowing again! Can we make a snow-man after church?" Bethany asked her mother. "Can Lisa come over after church, Mommy? We need to fi'nissh our spe'caall cards! There's one for our Sunday-School tea'ceer and we want to give it to her tooo'nite. It's 'portant, Mommy!"

Merry Beth couldn't tear her curious eyes away from the dark stranger's face. He was indeed very handsome, in a black and mysterious, rugged and jagged sort of way. His black stare made her shiver slightly. His stare was very powerful and silently screamed authority and predominance. It made her feel closed in—like she didn't have enough air to breathe and needed to escape to a bright, sunny, breezy and safer place. It was clearly evident he didn't want them here.

"We didn't mean to intrude on you and your family. Come on, baby—let's go." She turned quickly to leave and lost her balance on the icy, slippery step.

He immediately reached out to stop her fall, and she couldn't help but cry out against the terrible, slashing pain against her cracked ribs on her left side. Ever since she'd awaken after the accident her ribs throbbed as if someone poured boiling water or salt into an open wound. She paled to a ghostly white and knew her rescuer didn't miss her pain and discomfort.

She needed to sit down badly, but bravely smiled as Baron reached to steady her. His hands were strong and very powerful, yet gentle and caring at the same time. She needed to get a grip!

Bethany glanced way up at her mother and asked, "We leav'in now, Mommy?"

Merry Beth smiled despite her painful injuries. She was a woman who knew how to smile and said, "Yes, baby—now, give the nice man your gift. Church starts soon. We need to go now, or we'll be late."

Baron watched Merry Beth pale as she sucked in her breath in pain. He found his voice enough to mumble, "Are you all right?"

She smiled, yet didn't quite meet his dark eyes. "I'm going to be fine…really."

His temper snapped. She was in pain. "Are you *insane?* Why aren't you in the hospital?"

"Mommy and I thought you'deded like pears!" Bethany boldly placed a red wicker basket, decorated with a big red velvet bow attached on the handle, filled with fresh pears from Shop-'til-You-Drop in his hands. "Do you? Can Mommy and I come in and see your tree? Do you have a glittery pretty angel on top?"

"Hope Bethany Waters! You apologize, this instant. You don't invite yourself into someone's home like that. Say you're sorry, young lady, and then we have to go!" Merry Beth scolded.

"I'm s...sorry," Bethany softly whispered before she glanced up at the stranger with a lovely smile. "Don't you like the bass'ket? Mommy and I mad'deded it spe'caall for you. I pick'deded out the red bow at Wal-Mart. It's a spe'caall bow—see...it has cool gold glitter on it..."

Merry Beth searched for his dark eyes and smiled despite the black, icy stare Baron was throwing her way. Goodness! Didn't the man know how to speak? Didn't the man have any kind of manners? Didn't the man have any family? From what she could see, the house behind him seemed awful quiet and dark and forlorn—like his go-away-you're-not-welcome-here attitude.

Merry Beth mumbled an apology. "You'll have to excuse my baby—she gets kind of excited most of the time, especially around the Christmas season. But she's a treasure; to her—*everything* is special in one way or another."

A muscle under his left eye twitched. "I can see that."

Merry Beth and Bethany's genuine smiles bounced him off his lonely existence. Baron glanced down at the two on his porch and shook his head in disbelief. He noticed the woman's rosy yet bruised left cheek against her ghostly, pale complexion and didn't waste another second to invite them in. What a rude idiot he was. It was freezing out and he hadn't invited them in, and he couldn't remember the last time he'd shoveled or thrown rock-salt on his porch.

Life goes on and he groaned; fearing against all odds he was making a terrible mistake in doing so—letting them in. He wasn't a man who did letting in, friendship or kindness very well. He winced, remembering back to when there had been times he had. Deep inside he wanted that life back. Yet, he didn't dare touch either one again. Too dicey and dangerous!

And, he wondered if it really was this woman and child's special *God*, the same One who'd taken his wife and son away, that had lead them to his door. Doubtful!

Merry Beth turned away. "Come on, Bethany...time to go."

"You two might as well come in. It's freezing out there." He glanced over Merry Beth's shoulder at the old, ragged looking blue Toyota parked next to his new, shiny light-blue BMW. He flinched and rubbed a hand over his whiskered jaw and tired eyes.

Where's your husband, Mrs. Waters? And why isn't he here making sure you get home from the hospital safely? Why isn't he here making sure you're driving a safe, dependable, reliable car? He glanced at the aged looking and cheap coats the woman and child wore and winced. It was evident they didn't have much money. But their smiles—now that was another matter. They were priceless. Yet, he bit down hard on his tongue and rapid beating heart, holding back, not truly ready to let them in.

"Nice car," he mumbled as he placed the wicker basket on the table in the foyer, by his front door. "And yes, young lady, I love pears. Thank you; and the red bow is very beautiful." He stared down at the lovely child and her mother in awe and amazement.

She'd turned back, and he met Merry Beth's eyes, and pretty they were. At that moment he thought they were as transparent, like sea-glass. "I have something that belongs to you."

Merry Beth frowned in confusion. "You do?"

"Your rings…"

She glanced down at her bare left hand. "Oh, yes…my rings. Nurse Brackett told me how she thought you were my…"

"Husband…?" A muscle in his jaw twitched, violently. "I'm no husband, believe me." *Not anymore…*

Merry Beth whispered, "Oh, so you're *not* married then."

"Mommy—my feet are cold! When's the heater in the car gonna *ever* work?" Bethany asked as she switched from one yellow boot to the other, as if to warm them impatiently.

Merry Beth giggled. "Probably never, baby."

Here they were after being involved in a terrible near fatal car accident, two days later standing on his front porch, smiling up at him like he was something good enough to eat. Well, he wasn't and he wanted them gone! He'd been an idiot to ever invite them in.

The woman was bruised all over, broken, black and blue yet extremely beautiful. It was her eyes. They pulled him in. And the child was obviously unhurt, healthy, happy, and both were smiling up at him like he was Santa Claus delivering a huge bag of goodies on Christmas Eve or something, for goodness sakes! He rolled his dark eyes. He didn't need them barging in on his world like this.

And life moved on as each second ticked slowly past.

Both were standing on his front porch in the snow, giving *him* a gift of friendship, pears and warm smiles and sincere thanks. The least he could do was invite them in from the cold.

He reached for his black leather jacket, where it hung on a peg by the door, and unzipped the side pocket and handed Merry Beth her rings. "They're beautiful rings, Mrs. Waters. Your husband…he must love you very much to have given you these. Come on in, are you hungry?"

"Oh, we can't stay," Merry Beth said as she smiled up at him. He thought it odd that she placed her rings carelessly in her purse instead of placing them back on her left hand. Maybe her fingers were still too swollen or sore or…something. They did look swollen, from what he could see of them because of the cast. And there was bruising across her knuckles as well.

"The heater in your car doesn't work?" he asked with a raised dark right eyebrow.

"Our pastor is lending me the car until I settle everything with my insurance company—isn't that nice?" She glanced at the shirt he wore and smiled once more. "I just *love* this shirt! Green looks good on you, Mr. Williams." *No wife? No children? No wedding ring? No Christmas lights? No tree? No decorations? No smile? Just sadness—what can I do to make you smile?*

When she smiled like an angel up at him again, he didn't miss the warm glow to her now rosy cheeks, the shadows under her eyes and questions behind her creamy irises. All three made him feel very uncomfortable and his hand rose to the collar of his shirt, it suddenly choking his breath from his lungs.

"You should be in bed. You look like you're about ready to pass out at my feet. Come in and sit down before you do. You've suffered a terrible shock to your body, Mrs. Waters. Those ribs must be hurting like the old dickens. And you really shouldn't be driving with a broken left arm and sprained right wrist. I know you're in pain. I can tell. Where's your husband? *Why isn't he here with you and your daughter to help you get to church on time?*"

Bethany stomped snow off her boots and looked up at him to answer, "My dad'iee is in Heaven. He died before I was born'deded, and I miss him *very* much!"

Merry Beth swayed on her tired feet and her smile wavered immediately, and he regretted his harsh words, wishing he could pull them back in. "No husband. Just wonderful memories…"

He felt like a stupid jerk. "I'm so sorry…"

She paled again. "There's no need…"

"You still miss him, love him—need him?"

"He's been gone a very long time," Merry Beth whispered.

Air, she needed fresh air. Merry Beth said, as she reached for Bethany's yellow mitten hand, "Come on baby—we're going to be late for church if we don't leave *right now!*"

"But Mommy, we just got'deded here!"

They were leaving…already? A strong sense of urgency to reach out and make them stay caved inside his pounding heart. "No, wait—please, don't go." A frown creased his brow. "I'm sorry. I didn't realize your husband was gone."

"Pre'ttiee soon it will be Jesus'sis birthday! Mommy and me are giv'enn Jesus'sis very spe'caall gifts we made'deded our'selvees!" Bethany intercepted with a giggle.

Merry Beth had watched the many emotions flash across his black eyes in the last few minutes—anger, exasperation, resentment, animosity, irritation, displeasure, annoyance; panic and knew it was time to leave and once more reached for her daughter's hand.

Baron couldn't help but smile at the child. "I see."

"We apologize for intruding in on you this way. Come on, baby—let's go." Merry Beth turned to leave. "Merry Christmas, Mr. Williams. Thank you for all you did for my baby and me. Enjoy the pears. And no matter what you say— you are our hero!"

As she turned away she thought, *Get out of here, Merry Beth—before he bites your head off again. He looks like he's about ready to slash out at anything that moves or speaks to him—sad, real sad. Maybe my ideas to help him won't work after all.*

She's still in love with her husband. I can tell. I can see it in her eyes. She's running away like a scared rabbit. Baron didn't know why—but his hand shot out to stop the lovely woman and delightful child from leaving. Suddenly, being alone didn't appeal to his lonely, but mending heart anymore.

"*No, don't go! Please,* won't you both come in?" He flinched, wondering why he'd just said that, wondering why he'd just touched her again. Deep down inside his heart, he knew why! She was a beautiful, warm, friendly, available *sexy* woman. Or, was she?

Bethany turned back to him and looked up and said with an innocent, sweet smile, "We would have brought you a par'tig in a pear tree but Mommy said that was im'osssible. What's a dic'kensss? And how come you don't have any Cris'mas lights tink'eling in your windows?" The young girl searched his eyes with a frown suddenly. "Don't you like Cris'mas? Are you a grouch…a *green* one?"

"*You apologize this instant, Bethany!*" Merry Beth began to wonder if it was true, as she glanced at his dark, gloomy *undecorated* home and sad, lonely eyes. Somehow she knew, at that exact moment, this man was all alone in the world. He had no one. Her heart broke for him. She didn't understand it or question it, but wanted to help him smile again. In the midst of past pain and present darkness, a friendship was born.

"I'm sorry…" Bethany whispered her apology.

Baron glanced down into Merry Beth's now darkened emerald eyes and couldn't help but chuckle. She was a very beautiful woman indeed, and despite the darkness in them her eyes sparkled with life, laughter and smiles. He wanted to be a part of that. *Wrong!*

Baron's black eyes seemed to melt into her emerald, and his heart pounded wildly in his chest. She was a complete breath of fresh air in his lonely life—filled with such fire and beauty. It had been a very long time since he'd looked this close at anyone.

She was so close he could smell her soft fragrance, Jasmine—was that what it was? Its freshness soothed his pounding temples. Her warm and giving smile melted away his walls and defenses. What a deadly combination! His eyes of stone and her heart filled with life and smiles.

"It's okay, really. The child is just curious." He lowered his eyes to look at Bethany once more. He wanted to feel her softly breathing against his neck in his arms, in her sleep once more. She was a delightful bundle of excited energy, truly a happy and well cared for child, and curious.

"My wife and son are also in Heaven with your special Jesus, young lady. I guess I just—miss them." He watched the warm smile across the woman's eyes and lips quickly fade away.

Great, Williams! You're such a savage and scrooge. You've just taken away this woman and her child's laughter and smiles—great, just great! First visitors you've had in three years and you're scaring them away—now what? Get rid of them—that's what! You're doing a good job. I can tell that Mrs. Waters wants to bolt now that she knows…

Against his thoughts he made the move to shut the door. "Please, come in…its cold out there. I could make us some coffee or hot chocolate…" He wasn't even sure if he had any. For that matter—when was the last time he'd been to a grocery store?

"Mommy and I have white and red Cris'mas lights in ev'ree window at our house. We have ex'traas! You want some?"

She glanced up at her mother and asked, "We can bring'deded him some lights for his pri'tee house, can't we Mommy?"

Merry Beth glanced at her watch. "I'm sorry about your family, Mr. Williams. Come on, baby—we have to go. Church starts in about ten minutes. Thank you again for…"

"Do you know the song Par'tig in a Pear Tree? Mommy and I are going to bring you a spe'caall gift every day before Cris'mas b'cause you sav'deded us from my grand'deded da'dees car right bee'forr it ex'plodeded," Bethany innocently said.

Baron's heart fell in love with the little girl, right there and then. She was a treasure. Her cute little freckles would melt any man's hardened heart. For the first time in three years, his heart felt lighter. He wanted to smile and say thank you, but held it back.

"*Bethany! Where do you come up with these ideas?*" Merry Beth looked into his midnight black eyes once more with a warm smile. "We have to go. Thanks again for all you did for my baby and me. Have a nice Christmas, good-bye."

"But I want to see his tree!" Bethany argued stubbornly.

"Thank you for the pears, good-bye." He really did like pears, and it had been a long time since he'd enjoyed such sweet visitors!

As Merry Beth and her daughter walked towards the waiting old Toyota, slipping and sliding most of the way, Baron Michael Williams closed his door and for the first time in almost three years, gave in and smiled.

He rushed to the living room window to silently watch them, unnoticed. Despite the snow and cold and bitter wind howling to get in, suddenly he felt the warm sun on his shoulders. He felt no control over what was happening to his heart. He had no idea that Heaven's angels were singing praises and hymns because a true Christmas miracle had just happened, in his lonely life and broken heart. He'd smiled, truly smiled, from within.

He'd been a jerk to leave them standing in the cold and snow on his porch for so long, yet the woman and child's smiles never wavered. They were like sunshine after a summer rain, two budding tulips coming back to life through the cold and melting snow, a cool evening breeze while walking through the sand and surf, colorful leaves falling to earth at the end of fall…

His heart raced.

He didn't want to, but *needed* them to come back!

What now?

* * * * *

Unknown to Merry Beth, the first miracle had already taken place in Baron's wounded heart. She'd made him smile, but more importantly on the inside, and didn't even realize it.

It was 12:07 p.m., and just about everyone in the little Winter-ville Baptist Church in Winterville, Maine hugged her, and kissed her on her cheek as Merry Beth worked her way through the crowd to find her daughter after the service was over. She didn't have the heart to even try to stop them, even though her ribs hurt terribly. All throughout the service on 'giving and receiving of gifts' she thought about the strange, dark and mysterious yet handsome Mr. Baron Williams and his cold and uncaring, sad eyes.

She chuckled, he seemed to be a very complex man—filled with so many different emotions she didn't know where to start to help him. But there was one thing she knew for sure, as she searched through the heavy crowd of friends for Bethany, he was definitely a man who needed help and a little bit of Christmas cheer. He was a man on his own; a man who'd suffered terrible loss.

And *she* was the woman that God wanted to deliver help and miracles into his life, she was sure of it! *He* was going to smile if it was the last thing she ever did. After all, she'd been told her best quality was her smile and tender, caring touch. Would Mr. Williams flinch back if she dared touch him?

Pastor Todd's sister-in-law, Debbie, touched her lightly on her right arm and smiled. "How are you feeling today, love? You look really tired and *extremely* pale. You're doing too much! Todd wanted me to ask you if the old Toyota is giving you any trouble. Here's the insurance card he gave me to give to you."

Merry Beth smiled warmly and placed the card in her purse. "Are you kidding? That old car is a *treasure!* I'd be stuck if not for his kindness. And thank you for taking care of Bethany." She swayed in dizziness suddenly and reached for an empty pew.

"See—you're doing too much, Merry Beth!"

"I think—I just better—sit for a moment. My ribs, arm and wrist hurt like you wouldn't believe..." She glanced all around Debbie and asked, "Where's your lovely shadows—Kristi and Elyse? Oh, have you seen my daughter anywhere? I can't find her..."

"They're outside with their friends." Debbie helped Merry Beth sit with a worried frown. "You're over-doing it. I'll go find that sweet daughter of yours and my other two and help you to the car. I'll take Bethany home with me if you'd like, so you can go home and get some much needed rest."

Debbie's eyes challenged Merry Beth to try to argue with her. As Debbie turned to rush off the sun broke free from thick gray clouds and lit up the entire church with its rays through the twelve stained glass windows.

"Oh, Debbie—you don't have to do that, really. Besides, Bethany wants Lisa to come over. She said something about working on some kind of special cards or something?"

"Bethany and Lisa can just as well do whatever it is they're up to at my house. Better yet…why don't you come over for dinner? There's beef pot roast and potatoes in the oven as we speak. Then, after you get something to eat, you're going home to peace and quiet and rest. No arguing! I'll make sure Bethany gets to the church in time this evening for the children's Christmas choir and play practice," Debbie promised with a friendly smile.

Merry Beth sighed with relief. "Thanks, Debbie—quiet and sleep sounds wonderful. I guess I am a…little tired."

Merry Beth nodded her consent as Debbie rushed away, and leaned her head back. It would be nice to be able to just go home and sleep. But oblivion seemed an eternity away. She still had to finish all the angel costumes—fourteen in all—for the children's play on Christmas Eve at church, and reminded herself to stop at Wal-Mart on her way home to pick up the special gold and silver sequins and glitter she needed for the halo's and angel wings.

She still had to buy the stocking stuffers for Bethany's stocking and stop at the grocery store—her cupboards were looking a little on the bare side. She'd sold ten pairs of home-made hat-and-mitten sets to different ladies from the church that she'd knitted right before the accident, so she had extra money. And she needed to cash her paycheck from Friday. There was laundry to do and neglected housework to tackle as well.

She glanced up and smiled when she heard her daughter's soft, but excited voice closing in on her. "Bethany—there you are. I was looking everywhere for you."

"Mommy, Mrs. Thomas said I can'deded go to her house to finish mine and Lisa's spe'caall cards! Can I, Mommy? *Please?* I'll be real'liee good, I pro'misss!" Bethany made a move to jump in her mother's lap but Debbie gently and kindly held her back with careful restraining hands.

"Easy, pumpkin—your mommy's ribs are really sore." Debbie hugged Bethany tight when the little girl gave her a worried frown. "Your mommy will be better in no time."

Merry Beth reached out with her right hand and touched her daughter's freckled nose lightly. "Sure you can, baby. I think mommy will just go home. I need to take my medicine." She glanced up at her best friend, thankful beyond words for her friendship and kindness.

"Thanks for the offer for dinner, Debbie, but I think I'll just grab something at home. I'm kind of tired, and quiet and sleep sounds wonderful right about now. I just want to crawl in bed and sleep for a week!"

Ten minutes later, Merry Beth waved good-bye to her daughter and worked the little blue Toyota through the melting snowy slush and ice towards Wal-Mart.

God was silently working Christmas miracles in the little town of Winterville, Maine and Baron Michael Williams' life was about to be changed from pain, aloneness and darkness to relief, fellowship and bright light.

* * * * *

One of her favorite Christmas songs, *"Oh, Little Town of Bethlehem"* was playing softly from somewhere above her head, as she reached up for the shiny silver and gold glitter in the stationary aisle at Wal-Mart. Her hand stilled in mid-air when she spotted him. She smiled. Yes! Another chance to make him smile again!

There Mr. Williams was, as sure and as big as life itself, across her aisle reaching for candles next to the silly sign that read, '4 for a Buck'. She giggled. The playful sign was decorated with four colorful reindeer holding lit candles with their hoofs. She watched him as he placed several red candles in his blue carry-basket before reaching up for several more, ivory and green ones this time. She was very thankful for this second chance to make him smile.

She didn't waste another second to walk his way. She threw the silver and gold glitter in her blue carry-basket and couldn't help but smile again. *Yes! The man also owns a red-and-white flannel shirt. Everything else he wore was still black. I'll have to work on that part. You need color in your life, Mr. Williams. And here I am to help deliver that very thing. You need a friend; you need someone's caring, someone's touch; someone's laughter in your life...*

She couldn't help but notice once more how tall and handsome he was, and knew he had to be over six feet. Since she was watching him unnoticed, she didn't miss the aloneness, sadness and isolation across his troubled brow. She knew this man was grieving and very much alone and hurting. Her heart went out to him, like it often did to both human and animal in trouble. She felt this sudden need to rescue him again, to keep him from frowning; to keep him from being lonely and sad; to make him smile again.

Just as she cleared the end of her aisle to call his name, a stranger came from out of nowhere to her left and bumped really hard into her bruised ribs and broken arm. Merry Beth cried out in pain, as her purse, blue carry-basket and items inside went flying backwards on her way down.

"Oh, I'm so sorry ma'am. Are you all right?" The young woman who'd rammed her reached for her to help stop her fall. Before Merry Beth could even reach for something to break her fall, Baron was there and quickly lifted her up into his arms, like she weighed no more than a single piece of paper.

"Mr. Williams, you put me down this instant. I can walk, honestly!" Merry Beth exclaimed, exasperated and embarrassed.

"Is she going to be all right, sir? I didn't see her! I'm so sorry," the young woman apologized sincerely as she started picking up Merry Beth's fallen items. "She just quickly came from out of nowhere and…"

"She's going to be fine, I have her." Baron held Merry Beth close to his chest, firmly in his arms and carried her towards the front of the store. Like the fluffy snowflakes magically falling outside, little miracles were happening in his life and heart inside, and for the second time in years he'd reached out to help someone in need. He shook his head and tried to still the rapid beating of his heart by taking huge breaths. What was that perfume she was wearing? She smelled of roses this time. He winced; his wife had had perfume like that. Was it never meant for him to find any peace?

"What in the world are you doing here, Mrs. Waters? You should be at home in bed resting!" Baron glanced down at her rosy, flushed cheeks and frowned. "Are you all right? I heard you cry out in pain. I'll call for paramedics and an ambulance…"

She shook her head no and hid her face in the front of his leather jacket, evidence that she was embarrassed from him holding her in his arms, and he couldn't help but smile again on the inside. She smelled good, too. Oh, so good—and her eyes danced with that bright light again.

He chuckled. She was clearly embarrassed and flustered.

"I'd be fine if you'd put me down. Honestly, I can walk!" She fought and wiggled against his strong hold but he was too strong and too determined to make sure she was all right. Her painful ribs burned and she quieted in his arms. She couldn't help it and began to giggle. "You…you act like…like a knight-in-shining-armor!"

"Just be still…we're almost there."

"This is so silly…"

"I just want to make sure you're all right."

"I'm stronger than I look, honest. Please, put me down!" Man, oh man—did he ever smell nice. And strong, was he ever strong! And his eyes, though dark, danced with that light again. Despite his words, she struggled to be put down. "You don't have to do this—I'm really all right…honest."

"Hold still. We're almost there." He carried her towards the front of the store where McDonald's was. "I'll ask you again—do you have some kind of death wish or something?"

Merry Beth placed her flushed, rosy embarrassed face in the front of his black leather jacket once more. "Oh! *Put me down. This is so embarrassing. Put me down—people are staring. Oh, this is ridiculous!*"

When he remained silent she continued, "My stuff. I dropped all the stuff I need for the Christmas angels' costumes. I have to go back and get them. And my purse—oh, no, I've lost my purse, my wallet and my money!"

Her cries didn't go unheard, just ignored for the moment.

Baron carefully placed her gently in an empty booth in the McDonald's lobby and frowned down at her when she flinched in obvious pain. "Are you going to be all right?"

Merry Beth looked up at him through a wall of tears. "Yes, I will be—just let me catch my breath a minute…" She watched the muscles in his face twitch and lowered her eyes, wondering why he was so angry and so hard, like steel.

"Why aren't you at home in bed resting? How are you going to heal if you keep pushing yourself so hard?" He could feel her breath on his cheek and frowned when he realized he was so close, and backed up quickly. Her perfume—roses this time lingered near his brain as he turned abruptly away.

"I can't rest—there's too much to do. Christmas is coming!"

"I'll go and retrieve our fallen packages and your purse. Stay here—I'll be right back. Don't move from this spot!" he ordered.

Merry Beth smiled as she watched him walk quickly away. Her stomach grumbled and she reached for the money she had in her right coat pocket. She'd stuffed the change from a fifty in there, when she'd filled Pastor Todd's car with gas earlier at Irving's Truck Stop.

She'd already passed through the short line to order food by the time he returned with their blue carry-baskets and her purse. She smiled despite his frown and said cheerfully, "Hope you're hungry, Mr. Knight-in-Shining-Armor…my treat. I got us some Big Mac's, fries and fresh coffee."

He passed her a stern look when she placed the brown tray on their table with another killer smile. *Doesn't this woman ever feel sad, lonely, scared or alone? Does she always smile like this? Why does she have to be so pretty, so tempting, so nice; so needy?*

"You're one stubborn woman! Don't you *ever* listen?"

She grinned and lifted her chin. "Not if I can help it."

"You need to take it easy, Mrs. Waters. Are you sure you're all right?" he asked for the third time as he reached for the tray. "That woman hit your left arm pretty hard, and you shouldn't be carrying anything with a sprained wrist!"

"I'll be fine. It's only a *light* sprain." She nodded yes, fibbing through her pearly whites. "And it's only a serving tray, for goodness sakes! I made it through Bethany's birth without anyone holding my hand. I can surely carry a McDonald tray without hurting myself. I hope that you're hungry, Mr. Williams, because *I'm starving!* I bought you lunch—to thank you for rescuing me again. You *do* like Big Mac's, fries and coffee I hope…?"

He shook his head that he did and she asked, "So, what's it like to be a guardian angel *and* a hero?" As usual, her smile was bright and cheery as she sat. She didn't miss how he waited to sit after she had. So, he was a perfect gentleman as well. That was very unique in today's crazy world.

"I told you once—I'm no hero, and I'm certainly no angel." Baron just shook his head in disbelief as he took his seat across from her in the booth. He placed their two blue carry-baskets on the floor by their feet and removed his black Stetson and placed it on the table next to her retrieved purse.

"The woman who hit you with her cart had our things, and was looking for me when I went back to the aisle where we were." His eyes switched to her bruised yet pretty face.

He was stunned when it hit him right out of the blue, like a hurricane forceful wind, that he wanted to reach out and smooth away the bruises on the left side of her face. He wanted to pull her into his arms and give her comfort, caring and strength. He wanted to know this woman—*really* know this woman, and that frightened him beyond belief. He felt like his insides were trembling. Why he didn't just get up and leave was beyond his understanding.

"You are, too, an angel—surely, you know that you're mine?"

"I'll Be Home For Christmas" played softly above his head and he winced, hating the song. Suddenly, he felt like he couldn't breathe again. Her smile was too close and too comforting and made him wish for things he'd never find or feel again.

He winced after he angrily spat, "I'm nobody's angel, believe me! You're delusional if you think I am."

The smile she passed his way made sweat break out above his upper lip. "Well, whether you like it or not—you're mine. Every time I see you—you help rescue me from falling and…"

"Dying," he simply stated, as he reached for his coffee.

She winced at his single word but smiled at him anyway and passed him a Big Mac, large fries and ketchup. "Bethany isn't going to be too pleased when she finds out I ate at McDonald's without her. She just *loves* the Chicken Nuggets and fries and chocolate shakes, and you know what—her father was the same way. Do you eat out at McDonald's very often?"

Baron shook his head in disbelief; not able to remember the last time he'd ate out anywhere. "It's been a while." He ignored the creamers and sugars she placed in the middle of their table and removed the lid from his hot coffee. "Where is the little talkative, freckled, red-headed, cute-as-a-button, munchkin this afternoon? Don't all kids love to go to Wal-Mart…especially at Christmas?"

He watched her soft emerald eyes sparkle with life and a warm, friendly glow as she spoke of her daughter. "Bethany is with her friend, Lisa, at my best friend's home finishing her special Christmas cards." She reached for the salt and pepper and added both to her fresh burger.

"And you're right, Mr. Williams—I *am* supposed to be at home resting in my bed. Don't tell anyone," she leaned closer to whisper, "…it'll be our secret, just yours and mine. Okay?"

And then the miracle happened right in front of her this time—he smiled. It was a genuine, broad, sincere and friendly smile. One she'd never forget for the rest of her days.

Tears threatened. "You did it," she whispered.

He sipped his fresh black coffee. "What?"

She plopped three fries in her mouth. "You smiled."

Merry Beth's heart filled with hope. *Yes! Finally the man smiles! This is good, really good—thank You, dear Lord. Now, what miracle am I supposed to help deliver next? Maybe—oh, I know…laughter. Does this man even know how to laugh?* She thought back and frowned slightly, come to think of it he hadn't laughed once since she'd met him either.

"My best friend, Debbie—my pastor's sister-in-law, took Bethany off my hands after church so I could go home, relax, rest and take it easy…in bed! As you can see—I'm being a very naughty girl indeed." She talked a mile-a-minute, and always had bundles of energy. He craved that and sucked it all in, greedily.

He chose to ignore that statement. "What's the white feathers for?" he couldn't help but ask, as he glanced down in her carry-basket. She really had some interesting things in there.

After she closed her eyes in thanks for her food, Merry Beth took a huge bite of her Big Mac, chewed and swallowed before answering his question. "They're for the angel costumes I'm making for all the girls in Bethany's Sunday-School class at church. They're putting on a Christmas play with singing of hymns and the story of baby Jesus' birth in Bethlehem on Christmas Eve and..."

She stopped in mid-sentence when she heard him gasp and catch his breath. She watched him as he paled to a ghostly white. She didn't miss how his hand shook violently when he reached for his coffee and slowly lifted it to his lips. What in the world? What did she do or say just now, to create such pain in him so suddenly?

Baron ignored the white spots dancing suddenly in front of his eyes and sipped his coffee. "Your daughter—she's so filled with laughter and life and happiness. Tell me, Mrs. Waters; is she like this all year or just at Christmas? She looks a lot like you, you know—with the freckles and all..."...*that beauty.*

She asked between bites, "All what?"

He smiled again. "All that energy..."

He placed his coffee back on the table and reached for his hot fries, somehow knowing Bethany was a happy child all year long. He wanted to hold her in his arms again while she trustingly slept with her little face buried in his neck. "I have a feeling your daughter's happy and smiling and excited about life and living all year long. Am I right? Like you—she has this...glow about her."

"Yes, she's like her father in that way. Thomas Earl was filled with love and laughter, warmth, caring and smiles—all year long, and my sweet Bethany is very much like him," Merry Beth answered with a saddened smile, but only for a second or two. Her eyes sparkled when she glanced at him. "You think I glow?"

His dark eyes told her he did. "How long has your husband been gone?" Baron asked huskily.

There was no sadness in her eyes when she spoke of her late-husband. "Thomas died just before Bethany was born—congestive heart failure, almost six years ago now."

He paled, genuinely sorry. "I'm sorry."

She smiled and reached for more fries. "Don't be. I have wonderful happy memories, and I'll see him again some day."

They sat in silence as they both took a huge bite from their Big Mac's. "*Silent Night*" played softly in the background and Baron said huskily, "This is the song that brought tears to your eyes when you awoke from the accident in I.C.U."

Merry Beth just stared at him in disbelief. To think that he'd remembered something so special and private to her. "This song was Bethany's father's favorite, and also my dad's. He passed away three months ago. I still…miss him…"

Ah, the sadness was there this time. Baron didn't miss it or how she'd paled suddenly. "Are you all right?"

She smiled across the table bravely. "I will *always* miss daddy. He was my guardian angel my entire life—until *you* came along. He was everything good and decent and strong and dependable. Bethany misses her grandfather very much. She talks of him every day. They were very close."

When he remained silent she quietly asked, "How long have you been alone, Mr. Williams?" She heard him wince and catch his breath in again, and wished she could pull her hasty question back. She lowered her eyes to her fries. Her hand shook a little as she lifted two to her mouth. "I'm sorry…I didn't mean to bring the painful memories back."

"Three years, come Christmas Eve," Baron whispered. He swallowed the huge lump rising in his throat, choked on his Big Mac and reached for a napkin. She was right; thinking back only brought more pain. Maybe sitting here with this broken and bruised, yet beautiful woman wasn't such a good idea after all. She had a way to make him talk of things he'd just-as-soon forget. He couldn't, and that was why he lived the way he did—until he met Merry Beth.

It was her turn to cringe and she did it gracefully. "I'm so sorry…" Now she knew the reason her words a moment ago had created pain across his dark eyes. Now she knew why he never smiled or laughed. Now she knew why he was so alone.

"Don't be. I, too, have my happy memories."

Her eyes sparkled. "Did you like your pears?"

He smiled again. "I ate every one of them, thank you."

"No, it's *you* my baby and I have to thank."

All this was spoken without either one glancing at the other; their guardian angels' glanced at each other and smiled; unseen. The wonderful Christmas bells began to ring, but only God and the angels could hear them at that moment. Miracles were happening in both Baron and Merry Beth's hearts.

"No, *you* and *your baby* are the ones who helped bring *me* out of my dark state of aloneness. Until I opened my door and found you both on my front doorstep—actually, until I reached in and pulled you both from that crumpled wreckage, I'd literally shut myself off from family and friends. It's *you* that is *my* guardian angel, Mrs. Waters." He couldn't believe he'd just exposed so much about himself to her, and didn't even try to understand it. He squirmed in his seat, not liking it.

Green eyes met and clashed with black across the table.

"Please, call me Merry Beth."

"Okay, only if you'll call me Baron."

"Thank you, Baron—for saving our lives."

He smiled at her again. She smiled back.

He thought, *No, thank you for saving my life!*

A friendship had begun. A miracle had been granted.

"You know, they say if you save someone's life you are eternally responsible for it." She watched the emotions swim across his ebony eyes—the anger was now gone, replaced with a deep sense of sadness. His smile from before hadn't reached his eyes and her heart filled with new ideas of different ways to help him again. Her head buzzed with them and she felt dizzy from it.

"And who is *they*?"

"Well, you know…people."

He chuckled. "*Really*…what people?"

"Why don't you come to the Christmas play and concert at my church on Christmas Eve? Bethany would love to have you come. She talks about you non-stop you know," she suggested without lowering her eyes from his. Could one smile really make a difference in a life? "It's at the Winterville Baptist Church on Pine Street…"

"I don't think so. But, thanks for the invite." He pushed his empty Big-Mac container away and reached for his black coffee once more. Sweat broke out on his forehead. He didn't need all this *nice* stuff—he needed to get back to work. And he hadn't darkened the doorframe to a church since the funeral.

"Those extra Christmas lights that Bethany mentioned earlier this morning—if you want them, they're yours for the taking," she offered before taking another bite. "I'm not sure what kind of shape they're in—they're buried in my basement somewhere. My husband hung up hundreds of lights every year. He loved the lights. If you want them I'll dig them out. I'll give you my address and you can stop by to pick them up." She scrambled to find a pen and a piece of paper in her purse.

"I haven't decorated the house in," he began with a whisper. *Three years. Dear God, how did my life become this empty and lonely and forlorn?* "...well—it's been a while."

"Maybe it's time you did, Baron. Maybe it will help your heart to begin to heal," she lightly suggested with another killer smile, as she wrote her address and phone number down on a small piece of paper she found buried in the bottom of her purse. "Maybe it'll help you move past the pain and sadness I see in your eyes from losing your family, and live again."

She passed him the paper, and watched his jaw twitch and his eyes flared to hers angrily. "You don't *know* me, Merry Beth. So stop trying to be *my* rescuer or guardian angel. I don't need your help!"

She frowned and paled and tears filled her pretty eyes; he regretted his loss of temper immediately and wished he could snatch his heated words back. His empty and broken life wasn't *her* fault. He shouldn't take his anger and bitterness out on her.

He felt like a complete jerk again. "I'm sorry. I..."

"I beg to differ." *So much bitterness and anger! Don't you know that God has the grace to save you from this sadness and aloneness?* "You *do* need my help. *God* sent me to you."

"Oh, I just bet He did." *All this kindness, laughter and smiles can't be real!* He sucked in his breath. *Dear God—help me, what kind of man have I become? I'm so angry and bitter and cynical all the time...*

Their eyes met and clashed once more. "No one should be alone, especially at Christmas!" *He needs kind words and soft touches in his life to help him heal. Heal and move on...*

"I live and breathe alone." *Oh, Becky, I miss you so much. I can't do it. I can't let go—you're still here with me inside my heart!*

"You're one of those people who no longer care and have lost their way because of loss, hurt and pain." *Please, dear Lord, help me say the right words to help him to keep smiling!*

"It's sad, you know," she said softly.

"What is?" he asked nastily, biting back his quick loss of temper, wincing when he burned his tongue on his coffee.

She finished off her Big-Mac and reached for a clean napkin. "Living your life this way..."

His black eyes snapped like fire. "Since when has my life become your next problem to solve?"

Her stubborn chin lifted. "Life's too precious...we all learned that lesson on Nine-Eleven when those planes hit and those Twin Towers fell to earth in ashen death. I'll never forget that day, ever. So many dead—men, women, children..."

He closed his eyes, remembering back. "I know, and I lost my world three years ago on Christmas Eve. It doesn't get better when you lose the ones you love the most...trust me. Once they're dead...they stay dead. There's no getting them back...ever!"

His dark eyes burned into hers as he thought, *Why can't you just go away and pass all those wonderful, warm smiles to some other poor sucker who needs or wants them? I found all I needed in Becky's eyes and smile. I will never ask for more!*

"I know your pain—I lost my husband..."

"My reasons for living are gone with my wife and son."

"But it is Christmas, and life is for living!" *And I've already seen more than my share of miracles. It's your turn Baron—right here with you now is where God wants me to be. Let me help you!*

"So?" *I don't believe in Christmas and miracles anymore!*

There was so much to say yet there were no words between them. Only silence, so sad and lonely was his life.

Merry Beth gasped, knowing deep in her heart that he was going to be hard to reach. He had isolated himself for so long he'd lost touch with the world and human touch all around him. But had the isolation destroyed the man he was inside?

"Don't you believe in God and angels, love and kindness, hope and peace, rainbows and flowers, smiles *and* laughter anymore?" Merry Beth asked, knowing by the dark look in his eyes he didn't. She stuffed a few fries in her mouth.

"No." *And I never will again, so go away!*

"That's sad." *This is going to be harder than I thought!*

"No, it's reality. I live in the *real* world, Merry Beth. You give me one reason to believe again—*one*—and I'll hang up so many little blinking Christmas lights in my windows and on my home outside, that it will even make the tree in Rockefeller Square in Manhattan look bleak!" His hard black eyes challenged her with enough fire and determination that she couldn't help but wince and jerk back in her seat. Despite the pain slashing from within her sore ribs, she smiled across the table at him again.

She grinned. "All right, I can do that. For starters..."

She was too beautiful, and she'd made him care again. Feeling closed in again, he held up his hand to stop her as she started to speak. "Don't bother." He glanced at his watch.

"But…" she began as she chewed her fries.

"I have to go. Thanks for lunch."

"But you barely even touched your fries! Don't go…"

"Tell the munchkin thanks for the pears." Yes, life was for living. Baron gave in to the stubbornness that yanked at him, rose and walked rudely away without a backward glance.

Before Merry Beth could even blink he was up and out of the booth and walking away towards the front doors that would take him to the packed parking lot. She frowned and glanced down at his deserted carry-basket filled with red, green and white candles and other Christmas goodies—scotch tape, silver and gold ribbon—the glittery kind, sticker labels, a Christmas music CD by Celine Dion and small, red velvety bows…and Christmas lights!

A smile crossed her lips as she reached for his forgotten items and placed them in her own basket, silently telling herself she would be the one to deliver the message of *light* and *giving* Baron so desperately needed to make him truly smile again, from within.

Life was for reaching out and helping others in trouble. Life was about taking those chances. She wouldn't give up, not one to ever walk away from a challenge or risk or fight. She loved life, and wanted to live it to its fullest. She wanted the same for her new friend, no matter what it took.

Proverbs 25: 14-15 "Whoso boasteth himself of a false gift *is like* clouds and wind without rain. By long forbearing is a prince persuaded, and a soft tongue breaketh the bone."

Chapter Three

Matthew 1:22-23 "Now all this was done, that it might be fulfilled which was spoken of the LORD by the prophet, saying, Behold, a virgin shall be with child, and shall bring forth a son, and they shall call his name Emmanuel, which being interpreted is, God with us."

Miracle #2, laughter, December 14th, Monday, 7:33 a.m.

THE YOUNG GIRL stared at her mother—sometimes she just didn't seem to understand! "But...*Mommy!*" Bethany complained, rolling her pretty eyes to the high ceiling.

Merry Beth turned away from her sudsy sink filled with hot water and dirty breakfast dishes to give her daughter a stern 'I-mean-it-or-else-you're-in-trouble' look.

"Don't *but* me, young lady. You're old enough to help clean your own room. Now, I want you to go up there and pick up all your dirty clothes and put them where they belong in the hamper in the bathroom. Then, I want you to pick up all your toys and put them away where they go in your toy box and on your bookshelves. Mommy only has one arm and hand because of the accident, and it's kind of hard for me to do a lot of things right now with that one hand sprained. I need your help, baby…"

Her head spun with a dozen different things she needed to do today, and her right wrist and hand, no longer bandaged, was hurting unbearably, and she turned her head to hide her quick tears from her daughter, not wanting to frighten her. She hadn't taken any pain medication today; it made her feel sleepy all the time.

Bethany quickly jumped down from her bright-yellow booster chair and walked across the kitchen, and placed her dirty Cinderella juice cup and special Beauty-and-the-Beast cereal bowl on the kitchen counter. "All right, Mommy, but *then* can I go out and play? R'member—Lisa is com'innn over to build our spe'caall angels in the snow, and build our very own snow-girls. You promised!"

Merry Beth smiled and swallowed her burning tears back. Her daughter's speech was getting better every day, and often made her chuckle with laughter. Bethany rarely fussed or cried or gave her grief. Yet, she had to be stern!

"All right, baby—you can go out *after* your room is picked up." She sighed and rubbed at her throbbing right temple. There was so much to do and at the moment, she just wanted to crawl back in bed and sleep for days uninterrupted. She reached for the teakettle and filled it with cold spring water to heat for another cup of hot tea. Christmas was definitely the busy season. Yet she loved all of its wonder and joy and magic.

Bethany's eyes lit up with excitement and she jumped up and down and clapped her hands together. "Thanks, Mommy, you are the bestest Mommy ever!" She stepped close and hugged her mother's waist tight, forgetting about Merry Beth's sore ribs.

Merry Beth watched her daughter smile before she raced from the kitchen towards the stairs. "*And no running in the house, Hope Bethany—I mean it! Slow down!*"

She smiled as Elvis sang one of her favorite Christmas songs from the kitchen windowsill radio, "*Holly Leaves and Christmas Trees.*" The idea just popped into her head out of the blue, and she knew instantly, from hearing the song, how she was going to help deliver the second miracle called *laughter* in Baron's lonely life and broken heart. Her guardian angel also smiled, glad that Merry Beth was paying attention.

Oh, yes.

It was good to be alive.

It was good to have a new friend.

It was good that she could help him.

Baron needed that, a friend.

Although strong, he was hurting.

She wanted to erase that pain.

Could she help him love life and living again?

Oh, yeah!

* * * * *

Twenty minutes later, she smiled as she hung up her kitchen phone. It felt really good to be doing something special to help someone whose eyes silently begged for it. As she finished washing her dirty dishes with one hand she thought, *In*

60

exactly one hour and ten minutes be prepared to receive your very own huge, beautiful, tall, very tall, pine Christmas tree, Mr. Baron Williams. And maybe—just maybe—you'll add some laughter with that smile you gave me yesterday, and some day maybe that smile and laughter will reach your eyes, and after that your heart! You can't continue to give in to the sadness that losing your family has caused. You're alive, and God has something special planned for the rest of your life. I can feel it. I'm here, my new friend, to help deliver these miracles. I won't give up!

Three hours later, she stood at her back knotty-pine door watching her daughter and Lisa play happily in the snow, building their very own snow-*girls*. Their laughter, happiness and innocence warmed her heart as she turned away to make herself another cup of hot cinnamon tea.

She glanced at the calendar near the kitchen phone and counted the days until Christmas Eve. "Ten more days, Merry Beth—you need to get working on those angel costumes!" She blew her bangs from her eyes and reached on the top of the fridge for the bottle of Aspirin. The phone rang and she jumped.

"Hello…" She reached over and placed the teakettle on the big front burner on medium-high heat. "I know it's you, Debbie. I love this new caller ID I splurged for at Wal-Mart last week. It's nice to know who it is that's calling."

"Why—you getting weird calls again?"

Merry Beth winced. "Eh, no…not lately…"

Debbie smiled. "Is Lisa being good?"

"Our girls are laughing and having a ball outside playing in the snow building their very own snow-*girls*. You should see them. I gave them this old New England Patriot's baseball cap of daddy's, and also a old blue wool hat that was my mother's, two carrots for the noses, two old scarves, Oreo cookies for the eyes, grapes for the mouths, two old brooms, an old green Halloween wig and a white mop-head for the hair, and they found four long twigs for the arms. They're fabulous. I took a few pictures so we can both cherish the memory. Oh, and they added daddy's old fishing boots for the feet. These two snow-*girls* are truly masterpieces! I should call the newspaper office in town, for one of their editors to come out and take a shot and a story for the weekly paper!"

"The girls would love it!" Debbie roared with laughter. "I wanted to call and let you know I'm taking Kristi, Jason and Lisa to the White Birch Mall after lunch. Lisa wants to see Santa. She wanted me to ask you if Bethany can come along."

Merry Beth smiled at her best friend's laughter. "I know she'd love it, thanks. I haven't had the chance to take her yet with the accident and all. She has her own money. She's saved her allowance for months for Christmas shopping. I have some money put aside in a glass jar above the fridge—if she needs more."

"Good. It will also give you another chance to rest."

"I can't rest! I need to finish those angel costumes!"

"The Christmas pine tree you called about this morning has already been delivered to Mr. Williams' house, just a little while ago. Hugh delivered it himself," Debbie informed with a smile.

"Tell your brother I said I'll pay him when I see him at church Christmas Eve, or I can just give you the money when you pick up the girls after lunch."

"He said you don't owe him a thing, Merry Beth. He said not to worry about it. He said it's your welcome home gift."

"I wonder what Baron will think when Hugh knocks on his door with the tree." She glanced out the back door to check on the girls once more before reaching for her whistling kettle. "You should see his house, Debbie. It's terrible! It's so empty and barren and dark and cold." *Just like his eyes…*

"I'm sure he'll love it, Merry Beth—I have to go. Jason is yelling for me loud enough to wake the dead. I can't believe he's graduating in June and then off to college in September. I'll see you around one, okay? Bye…love you!"

"Bye, Debbie. Thanks…love you!"

Merry Beth glanced one more time out her back door before gathering all the necessary ingredients for the special Christmas cookie ornaments she wanted to make for Baron's tree. Every prayer she'd prayed recently had been answered. It was so cool!

Surely, God wouldn't stop now. In minutes she was covered with flour and cookie dough, as she prepared to make her special cookies for her new friend.

* * * * *

The Fort Kent, State Police & Border Patrol Headquarters station buzzed with excitement and laughter. Baron's 'welcome back' party was in full swing. Christmas decorations, hot food and gift swapping added to the festive spirit. Christmas lights of every color blinked on and off in every window, and candles cast their scented glow across the knotty-pine desk tops. The wives had been invited to the party and had added their own special touches, here and there.

"Baron, could you come into my office for a minute?"

It felt good to be back amongst the living again. Baron smiled and stood from his cluttered dark-oak work desk and walked towards Mitch's office. "Sure, boss, what's up? You look a little peeked and green around the edges, Mitch. What's wrong? Is Carolyn all right?"

Baron passed his boss a fresh cup of perked black coffee. "Here, take this, I just perked it fresh. And no, it isn't spiked."

"Good, Carolyn would have my hide hung in a tree if it was."

"She's not at the Christmas party and…" Baron began.

Mitch chuckled when Baron passed him worried look. "She's fine. She's shopping—you know how all women love to do that, especially now, during the Christmas season. Sit. I want to show you something." He took the cup and placed it on his shiny oak desk, next to his ringing phone.

"I just aced four hours on the firing range." Baron sat in one of the two empty leather chairs in front of Mitch's shiny oak desk and crossed his black boots one over the other. It felt good to be back. He never thought it would again, but wearing the badge was a big part of who he still was.

"You don't need to practice. If there's one thing you're good at—it's firing a weapon. You've always been one of the best on the force, you know that." Mitch smiled when he found the file he wanted. "Ah, here it is."

Baron sipped his coffee and remained silent.

"Listen to this—graduated at eighteen with high honors from Bangor High School, graduated at twenty-four with high honors from Radcliffe in New York, with a Public Defender lawyer's degree. You worked three years as Assistant District Attorney in In-town Manhattan. You joined the Navy at twenty-seven…" He glanced at Baron over the rim of his golden-framed glasses with raised silver eyebrows. "Twenty-seven…?"

"Yeah, so…?" Baron sipped his coffee. "Why are you reading my file, Mitch? What's up?"

"You must have been in perfect physical shape; Bear—most guys join the service when they're young around eighteen or twenty." Mitch raised his eyebrow in question again.

"Watch it, boss! I still am," Baron said with a wide grin as he sipped his coffee with one hand and patted his fit and flat stomach with the other. The one thing he hadn't not done since he'd lost his family was work out. He had an expensive gym at home with all the modern equipment, and also a membership to the local YMCA.

Mitch chuckled. "You're still what, young or in shape?"

Baron sipped his coffee. "Both!"

Mitch laughed and turned back to reading Baron's impressive file. "You've lost those extra fifteen pounds since I saw you last."

"I've been working out at the YMCA three times a week these past six months—tell the truth, boss. You're just jealous!"

Baron laughed lightly before asking once more, "Why you snooping around in my file, Mitch. What you looking for?"

Mitch just shook his head and continued reading. "You served eight years in the Green Beret, Special Forces. You retired with high honors. You married Captain Becky Lucille Paul on May twenty-sixth…"

At Baron's sharp intake of breath Mitch stopped and glanced at his friend above the rim of his reading glasses once more. Mitch frowned, worried about his best man. "Sorry about that…"

"Why are you reading my file, Mitch?" Baron asked with a nervous smile, ignoring the sickening feeling in the pit of his empty stomach that the department thought him too old or too washed up to wear a badge and gun again. It would never happen! This job was his life—it was all he had left. He'd wasted enough time as it was. He needed to get back to work!

"I never did really understand why you quit your job as Assistant D.A. in Manhattan, Baron. Want to tell me about it?" Mitch asked as he reached for his coffee and took a sip. "Why would an uprising attorney and Assistant D.A. want to move to Maine to become a State Trooper?"

"No, I do not! It's in the past. *Want to tell me what's really going on here?*" Baron jumped up from his chair and started pacing back and forth in front of the desk, frustrated beyond reason, anxious to get back to work, anxious to get back out there, and not stuck behind a desk answering the phone and sipping spiked punch!

Mitch just grunted and continued reading Baron's file. "You graduated from State Police Academy in Boston in May of '99, worked for this office for seven months until December—when you lost your…family…"

At Baron's murderous stare he murmured, "Sorry…you were so overly qualified for your job that you were promoted to Sergeant within a month."

"Yeah, so…why bring all this up, Mitch?"

Dark memories from the accident flashed in front of his sharp eyes—blood, there was always the blood! "I *know* why I left this office—*why do you have to bring Becky's name up in my face this way, Mitch? What is it you want from me?*" His heart drummed hard. He hated his loss of temper.

Baron had paled to a ghostly white and his eyes flashed across the desk like fire and brimstone. He knew he was on the edge—he needed to calm down and regain his bearings. He needed to get on with his life, but every time he thought back to the real reason he'd quit his job as Assistant D.A. his blood boiled.

There'd been too much he couldn't change, too much violence and death, too much pain, too much bending the rules.

"You need to get on with it. Leave the past—all of it, including Becky—in the past. Losing her and your son is slowly destroying you. You're on the edge, and I'm afraid you're like a walking time bomb that's going to explode at any moment!" Mitch never even flinched when Baron exploded in anger and frustration.

"That's what I'm doing! Getting on with it! Why the inquiry…?" Baron hissed through teeth that actually hurt. Several fellow officers began to stare through the open door and Baron passed them a 'butt-out-and-mind-your-own-business' stare.

Mitch turned away from his computer and stared at his good friend with worry and concern. "Look at you. I mention Becky's name one time—*one time*, and you're out of control!"

The muscles in Baron's face twitched. "Want to get to the point? And I am *not* out of control, Mitch, far from it!" Baron thundered through clenched teeth, knowing deep inside it was true. Had he lost his edge? Had he lost his depth?

"You're not ready," Mitch simply stated and reached for his coffee once more, relaxing back in his leather chair.

"What are you talking about?" Baron asked and rubbed his throbbing temples. "You always talk in riddles!"

"I need someone I can trust *not* to lose it under pressure, under fire—like you just did," Mitch simply stated firmly.

He slowly counted to ten. "You can stop worrying, Mitch. I'm fine. Didn't you get the report from that shrink you sent me to first thing this morning, around dawn?" Baron asked with impatience across his tongue as he rose and started to pace.

"Are you purposely trying to aggravate, annoy, irritate and provoke me into—what? *What is it you want from me? Blood? Hasn't there been enough of that shed?"* Baron thundered, breathing hard.

"Doctor Lewis, yes…I got her report," Mitch said with a worried frown across his brow, as he stared at the vanilla envelope that held the report.

"And…?" Baron pressed onward. The woman was a flake. Everyone in the department knew it.

"She thinks it's a mistake to let you come back. She says you're not ready. She says you're walking on the edge."

"Well, she's wrong. If I weren't ready I wouldn't be here, Mitch. You *know* me, and you know how much I loved Becky and my son. You *know* what that accident did to me! *It ripped my whole world apart, Mitch.* Look at me, *I'm almost forty-five years old and I have no wife, no children to carry on my name, and nothing to live for except this job! Can you say the same?*"

Mitch rose from his chair and zoomed in close to his friend's face. "You don't have to remind me. I was the one to rescue you from the liquor you swallowed and the bottle you buried yourself in after the funeral, remember? I'm your friend. I was at the funeral, I was there for you, and then you kicked me out of your home and life on my sorry butt and told me to go away and never come back!"

A muscle under Baron's left eye twitched violently. "Calm down, would you? I said I was sorry for that already…"

"You shut yourself off from friends, co-workers, what family you have left, you never smile and you drank alone! The man I once knew is gone." He didn't miss the black void in his friend's eyes where life used to be and winced, yet didn't back down.

These were the moments he wondered if God and Heaven truly existed. The muscles in Baron's jaw twitched as he tried to get his quick temper back under control. "All I see at the moment is *you* losing control. Want to back up? You're using up too much of my space and oxygen, and all this silliness is getting on my last nerve!"

Baron knew he needed to get a grip. For several moments the silence between them echoed in the room like a beating native drum. Mitch glanced at Baron from head to toe.

"Look at you! Your uniform all starched and pressed anew. Your badge all shined and polished; your sidearm all cleaned, loaded and ready to fire at a moment's notice. Your shoes all shiny and spiffy; your E.M.T. and driving courses all up to date, your lawyer's degree hidden in a forgotten drawer in your home office, still collecting dust I'm sure. Your military awards and medals tucked safely away on blue velvet in your wall safe, your…" Mitch clamped down on his own loss of temper when Baron interrupted his well-planned speech.

"You want to get to the bloody point sometime soon? Or are we just going to keep on wasting my time here babbling on and on and on about the past?" Baron thundered.

Mitch remained silent, eyes sharp and observant.

"Are you going to fill me in on that special case you've been working on, or what?" Baron asked angrily as he rubbed his pounding temples. "I didn't plan on you giving me the third degree like this. I just want to get back to work! Why you trying to hold me back? Are you my friend or my shrink? I don't need this added pressure, Mitch."

"You look the part—all polished, shined and pretty as a peach, but I'm concerned about the man, the *emotions* on the inside, Bear. I'm concerned you'll snap under pressure!" Mitch shook his head when Baron swore as he paced.

"You're not my shrink, but you're supposed to be my *friend!* Want to tell me why you're shutting me out?"

"I know you've seen and have been under more pressure than I could ever imagine in the Navy, Baron. Iraq, Bosnia, Iran, Cambodia, China, Afghanistan; places in the Middle East I've never even heard of, or care to…" Mitch began and groaned when interrupted again.

Baron stopped his pacing and leaned both hands down on Mitch's desk. "Why are you bringing up my past from the Navy, boss? And you and everyone in this department tell me that I need to put what happened to Becky and my son behind me. Well, the only way I know how to do that is to get back to work. There is nothing else, old *friend!*"

Little did Baron know that the angels watching over him and Merry Beth knew different, and planned on getting them together as a lot more than just friends in the near future, *if* he gave in to the stubbornness and accepted Merry Beth's smiles and friendship as just that. Only time would tell.

"I'm concerned about you—who you are and what you are on the inside. What you've become since losing Becky and Baron, Jr. You are a different man now, Baron. You're harder, colder, more distant, phlegmatic, and I'm telling you I know that you're walking that thin wire!"

Baron's dark eyes flashed like sizzling fire. "I am far from ever being unfeeling, passionless, listless, cold, lethargic, sluggish, slow or lazy, Mitch. I'm far from being any of those things. My absence from this job and my normal life in the past three years shows that I still have feelings. It shows that I still have a heart. For heaven's sakes, man, I lost my wife and son in a terrible car crash! Becky was my soul mate. My son was my life; they were both killed by a drunk drivers' hand. You know that!"

"I'm worried about you, my friend," Mitch searched Baron's black eyes with concern and added quietly, "...that's all. I swear. Carolyn and I both are...as the other men in this department are. We need to be there for each other in the field—with a clear head, ready and alert at a moment notice."

Baron sat as his legs gave way. "And pigs really do fly!"

"I think it's you who needs to *calm down!*"

Baron stared at his boss and counted slowly under his breath to ten again. *One, two, three, four, five, six, seven, eight, nine, ten...*

"You don't have to be concerned, Mitch. I'm fine. I want to join the land of the living again, old friend. And the *only* way I know how to do that is get back to what I do best—my work. If you take that away from me I'll be left with...nothing."

His heart sank. He didn't need this, not now and not ever. He closed his eyes, thinking, *Oh, Becky my darling, you promised to never leave me like this—you promised. Dear God, what I wouldn't give for just one more look, one more touch, one more kiss, one more smile! Why can't I feel you with me anymore, Becky? Where did you go?*

Mitch stood and searched into Baron's midnight black eyes across his cluttered desk. "You're on a two month trial period, Bear. It's the best I can offer you right now."

Baron exploded in anger as he rose to his feet once more. "*Two months, but why? You just read my file! You know I'm over qualified for this job! You know...*"

Mitch turned away and ignored his ringing phone. "It wasn't my doing, Sergeant Williams. It wasn't my decision!" he thundered through clenched teeth.

"Then tell me who ordered it, Captain McMillian!" Baron demanded with a hardened heart after the phone silenced.

"It came down from the top brass in Machias just after you left for the firing range this morning."

Baron turned away in disgust and defeat. "This is crazy!"

Mitch hated it too, but didn't give in. "You only worked here for seven months, Bear. You have to understand..."

Baron swallowed a curse and turned away. "Just give me my workload, Mitch. *And put me in the field! It's what I do best*—you know that. And let me worry about my cold, unfeeling, no-good-for-nothing sorry and pitiful, on-the-edge self!"

As Baron turned away his knees shook and his heart was heavy. Letting go? Starting over? The two walked hand in hand to him. And why did he see Merry Beth's eyes everywhere he turned today? What did it mean? It didn't make sense.

It angered him beyond reason. Lord, help him—he wanted to scream again. Her smile, it just wouldn't go away and it was so frustrating!

He loved Becky.

It had always been Becky in his heart.

There'd never be another woman for him but Becky—ever! She was, even in death, his wife and his life.

A two-month trial, what an embarrassing insult!

He deserved better than this.

He grabbed his back-up weapon out of his top desk drawer and slammed out of the office, more hurt than bitter or angry. He needed to make an important phone call! Two month trial, indeed—it was almost funny if it weren't so stupid! A blast of cold northern air took his breath away sharply, as he hurried to his truck, blinded with overwhelming anger.

* * * * *

It was just past six p.m. and Merry Beth and Bethany had stopped at the Shop-'til-You-Drop Supermarket for food and house-hold supplies. Merry Beth stared at Baron, who was standing at the other end of the long baking aisle reaching for a bag of sugar, in disbelief and shock.

A cop…? He's a cop? How is it possible that I didn't know that? Did he mention it— no, he sure didn't. A cop! He's so handsome, so strong, so big standing there. His life—is it filled with danger, bad guys, guns, ammo and secrets? Oh, boy, now what? She smiled, thankful for another chance to help him. A frown quickly creased her brow. He was a cop!

She stared at his sharp, impressive dark blue uniform, shiny black shoes and shiny silver badge shaped like a star with interest, and didn't understand why her heart was flip flopping around in her chest like she was some love-sick, silly young school girl admiring her first date or her first love.

"Mommy, look down there! It's him! It's Mr. Bear'ronn Will'amms!" Bethany screamed at the top of her lungs, just before running off down the long aisle towards Baron at quick lightning speed. Merry Beth winced then closed her eyes for a moment.

"Hope Bethany Waters! *You come back here—right now, young lady!*" Her heart raced so fast she couldn't catch her breath. Merry Beth's demand went unanswered and she stared after her daughter with an aggravated frown. She threw the cooking vanilla in her grocery cart before pushing her cart further down the aisle after her daughter. It was hard with only one hand, yet she managed.

69

As she passed the flour section she quickly reached for a bag of self-rising flour with her right hand, and as she turned to continue her chase the bag dropped from her hand when pain slashed up and down her wrist and up her arm, and the flour bag exploded as it hit the items in her cart. Flour flew through the air, silently and softly, literally everywhere. Oh, man—this was truly embarrassing...now what? She started to giggle.

There was flour in her hair, flour dust in her eyes and on her lashes, flour all over her worn black winter coat, flour on her bruised cheeks and freckled nose, flour on her blue tennis shoes, flour all around her feet on the shiny gray-vinyl floor.

Giggles surfaced but she pushed them down. "Oh, no—I can't believe I just did that!" She glanced up at her daughter once more with a frown. Bethany and Baron were walking her way and, may God help her, he was smiling from ear-to-ear! And his smile did funny things to her stomach and weakened her knees. Her hopes died down. Why did he have to be a cop?

Merry Beth smiled in spite of her present embarrassing situation. *Yes! Mission number two accomplished without even really trying this time!* Sergeant Williams was now laughing—laughing so hard he had tears in the corners of his eyes. She felt wonderful, wonderful but extremely embarrassed.

He walked slowly up to her and asked, as he reached out bravely to wipe away flour from her cheeks and nose, "You need me to rescue you *again*, pretty flour snowbird?" He chuckled once more and tried hard to keep a straight face but couldn't.

Her mending cheeks turned bright red. "No, I do not!"

"Every time I see you you're in some kind of trouble or another." He glanced down at Bethany and chuckled. "What do you think, Munchkin? You think we should help your mommy clean up this mess, or let her do it on her own?"

Merry Beth swallowed against her own rising laughter. "Stop laughing. It's *not* funny!"

"Mommy, you look like mine and Lisa's snow-girls!"

Merry Beth glanced up at Baron, way up since he seemed to tower over her like a tall building, and turned twenty shades of red. She then turned and glared at her laughing daughter in fun yet sincere embarrassment. "*Stop laughing this very second, young lady. And you, too, Mr. Williams—it isn't funny. I mean it—stop laughing. People are staring again!*" She blew her too-long bangs from her eyes. "I can't believe I just did that. I'm so embarrassed..."

Bethany giggled. "Mommy, you look sooooo fun-nieee!"

"I can't help it. This is priceless—if you could just see the look on your *white* and bruised and pretty freckled face." He turned to wink at Bethany and asked, "You have a camera in that back-pack of yours? I know women carry just about everything in those things."

Bethany giggled and shook her head no. Baron and Bethany roared with fun and laughter as they helped brush her off. "Mommy, you look so fun'nieee! You're all white—just like my angel costume you made'deded me."

Merry Beth couldn't help it and gave in with their fun and laughter. "I can't believe I just did that." She pointed at her daughter and stifled another strong giggle. "It's *your* fault, young lady. You know better than to take off running, away from me in *any* store like that. I've warned you time and time and time again!"

Baron started taking her groceries out of her cart one by one, shaking and brushing off the flour with his fingers. He reached in his back pocket for his clean handkerchief and wiped them off one by one and put her items in his cart without even thinking twice about it.

"Now, Merry Beth…you can't rightly blame this on the Munchkin. I think it's some kind of curse on you, or something. Think about it—since we've met you've been nearly crushed to pieces in that accident, you've broken your left arm, you've sprained your right wrist—which isn't wrapped as it should be by the way, you've almost fallen off my front porch by slipping on the snow and ice, you were nearly run over by that woman's cart at Wal-Mart, you have bruised and cracked ribs, bruises and cuts on your face, hands and arms, and now this…you're what a true knight-in-shining-armor calls a 'damsel in distress'. You're a pretty one though…"

Man, oh man—did he ever smell nice. What was that aftershave he wore? She tried not to, but couldn't help but flinch back from him when he stepped really close to whisper, "And through it all—you're still smiling and laughing. What's your secret?" he asked huskily, deeply, as he stepped closer to her when she backed up a few more steps. He could smell her perfume again—lilacs this time. Have mercy on his heart; it did funny things to his senses.

He had her backed up against the Jell-O's and Pudding's and four-for-a-dollar sign, and there was nowhere for her to go. His dark eyes held her captive. She was trapped, and there was nothing for her to do but lift her eyes to his…slowly…slowly…

And that she did. Man, oh man—was she ever pretty!

Baron couldn't help but think at that moment, *My, my, my—the fiery, stubborn, beautiful, strong-willed, pretty, bruised woman is shy? This is interesting. Very interesting indeed!*

Merry Beth thought at the same time, *This is dangerous but, so much fun. He smells so good. And those dark eyes are to just die for! He's handsome and quite desirable. He's vibrant and sturdy and strong. He's capable of breaking my heart in two!* Why did he have to be a cop?

Her heart hammered in her chest and her sore ribs cried out for mercy as Baron held her captive with his midnight black, inquiring eyes. She reminded herself to breathe before her lungs exploded. She blew her bangs from her eyes in exasperation before replying, "Back up, handsome. You're getting flour all over your impressive, starched, blue-crispy uniform!"

She tried to push him away but couldn't. He was too tall, too big, too powerful and much too strong. Her ribs throbbed and she paled. In reality, she didn't want him to back up. Lord, help her—she wanted him closer! She groaned and rolled her eyes to the ceiling, embarrassed and flustered beyond words.

"No way, no how—now answer my question—you aren't going anywhere until you do!" Baron demanded playfully.

"Mommy, can we buy some of these pret'tieee red or green little circle-star spin'kells for our spe'caall cupcakes? Please, Mommy! They are ree'llieee pretty!" Bethany reached for the little bottle of Christmas cookie sprinkles with a smile and threw them in Baron's cart without a second glance. "I like'deded the red ones the best, Mommy! They always make the cupcakes look really, really, *really* pretty!"

Merry Beth didn't take her eyes away from Baron's as she answered, "Sure can—put them in our grocery cart." His eyes—they were as black as unburned coal, like glassy sheets of ice.

Her emerald eyes pleaded silently, *Touch me, kiss me!*

His coal-black eyes whispered silently, *I want to touch you! I want to kiss you! What is this spell you've cast over me? I don't like it—not one little bit! Back away from her—right now, before it's too late!*

Baron watched her light green eyes turn to a darker shade of wet summer grass, and slowly swallowed against the huge lump in his throat. He suddenly remembered Becky, and didn't understand why he was thinking of touching and kissing and desiring another woman, and immediately backed away when he heard her sharp intake of breath like she was in pain.

"I'm sorry, Merry Beth—your ribs, did I hurt you?" In his heart he was still married to Becky, and to be this close to another woman, to desire and ever want another woman in any way, only meant one thing—betrayal. Suddenly, as sweat broke out on his forehead, he felt nauseous and a little dizzy.

Merry Beth blew her bangs out of her eyes again and finished shaking the flour off her winter coat with shaking fingers. "Don't be silly, I'm fine."

She watched her happy daughter throw a box of microwave popcorn in Baron's cart, the extra buttery and expensive kind, and stared at her in total embarrassment. "*Stop that this instant, you know better!* Put that back, Bethany. We have pop-corn at home on the top shelf in the pantry."

Bethany just stared up at her mother. "But not the *extra buttery kind*, Mommy…"

Baron turned away, sneezed and said, "It's really okay, Merry Beth. It's my treat."

Merry Beth shook her head no. "No, no way!"

Bethany continued to stare up at her mother and said, "We just *have* to have *this kind* of popcorn, Mommy! How can we deck'oorate our tree without it?"

Baron forced a smile and said, "Right Mommy! How can we decorate our tree without it?"

Bethany grabbed a bag of small, salty pretzels. "Mommy, you love these!" In the cart they carelessly flew.

Merry Beth cringed. "Bethany!"

Baron chuckled. "Yeah, Mommy—you *love* pretzels!"

Merry Beth reached for the box of microwave popcorn and the bag of pretzels and put them back on the shelf where they belonged with shaking fingers and much embarrassment. "We'll get a bag of buttery Jiffy Pop-corn, baby. It's cheaper."

Bethany took off running and she yelled, "Bethany! Come back here!" Her eyes sought Baron's. "She does this a lot. I tell her over and over not to run off like this when we're in stores."

By this time one of the store clerks was walking towards them with broom and yellow mop bucket in hand. "Looks like the Calvary is here at last." Baron smiled at Merry Beth before running after Bethany who'd raced off again—this time around the corner. "I'll get her. Just wheel my cart around the corner and meet me…never mind—I'll find you."

Merry Beth apologized to the store clerk for her mess and quickly pushed

Baron's cart around the corner. "*Bethany, where are you?*" Her daughter was nowhere in sight and her heart thundered wildly with icy fear, making her sore ribs hurt all the more. How many times had she warned Bethany about running off like this? Four dozen, at least! This week anyway…

She jumped a foot when someone touched her right arm lightly ten minutes later in the soda and chip aisle. "Easy, Merry Beth, she's right here," Baron said softly. He smiled as the fear in Merry Beth's eyes disappeared instantly. He wanted to yank her close and comfort her and kiss away her bruises and pain.

He clamped down on those feelings by brushing a hand through the young child's beautiful hair. "She's safe."

"Mommy, look what I found'deded! Can we buy it, Mommy? *Please!*" Bethany asked her mother, as she held up a box of silver icicles she wanted for their Christmas tree.

Merry Beth stared down at her daughter through a wall of glistening yet relieved tears, before reaching for her to pull her roughly into her arms for a huge, bear hug. "Bethany! You *know* mommy has told you and told you not to run off like that. You scared me half to death!"

Baron resisted the urge to yank Merry Beth into his arms.

Tears filled the little girl's eyes. "I'm sorr'rrieee, Mommy. Please don't cry, Mommy. I won't do it again, I pro'missee."

Merry Beth wiped away her tears and glanced at Baron. "Thank you for finding her. She does this all the time. I've told her and told her about the dangers but…"

Baron smiled. "I had a little talk with the Munchkin and she's promised faithfully to never do it again." He reached down and ruffled Bethany's waist length fiery red curls with his right hand again. "She's an angel, Merry Beth. You're very blessed."

"Thank you, Baron," Merry Beth whispered with a warm smile. Two miracles—smiles and laughter! What was next?

"You're welcome, pretty flour snowbird." Baron reached for a six-pack of soda and two bags of chips. The first—the ruffled kind that Bethany had asked him for, just a few minutes before, and the second—the sour cream and onion kind, his favorite.

"What chips do you like, Merry Beth? My treat!" He stared at her, resisting the strong urge to reach out and wipe the flour off her right cheek with his fingertips.

Merry Beth gasped. "You are not buying my groceries!"

Bethany spotted another favorite on a nearby shelf that she could reach. "Mommy, *gummy-bears*, the yellow kind...they're the best ones, Mommy!"

Merry Beth glanced at all her grocery items piled up in his cart and shook her head no. "You're getting my stuff all mixed up with yours, Baron, and *no! You are not buying my groceries. I won't have it—I mean it. Put them back in my cart!*"

"Can't, your cart is gone." Baron didn't even glance into his cart. "Come on, Merry Beth—what kind of chips? Look...a store clerk just took your floury cart away to clean it."

Her eyes whirled to where her cart had just been. "No way!"

His eyes sparkled with laughter. "Yes, way!"

"I can't let you do this. I have my own money!"

"I want to thank you and the Munchkin for the beautiful smelling, tall pine tree I found leaning up against my front door when I got home from work about an hour ago. I love the little card that came with it that said, 'A tree for our new friend, love, Merry and Bethany'. There really was no need for you to get me the tree, Merry Beth. But, thank you anyway—now, no arguing, come on—what kind of chips do you want? I want to thank you for the pears as well. We aren't leaving this spot without your favorite chips!" He crossed his arms over his huge chest and waited for her answer.

Her stubborn chin lifted higher, and she reached out and lightly brushed flour off his shoulders. "Bethany and I just wanted to see you smile again." She rolled her eyes towards the ceiling for opening her big mouth, and pointed to the Pringles. She gasped in shock when he threw three cans in his cart.

"Oh, *really*, and why is that, pretty flour snowbird?"

He placed two six-packs of orange soda in his cart as well when Bethany asked, "Mommy? Can I have orange soda to go with my chips? Please, Mommy! I clean'deded my room this moor'ning like'deded you ask'deded me to!"

Merry Beth cried out, "Hey, put those back!"

Baron smiled as Merry Beth placed the yellow gummy-bears back on the shelf next to the bagged popcorn. "Yeah, Mommy, she cleaned her room and everything!"

"Why are you calling me that?" Merry Beth asked as she put one of the orange soda six-packs back on the shelf. She turned towards her daughter and said crossly, "*Stop asking for stuff, I mean it, Bethany. Mind your manners, young lady, and not another thing!*" She reached for the chips and put two of them back on the shelf.

She winced; her right wrist was throbbing. She tried to hide her pain from Baron and her daughter and held her hand close to her chest.

"She does this, I haven't really taught her the value of the dollar yet. She's only five years old and…" Merry Beth explained and swallowed back her chuckles at Baron's next words.

"Because when I first saw you in that crumpled car amongst broken glass, blood and crushed metal—you were covered with snow and now…" He stepped bravely closer once more and brushed flour off her shoulders.

"Now, you're covered with flour. I can't help but wonder what might be next—cherries, hot-fudge and marshmallows? Do you like Hot-Fudge Sundaes, Merry Beth?" Lord, help him, he'd just found what he'd been searching for since losing his family—in *her* eyes! His insides began to tremble again. Suddenly, it was too stuffy in the store. He needed air and wanted to scream *and run* again! Yet, his feet remained planted to the very spot where he stood staring at the sunshine and beauty in her eyes.

Bethany jumped up and down with excitement and smiles. "Yummy! Can we, Mommy? Can we get some ice cream? Mr. Bear'onn Will'amms is nice, Mommy! Can he come to our house to live?" The young girl looked up at her mother with questioning, huge and excited eyes.

"*Hope…Bethany…Waters—honestly!*" Merry Beth turned twenty shades of red again and turned quickly away so he wouldn't see her embarrassment.

"I'd love to…" Baron wanted to snag the words back as soon as they passed his lips. "…take you and the Munchkin out for a Hot-Fudge Sundae, that is. Merry Beth—I know your wrist is hurting…come on, it's time to go."

He knew having this woman and her delightful child in his lonely life would be an endless adventure of fun and laughter, but it would also bring pain. He knew he had to somehow let go of his dead wife and son before he could move on and truly live again. It was harder done than spoken. It was hard to reach for and achieve when it hurt so much to breathe without them.

Baron turned away and placed two kinds of dip in his cart, ranch and cheese. Merry Beth glanced at his uniform and asked, "You never told me you were a cop. What kind of cop are you?" She glanced at all his shiny buttons, badges and pins.

He backed up a little and moved their now shared cart down the aisle. "I'm a Maine State Police Officer, stationed on the border of Fort Kent and Cair, Quebec Canada. I worked for the State Police and Border Patrol office up there for about seven months before the accident…" Baron swallowed hard before continuing, "…that took my wife and son. I started back to work today."

She watched the muscles in his jaw twitch and his eyes turn to that dark shade of gray, before looking at his nametag and whistling softly. His eyes told her he had a lot of secrets. She couldn't help but wince and jerk back from him a little when she noticed his holstered sidearm. She hated weapons of any kind. "Wow! You're a Sergeant. I'm…impressed."

"What's a Sure'gent, Mommy?" Bethany asked as she threw a bag of marshmallows in Baron's cart with an innocent smile. "We need these, Mommy—for our hot chalk'o'let on Christmas Eve. What's hot chalk'o'let without them?"

Merry Beth rolled her eyes and quickly tried to put the marshmallows back, but Baron gently patted her right arm away. "Leave it—I told you, my treat."

That stubbornness flashed in her eyes again. "No, you are *not* buying my groceries. I won't hear of it!" Merry Beth argued. She held her throbbing right wrist close to her breast again, as it throbbed from within. Suddenly, she felt dizzy and needed some air.

Baron didn't miss how she paled and held her right hand like she was in pain and said, "Yes, I am. Come on, let's go."

Merry Beth frowned and argued, "No, you're not!"

Baron chuckled. "You're a very stubborn woman!"

"You're a stubborn man!" *Very charming but stubborn!*

Bethany said, "No, Mommy—he's wonderful!"

Baron just smiled and shook his head and pushed the cart towards the checkout counter. His dark, black eyes smiled down on mother and daughter as he led them to the front to cash out.

Bethany tried to rush off to grab a bag of M&M's but Merry Beth snagged her coat collar at the last second and said, "Oh no, you don't!" She cried out from the pain in her mending wrist. "Enough is enough, young lady. You stay right here, and don't you dare reach for another thing to put in that cart!"

"But, Mommy, Lisa and I need M&M's for our surprise!"

Baron threw three bags of M&M's in his cart before he lifted Bethany up into his arms, and passed the cashier his gold Visa credit card when she was done ringing the groceries in.

"Come on, you two. Let's get these groceries paid for, separated and packed and loaded in our cars, and then I'm treating you both to dinner at the Irsing

Truck Stop on White Birch Lane by Eagle Lake. Have you ever eaten in there, Merry Beth? Their food is just delicious. Their seafood is the best in town." He lightly kissed Bethany's left cheek, thinking her freckles tasted of honey across his lips. Would Merry Beth's as well? Tempting indeed…

When the bag boy had the groceries packed and in their cart, Baron placed Bethany back to the floor so he could sign the visa slip and wheel their cart outside. "Come on, Munchkin. I'm starving for a cheeseburger and fries and chocolate milk-shake!"

"Bethany and I and our friends from church have eaten in there plenty of times; you don't have to do this…" Merry Beth chuckled as she followed Baron and her daughter back outside. It was chilly and windy and snowing again. She shivered a little and made sure her daughter placed her yellow mittens back on her hands. "It's cold, honey—put your mittens on and button up your coat, or you'll catch a bad cold and get sick."

"Why can't I do this, you don't like cheeseburgers and fries? You eat them at McDonald's—what's the difference?" he asked, grinning from ear-to-ear.

"Great job, Baron…let's eat the fattening stuff that'll clog all our arteries." Merry Beth winked and added, "*Real* healthy!"

After they divided the groceries and placed them in their individual cars, laughing the entire time, Bethany lifted her little fingers to Baron's right hand and asked seriously, before she innocently kissed his hand, "Are you gonna come and live with me and Mommy? I need an earth-daddy, and there's plenty of room at our house, 'cause *I love you!*"

Merry Beth turned white. "Bethany…honestly!"

"And I love you, baby." Baron winked at Merry Beth, his heart suddenly on his sleeve. "Come on. Let's get going. My stomach is growling. I'm starving!"

* * * * *

At the Irsing Truck Stop on Eagle Lake, thirty minutes later, as they waited for their orders of cheeseburgers, fries and chocolate shakes, Merry Beth couldn't take her eyes away from his face, as Sara Evans sang loud and clear from the music box in the far corner, "*I Could Not Ask for More.*" Baron and Bethany sat across from her in the back red-leathered booth, and all she wanted to do was reach out and touch him, but didn't dare. And to think—he'd paid for all her groceries; she'd have to think of a way to pay him back.

To be carefully touched, or kissed or loved by a man like him was a far, far away distant dream. One she dared not ever hope for again. *Well maybe just a little!*

She told herself she could dream if she wanted to, and continued staring at him. He was so handsome he stole the very breath from her lungs. She knew she was staring, but for the life of her she couldn't take her eyes off him to save her life. She drank in everything about him…

She soaked in his dark face and creamy eyes, rugged and leathery looking—99% of the time distant, cold and hard, except when he looked at her or Bethany. Then they suddenly became friendly and close, warm and soft, gray. His dark, coal-black hair was turning silver around his ears and sideburns. He had an interesting three-inch jagged scar on his left temple, and she couldn't help but wonder where and how he'd got it. She had the strong urge to reach across their table and smooth away its rough edges.

He'd gotten a haircut since she'd first seen him in the hospital and she smiled. He was very handsome and very tempting, extremely vibrant. Oh, yes—charming indeed! She heard him laugh lightly and watched him smile down at her daughter with warmth and kindness. His hands were big yet steady, as he helped her with her napkin and straw and ice water.

Bethany talked non-stop about everything from the weather to the promised hot-fudge Sundae's they were going to have after their supper, to the things she wanted for Christmas. Soft Christmas music played in the background when Sara Evans finished her song, and she couldn't help but smile. Elvis' *"White Christmas"* was another of her favorites. Tiny little red-and-white lights blinked from every window in the restaurant, and every table glowed intimately from the dancing lights from the red-and-green candle centerpieces.

Green holly wreaths decorated with red cranberries hung in every window, shiny silver icicles and brown pinecones hung from the ceiling, and every time the front door opened to greet another customer the icicles softly danced from the cold wind and blowing snow that blew in.

"So, Merry Beth, you going to tell me why you and the Munchkin wanted to see me smile so bad…?" Baron asked as he reached for his black coffee. He'd almost reached for her right hand but lifted his coffee to his lips instead. She held it to her breast like she was in pain again. He watched her eyes, and feared he was drowning fast, fast and deep; white-hot furious. He felt the madness from the raging running-wild river pulling him under…

"Why isn't your sprained right wrist in a bandage or sling, Merry Beth? How can it heal if you don't slow down?" Baron asked, meeting her eyes head on, as stubborn as she.

Merry Beth stirred her hot chocolate. "It's fine, really."

Bethany followed her mother's lead and reached for her hot chocolate. "Mommy said you look'deded kind of sad and blue." She glanced quickly up at him and frowned. "You don't look'deded blue to me, Mr. Bear'onn Will'amms. Your clothes do, though. What did Mommy mean?"

"I think your mommy just wanted to see me smile."

"She doesn't smile when I don't clean my room!"

Baron put his head back and roared with laughter, and Merry Beth smiled from ear-to-ear, trying hard to hide her laughter. "It's happening," she whispered, as she reached for her change purse to play more Christmas songs.

"What's happ'eeenin, Mommy?" Bethany asked and cried out as she reached for her ice water. "Ouch, Mommy...I burn'deded my mouth!" Tears glistened across the young girl's soft green eyes as she sipped her water through her straw.

Baron immediately reached for the injured child. "Be careful, Munchkin. The hot chocolate is really hot! Easy," he said as he lightly rubbed her on her back to add, "...just sip it really slow, but wait a few minutes to let it cool a little more first."

He turned his eyes to stare at the beautiful woman sitting across from him, and couldn't help but compare her with Becky. He winced, wondering if he would always do this. What was it about Merry Beth that had him wishing for things he'd already had, loved and then lost? He couldn't do this again. It hurt way too much. Losing the ones you love hurt way too much.

Becky had had short, black, straight hair. Merry Beth's was fiery red, thick and curly to her waist. Becky had had chocolate brown eyes that were always controlled, reserved and hard—he knew it was because of her extensive military training. Merry Beth had sultry, deep, tempting and warm emerald eyes that screamed silently for him to kiss her and so much more.

He knew it—he'd heard her silently whisper for it when they were at the grocery store and he'd had her backed against the Jell-o and puddings. And, even now, it frightened him that he wanted to kiss her. He looked at her lips and cursed his fate.

Have mercy, what that light-pink lip-gloss did to a man's heart. Dangerous—that's what this was. Had he sealed his fate when he'd lifted her from that wreckage, and also in the grocery store when he knew he'd found what he needed in her emerald eyes? He winced. What had he gotten himself into here? He felt...reborn, alive. The darkness in his life seemed to be fading, right before his very eyes.

Becky had always been an extremely serious minded woman—never laughing or letting go too often. Merry Beth constantly glowed with laughter, life and fun *and* pretty light-pink lips. Kissable lips at that! He couldn't help but wonder if they were soft—somehow, he knew that they were—like rose petals. He couldn't help but wonder what they would feel like under his in hardness and heated passion; for some reason that he didn't want to ever try to under-stand he knew he wanted to find out. He was falling for this woman, and falling hard and falling really fast! He needed to back off.

Becky never took the time to stop and smell the roses. Merry Beth, on the other hand—at least today, smelled like soft, velvety roses. Oh, man—he knew he was in serious trouble!

"Well, Merry Beth, my pretty flour snowbird—about that smile?" he asked again with a raised dark eyebrow.

"I wanted to see you smile because you seemed so, I don't know—lost, alone, sad, isolated, secluded, apart from others and the world around you, separate..."

Merry Beth lowered her dark lashes so he couldn't see the truth in her eyes— she cared for him, *really cared! Too much! Too soon!* And that knowledge scared her— a lot. There had never been anyone for her but Thomas Earl, but he'd been gone for so long, and she *was* lonely, and missed having a man in her life to laugh with, share things with, talk with, spend time with, care for and love on a one-on-one, daily, forever-after basis.

"Not anymore." He reached boldly across the table and took her right hand in his and squeezed it tight. She winced from the pain and he immediately let go. "Sorry...I didn't mean to hurt you. Are you all right? You really need to have that hand and wrist bandaged. It'll heal faster if you do."

She passed him her best smile. "I'm fine, really."

She lifted her pretty but questioning eyes and he searched in their darkened depths. "Because of you and the Munchkin, I'm slowly finding my way back."

Bethany, being the young girl of only five years old—loving, giving, sweet and innocent, reached up and kissed him softly on his left cheek. "Why? Were you lost?"

He smiled down at her and kissed the tip of her cute little nose. "Yes, baby. I was lost."

Merry Beth smiled. "Not anymore."

"Mommy, I'm hungry! When we gonna eat?"

Baron and Merry Beth both roared with laughter, as their young waitress delivered their meals with a friendly smile.

Baron felt alive for the first time in almost three years.

Merry Beth fell in love, right there and then.

Bethany reached for the ketchup and poured a generous amount all over her burger and hot, salty fries.

James 4:8-10 "Draw nigh to God, and he will draw nigh to you. Cleanse *your* hands, *ye* sinners; and purify *your* hearts, *ye* double-minded. Be afflicted, and mourn, and weep: let your laughter be turned to mourning, and *your* joy to heaviness. Humble yourselves in the sight of the LORD, and he shall lift you up."

Chapter Four

Matthew 1:24-25 "Then Joseph being raised from sleep did as the angel of the LORD had bidden him, and took unto him his wife: And knew her not till she had brought forth her firstborn son: and he called his name JESUS."

Miracle #3, friendship, December 15th, Tuesday, 6:27 a.m.

CHRISTMAS WAS ONLY ten short days away, and there was still so much to do! How would she ever get it all done in time? "You be a good girl, baby. Mommy loves you."

Merry Beth tried hard to smile as Debbie led Bethany out the back kitchen door towards her waiting black Chevy truck. It had been snowing heavy since past midnight, and everywhere she looked was covered completely with a soft blanket of white, warming the earth.

She tried hard to hide it from her friend, but knew that she hadn't—she was exhausted, sore, in pain and miserable today. She knew it was a delayed reaction from the car accident because her broken left arm, cracked ribs and sprained right wrist throbbed terribly. She hadn't gotten much sleep and it showed with dark circles under her eyes and ghostly-gray complexion, but she hated taking the pain medication; hated how groggy they made her feel.

"Thanks for being such a good friend, Debbie. Bethany loves to play with Lisa at your house. She's her best friend, like you are mine. We'd both be lost without you guys." She spotted Kristi sitting in the front seat and waved a friendly hello.

"How are the kids coping since the loss of their father?"

"Better. Don't worry; love—she'll be just fine at my house. Now, *please*, try to get some rest. You look tired, my friend. I'm worried about you." Debbie kissed her softly on her bruised but mending left cheek. "*Go to bed and stay there!*"

Merry Beth reached out and hugged her best friend tight. "I promise. As soon as you leave I'm hitting the bed."

"Go to bed and *sleep!* I've already taken care of getting those angel costumes done, your tiny apartment is decorated more than the White House, you've sold every hat and scarf set that you've made. You've baked, cooked, cleaned, shopped 'til you literally dropped, and now that I am kidnapping your daughter again—you can finally *get some sleep! I mean it!* You need your rest."

"I admit it, I am a little tired. I just miss my baby when she's not here—the apartment is so empty and quiet without her." Merry Beth scolded herself for her silly glistening tears and wiped them away. She blew her daughter a kiss as Bethany followed Lisa to the warming truck and jumped in the back seat.

Christmas and snow came hand in hand, for Mainer's anyway. Music played from the radio in the truck and both women smiled, liking *"Silver Bells"* tremendously.

"Don't forget your seatbelts, babies, and have fun. See you tomorrow, Bethany, and I'll make sure Mr. Williams gets his special cookie ornaments for his tree." Merry Beth frowned as white spots danced wildly in front of her tired eyes. Her head pounded with a promised migraine and she swayed a little and reached for the open truck door to steady herself.

"Merry Beth, you *know* how Lisa and Bethany are during their many sleepovers. They enjoy their favorite Walt Disney movies, popcorn, soda, coloring and painting, whispering secrets back and forth, puppets, play-dough castles, make-up and dress-up, and now making those special Christmas cards!" Debbie turned to leave. "Bethany will be fine. Now, bye, love…go, and sleep!"

Merry Beth swallowed against the sudden sob in her throat. With her daughter gone the quiet seemed to scream all around her, yanking her under like quicksand. She didn't like those quiet moments to herself, but didn't want to be an over-protective and clinging, fussy mom either. "I will. Bye, girls. Have fun. Bethany…you mind, and be good."

Merry Beth ignored Debbie's stern, "Get back in there now. It's freezing out here and you're not wearing a sweater or jacket—honestly! You're going to catch a cold and get sick!" as she rushed through the thick snowfall to the driver's side.

Merry Beth reached in the back door and gave her daughter one last hug and kiss. "I love you. Be good, and make sure that you mind Mrs. Thomas." She touched Lisa softly on her nose. "Have fun, you two, and don't eat too much popcorn this time. Or you'll both get sick again."

"I love you, Mommy—bunches and bunches!" Bethany smiled as Merry Beth checked the seatbelts.

"You're pretty today, Mrs. Waters," Lisa said with a shy grin and giggle. Bethany smiled at her mother. "She's always pretty!"

Kristi turned in her seat and asked, "You feeling any better, Mrs. Waters?"

Merry Beth smiled at Kristi and said, "Much." She turned to search for Lisa's eyes and said, "So are you, sweetie." She blew all three girls a quick kiss before closing the door, and waved one more time before turning back to the apartment. "Thanks, Debbie. Call me later, okay? After lunch…"

"Bye, Mommy. I love you!" Bethany yelled, waving good-bye as her mother locked and closed the truck door.

Debbie glanced at Merry Beth with her pale cheeks, dark eyes, wearing only thin nightgown, white housecoat and slippers and frowned. "Sure will, love. Now, get in there and please get some sleep. I put some of my homemade chicken noodle soup in your crock-pot to heat on low. It should be nice and hot by noon for your lunch. Now—*go to bed!* Unplug your phone so you won't be disturbed. I'll be by later to check on you."

"I will, I will! I promise." She waved her friend to stop worrying and leave. "The second I get inside I'm going to bed—*I promise! Stop worrying, I'm fine!* And thanks, Debbie." She stepped back and waved as Debbie pulled out of her driveway.

Merry Beth waited until the truck was well out of sight before she turned back inside. The weather report called for only two more inches of snow by noon. But by the looks of the gray clouds, threatening sky and thick flakes falling down, she knew they'd get more than that. With closed eyes she lifted her cut and bruised, mending face to the sky for a few moments, and enjoyed the taste of snowflakes on her lips and tongue.

Creamy yet dark eyes and a strong yet caring touch came into view in her mind, and she shivered and quickly raced inside. She closed the door, locked it and turned out all the lights on her way towards her bedroom upstairs. After quickly swallowing two of her prescribed pain pills, she set the alarm for noon, unplugged the phone and took off her robe and slippers and crawled happily into her double bed. She was warm in seconds. The new white Down-Comforter that her father had given her last Christmas was a treasure.

Oblivion and blessed forgetfulness was a much craved and desired wish, as she'd slowly crawled into her unmade bed. She'd shivered from the dampness and cold in the air and pulled the sheet and blankets and comforter over her tired body. The blankets were warm because she'd left the electric blanket on, on low.

She closed her tired and burning eyes and snuggled as far down under the covers as she could without suffocating herself.

In minutes, blessed darkness carried her away into a deep sleep. Little did she know a burning fever was raging close from pure exhaustion and sickness, pulling her further down, down, down; slowly—she was alone, except for her guardian angel, as the silent fever slithered its way through her exhausted, broken, bruised and worn out body.

* * * * *

Baron drummed his fingers hard, impatiently against the switchboard desk while he waited for Merry Beth to answer the phone. It was 10:22 a.m. and she hadn't answered one of his calls all morning. He jerked back from the constant unanswered rings once more, and slammed the phone back in its cradle, frustrated to no end.

He'd tried to call her at least ten different times since earlier in the day, and her line had rung off the hook every time. He was on the edge, and about ready to explode with built-up worry and frustration! He'd been back to work only a day, and Mitch still had him working switchboard. Maybe it was time to move on to another job somewhere else. Yet, he knew he couldn't. Not yet.

His cops' instinct told him that something was wrong with Merry Beth, but what? He hated the visions of her being hurt again. Any number of things could be wrong—another car accident, another round at the hospital emergency room or I.C.U., a burglar or thief catching her unaware. Dear Lord, no!

He didn't understand it but suddenly in his lonely, dark, pathetic life Merry Beth and the Munchkin had become the reason for him to care again, live again, come out of his cocoon and join the land of the living again, smile again, laugh again. He fought it all the way, not wanting to give in.

He glanced at his watch and frowned. He was scheduled to work until five. There was nothing he could do until then. Because of the storm they were shorthanded four men today. He didn't know any of her friends or neighbors so there was literally no one he could call to check on her, to see if she was all right. He'd never even been to her apartment. As he impatiently waited for Mitch to send him out in the field throughout the day, he prayed for the safety of his new friend. She was so beautiful, so loving; so kind and giving…

He knew in his heart he liked Merry Beth—*really* liked her. It scared him. He hated that it did. For almost three years his every breath and thought had been nothing but Becky and his son. And now, was his heart controlling his hand? It wasn't easy letting go of the past. He wasn't sure if he'd ever be able to completely let go.

There was Merry Beth and the Munchkin. He couldn't get them out of his head. And now they were creeping inside his heart. The darkness and pain the accident and losing Becky and his son had caused seemed to be disintegrating because of Merry Beth and Bethany's laughter and smiles. They loved life as he once had, and he wanted that again. The loneliness in his heart and life seemed to be drifting, falling silently away because of their faces. He didn't understand it, but knew he didn't want to run from it either.

He was hooked, line and sinker.

Why wasn't she answering her phone?

He had a *very* bad feeling…

…a bad feeling indeed.

* * * * *

Around 5:12 p.m., as Baron drove slowly south on Route 1, he reached inside his uniform jacket pocket for his ringing cellular. The snow was coming down thicker and heavier now, and he was barely creeping along at fifteen miles per hour. He eased up on the gas pedal a little as he turned the cell phone on with his right hand.

"Hello…"

"Is this a Mr. Baron Williams?"

The woman's voice was soft, but sounded a little hurried and frantic to him. "Yes, it is. Who's calling, please?" He held the cellular under his chin and reached over to turn down his car radio. He frowned; the weather report stated another snowstorm with at least six more inches coming in right after this storm passed by, sometime after midnight.

"This is Merry Beth's best friend, Debbie Thomas," Debbie explained while chewing on her lower lip.

"Yes, Mrs. Thomas. Merry Beth has mentioned your name on several occasions. I'm sorry about the recent loss of your husband." He reached over and turned up the defroster a few notches, ignoring the panicky feelings inside his gut. *Something's wrong with Merry Beth. I just know it. I can tell by her voice. Something's happened, but what?*

"What is it? Has something happened to Merry Beth?"

"Thank you for your concern about losing my husband. Listen, I got your address from my younger brother, Hugh. He's the one who delivered your

Christmas tree from Bethany and Merry Beth yesterday morning…" Debbie began to explain, anxious and worried.

"Is something wrong with Merry Beth or Bethany?" He knew he cared for them more than he wanted to, more than he could ever understand, much more than just a friend, much more than he should—he couldn't help it. He felt connected to them now.

Holly leaves, Christmas trees, white-and-red blinking lights a glow, pine mistletoe, colorful wrapped presents under the tree, red-and-green stockings hung in front of the fireplace, scented candles with their dancing light, fir or pine wreath on the front door—he missed all of it. But most of all he'd missed human contact, that soft and loving touch—like Merry Beth's.

"I hope you don't mind, but Hugh gave me your address, and it took me at least three hours of begging with at least twenty different calls on my hands and knees to get this number from your service." Debbie sighed heavily in her frustration; worried that Merry Beth would be deeply hurt by this strange man that had suddenly popped into her life.

"I don't know you, but I don't know who else to call and…" Debbie began to explain, hesitation across the line.

"It's all right, Mrs. Thomas." *She's stalling, but why?*

"Oh, good, anyway, I'm in a real bind here and…" *If you hurt my best friend you're dead meat, I mean it. I'll personally strangle you myself!* "…with the raging storm and my truck that won't start…"

"Just tell me if Merry Beth's all right." *The world is too cold, and I need a friend to hold. Merry Beth—I need Merry Beth!*

"I'm not really sure," Debbie hesitated. *Who are you, Mr. Baron Williams, friend or foe?*

"What do you mean you're not really sure? Tell me!" Baron demanded over the line, slowly counting to ten to calm his rapid beating heart. His left hand tightened on the steering wheel when his back tires began to slide on the snow and ice.

"I've called her apartment at least twenty times since lunch and it keeps ringing every time. I should have *never* told her to take it off the hook. She must have unplugged the stupid thing…I hope. I don't know whom else to call. I can't get a-hold-of my brother-in-law—Pastor Todd Thomas, has Merry Beth ever mentioned him? Anyway, I've called everyone I know of from church that knows Merry Beth and Bethany, but no one's home. I've even called my brother, but even he's not answering. I have three children plus Bethany here—there's no way I can make it over there to check on her like I'd planned and..."

"You have the Munchkin there with you?" *At least Bethany is all right—thank you, dear Lord!*

"Yes, I've had her since about six-thirty this morning. She's spending the day and night with us. My daughter, Lisa, and she are best friends. When I left Merry Beth this morning she seemed fine—a little tired and pale, but fine. She promised faithfully to go right to bed and get some much needed sleep and rest. I have my own three and Bethany and two of my son's friends here, and my truck won't start. There's no way I can get over there to check up on her, and I've called 9-1-1 but they're really backed up with accidents from this crazy storm..."

"Give me her address again, I'll do it. She gave it to me once but I don't have the paper with me. I left it at home." Baron frowned. There could be a number of things wrong—a thief or burglar catching her in the house unawares. The thought put chills up and down his back. She might have fallen and hurt herself, sickness or another car accident. The thought of that rugged looking, old, raggedy, rusty blue Toyota gave him the willies every time he thought of her driving in that death trap. Or, the phone could simply be unplugged. He took huge breaths to still his rapid-beating fearful heart. He hadn't cared like this in a long time.

"Maybe I'm just being silly, but with the accident and her injuries—I told her she came home from the hospital too soon. She's so stubborn and *never* stops! I just want to be sure she's really okay. You don't mind going by to check on her?"

"I'm sure she's all right." He knew it wasn't true, he could feel it in his gut. Something was wrong, and he was a man who always listened to his heart when it whispered a friend was in trouble. "And no, I don't mind. Just give me the address and I'm on my way."

When Debbie remained hesitant to give out Merry Beth's address, he continued, "You really can trust me, you know. I won't hurt her, I promise." The world still wanted too much and he silently prayed for another chance with someone as sweet, lovely, kind and beautiful as Merry Beth—well, it was just too good to be true.

"I'm a friend. I'll just swing by and make sure she's okay." *Oh, dear Lord in Heaven—let it be true, please!*

"It's 252 West Chestnut Drive, Apartment One. You can't miss it. It's a huge house divided into two apartment complexes. It's white with red trim. The apartment next door to her is empty."

Baron mentally memorized the address. "Got it…"

"You can't miss the empty windows from the street. Merry Beth's apartment is usually lit up like the Fourth of July at Christmas time; it's three miles past Winterville High School on the right, off Route One north." *Please, don't hurt my friend! She's too trusting, she's been alone for a very long, long time, she's going to be hurt by you, I can feel it in my bones! You're going to break her heart in two, aren't you?*

"I'm in the southbound lane so I'll just take the next exit and turn around. I figure I'll be there in about ten or fifteen minutes, give or take a few. The roads are pretty bad and visibility is terrible. This storm is turning out to be a real nor' easterner, and the plows and sanders haven't passed this way in quite some time, it seems."

"I'm really worried about her…" Debbie confessed.

Why did it seem every step he took in the last three years was an up-hill climb, and the last three days as smooth as a light breeze going downhill? Every protective instinct he had buried deep inside him came crashing to the surface in his thundering heart front and center. "Try not to worry, Mrs. Thomas. I'm sure she's either asleep or out shopping. You know how you women are at this time of year. I'll call with news one way or the other."

"Let's just pray, and I'm thankful this storm isn't another terrible ice storm like we had back in January of '98. I'm so glad I finally reached you, Mr. Williams. Bethany said if anyone can save her mother when she's in trouble, it's you…"

He smiled again, this time from within. "Is that so?"

"She seems to think that *you* are solely responsible for getting her mommy to wake up after that car accident. Bethany talks about you all the time. It's Bear-on this, and Bear-on that—she's standing right here next to me with tears in her eyes, worried for her mother."

He heard this woman named Debbie whisper to Bethany that everything was going to be all right, and smiled. He'd never met this Debbie but liked her immensely, and with her deep, rich, caring and concerned voice he knew that she was a friend concerned for his pretty flour snowbird.

"Tell the Munchkin I'm sure everything is fine. Give me your number, just in case." He memorized it as Debbie gave it out. "Thanks, I'll call you soon."

"I've been praying. I've told Merry Beth a dozen or more times since the hospital released her to take it easy and get some rest. She's over-doing it—I just know it. She doesn't know when to quit. I've taken Bethany as much as I can over the last few days to give her some breathing space and quiet to rest, but you know

Merry Beth. She's stubborn and strong and independent and bull-headed, and it's typical of her to overdo it!"

Baron smiled slightly. "Well, actually—I don't know her all that well." *But Lord only knows how much I want to!* What was it about Merry Beth that had his heart racing and sweat breaking out across his brow and his palms also sweaty—in the middle of winter-wonderland, for goodness sakes?

Debbie hit herself in her forehead and continued, "No, of course you don't. Anyway, she doesn't stop or slow down. Ever! She keeps right on cooking, cleaning, shopping, doing laundry, selling her knitted hat and scarf sets, holiday decorating, making you those wonderful Christmas cookie ornaments…" She gasped and covered her mouth, knowing she'd just revealed another one of Merry Beth's secret surprises. "Oops, I've gone a spoiled it!"

His heart did a funny flip-flop inside his chest. "What ornaments?" *Oh, Merry Beth, what have you done this time? Your friend is right—you need to slow down. You need to give yourself this time to heal!*

"Oh, no, I've spoiled the surprise. Merry Beth is going to laugh at this one." After a few seconds of silence she continued, "You aren't going to hurt her…are you?"

Lord, give me strength… "I give you my word—I won't hurt her, not intentionally."

Debbie let out her breath. "Call me, please, and let me know she's all right. Bethany and I will be waiting right here by the phone for your call."

"Will do—thanks, Mrs. Thomas, and give the Munchkin a hug and kiss from me."

"I will. Good-bye, Mr. Williams."

"Bye…talk to you soon."

Baron frowned as he took the next exit to turn around. "Please be all right my pretty flour-snowbird," he whispered as he worked his truck through the blistery snowstorm. He winced as his tires slid on a patch of ice. Merry Beth wasn't *his* anything!

He was surprised to realize he no longer wanted to hang on to the heartbreak he always felt from losing his wife and son—not when there was still so much of life to live. Three years, he'd spent three years in mourning—not wasted years, just years that were gone from his grasp forever.

He was surprised to realize he was no longer afraid of the mysteries tomorrow might hold—for some unknown reason, God was giving him another chance to begin again. He wasn't totally sure that he was ready.

He was surprised to realize, even though he'd never forget Becky and Baron, Jr.—he'd hold them close inside his heart forever, it was time to stop mourning and get on with living. And he knew that Becky would have wanted it that way.

Love was on the way to him silently, softly, carefully, on the wings of angels. Love was on the way to him through smiles, laughter and friendship. Love was on the way to him calmly, peacefully, motionlessly in the belief of God's mercy and never-ending promises.

With every breath he now took, Baron Michael Williams was getting stronger. It was truly another Christmas miracle.

Life did indeed move on; for that he was very thankful.

Very thankful indeed. . .

* * * * *

Baron frowned with worry fifteen minutes later, when no one answered his loud knocking on Merry Beth's front and back doors. The old Toyota sat in the driveway and it was covered with snow and ice so he knew she hadn't gone anywhere today. There were no footprints in the snow anywhere near the apartment building so he knew there were no intruders, recently, anyway. He stared at the broken side window on the right side of the apartment complex with deep concern. Had someone broken in or had the window broken from the snapped tree branch lying nearby?

He didn't want to take any chances and quickly reached in his uniform jacket pocket for his cellular and dialed 9-1-1 for back-up. His instinct warned him that something was wrong, and he didn't hesitate to call for the local police and ambulance. He closed his eyes in disbelief when the dispatcher informed him it would be at least two hours before anyone could come to help.

With the snowstorm there had been nine different vehicle accidents along Route 1, and at least two-dozen calls for help in the last three to four hours. There were only three police officers in Winterville, and they were backed up beyond belief. They'd called in officers from Caribou to help, and as soon as they could they'd send someone to answer his call. But, since Baron wasn't even really sure something was wrong with Ms. Waters, his call wasn't a high priority.

He was on his own. But that was okay. He liked it that way, didn't he? He quickly walked through the heavy wet snow back to his car and opened the trunk and reached for the blanket inside. In less than ten seconds he'd placed the blanket so he would avoid getting cut, jumped up and in the broken living room window, and fell to the bare floor with a thud. He winced from the sound of shattered glass on the bare floor under his work boots and silently promised Merry Beth that he'd replace the broken window first thing. He worried that she didn't have much money, and a broken window would put a dent in her wallet. It was cold in the apartment, cold and dark.

His alert eyes scanned the living room. *Come on, Merry Beth—where are you? Are you all right? Please be all right!* He didn't like the eerie feeling in the pit of his stomach or the goose bumps on both of his arms. The silence echoed in his rapidly beating heart—like native drums, and as he carefully stepped through the broken window into her dark living room he held in his breath.

He winced from the chilliness and dampness of the apartment. *Have you run out of oil, Merry Beth? How long has this window been broken?* He felt the fireplace hearth—dark and cold. He called her name softly at first, and reached for his loaded 9 mm Smith & Wesson in his black leather holster on his belt, when there was no answer to his call.

The tall, pine Christmas tree stood bravely and proud to the high ceiling in the far corner. It was beautifully decorated with dozens of little ornaments—he knew in his heart Merry Beth and Bethany had made each and every one of them. The popcorn strings hung in little loops here and there and he smiled briefly, remembering the Munchkin's debate on which kind of popcorn to buy at the grocery store. The red, green and ivory candles on the fireplace mantle were lifeless and cold. There was a thin layer of dust on every piece of furniture.

He glanced up quickly to the top of the tree at the white- and-golden angel sitting there and frowned. The apartment was too quiet, too dark, too empty, something was wrong…

"Merry Beth…? Are you here?" The only sound he heard was his own rapid beating heart. He stepped silently towards the kitchen. "Answer me if you can, Merry Beth…?"

The dark-green holly, decorated with little brown pine-cones spray-painted gold-and-silver, sat around the candles that lay across the fireplace mantle—decorated with red-and-silver bows. There was not one space in the entire living room that wasn't decorated for the Christmas season in one way or another, from the lights in the windows to the mistletoe above his head. Snow blew inside the living room from the shattered, broken window, and the bitter wind blew the fluffy white curtains back and forth. A feeling of doom washed completely over him. His hurried footsteps were silent, and the howling bitter cold wind blew unmercifully against the apartment building windows and roof, as he raced across the living room towards what he guessed to be the kitchen.

"Merry Beth...?" Silence answered his calls. "Are you here? Are you hurt...?" Fear slithered into his uncertain heart. He knew he'd never heard such dead silence, even after he'd lost his wife and son—after the funeral, at the house alone. It was eerie.

He quickly scanned the tiny kitchen and frowned when he found it empty and cold. He glanced at the stove. It was covered with dirty pots and pans. He glanced at the kitchen table. There wasn't a clean available spot in sight. It was clearly evident that either Merry Beth was a terrible housekeeper, which he seriously doubted—the living room had been immaculately clean—or, something was terribly wrong here...

His heart hammered in his chest as he scanned the kitchen. It was a beautifully decorated room with bright, sunny yellows and blues and healthy green plants hanging in the windows. The room was inviting and friendly, it seemed to pull him in.

The counters and table were covered with dirty dishes. The Munchkin's Cinderella cup sat dirty from orange juice she'd obviously not finished. The Beauty and the Beast cereal bowl sat with uneaten cheerios and milk still inside— now warm and mushy. Half empty coffee cups—two, half empty milk and juice carton—now spoiled, half eaten bowl of what looked to be Chicken Noodle Soup, bread bag opened, unread newspaper next to one of the coffee cups. He frowned, somehow knowing in his heart Merry Beth was a very neat and organized and clean housekeeper. Then why the mess, and where was she? The light above the sinks was on. Was she hurt, sick, unconscious?

The quiet bounced off the walls. As his eyes scanned the kitchen his heart literally stopped inside his chest when he spotted the blood...

He cringed and jerked back from the sight in one of the white kitchen sinks. One was filled to the top with sudsy water. He stuck his finger in and jerked back. It was still hot. The other sink held broken glass and a lot of red blood. The blood was scattered all over the sink and sideboard and, he glanced down, across the floor. Drops of blood trailed across the vinyl floor towards the hallway that led to the stairs.

His feet moved in less than a heartbeat. The dark, red blood called out to him like a foreboding thing. It was misgiving, suspicious, apprehensive, and it left his thundering heart filled with fear, uneasy and troubled doubts and uncertainty— as his dark, expert eyes followed the blood trail.

The blood trail led to the second floor. He didn't waste a second to climb to the second floor. His feet moved silently up the old oak-brown stairs, yet quickly. *"Merry Beth, answer me if you can! Are you here? Are you hurt?"* The complete silence was disturbed by what sounded like…music. He listened to the soft music. *Silver bells?*

He listened once more. Crying, tears, sobbing…

"Merry Beth—answer me if you can! Are you hurt?"

"I'm in here," Merry Beth whispered through her pain and tears. *Oh, Baron, thank you for coming, but how—how did you know I was in trouble?* She closed her rested eyes with relief, afraid that she needed stitches. She lifted her tear filled eyes to the mirror and winced at the terrible sight.

"Oh, just great, Merry Beth—just perfect…you look like death warmed over. Quite the impression you'll make. You're going to scare him away. What a mess! Oh, why me…?"

Baron quickly closed his eyes in relief, but only for a few seconds and swallowed the fear and panic gripping his very soul like a crushing bulldozer. He raced towards her voice and glanced into her bedroom at the unmade bed and soft, white wicker furniture. She was nowhere in sight.

"Where are you, Merry Beth…?"

He didn't know what to do about the beautiful woman who'd invaded his cold and lonely, dark world. The woman who'd invaded it with her beauty, her warmth, her kindness, her smiles and laughter.

He didn't miss the expensive, eight-by-ten, silver framed photo—a wedding photograph of Merry Beth and her late-husband, sitting on her white-wicker nightstand. Her beauty in the photograph stole the breath from his lungs. The sharpened jealousy that ripped at his pounding heart surprised him, as he searched for her with his dark eyes. The queen-sized bed was unmade and crumpled. Was she a restless sleeper?

"Merry Beth…?"

"I'm in here—in the bathroom…"

"Are you all right? I saw the blood in the kitchen, and in the hallway and on the stairs. Did you cut yourself?"

She rolled her eyes, embarrassed. It seemed he really was becoming her white-knight-in-shining-armor. What was the old myth about that, anyway? "Yeah, I guess you could say that…"

As his steps carried him quickly towards her voice, he clamped down hard on the jealousy that raged across his heart. He had no right to be jealous—none whatsoever. Her husband was dead, for goodness sakes! She still wore her stunning wedding rings, and the photograph was more evidence that she was still in love with her late-husband. She hadn't put the photo away after his death, like he had all of his. He needed to get a stronger grip!

"Merry Beth...?"

"I'm in the bathroom. I cut myself. I was trying to clean up the kitchen a little, and you'll never know how hard it is to wash dishes and clean a kitchen with only one hand—a sprained one at that!" She held up her injured right hand and blood dripped down her fingers and arm immediately.

Tears burned her eyes. "I cut it on a broken g...glass..."

Baron stopped dead in his quickened steps when he saw Merry Beth leaning over the bathroom sink, wearing a fluffy white housecoat and slippers, holding up her right arm so he could see the damage from her cut. Dark red blood dripped down her hand and arm, and dripped on her housecoat and slippers, and he winced yet sighed with relief. She was pale and had dark circles under her pretty eyes, but she was alive! She looked fragile and exhausted, weathered and worn out. It looked like the sink was holding her upright, yet he'd never seen a more beautiful, desirable woman.

"*What did you do, let me see?*" In seconds he put the safety back on and placed his loaded 9mm Smith & Wesson back in his hip holster, and reached for her injured right hand. "Rinse it off again so I can check how deep the wound is."

"I think I've sliced it really good this time." She swayed a little and winced from his close inspection. He towered over her, his hands were huge and swallowed her own, but she liked having him here, liked having him this close. She closed her eyes, knowing deep in her heart she was falling in love with him. Was he her second chance at love since losing Bethany's father? How in the world could she be falling in love with him so fast? She'd just met him after the accident. It was too soon. In reality, he was a stranger.

She smelled of roses and freshness and honey shampoo, despite her weariness, mending cuts and bruises and tear-filled eyes. He took several deep breaths in before he spoke to lightly tease her.

"It's obvious to me *now* that you're doing all of these things on purpose, pretty flour snowbird. You just wanted me to come and rescue you *again*, admit it. We both know it's true."

She winced as the cold water burned her hand where the cuts inflicted sharp pain. "No...I...really...I..."

Baron smiled down at her and winked to ask, "Didn't you? I'll gladly come any time you need me, Merry Beth, but *this* is a little silly, don't you think? You have Debbie and the Munchkin worried out of their minds." *And me—you scared me half to death. Dear Lord—give me strength to say no, she looks so beautiful standing here like this with those huge grass green eyes begging me to kiss her!*

Merry Beth smiled. He smelled so good. It was so nice to have someone else to lean on for a change. He was so handsome. Goodness—the man was tall! He towered over her and she couldn't catch her breath as her eyes slowly lifted to his. Have mercy, would he ever kiss her? What was he waiting for?

She snatched her hand quickly away and cringed. "Ouch!" She glanced at him for a quick second or two and asked, "What are you doing here, Baron? How do you know Debbie? Is my baby all right? I slept most of the day away and when I woke I was hungry, so I ate some of Debbie's soup and then tried to clean up and…"

She placed her hand under the faucet once more, and cried out from the pain and jerked her hand back from the cold water. "Man, oh man, that hurts like the…dickens!"

She chuckled lightly, remembering Bethany asking her what dic'kensss meant. "Go away! I can take care of myself!" she said stubbornly. Her eyes told him she didn't mean it.

"So many questions, and she's cut and bleeding all over the house, and what does she do? She laughs…it is unbelievable!" He knew by the first look, after she rinsed off the blood from her hand, that she didn't need stitches. Why did she have to be so pretty, so loveable, so soft and fragrant?

"These cuts aren't deep enough for stitches, Merry Beth. But you sure did slice it pretty good, in three different places." When he reached over her shoulder and touched her hand, both felt the tingling sensations—which quickly ripped them apart. Baron stepped back and took in several long calming breaths.

Merry Beth smiled despite her racing heart, despite how close they were in the bathroom. Man, oh man—did he ever smell good! And, as before in the grocery store, he looked quite handsome in his spiffy, impressive dark-blue uniform. Why did he have to be a cop?

Her hair was wet, uncombed and wild from her recent bath, and why did she have to smell like those silly roses as she lifted her darkened, searching emerald eyes to his gray? He was so relieved to see her alive, and safe and unharmed— well, almost, that he reached for her and without even thinking twice pulled her roughly to his chest for a bear hug. He heard her gasp in pain and remembered about her cracked and mending ribs and let her go immediately.

"Your ribs…I'm sorry, Merry Beth."

"What was that for?" she asked as he let her go. His hands lingered longer than they needed; to steady her. But he didn't want to let her go just yet. He *had* to, and did.

He immediately stepped back a little. "You scared us all half to death! What's wrong with your phone? Debbie and I have been calling and calling…all day." Baron lightly scolded her. "Sit! Where's your first-aid kit?"

"Why you guys calling? I can take care of myself!"

He closed the lid on the commode and gently pushed her down on the seat. "You *do* have a first-aid kit, don't you?"

She was beautiful. There was no way around it. He feared he was falling in love again, and he didn't want to!

"Of course I do. I have a child in the house, you know."

Merry Beth smiled, knowing he cared meant everything, and she knew that he did—she heard it in his voice and saw it in his *gray* eyes and trembling hands. She suspected that he was fighting against any feelings he might be feeling for her and smiled, thankful for the miracles taking place in his heart.

"Merry Beth…the kit…? You should be in the hospital!"

She leaned a little closer. "So many questions, are you *always* this bossy, Sergeant Baron Michael Williams? Your eyes—they turn from black to gray when you're…"

"Yes! And if we're to remain friends you better get used to it. Now, the kit…?" He raised his dark eyebrow and crossed his arms over his broad chest and crispy starched uniform shirt. Her best friend was right; she was too stubborn and strong-willed!

"I was just going to get it when I heard you call my name. It's under the kitchen sink. I came up here to get some clean towels to wrap my hand in, because I'm out of paper towels and napkins. My phone is out, I don't really know why."

"It's probably because of this silly little storm—honestly! It snows a little and everyone panics. You'd think that anyone born and raised in the state of Maine wouldn't panic because of a few inches of fluffy white snow." She smiled up at him and swallowed the words that popped to her lips next. *I'm glad you're here. I need you, and I'm falling in love with you!*

He glanced outside at the raging snowstorm. "Merry Beth, this is no little storm—this is turning out to be a true nor' easterner and a broken branch has broken one of your living room windows. I'm afraid your television and VCR are soaked with melting snow and need to be replaced."

"I heard the loud crash, but didn't go look because of this mess…" She held up her bleeding hand again.

He rubbed the bridge of his nose, like he was fighting off a bad migraine. "I won't lie to you—it's a mess down there."

She winced at the thought of the unwanted expense, and he glanced at the tiny, but oh so pretty freckles across her nose and cheeks, and immediately wanted to feel their softness under his fingertips. Even better yet—under his lips! Yes, that sounded nice. He backed up a few feet instead and the doorknob hit his lower back.

Easy Williams—back off from those kind of thoughts. She's just a friend. Don't do this; don't get too close, it's much too risky and dangerous for everyone concerned. He frowned a little, knowing in his heart he liked risk. It was his middle name on every level of his work as a police officer. "Come on, Merry Beth…sit down."

Merry Beth turned back to the sink and running cold water. "So, Debbie called you? How'd she get your number? She's such a worrywart. Is my baby okay?"

"Your friend is very persistent. The Munchkin and your friend are waiting for me to call, speaking of which…" He reached inside his uniform jacket pocket for his cellular and dialed Debbie's number. "You talk to them while I go and get you that first-aid kit."

Baron wrapped Merry Beth's injured right hand with a small towel and turned away. "I'll be right back, don't go anywhere. Sit!" She smiled at him before he quickly raced away.

Merry Beth sat on the lid of her commode and waited for Debbie to answer. She answered on the second ring. "Hello. Merry Beth—this *better* be you if you know what's good for you!"

"Yes, Debbie, it's me." She frowned when she noticed the drops of blood that had dripped on to her fluffy white bathrobe. She noticed the blood on her slippers as well and winced, both had been gifts from her father last Christmas.

"It's so good to hear your voice! Are you all right? What's wrong with your phone? I've called and called and called and it just rings and rings, since lunch."

"Baron is here, I'm using his cellular. I plugged my phone back in and it's out. Thanks for calling him, by the way."

Debbie blew out her breath. "And you're okay?"

Merry Beth smiled. "Yes, I'm fine, Debbie. You worry too much, but your friendship means the world to me. Is my baby right handy? Baron said she was worried?"

"Hold on, I'll go get her…"

"Thanks Deb."

Merry Beth smiled as she waited for Bethany to come to the phone. The Christmas bells, pretty silver and gold ones, were ringing inside her hopeful heart, despite the raging storm and blistery chilly wind that rattled against the old bathroom window. The more snow the better. She loved the snow. Except for when she had to drive in it or shovel it, of course. She rose to her feet and quickly glanced out the tiny window, and couldn't help but wonder why she still had electricity. It looked like it had been snowing steady for a week or more. There wasn't anything out there that wasn't covered with white. It was indeed a white-out!

"Wow, it's beautiful! Thank you, God, for this beauty."

Despite the beauty from the storm, the howling wind and blowing snow made her shiver. Her entire body ached from head to little to ease the throbbing in her head, ribs, broken arm and sore wrist. She'd awaken from her deep sleep after four, covered in sweat and a fever that raged around 103.

"Merry Beth, she's right here."

Her legs felt wobbly and she quickly sat back down on the closed commode lid. "Mommy…?" Bethany's voice was soft and Merry Beth knew from its sound that her daughter was scared. "Are you all right, Mommy?"

"I'm fine, baby. Are you having fun with Lisa?"

"Yes. What's wrong with our phone, Mommy?"

"I think the snowflakes messed up the wires, baby."

"I miss you, Mommy."

"And I miss you, baby."

"Lisa and I bake'deded some *homemade* pretty star cookies and decorat'deded them with tiny green-and-red spin'kleess a little while ago, Mommy!"

"I'm sure they're pretty, baby. Save me one."

"I will, Mommy."

"I love you, baby—let me talk to Mrs. Thomas again. Have fun with Lisa, and I'll see you tomorrow." Merry Beth didn't see Baron standing close to the doorway listening to her every word. "Bye, baby…be good—love you!"

"Merry Beth…"

"Debbie…thanks for taking such good care of my girl."

"She's one of the family, you know that. You both are."

"Baron came to my rescue *again!* It's embarrassing but I sure am glad he's here. I have a slight fever and…" Merry Beth jumped and rolled her eyes at Debbie's worry coming across the line, interrupting her. Debbie had always been the strong one, the leader, the courageous one—the worry wart!

"You have a *fever?* How bad is it? How high is it? Do you need to go to the hospital?" Debbie asked immediately, anxious.

Merry Beth rubbed her throbbing left temple. "No! No more hospitals. I hate it there. It was 103 last time I checked and…"

"Put Mr. Williams on the line! I want to talk to him."

"No!"

"Yes!"

"Honestly. I'm all right, Debbie."

"You sure? 103 isn't anything to brush aside like old news."

"I just took a cool bath and it helped bring it down a bit. I'm feeling much better. And you'll be glad to know I slept most of the morning and afternoon away. I slept from seven until four-twenty-two…to be exact." Merry Beth closed her eyes and wished for another bout of oblivion. "Can you believe it?"

"Well, no…"

"I cut my hand a bit trying to wash dishes and…"

"How much is a bit? And you *know* how dangerous a fever can be! You were so sick with the pneumonia and…" Debbie began with a hurried and worried tone.

"I'm calling for an ambulance!"

"No, no ambulance! I'm fine, really…"

Merry Beth smiled. It was wonderful to have a close friend like Debbie. She truly was an angel from above. "Debbie, I don't have pneumonia again—stop worrying, okay?"

"What's your temperature now?"

"I don't know. I haven't checked it again. I just got out of the tub a little while ago…"

She heard Baron quietly step through the bathroom door, and looked up at him and smiled as he stepped close to her once more. The bathroom was tiny and it seemed like he took up all the empty space and oxygen, as she fought hard to catch her breath. Besides her father, Debbie's late-husband and brother, and Pastor Todd, there had never been a man in her apartment.

He was definitely a handsome first that God had thrown in her path to save her more than once! She couldn't help but chuckle, hoping he'd stay and be the last. She turned her eyes and flushed face away so he couldn't read her thoughts.

"I have to go, Debbie. Thanks, again. Try not to worry about me so much. I'm as strong as an ox, and I can take care of myself, you *know* that. I've been on my own for a long, long time. I love you and I'll call later, as soon as the phone line's working again. Bye," Merry Beth promised with a smile, despite her throbbing body from head to toe.

"Okay, if you're *sure* that you're all right?"

"I'm sure."

"Love you, bye."

"Love you more, bye."

Baron smiled. "I found the kit."

Merry Beth glanced at Baron and smiled as she turned off the small cellular and passed it back to him. "Honestly! She worries too much. I'm fine, *really!*"

Baron placed the first-aid kit on the sink and opened it. "She's a good friend. You're lucky to have someone like her in your life. You're *very* lucky, Merry Beth."

Merry Beth smiled. "No, I'm blessed, Baron, so blessed."

He raised his dark eyebrows. "What's this about you having a fever of 103?"

Merry Beth hid her eyes from him and mumbled quietly, as she wished she'd at least brushed her hair, "It's nothing…"

"And the pneumonia…?"

"Two winters ago…"

Baron shook his head and reached for the peroxide. "A temperature of 103 isn't nothing pretty flour snowbird. Where's your thermometer?"

She pointed towards her bedroom with her right hand. "It's on my bedroom nightstand by the phone, why?"

"I'll be right back."

"You don't have to check it. I'm really all right!"

"You are a very stubborn woman!"

"Well, you are a very stubborn man!"

Despite her best efforts to show him she was really all right, he checked her temperature anyway and nursed her cuts and treated her like she was *his* angel.

Yes, it was nice to have a man around the house.

Yes, it was comforting to know he cared.

But how much did he care…?

Why was he really here?

* * * * *

Twenty minutes later, Merry Beth was sitting at a cleaned kitchen table eating another bowl of hot, homemade chicken noodle soup and sipping hot tea smothered with lemon and honey.

Baron had taken charge and doctored her cut right hand. He'd taken her temperature and carried her down the stairs—grumbling and mumbling all the way. He'd cleaned off the dirty stove and table, made her the tea and given her a hot bowl of soup, and now was elbow deep in sudsy bubbles washing all of her dirty dishes and pans from the last few days.

It was nice to have someone to talk to, an adult, someone to laugh with and someone to care for and lean on for once. It seemed like years since Bethany's father's death. He'd been the sweetest gift in her life, until Bethany. Now, God had given her Baron. What, *exactly*, was she supposed to do with him?

"Thank you so much for you help, Baron. This soup tastes delicious. You sure you don't want some? Debbie's a good cook. I don't know why she worries so about me. I'm fine, really. A little temperature isn't a reason to call in the National Guard.

"I love the snow, don't you? I love this time of year, don't you? Bless the little Chickadees' hearts—they must be freezing out there. Did you know that God watches out for the birds in any storm, Baron? He knows where each and every one of them are and…" she knew she was rambling and bit down on her tongue.

"Is that so?" he asked, without turning around. Her ramblings were having the strangest effect on his mending heart.

"It's true! My grandfather's favorite hymn of all time was 'His Eye is on the Sparrow' and…" She clamped down on her tongue again, embarrassed that she'd been rambling on and on and on since he'd carried her downstairs, and making a *complete* idiot of herself. He must be looking for the closest exit!

"Sorry, I'm rambling. I'm just wired I guess. I haven't been myself since the accident. If I get on your nerves just tell me and I'll put a muzzle on it. It's been so long since I've had an adult to talk to, besides Debbie and my Pastor, that is. It's kind of…nice."

He reached for a dirty frying pan and shook his head in disbelief. The woman never slowed down. In one sentence she talked about food, best friend, snow, the birds, God watching over the birds, and her grandfather's favorite song. Unbelievable!

"No, it's fine." *Oh, Merry Beth, I could listen to you talk for hours—please don't stop, keep talking, I love the sound of your voice, the sound of your laughter, the smell and feel of you!*

"I love the carolers; we go out every year from Pastor Todd's church to sing Christmas songs on Christmas Eve, have you ever done that? Debbie, her kids and Bethany and I always go. We sing at the grocery stores, outside Irsing's, the Post Office, Town Hall, the Fire Station, the sheriff's station, and the two diner's Winterville has. Oh, and I love the pretty blinking lights in the windows, don't you? I love wrapping presents on Christmas Eve after my baby is asleep, and filling Bethany's stocking is so much fun—oh, turn that up! I love that song." Merry Beth smiled as Faith Hill sang "*Just to Hear You Say That You Love Me*" from her kitchen windowsill radio.

"Music—where would any of us be without it?" she asked.

Baron smiled, liking the song as well, liking the sound of Merry Beth's ramblings, and reached up towards the radio on the kitchen windowsill and turned it up.

"How would you like to come over for Christmas Eve and hear the carolers, Baron? Usually Bethany and I go with them every year, but…" She lifted her broken arm and sore right wrist. "…with this silly thing and my mending right wrist—I really haven't felt much like myself since the accident."

He closed his tired eyes and sighed a little. Even though he welcomed this woman and her child in his life, he felt exhausted to the bone. He didn't have the strength to *do* Christmas again. He didn't turn to answer. "I don't know, Merry Beth…we'll see. My singing leaves much to be desired. I can't carry a tune."

"Won't you let my daughter and I help you heal the wounds? We could bake a turkey or ham, apple pie or pumpkin, whatever you like? We could light some candles, wrap some gifts, pop some pop-corn, watch 'One Magic Christmas' or 'It's a Wonderful Life', *and* if you're *really* good, Santa might even let you go with me to the Christmas play and concert the children are putting on at my church before the caroling! So, what do you think? You think you might want to go with me…*us*? You think you'd like to spend Christmas Eve with Bethany and me? You don't have to buy a thing…just show up and let us spoil you rotten!"

Merry Beth lowered her eyes to her soup bowl, thinking, *Oh, God in Heaven—please let him say yes. I know that I'm falling in love with him. I want to help him, Lord. I don't want him to ever leave. What if he says no? Please Lord—don't let him say no!*

He remained silent, whistling to the music. He didn't answer until the song ended. "I haven't celebrated the Christmas season, or any other season, since losing my family and…"

"If you say no you're going to break my heart. I haven't ever asked a boy on a date before, and I'm kind of nervous here…" She looked at his broad back with eyes filled with laughter, life and pleading. "You aren't, are you?"

Baron didn't glance her way to ask, "What?"

"Going to break my heart?" Merry Beth whispered.

He sucked in his breath and closed his eyes for a moment. And when he did it wasn't Becky's face or smile he saw, it was Merry Beth's. Lord, help him. It hit him like a thunderbolt. He was already in love with her. How in the world was that possible? He'd known her less than a week! No, it just wasn't possible.

Baron turned and met her eyes across the kitchen, and knew then that he loved her powerfully, yet softly; it scared him. Their guardian angels' standing right beside him smiled from ear-to-ear, but of course Merry Beth and Baron didn't see them. How could this have happened so fast? It didn't make sense. He needed to figure it out. He needed some air. He needed to distance himself. He needed to get out of here!

His heart hammered in his chest as he turned down the volume on the little radio sitting on the windowsill. Somehow he just knew that Merry Beth and her daughter were what he'd been waiting for, to help heal the wounds and take away the darkness and loneliness in his life. He couldn't help but wonder what Merry Beth was doing…

Was she waiting to win his heart? He didn't have one. Was she waiting for him to say the words 'I love you'? He never would. Would she do all those things the song said? He hoped not. Would she climb up to the sky and take down the stars, capture the moon, walk across the world to feel him close to her in her arms? He hoped not—he didn't want to hurt her. Were the strong and binding feelings he felt for her real? He feared they were. Did he *really* love her? He shook his head no. Of course he didn't! He was just lonely and tired of being alone. He hadn't been with a woman since before Becky died. Three years was a long time to be without a woman.

He knew that he wanted to protect Merry Beth, pull her into his arms and never let her go, kiss her senseless over and over and over again, touch her—body and soul, kiss away the bruises and hurt; smile and laugh *with* her. He shook his head to clear away these thoughts. He couldn't.

He frowned, knowing he wanted to do all of those things for her—and so much more. As he wrung out the wet and sudsy dishcloth he thought, *I'm in trouble, deep trouble here, it can't be true. How can I love her? I only met her forty-two hours ago. I still love Becky, don't I?* He shook his head to clear it. *Yes, of course I do. I will always love Becky!*

He swallowed his panic and rising doubts and lingering un-certainties, and huskily answered as he wiped down the kitchen counters, "No, pretty flour snowbird. I promise you I'll do my best not to break your heart."

A few seconds passed before he asked, as he turned around, "Who's going to fill *your* stocking, Merry Beth?"

She glanced up from eating her hot soup and didn't hesitate to say, "Why, Santa of course, who else?" She flashed him her pearly white smile once more. "Who's going to fill yours? You *do* still believe in Santa, don't you?" She batted her grass-green eyes at him playfully and passed him that smile he loved so much.

He wanted to kiss her hard and fast, to frighten her, so she'd go away and stay away! Yet, he knew he'd never purposely hurt her.

She wanted him to pull her close and kiss her senseless so he'd stay here forever. She liked having him here. He wouldn't stay—she saw it in his gray eyes. Why did he have to be so strong, so brave, so caring and giving? He truly was her white knight!

Me, Merry Beth—I want to be the one to fill your stocking. I want to be the Munchkin's Santa! "You want some more soup? You're thin as a rail. I could make you some toast to go with it."

No, all I want is for you to open your arms and heart and let me in! "No—this is enough. I can't believe I slept from early this morning around seven 'til after four. That's nine hours sleep—wow! I must've been…" Her words stilled when he turned away from washing the counters to walk swiftly towards her.

His eyes had turned to gray again and his face was shadowed and dark, determined. Her heart began to pound in her chest and she dropped her spoon in her bowl and met his creamy eyes as they drew closer and closer and closer.

"What…what's the matter? What are you doing?"

Before she knew it Baron was squatting down on the vinyl floor in front of her at the table, on his knees. He searched her dark emerald eyes and said, "You're doing too much, Merry Beth. You need to take it slow and easy. You've had a rough, busy—*much too busy* three days, and I would *love* to go to the children's play and concert with you. I'd *love* to spend Christmas Eve with you and the

Munchkin." *Lord, help me. I want to spend the rest of my life with you and your daughter! What have you done to my lonely heart?*

Against all odds and that tiny voice whispering inside his head not to, he took the chance of his lifetime and reached up slowly with his left hand, and touched the left side of her bruised but healing cut face softly. Have mercy—he wanted to kiss away her bruises, and that knowledge left him breathless and scared spitless. And yes, he smiled; her freckles *were* soft-as-melted-butter under his fingertips.

"The bruises and tiny cuts are fading, but it's evident from these dark circles under your eyes that you're not getting enough rest or sleep. That fever was a warning. You need time to heal Merry Beth. You need to take it easy. Who's going to take care of the Munchkin if you get sick?"

"I'll be all right, really." He dropped his hand from her much-too-soft-skin like it had burned it, yet he smiled at her.

"I've lost count of how many times you've said that."

She searched into the depths of his creamy eyes and smiled. His eyes weren't black, cold, uncaring, hard or distant like they'd been when she first glanced in them at the hospital after the accident. Now, she only saw gray-warmth, caring and friendship in their depths. She wanted, needed, and yes, even desired more with this man. Were her feelings for this man genuine? Was she falling in love? Was it really possible?

It hit her, hard, across her beating heart. Yet, she smiled, welcoming it—she loved him! Wow—that was fast.

Without even realizing she'd done it, she lifted her bandaged right hand to his left cheek. She was very pleased to see he didn't wince and flinch back from her touch. "You're just like Debbie—stop worrying! I'm fine. You're a good man, Baron…a true friend."

It seemed that love had whispered to them both, on the wings of angels it had been born—unknowingly to each other. He didn't want to let this chance at a new life pass him by. She wasn't willing to let go of this second chance at love.

Together, could they find the way to heal the wounds?

"I'm worried about you…"

"Stop worrying. I'm going to be fine, really."

She was being stubborn again. "You bet you're going to be fine, because *I'm going to make sure of it!* Thank you for thinking of me and inviting me on this *first date!* It really means a lot, pretty flour snowbird."

She blushed red. "It's not a date...not really..."

He slowly smiled and winked at her. "Yes, I think it is."

"Baron...?" She watched his black eyes turn to gray again, and those bells in her heart began to chime.

"Yes, Merry Beth?" He watched her beautiful eyes darken to that shade of wet summer grass once more, and he knew it was true—he'd done it...he'd gone and fallen in love with her. He wanted to kiss her, *really* kiss her, so she'd know.

"You're stuck." She swallowed a giggle and dropped her hand back to her lap.

"I'm what?" He frowned. He had to be at work at precisely six in the morning at Fort Kent.

"We're stuck." She couldn't break the spell as they stared at one another in silence.

He paled a little. "Stuck...?"

She giggled. "Yes, stuck. So put your feet up, because you're not going anywhere."

"What exactly do you mean, pretty flour snowbird?" he challenged her, as he slowly rubbed his index finger down her cheek, down her cute freckled nose. "How stuck, stuck with your ever smiling, laughing, happy glow on that beautiful face of yours—or, stuck as in sleeping on the back porch or sofa with a lumpy bed roll and hard pillow and borrowed warm blanket?"

He laughed lightly when she smiled ear-to-ear at him. He knew he'd never get enough of her sweet tempting smile, and man, oh man...how he wanted to yank her close and kiss her senseless right about now. It had been snowing heavy for hours—he liked being *stuck* with this pretty woman. He knew it'd be an adventure he'd never forget for the rest of his days.

"You're going to have to stay here tonight. I think we're what you call— *snowbound!*" She smiled at him and added, "You *have* glanced outside recently haven't you?"

"Ah, yeah, I have. I was driving in that madness not a half-hour ago to come and rescue you... *again!*" He roared with laughter, enjoying her sweet smile and tempting, soft perfume.

"Got any extra blankets, sheets and pillows? I always wanted to be totally snowbound with a pretty flour snowbird. This night is going to be adventurous and fun—isn't it?" he asked, searching the depths of her beautiful emerald eyes. The temptation to kiss her overwhelmed him again, but he managed to hold it back.

"I hope so. You can sleep in Bethany's bed. It's a single and should be plenty big enough for you. There are railings on the sides that need to be unscrewed so you'll fit, don't worry—I won't let you fall." Her words and dark eyes at that moment melted any resistance he had left in his heart right around his shiny, black work shoes.

He'd never seen a more beautiful woman. She was like a breath of warm summer air on a cool day, like a spring flower blowing gently in the afternoon light breeze, like a cool snowflake landing on his hot tongue. It was true. He loved her. His heart literally stopped in its beating, and it was a few moments before he found his voice to speak once more.

"Thank you, Merry Beth," he whispered huskily.

She didn't lower her eyes as she softly asked, "For what, Officer Williams...?"

He leaned closer and kissed her—on the tip of her nose. "For being my friend; for making me smile and laugh again."

"That's easy. You're a very nice and likeable man, despite the pain I see in your eyes and the sadness I feel in you—you just have to keep trying and never give up. God has richly blessed us with so much, Baron—life and living, smiles, fun and laughter, friendship, this beautiful snow..." Her words were stilled when Baron lifted his right-hand fingers to her lips. Why were they so soft and tempting—when they were so strong and masculine?

He couldn't help but chuckle. "Merry Beth—how can anyone in their right mind be thankful for a blizzard like this?"

Her eyes danced with happiness. "Don't worry, my friend. Without the cold, snow and winter—we couldn't look forward to the green grass, spring and flowers." She smiled, trying hard to ignore the sizzling sensations ripping up and down her spine from Baron being so close. She liked it—too much. He'd touched her cheek, her nose; her lips. He'd kissed her nose. When would he ever kiss her lips, for goodness sakes! Did she have to make the first move?

His voice replied huskily, "Merry Beth...?"

Was he going to *finally* kiss her? "Yes...?"

Their eyes clashed. "I won't let *you* fall."

Emerald eyes remained locked with wolf-gray, as she softly whispered, "Baron...?" As he broke eye contact and stood she said, "Thank you for being *my* friend. We'll help each other be strong, okay? Because that's what friends are for. I'm glad you were there to pull Bethany and me from daddy's car." *Kiss me. I want you to kiss me!*

He didn't, and quickly turned back to the sink, to wipe and put away the clean dishes, silverware and pots-and-pans.

He'd withdrawn from her, back into his silent world.

What now? Had she done or said something wrong?

Proverbs 17:17a "A friend loveth at all times…"

Proverbs 18:24 "A man *that hath* friends must shew himself friendly: and there is a friend *that* sticketh closer than a brother."

Chapter Five

Luke 2:1-5 "And it came to pass in those days, that there went out a decree from Caesar Augustus, that all the world should be taxed. (*And* this taxing was first made when Cy-re-ni-us was governor of Syria.) And all went to be taxed, every one into his own city. And Joseph also went up from Galilee, out of the city of Nazareth, into Judaea, unto the city of David, which is called Bethlehem; (because he was of the house and lineage of David:) To be taxed with Mary his espoused wife, being great with child."

Miracle #4, hope, December 16th, Wednesday…

"THE WHOLE WORLD is dying, Merry Beth, with greed, envy, disease, sickness, famine, racism and hatred. HIV and AIDS are killing both the young and old. There's endless murder, rape, war, unemployment, pollution, contaminated water, threat of nuclear war and mass destruction, mass suicides, fire, floods, earthquakes, and just plain old random acts of violence and hatred against children, animals and people of every race. On and on—it doesn't ever stop. And if it does it doesn't end. Remember the murder, death and destruction on 9-11? And you're actually telling me to believe that there is still *hope?*"

Baron laughed bitterly and stared at Merry Beth. His eyes couldn't get enough of her beauty, his heart wanted to believe like she did; it couldn't. He'd seen too much of the violence while in the Navy, and also as an Assistant D.A. and police officer in Manhattan. He'd lost good friends when those Towers had burned and crumbled to nothing but broken steel and human ash.

"You have to believe, Baron. You *can't* give up."

He shook his head. "If hope is still out there it's very hard to find. Even on my job—you wouldn't believe the things I see!"

"Yes, I believe there is hope." She smiled at him before lifting her yellow sunflower cup to her lips. "This hot chocolate is delicious. Aren't you glad I have a gas stove?"

The electricity had gone out just after midnight, and the candles' dancing light waltzed softly all around them from the four red-and-green candles in the middle of the kitchen table. She pointed to them and said, "See—a blessing. If I had electric we wouldn't be sitting here enjoying this wonderful candlelight and fellowship, and this hot-chocolate, cinnamon toast and cheese omelets you made for us on my *gas* stove."

He watched her take another bite of her omelet and wanted to pull her close for a first earth-shattering, over-the-fence, feel-the-earth-tremble-under-your-feet kiss. So far he'd managed to keep a tight lid on the temptations her eyes awakened in his heart. That memorable quick kiss on her cute little freckled nose had opened a door he knew he should have kept shut and locked.

"Come on, Merry Beth. How can you sit there and say there is hope? I've worked my entire life to strive to be better, do better, and have better things—a better education, a better job, a better house, a better car, and a better salary. I've worked fifty to sixty hour weeks, sometimes twenty-four-seven, to try and change things out there—not only in my present job, but while I was in the Navy. While working as Assistant D.A. in Manhattan I've seen some terrible benign things, Merry Beth."

She didn't speak and he added huskily, "I was there on 9-11 and lost a lot of fellow police officers that day. They and the lost and fallen fire-fighters were my *friends*, Merry Beth. The world is filled with corruption. It's dying, can't you see that? For every five good men—there are twenty evil ones. Isn't your God listening?"

"Yes, He is…and He is your God, too." Her sad eyes lifted to his, begging him to understand. "I understand everything you've said Baron, but…"

"Everywhere you look there is extortion, espionage, treason—there's no one left to trust, Merry Beth! I've paid my bills and mortgage and car payments on time, I've saved what I can, I've helped whomever I could along the way. I've served my country, I fell in love, I got married, and I had a son—a family! And in one single instant…" *How do I find hope after losing my wife and son? How can I truly be in love again? It's just not possible. I don't have the strength to do this again. Lord, help me—please!*

Her heart broke in two for him, for his sadness and lack of faith. "A drunk driver comes along and snatched it all away. Baron, you can't go on blaming God for losing your wife and son. The Bible says that life is but a vapor—it's here one moment and gone the next. You can't question God's motives. He can see into the future, we can't, and all those *things* that you mentioned just now—*they* are not what's important in life. You can survive and be very happy without a new car, a beautiful fancy house, lots of money in your wallet or savings account, prestige, reputation, fame, fortune, expensive jewelry or clothes—look at me and Bethany. We are very happy and..." She sipped her hot chocolate when he interrupted her.

He shook his head in disagreement. "You have to *live* in the real world, Merry Beth. You can't separate yourself from it and live like a hermit." He winced, knowing he'd done just that since losing his family. But, no more!

She smiled. "I know that. That's not what I meant..."

He shook his head. "I agree that you can separate yourself from certain aspects and temptations...*sin* of the world, yes—smoking, gambling, alcohol, pornography, what music you listen to, what movies you watch, how you dress, your attitude and speech, but you still have to *live* in the real world, Merry Beth!"

Her dark eyes snapped to his with heated fire. "What are you saying? You don't think I live in the real world? I do—believe me. I don't have much money; it's true. It wasn't much but Thomas Earl left only one life insurance policy, and so far I have managed to leave it untouched for Bethany's future and education.

"In the winter I knit and sew to make extra money—blankets, patched quilts, hat and scarf sets, afghan's and pillows...I *enjoy* sewing, and I make enough from my teaching job to pay my monthly bills and buy food. Usually I work extra, making wreaths this past week—but with my arm in this cast and sore right wrist; God always provides. I live my life as a testimony to that fact!"

He pushed his empty plate away and reached for his hot chocolate. "Merry Beth, you shouldn't have to count every dime and nickel and penny to just barely get by. What kind of life is that? Surely, God doesn't mean for anyone's life to be this way? Some live in greater riches than we've ever seen or could ever imagine, and some live in poverty with no hope of ever finding a way out, with no roof over their head, or no table to eat on, or no food or safe water at all. There's prostitution out there—just babies some of them!

"There's hate crimes, slavery, the endless war with drugs and terrorism— these men and women aren't afraid to die to hurt and maim and destroy others...and there are people that live in filth, Merry Beth. I've seen it with my own eyes!"

She shook her head and reached across the table for his hands. She lightly caressed them; sizzling sensations immediately jumped up and down her right arm. Why was that, you suppose?

"God created a perfect world with no sin, Baron. It was Satan who tempted Eve in the Garden of Eden—her and Adam's fall was what brought sin into the perfect world. And I have greater riches than the richest person alive on the earth—because I have God in my heart and in my life, on a daily basis. I don't need money or a fancy car, or diamonds or gold or power and wealth to be happy. My happiness comes from within, inside my soul. Don't you see?"

He didn't want to give in and argued stubbornly, "I see that you struggle to barely get by counting your pennies!"

"You can't put a price tag on God's love. It's bountiful and endless and *free*. I believe...I *know* He gave His own Son to die to take away the sins of the whole world, Baron. But, God deals with each one of us on an individual level. Each one of us must ask in faith, believe and accept God at His Word." Despite the way Baron was shaking his head no and disagreeing with her, she smiled. He was hearing her, but he was just refusing to let go and believe.

"I envy you...it's clear to me that you have suffered from that terrible accident. You have a broken arm and sprained wrist, cracked ribs, barely getting by counting your change, living alone with no husband to help support and take care of you and the Munchkin, you work hard, you strive for a better life for your little girl, you're *struggling*, Merry Beth. Yet, you're truly happy. You smile and laugh and never give up, despite the pain life throws your way—you still believe there is hope."

He wanted what she had—he wanted to be able to really smile from within. He wanted to find peace in his troubled life and heart. He met her eyes. "You're a strong woman, and very brave."

Merry Beth just smiled and sipped her hot chocolate before continuing. "In the spring and summer I grow and sell my vegetables and flowers—tomatoes, cucumbers, potatoes, beans, and carrots. I make and sell flower arrangements, baskets and wreaths. I love my job teaching kindergarten. It's true that a teacher's salary isn't much, but it's the children's smiles and laughter and warm hugs that I love the most. God always, *always* supplies my every need, Baron. Bethany and I never go without."

He shook his head. "Maybe not, but don't you ever wish for something better? Aren't you ever tired of always trying to make something out of nothing?" Her eyes saddened a little and he wanted to yank his words back, but couldn't.

She shook her head no. "No, I love my life, I love my daughter, I love my job, and I wouldn't change a thing. I have more riches than any amount of money can buy because I have my daughter's love. Her love means everything to me—as God's does. Don't you see—without *Him*...we're all just drifting with no purpose, we're empty, we're sad, lonely...and lost."

"Yes, but that doesn't change the world, does it?"

"You *have to* believe there is still good in the world, Baron. You have to, or you'll go quietly insane." Her eyes begged him to understand. "You have to believe, even through your loss. This world *is* worth fighting for, Baron. It is!"

Memories from the accident turned his eyes to a darker shade of gray. "*You* of all people know how cruel the world can be, Merry Beth—you and Bethany were hit and almost killed...not by one drunk driver but by *two*...only six nights ago! What would you have done if you'd lost the Munchkin in that crash? Would your faith have seen you through then?" He watched her pale to a ghostly white and regretted his words once more. He stopped his hand at the last second from reaching out to comfort her.

"God's grace is with me, Baron. Don't you see?"

"I see that thunder always rolls in before the storm."

"God creates the storms."

"I see that evil rules the world."

"Satan's time is limited here on earth."

"I see that hate and violence overshadow love and peace."

"You'll find forgiveness at the foot of the cross."

"I see that the mountains are too high."

"Faith can move those mountains, Baron."

"I see that no matter what I say—you'll disagree."

She smiled. "Perhaps..."

She often wondered if God ever cried when He looked down at all the destruction and sin in the world. So much had been done to destroy the earth He'd created and yes, it was hard to believe in miracles, it was hard to believe and trust; it was hard to depend on Him for everything in this day and age, hard yes, but still possible.

"Anything is possible with God, if you have faith *and* hope in your heart. God is loving and merciful and forgiving. He will show you—*us* the way," she whispered softly, meaning it with her whole heart. God lived inside her heart, and she wanted that for Baron, too.

Merry Beth closed her eyes for a moment. It was early, just a little after seven a.m. and it was still snowing outside. She shivered suddenly against the chill and cold, the brittle wind howled and begged desperately to get inside where it was safe and warm. Baron had built a fire in the living-room hearth and kitchen wood stove, and it was snuggly and warm in spite of the storm and loss of power. Her fever was gone and she'd slept peacefully without medication. She felt rested for the first time since the accident.

Baron, on the other hand, had slept miserably in Bethany's tiny bed—dreaming of and reliving the seconds before the accident happened that ripped apart his entire world. When he'd turned in his seat to reach for his wife, it wasn't Becky's smiling face that instantly turned to pain, blood and death—it was Merry Beth's. He'd also dreamt of his son's last cries in life before death snatched him into eternity forever. He'd given up trying to sleep somewhere around three a.m. and had stumbled his way to the living room, sitting in front of the blazing fire until the light of dawn…thinking of all he'd lost. He'd spent the last three years trying to erase every memory he'd ever made with his wife and son—it hadn't worked. He loved them. He would always love them. They were a part of his soul.

He rubbed his right hand over his tired eyes. "You cannot know how deep the pain is from losing your family," he began. He noticed the sudden sadness in her grass-green eyes, remembered her lost husband and father, and bit down hard on his tongue.

"I do. I lost Thomas, my mother, my father, and God gives and takes life, Baron. Some live a hundred years, some only days or hours. It's not up to us to decide fate. We have to thank God for every second He gives us in this life. And we must make every second count—we all learned that on 9-11. Because, yes—it could all be over tomorrow. Yet, we are not promised tomorrow, are we? You're right though—we are living in a dangerous, cold, uncaring and unloving world, but there *is* still hope in it. There's goodness out there—it's worth looking for and worth fighting for."

He stood from the table and walked to the back door to stare out into the blinding snowstorm. "It's not that simple when you've lost your family along the way, when you're left alone to face life every day and night without them. When you see their faces every time you close your eyes, and hear them breathing or whispering to you in the darkness of the night…and in your dreams."

"They are gone from this earth, Baron—but you haven't lost their love because they live inside you…they always will. My parents and husband do…to this very day."

As he watched the snow fall he thought, *The world doesn't make much sense, Merry Beth, and there's too much loss and pain in it. My heart is broken. There were days I feared I'd never be able to go on—until I met you...*

He turned back and met her dark eyes across the kitchen. "You lost your husband, your parents—you know how hard it is to go on alone, without them. I see it in your eyes...even though they're still with you—even now...you'll always miss them."

She remembered back to a time when it was that way for her after Thomas Earl had died. But as every year passed it got easier and easier, and his memory would always be inside her heart. He'd been her high school sweetheart and a good husband; he'd been loving, faithful, strong to the end and sweet. She'd never been with any other man than Thomas Earl. He was her first and only love.

"You have to let go, Baron. Until you do..." She knew she'd do anything to help this man, this wonderful yet sad man she'd suddenly fallen in love with.

"I don't live one day at a time. I live second by second."

"You've lost sight of your dreams because of your loss. Let me help you find new ones. Let me be your friend. I want to help you...you *need* me—you rescued Bethany and I from my daddy's car just before it exploded for a reason!"

His eyes sought hers. "You're telling me this is fate—you and I—being together like this?"

She smiled and finished her hot chocolate. "Yes, it is."

He walked back to the table and cleared it and placed her dirty dishes in the sink. "I'll never find peace—I know. It's easier said than done, pretty flour snowbird." *The aloneness and quiet bounces around inside my soul and head, Merry Beth, and it's hard to find new dreams, new beginnings, but in your eyes I'm finding them again, aren't I? What now?*

"God can give you this peace you so desire, Baron, if you let Him in—please, take a leap in faith and trust in Him!"

He turned towards the back door again, with his hands as fists' in his pockets, as he watched the white-out storm. "The things you bury away deep inside you—pain, loss, regret, anger, the sense of being alone—they always rise to haunt you again, Merry Beth, if you don't face them. I know that. There's not much out there that's strong and lasting any more. Surely, even you can see that?"

Another headache threatened. "Even me...?"

"A woman who lives by faith in an unseen God—I can't do it. I don't know if I ever really did," he admitted quietly.

Tears burned behind her dark eyes. "Please don't say that—it's not true. You'll find the answers. I know you will. You can't give up, Baron," she bravely added, as she rose and walked to him and reached out to touch his left arm, "I won't let you."

He turned away from the raging, powerful storm and looked into her pretty eyes; her kind touch that burned his arm touched his heart. "You're too good to be true, Merry Beth." He reached for the warming milk that sat in a copper pan on the wood stove and refilled their hot chocolate mugs. As he dumped two spoonfuls of cocoa in each cup he explained, "I know that Becky and my son are in Heaven. Like you, she was strong in her faith when she was a young teenage girl. Not a day went by she didn't mention God did this, God did that, God is with me, God loves us…"

She knew he still loved his wife—his sad wolf-gray eyes told her so. She returned to the table. "Tell me about her…please."

He forced a smile, as he sat across from her at the cleared table and stirred his hot chocolate. "Becky became a career woman who loved Navy life. I loved her desperately, but near the end…there were many times she was a hard and cold, distant woman, Merry Beth. The last few months of her life she became rigid and with-drawn, silent and sadly, apart from me. I've yet to understand why. It haunts me to this very day."

Merry Beth frowned as she slowly stirred her own hot chocolate. "Maybe she was trying to find her own sense of purpose, meaning and peace inside her heart. Maybe she was trying to find her way back to God…if she'd fallen away from Him. The struggle between God and Satan for the human heart is very powerful."

Baron rubbed his whiskered face, combed his right hand through his hair and lit two more candles. "Surprisingly, after she found out she was pregnant she didn't re-enlist and retired from military life to become a full-time wife and mother. Her entire world seemed to become our son, our home and our life together, but I always wondered deep in my heart if she was truly happy once she quit the Navy."

She sipped her hot chocolate, thankful for its warmth as it soothed her beating heart. "You saw it in her eyes…she wasn't?"

Worry creased his brow. "Yes. The Navy was in her blood you see, her father and grandfather before her, and her three older brothers'—they are…were all Navy. She was an excellent electrical engineer, and her passion was the fighter jets.

She could tear apart a coughing engine and rebuild it to purr like a baby kitten. There were times she was so strong, so brave; then there were times—right before her death, that she seemed so lost, so alone, so withdrawn from me and the world around her. She distanced herself from me—I couldn't reach her, and near the end she never smiled or laughed anymore…"

His hand shook when he lifted his spoon to his lips. Did Merry Beth see, he wondered? Did she think him weak? Did she think him a wimp? Did she think him foolish? "…except for when she glanced at our son."

She passed him a smile that told him she cared, *really* cared—for him. "It sounds like your wife wanted both sides of that coin, Baron—career and family life, as wife and mother and engineer. To some women it's very hard to give up a promising career and stay home and change diapers and clean house and bake cookies, and become someone like Betty Crocker. Now, don't get me wrong— it can be done, but it's a constant struggle."

"Becky had it all, and like I said, in the last months her eyes only smiled when she looked at our son," Baron lightly confessed.

"Like yours," she whispered as she reached for another piece of cinnamon toast. This man, when he loved, loved deeply—for life, forever, for always. His story was indeed a sad one.

He sipped his hot chocolate then glanced at her with a frown. "What do you mean—like mine what…?" He searched for her soft emerald eyes across the table, the dancing light from the candles reflecting off her pretty eyes.

"I said—like yours. *Your* eyes never smile, Baron. I remember when I first met you I kept trying to figure out a way to make you smile, *really* smile. Even now, when you smile your eyes are always sad and forlorn. Even after almost three years, you're still in mourning."

She watched him pale and flinch back in his seat, as if she'd struck him across his face, and knew her words raged true in his broken and angry heart. The love he'd shared with Becky was hard to walk away from. This was a man who loved and loved for keeps. Yet, his left hand was bare of a wedding ring.

Merry Beth's love was what Baron needed to help heal the deep, dark wounds. He knew it, sensed it in her look, her touch, her smile—everything about her whispered, '*trust me.*' He didn't dare take the chance. Not yet. His heart was still healing. He felt, at that moment, sadness engulf him.

"I've lived alone in solitude for almost three years, Merry Beth. You and the Munchkin are the only two people I've let in." *And I've fallen deeply in love with you.*

I don't know how, but I have and it hurts, pretty flour snowbird. I can't take the risk to ever love again. I can't. I have to go and never return!

"I'm glad." *Because I've fallen deeply in love with you!*

"Why?" *You're so easy to love, Merry Beth. I thank God for bringing you into my life. I don't want to lose you, but I'm afraid to love again, touch again; reach out again.*

"I'm glad because I believe that God is working miracles in our lives this wonderful Christmas season." *Oh, Baron, don't you see? You can't lose your way. You can't lose faith!*

"Miracles…what are you talking about?" *Oh, Merry Beth, don't you see? I've lost my way. I lost my faith in ever finding hope again the day I lost my family!*

"There are so many—where to start…"

"Let me guess—you believe in true-blue miracles as well."

"Yes! It's the little ones that count, by the way."

He stirred his hot chocolate and said huskily, "I don't believe in miracles anymore, big or small." He shook his head to clear it. "You really are a rare one, aren't you…and so talkative?"

She shook her head that she didn't agree. "Well, I do believe! For starters— you're smiling again, you're laughing again, you and I are friends helping each other in different ways," she said with another killer friendly smile.

"How am I helping you, Merry Beth? Name one thing I have done for you?" His dark eyes challenged hers across the table as he lifted his hot chocolate to his lips.

"You helped me when I was hit by those two drunk drivers. You helped my baby girl stay warm and safe until I woke afterwards. You helped me when I cut my hand, you helped me clean my kitchen and washed all my dirty dishes and pans, and you fed me and nursed me through my fever last night. You chopped enough wood to last a month to help keep my house warm, you…"

Her words were stilled when he reached across the table and lightly touched her lips with his fingertips, silencing her. Creamy gray eyes clashed with emerald, locked together.

He knew in an instant he should have never touched her. "What about *you*? You and the Munchkin gave me those pears, and you gave me that tree—which is yet to be decorated, by the way. And by the looks of this storm, I might be stranded here for days! At least Mitch understood about me calling in to work." He dropped his hand and took a huge breath in before continuing.

"You, a virtual stranger, became my friend—something I needed to jerk me awake again, to open my eyes, to help me get past the pain and loss and darkness I've lived in from losing my family…"

"See, you're getting it. You *do* understand!"

"You gave me the gift of *wanting* to smile again, the gift of your laughter and friendship, the gift of realizing there is still hope in this world, Merry Beth." He raised her right hand to his lips and kissed her knuckles softly. "No matter what I said, I do believe in hope. Thank you, Merry Beth. The road ahead seems a little less—*long* because of your friendship, your smiles, your caring; your touch."

He dropped her hand and it was several minutes before she said, "Oh, I forgot to tell you—my baby and I made you some special tree ornaments. They're in a box under my tree." She searched his eyes and smiled. "I'm glad you're back amongst the living again—it isn't good for anyone to be alone."

As her eyes took his handsome face and unique eyes in she thought, *You're so strong, and brave, and kind, and handsome. I can't believe that God has brought you into my life. I've been alone for so long. Maybe everyone in town has forgotten. Maybe it's truly over.* She knew better. *I have to keep the truth buried, for Bethany's sake. I pray it isn't dangerous for me to love you, Baron, but I feel like God has brought you to me. With every breath I take I feel it. I want it. I want you in my life as more than just my friend!*

He reached across the table for her right hand again, and held it in both of his. "Thank you, Merry Beth."

"No, it wasn't me. It's God working in your heart."

He wasn't sure about *that*, but smiled anyway. "Thank *you*, Merry Beth." He felt her shiver when he lightly rubbed her right wrist with his thumb, her rapid pulse under his touch.

She smiled and made the move to stand. "God is doing most of the work, Baron. I truly believe that. I'm just helping a little. Don't you see—the gifts from the heart, the kind that don't cost money, *they* are the most important…the most treasured ones of all."

"What do you mean?" He watched her eyes light up, and they sparkled with warmth and life and living. His heart beat faster. Man, how easy it would be to love this unique woman. Her pretty eyes and stunning smile just pulled him in, like the strongest magnet.

"A smile, friendship, soft laughter, a warm hug, a gentle touch, a homemade ornament for the tree, baked goodies, a soft kiss on the nose when someone's a little down, wild flowers that you can pick in the meadow. Music, a sea-shell, a sand-dollar, a letter to a far away friend, colorful balloons and pretty flowers when someone's sick, homemade chicken noodle soup like Debbie made for me, a special new friend…"

She lifted her dirty mug and carried it to the sink. "…like you." Her steps weren't wobbly or unsteady. She was a brave, caring and strong woman.

Baron just shook his head and quickly rose to help wash the remaining dirty dishes. "You're such a treasure, pretty flour snowbird. Now that you've given me more than one good reason why I should believe in God and angels, love and kindness, hope and peace, smiles and laughter again—it looks like I'm going to have to decorate my house with Christmas lights like I promised. You and the Munchkin want to help me?" he asked with a chuckle as he wiped the table clean with the wet dishcloth.

"Love to, and my baby *loves* Christmas lights so you better prepare yourself. She's a Christmas baby—she'll be six in exactly nine days. I still have so much to do!" She passed him a gentle, soft smile, knowing the miracles were truly happening in his heart. He was starting to heal. "*You* want to help me plan a surprise birthday party, Sergeant Williams?"

"Thank you for being my friend." He reached for her right hand once more and bravely lifted it to his lips and kissed her knuckles again. "…and I'd love to help."

He met her eyes to add, "Why isn't this hand still wrapped tight in a bandage like I wrapped it yesterday evening? How's it going to heal when you keep taking it and the sling off?"

She loved the feel of his lips on her skin, and wished—just this one little wish—he'd catch her under the mistletoe and kiss her, *really* kiss her—in trust, in love, and with hope in his heart. Hope for a future together, for them as a couple. She didn't want him to let go of her hand but he did, and she turned away from his creamy gray gaze slowly. "It's fine, really."

"You always say that, even when it's not true?" he quietly asked. "You don't have to put on a brave front…not for me."

Her heartbeat tripled. What would he do or say if he knew the truth about her past? Would he call her *friend* then? Would he stand by her or walk away and never look back—like many of her friends had?

She remained silent as she filled the sink with lukewarm and sudsy water, and he said, "I love birthday parties. Tell me, what does the Munchkin want? What's her favorite music? Maybe I'll get her some CD's," he suggested, as he gently pushed her aside so he could wash and rinse the dishes. In less than a minute he had sudsy water and dirty dishes up to his elbows again. "All kids her age like music."

"What are you doing? I can do those…"

"Go sit—I have kitchen duty today, and rewrap that hand!"

She smiled and sat and obediently wrapped her sore wrist. The house was much too quiet with her daughter gone. She missed the sound of her laughter and running footsteps overhead.

"She likes worship and praise songs and hymns, like her mother. *You* can blow up all the balloons if you want. Let the dishes soak, let's go call Bethany and see how it's going at Debbie's house," she suggested as she rose from the table.

He turned and smiled at her and she knew she'd never loved like this—so fast, so powerful, so vibrant and sonorous. This man's eyes seemed to read her very thoughts, her very soul. This man's heart was healing, he needed time and space. She'd wait, knowing it would be worth it.

She turned away from his creamy yet dark eyes towards the living room. "I wonder if the phone is back on yet. I'm glad you have your cellular with you. Does it need to be charged? Hey, I bet you don't have your charger with you."

"I don't, and the last time I checked the phone's battery was halfway charged." He wiped his hands and followed her from the kitchen and despite her wishes for that kiss; Merry Beth stayed clear of the pine mistletoe, telling herself neither one was ready for that kind of human touch. Not yet.

Her heart raced. Desire for his kiss weakened her knees. They were still stuck because of the storm. What now?

* * * * *

Later that same afternoon, around four-thirty, Merry Beth glanced at Baron and asked, "Since we're stranded here for only God knows how long—tell me about your life, Baron. What was Navy life like?" She loved the blazing fire and lit candles. It was cozy and warm in the homey living room.

Baron and Merry Beth were enjoying the warmth from the hot, blazing fire together. The snow and howling wind had stopped about an hour earlier and the world around them was now quiet in its blanket of heavy, icy white. They'd spent the morning playing Solitaire, Scrabble, Rummy and Othello. They'd each talked about their life over a light lunch of green salad, tuna sandwiches, and hot tea earlier.

The electricity was still out and while Merry Beth slept from one to four, Baron prepared homemade beef soup, which was warming on the wood stove in the kitchen, in a huge black cast-iron kettle. He swept and mopped her kitchen floor and took out the garbage. He filled her wood box and chopped up the remaining wood that was stacked in a huge pile by the barn. He'd placed most of her refrigerator food outside in the icy snow to keep it cold.

He shoveled her front porch and sidewalk and unburied both of their cars from underneath snow and ice. His had started right up. The old rusty Toyota on the other hand remained cold as stone with a dead battery. He called a local friend and made the arrangements for her long driveway to be plowed as soon as possible. He called the electric company and was told the electricity should be restored in the next few hours.

After she'd finally awaken from her much-needed three-hour nap, he checked her temperature again and was pleased to see it was normal. He'd covered her with a warm patched quilt from the back of her couch after she'd fallen asleep, and she was still snuggled under it warmly and comfortably. He glanced into her soft green eyes as he placed a fresh cup of hot tea on the coffee table close enough so she could reach it.

"Why do you want to know about my life while in the Navy?" he asked as he settled in the lazy-boy chair by the sofa.

"I'm just curious, I guess. How does a man go from being an important D.A. to Navy to State Police Officer? *Exactly* how old are you, anyway?" She swallowed a giggle at his shocked expression.

"What? What's the matter? Are you way over the hill or something?" She liked teasing him. His eyes always darkened to that creamy shade of gray when she did.

She heard him chuckle as he settled in the recliner chair by the fire with his feet up. "I always thought it was against the rules to ask someone their age. How old are *you*, pretty flour snowbird?" *When you look at me like you do, I can't help but want to pull you into my arms and hold you close for always, and kiss you senseless!*

He loved her laughter and knew he'd never get enough. "I'm thirty-nine. See how easy that was. Come on—don't be chicken. Tell all. You know all about my life!"

She smiled when he talked about her life from his memory. "All right, let's see if I remember everything you told me. You were born and raised in Winterville. You graduated from Winterville High. You graduated from University in Old Town with a degree in Elementary Education. You married your high school sweetheart in the month of May. You worked for six-and-a-half years as a bank teller for First National…"

Merry Beth smiled. "Wow, you have quite the memory!"

"You were married for seven years until Thomas died in May of '99 due to congestive heart failure. You gave birth to a healthy seven-plus-pound baby girl in December of '97. You went back to work at the bank when the Munchkin was just a month old but only for three weeks. Why is that, by the way? You never said."

Panic crowded her vision, but she pushed it way back behind her. As she sucked in and held her breath, life moved on. She closed her eyes against the dark pain and familiar feelings of humiliation, and terrible memories from the years before and the weeks after she'd been literally forced to give up her job. A girl had to have some secrets didn't she? "It's in the past, Baron. I don't talk about it or think about it anymore."

Her heart was beating so fast she couldn't catch her breath. To tell would put her baby's life in turmoil; she couldn't do it. It saddened her that she couldn't tell her new friend the truth about her past. She wanted to trust him with it. She really did! It was hard to open up those old wounds again. Maybe someday she could, but not now. Thinking back made those old wounds bleed again.

He didn't miss how her eyes clouded over with pain and sadness, and his curiosity got the best of him when her smile disappeared and she paled to a foggy white, and he pressed her further for answers.

"Come on, Merry Beth. Spill the beans. What happened to you, to make you quit a job you loved and worked at for over six-and-a-half years? You said you were making good money, why quit? Why quit the job at the bank and turn to teaching? You said that you were in line for a huge promotion and had wonderful friends there. What happened to make you turn your back on all of that? Or is teaching your passion, your dream?"

She looked everywhere but at him. "I thought we were going to talk about *your* life! How did we all of a sudden start talking about mine? I want to talk about *you*."

"Stop stalling, Merry Beth. We're talking about *you* now. What's wrong? I'm your friend, aren't I? You can tell me anything. You're frightened—care to tell me why?" he asked, curious now.

He didn't miss how she shivered and snuggled further under her quilt, avoiding his eyes. *What happened to you to put that look of panic and fear in your eyes? Come on, Merry Beth, talk to me, trust me enough to tell me. I've fallen in love with you. Won't you let me help you?*

Maybe she could tell him, a little…

"The new bank manager—you see, my old boss retired in December of '97…" She closed her eyes against the memories, not understanding why she was about to tell him about her past so easily and trustingly. She'd kept it a secret for so long, yet didn't everyone in town know? Evidently not…

Every protective instinct he had came crashing forward front and center in his heart at that moment. He didn't like how she paled and avoided looking in his eyes. He didn't like the fear she tried to keep hidden from him by looking away. He waited for her to continue, fearful in his heart what she was going to say. She was scared, truly scared. He also didn't miss the look of pure panic across her lashes before she'd turned away. Something bad had happened to her at the bank, but what? Her next words filled his entire being with white-hot disbelief and rising anger.

"He…well, he touched me in…certain ways that weren't…appropriate, Baron. For some women, in the business world where survival is the key, it's called 'just-ignore-it-and-look-the-other-way-or-lose-your-job'. In my world it's called *sexual harassment*. I filed charges against him while I was on maternity leave, but…"

She buried herself deeper under the warmth of the quilt and leaned her head back and closed her eyes, hating it that just talking about the past brought uncertainty and fear back in her heart, her world. She didn't want to remember or relive those old memories. She truly didn't.

They brought her nothing but pain and humiliation.

"You were forced to drop the charges or lose your job. *You actually lived with this man's harassment and hands on your body for years! How is this possible, Merry Beth?*" Rage he never knew existed inside him crushed his very soul with anger and hatred against the man who'd hurt her. It consumed him to the point he swore he was drowning in its darkness, right there and then. He quickly stood and began to pace across her worn brown carpet in front of the fireplace hearth.

When she didn't answer he asked, "It's true, isn't it? You were forced to give up your job."

"Yes," her whisper slashed across his heart.

"And when you went back to work after the Munchkin was born…?" he pressed, holding his breath in.

"The sexual harassment only got worse. I quit after three weeks," she admitted quietly, not meeting his now gray eyes. She cringed, hating it that he might think less of her in any way. Why did she have to open her big mouth and tell him?

In seconds he was at her side pulling her into his arms. "How terrible and degrading it must have been for you, Merry Beth. All alone, widowed, being a new mother and forced to deal with a sick, twisted..." The muscles in his jaw twitched as adrenaline turned the warm blood in his veins to pure ice.

"Why didn't your husband do something? This was going on well *before* he died. Why didn't he put a stop to it one way or another?" He searched her darkened emerald eyes and didn't miss how she winced against his sharp hold on her shoulders. He eased his hold immediately.

"I'm sorry, Merry Beth; it's clearly evident you've suffered terribly from the hands of this man. I didn't mean to hurt you. I know your ribs are still very sore— you all right?"

She shook her head yes and whispered, "I didn't tell Thomas about the sexual harassment, Baron."

"For goodness sakes—*why not?*" he thundered as he searched for his answer in her eyes. He prayed for the chance to be alone with this man for just five minutes in some dark, shadowy alley somewhere. He knew it would be wrong to take the law into his own hands, what was that Bible verse Becky always quoted again about seeking revenge?

"I faced it alone and kept it a secret until after he died. He also had colon cancer, Baron, and he was very sick those last months from the chemotherapy. So sick he couldn't work. The only money we had coming in was from my salary at the bank. I couldn't afford to quit. We needed the money. I was forced to keep my mouth shut, take the harassment and swallow my fears and tears—and shame...to survive. It was the only way..."

His temper snapped. "*This isn't right! It's wrong!*"

She swallowed against the rising sobs in her dry throat. Remembering back and talking about it only brought back the shame and humiliation, and she didn't want to remember.

"Tell me why you kept it from your husband, Merry Beth," Baron asked firmly, not letting her confession drop away so quietly. He knew it had cost her a great deal to confess the truth to him just now. Yet, she was holding back.

"I know you well enough to know you're holding something back from me, Merry Beth. Come on, spill it!"

Her dark eyes snapped to his in frustrated defiance. "I kept it from him because Thomas Earl was a good man, Baron! He was honest, caring, very loving, dependable, faithful, hard working, smart, well educated; funny—he always made me laugh. I fell in love with him because he could *always* m…make me l…laugh."

Her voice cracked. She felt like she was lost in his creamy eyes, and smiled through her glistening tears. Every time Baron was angry his black eyes turned to creamy gray.

"You're angry," she whispered close.

He closed his eyes. "Yes. Not at you, but *for* you."

"I didn't want to hurt him, didn't want him to worry; he suffered enough pain, Baron," she added quietly, once more hiding her eyes from him by glancing in the blazing fire.

"You're stalling. What's the truth, Merry Beth?" he pressed. "You've come this far. You might as well tell all."

Her temper flared and she tried to push at his chest but he wasn't letting her go, and it hurt her mending ribs too much. "I told you—Thomas was sick! He'd gone through remission twice and I didn't want to put any more burdens on him. I loved him, don't you see? I couldn't do that to him. There was nothing he could do. He was too sick, Baron!"

She lost control and crumbled right in front of his eyes. She'd never told another human soul, except her lawyer, not even her father or Debbie, until now. It had been a long, hard battle she'd carried alone all these years. Tears burned her eyes and she finally gave in and let them fall. *Oh, Baron, to tell you the whole truth— it's too shameful. I can't do it. How can I tell you the man who did this to me is Bethany's own grandfather? How can I tell you that he's a drunk and a terrible, evil, sick and twisted man, so unlike his son—my wonderful Thomas Earl?*

He pulled her carefully to his chest and rubbed her back slowly and softly with both hands until she quieted. "Don't cry; my pretty flour snowbird. It's over now. I'm sorry I brought up all this past hurt and pain for you. I never meant to make you cry. You talk of me letting go—you need to do the same."

"I don't want to talk about it anymore," she mumbled in the front of his uniform shirt, accepting his clean handkerchief when he passed it to her.

"Try to rest, Merry Beth. You're exhausted," he suggested.

He held her in his arms until she sobbed herself to sleep, and a little more hope within him died. He watched her sleep and wondered why she smiled, why she laughed, why she gave him warmth, friendship and yes, even a sense of *hope* again—when she'd been hurt and humiliated beyond belief. He didn't understand why she was so trusting and so giving and so sweet and kind and outgoing when she'd been through so much pain and humiliation.

She was truly a unique treasure, one he didn't want to let go of, but would because he loved her. To keep her and call her his—it wasn't going to happen.

Not now, not ever.

* * * * *

Merry Beth slept soundly until Baron woke her two hours later, when Bethany wouldn't take no for an answer.

"Merry Beth, wake up—it's the Munchkin. She's called three times and adamantly expresses her wishes to speak to her Mommy this time."

She opened her rested eyes in surprise that she'd slept, and rubbed her right hand over them to wake herself up. "Oh, my goodness—did I fall asleep, *again?*" She sat up slowly and reached for the cellular in Baron's outstretched hand.

"Thanks," she mumbled softly, her voice scratchy from sleeping so sound.

He turned away and placed two more logs on the fire. His eyes were gray again, and she wondered why he was angry. Had her words about her past earlier sickened him, and he was anxious to leave and never come back?

"Mommy...?" Bethany whispered over the line.

"Hello, baby, how did your day go? Did you make angels in the snow?" She watched Baron as he placed two more logs on the fire before reaching for his uniform jacket. Her heart broke with disappointment, knowing he was preparing to leave.

She glanced at her watch and flinched when she realized how late it was. It wasn't until then she realized that the power was back on. She searched for his eyes again, but he kept them hidden from her by glancing away towards the kitchen. He seemed like a stranger again—so distant, so cold and withdrawn from her, his back rigid, his eyes wolf-gray and...angry. She shivered, wondering why.

"I want to come home, Mommy. I miss'deded you," Bethany cried over the wire.

"I miss you, too baby. I'm coming to get you first thing in the morning. I promise—as soon as I shovel myself out and the roads clear a little, I'll come to get you."

Baron pointed to his watch, signaling he had to go.

"It snowed a lot, baby—but I'll try in the morning."

Baron sat by the fire and put on his shiny black boots.

"Okay, Mommy. What time, Mommy?"

"I'll come get you after breakfast. Then we'll go to the Mall and shop, and eat lunch at McDonald's. You can have your favorite—Chicken Nuggets! How does that sound, baby?"

Bethany jumped up and down with excitement. "Can I see Santa again, Mommy?"

"I don't see why not. Let me talk to Mrs. Thomas, baby. I love you. Be a good girl, and I'll see you in the morning!"

"I love you, Mommy—bye!"

Baron whispered from across the room, "I have to go."

It had to be because of the story she'd told him about the sexual harassment. Her heart broke and her eyes filled with unshed tears. She quickly answered as he turned away, "Wait! Your phone—I'm using your cellular!"

Fate had drawn them together.

Now he was leaving. Was it for good?

He glanced back at the woman he'd fallen in love with and didn't smile as he turned away. She didn't miss how the light had gone out of his eyes. Something was wrong, terribly wrong!

"Keep it—in case of an emergency. The charger—an extra one I have, was in my glove-box. I wrote the number down for you and it's posted on your fridge. I have to go now, Merry Beth, duty calls. Your driveway has been plowed, and you have enough wood chopped to last you for a month. I made another soup and it's warming on the stove. I unburied the Toyota and jump-started it for you. Eat before you go to bed, okay? Take care of yourself. Stay warm and be well…and keep that right hand wrapped!"

And just like that, he turned away and was gone. Merry Beth just sat there and stared after him in shock; the sound of his footsteps walking away sure sounded like a final good-bye.

What in the world? What happened while I slept just now, are you ashamed of me because I didn't follow through with my harassment charges? Oh, Baron, please come back. Come back—don't leave if you're in pain. Stay, and talk to me, please. Let me explain, let me try to make you understand, don't walk away. Are you coming back? I've fallen in love with you. Please, I can't deal with your good-bye!

"Merry Beth, are you still there?" Debbie asked for the third time, anxious because of the silence over the line.

No answer. Debbie asked again, "Merry Beth! Are you there? What's wrong?"

"I'm here," Merry Beth whispered, as she wiped away her tears with Baron's handkerchief he'd left on her coffee-table.

"Are you all right?" Debbie knew by the sound of her voice, she wasn't. "Something's wrong—what is it?"

"I'm fine," Merry Beth lied, swallowing the sobs in her throat. This was hard. Loving someone shouldn't be this hard!

"You don't sound fine. What's wrong?" *He's hurt you, hasn't he? He's hurt you and I'm going to ring his neck!*

"I just woke up, Debbie—from a deep, sound sleep."

"Oh…" *What else? What's really wrong?*

She wiped away her tears. "How's my baby been? I'm sorry I haven't been able to get out, to come over and get her."

"She's fine, love. Are you alone?"

"Yes. Baron just left."

"You're—*sure* you're all right. The fever's gone down?"

"Yes, it's gone. Baron has taken wonderful care of me. I have enough wood chopped for a month and plenty to eat and it's nice and warm in here. How's it going at your house? If you lost it, did you get your electricity back yet? Are you calling me on your cell or your home phone?" The sound of Baron's truck leaving made Merry Beth flinch and she leaned back and closed her eyes once more.

"Jason went out with his friends from church—sledding I imagine. Kristi just left with Elyse—ice skating and eating out at Burger King. Lisa and Bethany are once more upstairs in Lisa's room playing everything from Barbie's to Up-Words to Uno and doing puzzles. Todd was here to help Jason shovel us out, but is gone helping unbury the church from the snow. I'm now cooking a decent meal for the first time in days it seems like—the power just came on about an hour ago…" Debbie informed with a smile. "You still buried, you need help getting out?"

"It seems I've slept most of the early evening away. Baron told me just now that he had my driveway plowed out. I'll be by first thing in the morning to pick up my baby, if it's okay that she stays one more night?" Merry Beth wiped her tears away, the look in Baron's eyes before he left she knew she'd never forget. She shivered. He was angry, very angry—but why? Something was wrong, but what? They'd come so far, hadn't they?

"Of course it is. Come for breakfast. I'll make those blueberry muffins that you love so much," Debbie suggested. "Kristi has plans to make her famous homemade apple pancakes, and Lisa and Bethany want to help cook the bacon and sausages and help set the table. I'll squeeze homemade orange juice…your favorite."

That sounded wonderful! "Okay, what time?"

"Around seven-thirty, is that okay? Jason has a doctor's appointment at eight-fifteen. Bring some of that hazelnut coffee that you have in your freezer—it's delicious!"

"I'll be there, and thanks for everything, Debbie. You're an angel! See you in the morning. Love you, bye."

"Love you, too…bye."

As she closed the cell phone she shivered against the sudden coldness and emptiness and quiet that zeroed in on her. She leaned her head back against her pillow and covered herself with the warm quilt. She wasn't a woman who did *alone* very well. It was much too quiet. What had happened while she'd slept to make Baron leave so quickly, to make his eyes turn to such an angry gray?

"Oh, Baron—are you coming back? Have I lost you for good? Did I ever even have you to begin with? Why did you leave so quickly? What happened while I slept? What happened to make you so angry and distant? Please, come back…I need *you!* I've fallen in love with you!"

Too quiet—it was much too quiet with him gone.

* * * * *

Answers—he needed some answers, and he needed them *yesterday!* How was it possible? What was it that Mitch was playing at this time? How many buried secrets must he dig deep to unravel, before he could finally put his past to rest?

Baron pulled his light-blue BMW to a stop in front of Dunkin' Donuts on Main Street in downtown Winterville twenty minutes later, and tried to force back the thundering adrenaline that was quickly pumping through his veins.

Like a low-life coward, he'd left Merry Beth's apartment; he knew he was only running, running hard and fast. But the thought of any man touching her in *that* way, in *any* way; he silently prayed for forgiveness for his blinding anger. He wanted to strangle the bastard with his bare hands, he wanted to make him pay, and would if he found out who the low-life was!

He was tired and needed a hot shower, change of clothes and blessed oblivion. But to find that comfortable state of forgetfulness seemed an eternity away now, after the phone call he'd received from Mitch less than an hour before. Once more, his entire life had shifted under his feet, violently.

He quickly turned off his lights and turned the ignition off with shaking fingers. In seconds he worked his way through slush, snow and ice to the warm lobby where he ordered a large black coffee. He sat at the back booth and waited for Mitch.

While he waited, despite what Mitch's urgent phone call had revealed, his thoughts were on Merry Beth and the Munchkin. He didn't dare hope that this was his second chance for a family. He didn't dare hope that she would ever love him back in return. He didn't dare hope for anything until he cleared up his past.

He watched Mitch, as he pulled into the parking lot in his black Chevy 4X4 truck. His heart beat like a rapid drum in his chest as he watched him walk slowly towards his booth after ordering a coffee. He was still in uniform and looked tired with blood-shot eyes and darkened circles under his oak brown eyes. His face was rugged looking and masked with shadows.

"What's going on Mitch? You're talking in riddles again."

"The roads are icy and treacherous—sorry I'm late. We need to talk." Mitch removed his black leather gloves and rubbed his hands together as he shivered.

"Carolyn's gonnah have my sorry hide for being late for suppaah again." His Maine accent slipped from his tongue naturally, and he stared across the booth at Baron with a worried frown, after he sat and removed his uniformed jacket and old yet impressive brown Stetson.

Baron's black eyes had changed once more to a darker shade of wolf-gray. He stared at his friend and boss with shock and disbelief before asking, "What exactly did you mean when you said Becky and my son were murdered, Mitch? Talk to me—tell me what you meant… *now!*"

James 4:14 "Whereas ye know not what *shall be* on the morrow. For what *is* your life? It is even a vapour, that appeareth for a little time, and then vanisheth away."

Chapter Six

Luke 2:6-8 "And so it was, that, while they were there, the days were accomplished that she should be delivered. And she brought forth her firstborn son, and wrapped him in swaddling clothes, and laid him in a manger; because there was no room for them in the inn. And there were in the same country shepherds abiding in the field, keeping watch over their flock by night."

Miracle #5, compassion, December 17th, Thursday, 7:56 a.m.

"I DON'T LIKE it, Merry Beth. You have a sad, lost look in your eyes for the first time since Thomas Earl and your father died. What has that man done to you?" Debbie hurried quickly to finish clearing away the dirty breakfast dishes from her knotty-pine kitchen table with a worried frown across her brow. In seconds she'd cleared and wiped it vigorously down and replaced her red-and-green lacy Christmas mats.

"And he's a cop, love! That means danger, guns, calls in the middle of the night, long hours, shady and dark characters lurking about, mystery, jeopardy, risks, hazards, uncertainties, unending threats, critical care, unsafe cases; perilous criminals sneaking and prowling around and…" She took in a long breath then blew out of breath. "There goes your quiet, safe and *peaceful* life!"

Merry Beth glanced at her best friend and sighed heavily while rolling her eyes towards the ceiling. "Oh, for goodness sakes, you sound like a mystery, murder novelist or something! You watch too many movies. Come on, Debbie. Have a little bit of compassion here—don't you feel any kind of sympathy or condolence for him?"

Debbie's stubborn chin lifted. "I just don't want to see you hurt, that's all. Your eyes tell me you already are."

"As long as I've known you you've never been a woman who's harsh, indifferent or unconcerned for a friend in need. *He lost his wife and son in a terrible car crash three years ago on Christmas Eve!* They were hit and *killed* by a drunk driver, Debbie, just like my baby and I were hit last Thursday. Right out of the blue it happened. *Sergeant Baron Williams saved me and my baby from burning up in that crash, Debbie—he saved us!*"

Debbie finished her black coffee in one huge gulp, and dumped the dirty cup in the sudsy water in her kitchen sink.

She turned back to her friend. "This stranger—this man you call your new friend; I don't know him, love, and neither do you—not really. I'm just warning you to be careful, that's all. I'm not saying I'm not grateful for what he did; God knows I am. I just don't want you to be hurt by him. I'm trying to warn you to be careful, that's all. You're my best friend and I want you happy *and* safe!"

"I'll be careful." Even though Baron had hurt her a little by the way he'd quickly left last night without so much as a single kiss or kind look or word, she loved him, and her heart overflowed with worry and compassion for him.

When Debbie passed her a 'you aren't really listening look' she said, "Will you stop worrying and being such a fuss-pot. Honestly!" Merry Beth finished her own coffee and dumped her dirty cup in the sudsy water as well. "You want me to help with these dirty dishes? The muffins and juice were the best, Debbie. Thank you."

Debbie lightly pushed her away from the sink. "No! You've already damaged that right hand trying to wash dishes at your house. I'll do them later when I get home. I have at least a hundred things to do today. Oh, by the way—Azelia Ka'ke has the angel costumes almost done—remember; she and her mother, Lovina, and sister, Janet are sewing on all the buttons, sequins and feathers. You *are* still coming to the play and children's concert, aren't you?"

Debbie turned off the coffee maker and checked the stove to make sure it was off, as she yelled above her head to her son. "*Jason—move it or lose it! We have to leave—right now!*"

"I'll be there." Merry Beth smiled as Bethany and Lisa walked side by side into the kitchen giggling and whispering to each other. "Come on, you two little sweeties. Let's get our coats, earmuffs, mittens, scarves and boots on. It's time for the three of us to go Christmas shopping!"

Bethany glanced at her mother and asked, "Where we going first, Mommy?"

Marry Beth answered, "Why, Wal-Mart—where else?"

Debbie laughed. "Is there any other store for working mothers? I just love it when those smiley faces and price tags keep falling down at our feet, don't you?"

Merry Beth giggled. "Oh, yeah—what woman doesn't? Come on girls, let's get cracking!"

In under two minutes the kitchen cleared as everyone rushed out the back door at once. Their day had begun. What would it hold?

* * * * *

Earlier that same morning at Dunkin' Donuts, around 12:30 a.m., Baron asked his boss, "How could you keep all of this from me, Mitch? *How...?*"

Now was one of those times Baron felt he was falling swiftly and silently away, like he did when the E.R. doctor had told him Becky and his son were dead. He was slowly falling through thin air again, with no one or no net underneath him to catch his fall; he was alone, he was drifting, he was isolated, and he didn't hear the soft Christmas music playing *"The First Noel"* in the background, as his burning eyes and his broken heart ached from the razor-sharp pain Mitch's words had inflicted.

He only heard the rapid beating of his heart, loud and fierce in his ears. He sucked in all the cool air he could into his lungs when he couldn't catch his breath. He could barely whisper, "I had a right to know."

Baron sat in the Dunkin' Donut back booth, and stared at the vanilla folder he'd just spent the last three hours reading carefully, two times over. He felt like his heart was once more ripped wide open and left bleeding, cold, and exposed. He'd been betrayed, betrayed in the worst way, betrayed by a woman he thought he knew and loved, once. Any love he'd felt for her at one time was now crushed and broken away because of that betrayal.

It was truly over, and Merry Beth was wrong, there was no hope. Not in his past, not now, and probably not ever again. She was right about one thing though—the world was indeed a cold and uncaring, dangerous and dark place.

There wouldn't be any peace in his life again until he found his wife and son's murderer. Becky was gone. Not just from the accident, but, long before. This kind of hurt, he knew, wouldn't be going away for a very, very, *very* long time, if ever. He'd lost her long before her death, and didn't even know it until this very moment. She'd slept with another man and betrayed their marriage vows. How could she do that? This was wrong...very, *very* wrong.

This couldn't be fixed, not ever.

Baron's vision blurred. Dear God, no!

Mitch and Baron spent the better part of those hours sitting in the back booth, drinking endless cups of coffee and smoking cigarette after cigarette. Baron knew he'd never be able to let the past go and rest easy, not now, not after reading the file. And now that he knew the truth, there was only darkness. There were only shadows lingering close once more.

Any hope or love that he thought he could ever find with Merry Beth was over as well. Any hope he thought he could find in the wonderful Christmas season was gone. It was replaced with sadness and an overwhelming sense of loss and...anger.

The sign above Baron's head read 'No Smoking' but was ignored by both men. The clerk behind the counter just shook his head and had looked the other way hours ago.

"I've been working on this since the funeral." Mitch passed him a computer CD disc. "Take this—everything I have is on this disc. *Everything!* Take it and bury it in a safe place, Bear, just in case. And make sure you burn every paper in that file you just read, because believe me—in one moment, your life can change forever." Mitch's dark brown eyes burned into Baron's creamy gray, before passing him a small white piece of paper.

A muscle under Baron's right eye twitched. "Yeah, I know that firsthand. One minute I was happily married with a young son. I loved my work, I loved my life, I loved my *faithful* and *trusting* wife...the next—I lost it all and was left alone because of a drunk driver. I also lost a lot of my friends from work when those Towers crumbled...and now...*this.*"

"This is the name of the private investigator, an old friend of mine from my unit in Vietnam, he and four other...war time buddies of mine are responsible for all the snooping and digging on the General. They call themselves the *Redemption Force.* They are the one's responsible for finding out everything you just read in that file, Baron. They put their lives on the line, and their wives lives, their girlfriends and children's lives on the line, to dig out this important information for me...for you."

When Baron remained silent he continued, "Be *sure* that you go over every file, on paper and computer disc, that Becky left behind! There might be something somewhere..."

"We missed." Baron glanced at his watch. "It's late..."

Mitch's chocolate eyes scanned the Dunkin' Donut lobby and parking lot. There wasn't a car or person in sight. He glanced at his watch and winced. "Carolyn is gonnah skin my hide—it's after 12:30 in the morning! I need to get home. I have several friends watching over the house while I'm gone, and I need to relieve them. It's late; they'll want to be getting home to their own wives and families."

Mitch stood to leave. "I need to get back. Keep me posted. This is important; you need to stay focused, and strong."

Baron didn't miss the quick flash of fear across the old man's dark eyes, and reached out to stop him from leaving. "Just in case what? Are you being threatened in some way?"

Baron was a man who wasn't easily threatened and usually ignored caution, warnings, intimidation and fear—unless someone he loved was being hurt or threatened. He heard the shivers whisper softly but rapidly up and down his spine, and knew it would be a grave mistake to ignore them as they made him shiver with doubt and uncertainty.

Mitch said, "It comes with the package of being a cop."

Baron rubbed a hand over the stubble on his chin. "I, too, have a lot of *friends*, Mitch. I make one phone call and at least seven of my SEAL Team friends from the Navy will be on my doorstep before the sun comes up. Now, talk! What kind of threats?"

Mitch groaned and sat once more. "I've been getting little—signals to back off in the last few months…"

A muscle under Baron's left eye twitched. "What kind of *little* signals are you talking about? How bad…?"

A tall, dark stranger dressed in black from head to toe walked slowly in the lobby, and Mitch immediately reached for his holstered weapon. "Just last night, Carolyn and I found our neighbor's Shepherd dog, dead on our porch and…" He rubbed his right hand down his whiskered face.

"Easy…" Baron touched his right arm in a tight grip. "Take it easy, Mitch."

Mitch shook his head as if to clear away bad thoughts, and placed his loaded .45 back in its leather holster on his hip. "Sorry, I've been just a little jittery and on edge lately. All this stuff is driving me nuts! Every stranger I meet—I can't help but be suspicious and overly cautious. Do you blame me?"

"Look at his shoes, Mitch. And his coat is ragged, torn and worn. His fingernails are black from dirt. He's only an old homeless man looking for a cup of warm soup or coffee." Baron stood and walked to the serving counter and gave the clerk a five-dollar-bill. "Give the old man whatever he wants." He nodded to the homeless man before turning back to the back booth.

When Mitch remained silent Baron continued, "*Talk to me, Mitch! Tell me the truth—tell me what's going down!* What kind of threats?"

"Flat, sliced tires, water in my gas tank, Carolyn's car being vandalized with acid, our collie dog—Maxwell, found shot and left to die on the back porch three nights ago, our mail being ripped open and left in the mailbox as evidence that someone's been there snooping, broken white roses left on the front porch in the morning paper, 'silence or die' painted in red across my garage doors, mysterious hang up phone calls. You know—stuff like that, and I'm pretty sure my home has been bugged. We had a break-in three weeks ago and..." Mitch rolled his eyes when interrupted.

"This is ludicrous! Why didn't you tell me? Things like this don't happen in Maine." Baron winced. "I could have—I could have done something to help you, Mitch. You should have told me about all of this, months ago!"

As soon as the words passed his lips, Baron knew they weren't true. Things like this happened everywhere, worldwide. What kind of sick game were they playing at this time? Who wanted Mitch to remain silent and about what exactly, and why? Had Becky been involved in all this madness? Is this why she'd been murdered—to keep the truth from coming out? And what truth was that?

He carefully placed the shiny gold disc inside the clear case marked 'B & Jr.', and the tiny piece of paper in his uniform jacket pocket, knowing the letters stood for Becky and Baron Jr. He rubbed the stubble across his face and chin, and burning eyes with his right hand, before reaching for his black coffee once more. His hand was less than steady and he frowned. Becky had died to keep the truth silent about what, exactly?

"You and I have seen what war can do to a man, Bear. Me in Korea and Vietnam, you in Desert Storm, and in those holes they call Iraq, Bosnia, Cambodia—we both know what makes the world turn. It's called greed, for money and power. The war that police officers' rage to try and stop the illegal sale and distribution of drugs and weapons worldwide is out of control. There's no stopping any of it; you *know* that..."

Merry Beth's pretty eyes and stunning smile flashed in front of Baron's. "There are some who believe there's still hope."

Mitch shook his silver head no. "No, we wear our cute little uniforms and shiny badges, and carry our loaded lethal handguns to tell ourselves we're making a difference to finally make the world a better place. It's never going to happen, Bear. Never! It's all such a joke really. What did we do it all for? Freedom? Peace? Are any of us really free?" Chocolate eyes sought blackish gray and locked—like steel prison doors.

Baron found it extremely hard to smile through the darkness surrounding his soul. "I have a friend. Her name is Merry Beth—she tells me there is still hope out there. I was starting to believe it earlier—well, after what you've just told me I don't *see* it. I don't *feel* it. I don't *sense* it. It's just not out there, or in here…inside me anymore."

Baron pointed to his heart and ignored the tiny little voice inside whispering, *Trust in the Lord with all your heart and lean not until thine own understanding. In all thy ways, acknowledge Him, and He shall direct thy paths…*

He was no longer a man of faith. He was a man of action! He'd take care of his wife and son's murderer himself, or die trying. "I know that now, more than ever—especially after reading this file," Baron whispered with hurt blinding his vision.

"This is Christmas—a time for peace and hope. Don't let your heart grow cold and distant over this, Bear. Even though there are many wrongs and unstoppable evils in this world—your friend is right. There *is* still good *and* hope!

"But we cannot ever shut ourselves off from the evils and injustice and hatred and darkness in the world, and pretend it's not there and pretend that everything is going to be all right, and sit around and wait for someone else to clean up this mess, while we look the other way. It's been dropped in our laps and it's up to *us* to fix it! We are sworn to serve and protect the innocent—your son is…*was* included in that sacred oath." Mitch stood to re-fill his coffee.

When Mitch came back to the back booth he carried two steaming hot cups of soup. "I don't know about you, but I'm starving. Here, I bought us each a cup of creamy broccoli soup and some crackers."

Baron's empty stomach grumbled. "Thanks."

Mitch placed the napkins, hot soup, crackers, spoons and salt-and-pepper on the small table. "This won't be as good as Carolyn's, but it will erase that grumbling in our stomachs I've been hearing for the past few hours." He reached for his cell and punched number one. "I need to let Carolyn know I'm all right and will be home shortly."

"I can't remember the last time I got a good night's sleep." As Mitch talked quickly to his wife, Baron ate his hot soup and winced against his grumbling stomach. He glanced at his watch. Was Merry Beth now asleep under that warm quilt, on her lumpy old couch, in her homey inviting living room that was decorated to the rafters for Christmas—was she warm enough from the blazing fire he'd started before he'd left?

When Mitch finished his call to his wife, Baron said, "Merry Beth's friend, Debbie Thomas, made her a pot of homemade chicken noodle soup; now *that* was delicious—just like my mama used to make when I was a boy. What I wouldn't give right at this moment to see mama walk through that door."

"As you very well know, Carolyn is a wonderful cook. When are you coming over for dinner? It's been a long time, Bear. She asks about you every day, and told me if I didn't drag your sorry butt home with me one night soon for dinner, that I was grounded from watching football for the remainder of my life, and she means it."

Both men laughed lightly and finished their soup before Baron asked; once more getting back to the terrible truth.

"What are we going to do to stop them, Mitch? Tell me? What are we going to do? Who do we trust?"

Mitch was right—they didn't know whom to trust. This was a deadly game they played, and two people were already dead, if not more. Had he lost his wife and son because of what was on the disc that now lay in his jacket pocket next to his rapid beating heart?

"What can we do to stop them, my friend? You and I don't know who *they* are!" Mitch said with a pounding heart.

Baron pushed his empty soup bowl away. "I can't believe this—this is completely insane! To think what Becky must have gone through—all alone. I know now, I know why she was so cold and distant those last months before she died." He dropped his pounding head in his hands, thinking, *Oh, Becky—why didn't you just come to me? I could have done something to stop this. I was your husband. You should have trusted me to help you and keep you and our son safe!*

"I loved her too, remember? And now my family is also at risk. I've taken necessary measures to keep Carolyn safe. Do you understand what I'm saying to you?" Mitch's brown eyes warned Baron that anyone he was connected to was in danger.

Baron understood and shook his head in disbelief. Any ties he had to Merry Beth and her daughter had to be cut, now, to keep them safe. That dark truth didn't seem fair, somehow.

"How is this possible, Mitch? Becky was my wife. It was my duty to protect her and keep her safe, *and alive!*"

"Oh, Come All Ye Faithful" started to play softly in the back-ground and Baron flinched back in his seat from the pain crushing his broken heart. "Why didn't she

come to me? It's clear to me now that she didn't trust me or have faith in me. She let evil and immorality, wickedness, corruption and indecency into our home, into our bed! How could I have not seen it? Felt it? How could I have not known?"

"I'm so sorry, Bear. But, if we're going to expose them and this General— I need your help. Now you know why I needed to be sure your emotions are under wrap?"

Mitch pushed their empty bowls of soup further away, and reached for his coffee once more. "We'll also be exposing corruption in the local police force here in Winterville. They covered up the truth. You read the report. You know…"

Anger exploded inside Baron's heart. "The man who hit our car that night wasn't drunk. You're actually telling me he was as sober as a judge—that the accident wasn't an *accident* at all? That it was a *mob hit—was it a mob hit, Mitch, or a secret Military Militia hit?* Who put that bullet in his skull to keep him silent? The General…?"

"The man who rammed your car that night is now known to have been a member of a militant group that moves across our land, Bear. His real name was Jai Sung. He was Chinese. Markings on his body clearly stated Chinese Underground Mob. I'm telling you that this thing is huge, and almost impossible to trace, or stop. They're ex-military men and women who no longer believe our legal system works. They make themselves to become the law, Baron. They're warlike creatures, they're belligerent, hostile, pugnacious, aggressive, combative, and I'm afraid that your Becky got caught up right in the middle of it!"

Everything Mitch had just mentioned reminded Baron of his Navy SEAL days. He shivered, not wanting to believe any of it.

"You're telling me Becky found out incriminating evidence that an American Five-Star General was…*is* selling top-secret information about secret chemical weapons to foreign countries, mainly Iraq? That's high treason, Mitch! You know that.

"It's betrayal at the highest level; its sedition and disloyalty to our own government. You're telling me that this General is the one responsible for Becky and my son's deaths…*murders?* And there's information in this file stating clearly that Becky was ordered to sleep with him to get information? Tell me, my friend—*how could I have been so blind to the terrible truth?* How, Mitch? Don't you understand—I love…*loved* her!"

Baron felt sick to his stomach and empty inside, as tears burned the back of his eyes. His wife, the woman he thought he'd known better than himself, had had sex with another man to get secret information out of him for the government she was sworn to protect and to serve. It was unimaginable! "Explain this to me clearly, one more time, slowly…so I'll understand."

"Yes, I'm sorry, Bear, it's true." Mitch winced and jerked back in the booth away from the pain he clearly saw in Baron's dark yet creamy wolf-gray eyes. "I'm sorry I kept the truth from you for so long. But there are things happening now…things in motion; things that I can't stop…"

Baron's temper snapped in two. "*Who ordered my wife to sleep with this sick bastard? And who ordered the hit that killed my family? Who ordered the hit on the man who killed my family? I want answers, Mitch. And I want them now!*"

He leaned closer to whisper through clenched teeth, "It doesn't matter who he or she is, Mitch—they're going down." The muscles in his jaw twitched and his eyes spoke volumes of anger and hatred. Brown eyes locked on gray. "I swear to you on my son's grave—they're going down…by *my* hand, Mitch."

Mitch reached across the booth for his friend—the man who'd been like a son to him. He shook him roughly by his shoulders. "You need to calm down, Bear. We can't do anything about any of this until we both get a-hold-of our emotions! We both need sleep; we need help here, Bear. There's no way we can do this alone. There's too much at risk. This corruption goes right to the very top. This General is the President's first in command. Do you know what that means? It means death, for the both of us and anyone we love, if we're not careful…*very* careful."

Baron stared at his friend with gray eyes that now sought revenge and restitution. "I can't believe this is happening. Just when…" Merry Beth and Bethany! Dear Lord, had he in some way already put them in grave danger? Fear crept across his thundering heart and despite his training, panic set in. No, this wasn't happening!

Baron's eyes felt like they'd been scraped by heavy, thick sandpaper. His stomach grumbled for more food. His head split with a threatening migraine. His heart ached with a new pain. He needed sleep; he needed answers! He needed…hope! His hands shook every time he reached for his coffee. His heart hurt. It hurt to breathe, to think and to hear the truth. It hurt to let Merry Beth and her sweet daughter go. But he knew he must, to keep them safe.

"Just when what…?" Mitch asked, as he quickly gulped and emptied his coffee cup.

It was over. Baron knew the dark risks and bloody dangers. To keep Merry Beth and Bethany safe, he had to stay away, far away.

Just when I've fallen in love with a wonderful, warm, caring, gentle, laughing, smiling, tender, happy, loveable and tender woman—I have to let her go. Merry Beth! Oh, Merry Beth, this means it's too dangerous for me to be anywhere near you until I figure all this out. I can't come back. To keep you and the Munchkin safe—I can't come back!

"*Just when what*…talk to me…?" Mitch thundered loudly through clenched teeth, heart racing. "Talk to me!"

"Never mind, it's not important anymore." Baron pushed the over-flowing ashtray away in disgust. To go near Merry Beth or Bethany—to see them, touch them, be with them again could mean their deaths', just like Becky and his son.

"Everything I knew about Becky and our life together—was it all a lie, *all* of it?" Baron could barely whisper through his pain that slashed at him like a snake's venom. He jerked back in his seat and rubbed his pounding temples.

"Everything's important, Bear. Let me help you," Mitch begged. "We don't have much of a chance unless we stick together on this. There can be no more secrets between us!"

"You've just blown apart my entire life, my entire image of my wife, my entire world and my entire marriage in one word, Mitch. Betrayal! And you say you want to *help me!*" Baron laughed bitterly and reached for his cigarettes and lit another one up.

Mitch flinched in his seat. "Take it easy, Bear! Please, try to stay focused here. I know this is painful, and I'm sorry, but…"

It was evident on his face that Mitch was pretty shaken. "I haven't touched a smoke since my days in Iraq! And since Becky and B.J.'s deaths'—*murders*, just look at what I have become, Mitch—an angry, bitter *old* man! And all because of what—some mysterious, unknown, nameless, faceless, gutless, foreign country's pathetic little bastard's greed for money and weapons and power?"

"Becky was *forced* to do these bad things against your marriage vows, Bear. *Forced!* You must keep remembering that. She was pushed into a corner—it was do or die. She did and died anyway. *She* was betrayed, betrayed by the very government she was sworn to protect, serve and defend. Don't you see?"

"Oh, I *see* all right," Baron snickered in bitterness.

"It's like Vietnam…all lies—nothing but darkness, death, destruction and lies!" Mitch hissed through his own sense of anger and betrayal, past memories clouding his vision.

"What are you saying? Are you trying to tell me that Becky was what—*threatened*—they threatened to what? Kill me? Kill our son? Kill our friends? *What?* She slept with the General…how many times, Mitch? Once, twice, three times, a dozen—*how many*, and in whose bed—ours? How many times before she refused, backed down, got out and then what…?"

"Take it easy! *Please! This isn't helping matters any!*"

"They silenced my wife all right. *To keep her silent for all of eternity, they killed her!* This *is* what this report says between the lines, Mitch. Becky was killed to keep the truth from being exposed!" Baron buried his throbbing head in his hands and pushed back the tears so the anger could whisper through in a low, soft, sibilant voice.

When Mitch remained silent he lifted his head and asked, "What truth, Mitch—the truth about the General's drug cartels? The truth about the inside connections the General has to sell information about chemical weapons to other countries, the truth about how corrupt *our own government is?*"

"Yes, it's all true. I'm sorry, my friend," Mitch replied through his own pain and sudden sense of loss.

And life moved on, despite the terrible truth called betrayal. A hard, cold, terrible thought flashed through Baron's mind and he jumped up from the table so fast he spilled his coffee. *My son! What if, what if that sweet, innocent little baby wasn't my son? What if, what if he was the General's son? No, no, no, no, no! Please, don't let it be true. Please, don't let it be true! Dear God—don't let it be true!*

Baron paled and swayed on his feet. "Dear God…no…"

Brown eyes clashed with dark-gray. Mitch jerked in his seat and asked, "What is it? What's wrong?"

"I can't…I need to get out of here…I need…air!" Baron could barely catch his breath as he quickly turned away from the back booth table. Panic set in quick and deadly. There was no stopping it. He was drowning again. This wasn't happening. It couldn't be true. It had to all be a lie! Becky didn't cheat. His son was his blood. That precious baby boy was *his* son…he was!

Mitch jumped up before hot coffee spilled all across his lap. "*What the devil is wrong with you,* Bear…? You look as white as a ghost. What are you thinking? Tell me!"

Baron shook his head and turned to walk away. "I need some air. I need some sleep, Mitch. I can' think. I can't breathe. I can't do this anymore. I'll call you later. I won't be at work today, I'm sorry…" He picked up the vanilla file and walked quickly outside before he threw up all over the Dunkin' Donut lobby floor.

Mitch called his name, but Baron kept on walking and didn't look back. "Baron! *Baron, please—come back! Baron!*"

At that moment, as he walked away to his truck, Baron couldn't remember ever being in love with Becky. It was truly over. Merry Beth's sweet and warm and beautiful smile filled his senses, as he jumped into his truck and searched in his pants pocket for his keys, yet he ignored it. He couldn't love her! To love her, at this moment in time, could mean her getting hurt, possibly even killed.

There was no way he'd be responsible for hurting Merry Beth and the Munchkin—no way! He had to stay away—he had to figure it all out, he had to find a way to fix it. Dear God, his heart actually hurt inside his chest. He felt like he might be having a heart attack, it hurt so bad and so deep. Tears burned as he started his truck.

It started to snow again, lightly, as the sun rose and broke through the dark gray clouds, as he slowly drove in a misty fog and white daze towards his home, hours later.

But he didn't see the new promise or hope of another day, as he sat in his cold truck outside of Merry Beth's apartment house, watching the snow and wind rage against the old shutters, aged roof and chipped paint. He didn't see the bright sunshine sparkling like diamonds on the snow across the fields. He didn't see his guardian angel sitting close by, by his right side. He didn't feel comfort in the knowledge that he loved Merry Beth.

He only saw and felt the black darkness, deep pain and unending emptiness as he turned the key in the lock of the home that now meant nothing. Everything the house had once stood for was now null and void. It was as if someone had stamped *insufficient funds* across the check he'd written to make the down payment on his and Becky's dream house, their entire life together was a lie. There were no memories of happy times he'd shared in the house with Becky and his son now.

Everything was a lie, all lies!

Everywhere he turned inside the dark, cold house—soft whispers of those lies, deceit and betrayal met him square in the face. He wanted to be sick. He wanted to weep. He wanted to run. He wanted to burn the house to the ground, hoping to bury Becky's betrayal deep enough so he'd never have to face it again.

Before Baron fell into an oblivious state of sleep before six a.m., he called his SEAL Team friends and made the arrangements to meet at the Fort Kent Baptist Church on the 21st. He called the hospital where his son had been born and made the necessary arrangements for his wife and son's medical records to be sent by overnight express mail. He called his accountant and Winterville's Ford Dealership, and made the arrangements for a brand new truck, a 4x4 Ford Bronco, to be delivered to Merry Beth and Bethany. He told himself that it was time the woman he loved with all of his heart and soul—the woman he knew he could *trust*, to drive a safe, dependable vehicle. And despite Becky's betrayal, life moved on.

There were at least a dozen different things he wanted to do for Merry Beth and the Munchkin. After—after he got some sleep, after he straightened out this little murderous hellish mess Mitch had dropped in his lap, after he faced the man or woman who was responsible for Becky and his son's murders; then, and only then, would he breathe easy again.

He dreamed of a beautiful, white Christmas morning, filled with smiles, laughter and warm sunshine beating through the fluffy white snow. He dreamed of Bethany's happy shouts of glee and surprise while opening every gift that he'd placed secretly under the pine tree and in her stocking. He dreamed of slowly placing a diamond engagement ring on Merry Beth's left hand. He dreamed of a new life—one he wanted to share with Merry Beth and her precious little daughter. A new life built on shared commitment. A new life filled with the promise of a happy and safe future. A new life filled with everything he thought he'd once had with Becky—*trust*.

Where was the hope? Gone, as his happy dream turned dark and nightmarish...there was now blood and screams, bullets and fog, uncertainty and doubt, pain and tears. Becky stood on the edge of a rocky cliff, overlooking the raging ocean below. She wore a beautiful gown of white and had yellow flowers in her hair. She held their son tightly to her breast, and when he called out her name she turned and smiled at him. But, dear God...the cliff...the cliff was too slippery! She and his son were both covered in blood. He screamed their names as they fell to their death.

* * * * *

At the Wal-Mart McDonald's, inside the Northgate Mall, around 4:30 p.m., the miracles continued to blossom, unseen.

Merry Beth counted her money while Bethany and Lisa ate their Happy Meal's of Chicken Nuggets, fries and milk with more gusto than even she could muster. She felt exhausted.

Christmas shopping with two little ones under foot was fun but tiring. Her feet ached and she still needed to figure out what to buy for Baron. She winced when she realized she only had less than twenty dollars left. But it had been so much fun picking out all of the new Christmas lights for Baron's house.

Lisa and Bethany had picked out red-and-blue. She had picked out the white icicle lights, dreaming of how beautiful they'd look all across the front of Baron's house. She longed for the moment she saw him smile and heard him laugh again. She dreamed of the moment he'd kiss her; *really* kiss her for the first time.

She glanced out the front doors and scolded herself for taking so long in the many stores they'd hit since lunch. It was snowing again and Debbie probably wondered what in the world had happened to them. She smiled; remembering Baron's cellular tucked safely away in her purse. As she punched Debbie's home number she plopped three fries in her mouth and watched the girl's laugh and giggle and whisper back and forth about their special Christmas cards. Oh, the joy of such sweet innocence and fun and friendship.

"Hello…"

"Hi, Debbie, it's me."

"You *are* still alive! Is Lisa having fun with Bethany?" Debbie laughed lightly and smiled as she said, "They're quite the pair, aren't they? Since when do those two *not* have fun when they're together?"

"We're at the Wal-Mart McDonald's in Northgate Mall and everything's fine. The girls have had a ball today. My aching feet and sore ribs are a testament to that fact. How did Jason's doctor's appointment go this morning?" Merry Beth reached for her coffee and took a sip.

"He's fine, nothing to worry about…just a slight head cold. You're doing too much again. What am I going to do with you?"

"We're eating our early supper now. Give me some ideas on what to buy for Baron for Christmas."

"I've never met the man. I can't help you on this one. You're on your own."

"Gee, thanks a lot!"

"Buy him some Taz or Tweety-bird slippers."

Merry Beth's eyes sparkled. "Oh, now—hey, that's a good idea. I could get him those from Bethany."

Debbie rolled her eyes and grumbled, "You've fallen hard, my best friend."

"What are you talking about? I have not!"

"Have, too."

"Have not!"

"*Have, too!*"

Giving in, Merry Beth said, "Well, what's wrong with that? Baron is intelligent, warm, sensitive, kind, giving, strong, rugged and *very* handsome, and he's a State Police Officer, Debbie. Now I must ask you—what could go wrong with him around? He's also ex-Navy SEAL, *and* he's a lawyer!"

Debbie worried. "Oh, do tell. This guy sure has *some past!*"

Merry Beth rolled her eyes. "Oh, for goodness sakes, you sound more and more like my father as every day passes."

"Your father was a good man. You were the apple of his eye. You and Bethany were his life. He knew how easily you trust people, and it worried him to no end."

"That's not entirely true—mom was his life."

"Yes, but you were always his *little girl*—right up to the very day he died."

Merry Beth missed her father more and more, as each day passed. "I know Baron is a good man, Debbie. *I know! I feel it with every breath I take!* He's hurting right now, still finding his way past losing his wife and son. But, I care for him and am willing to wait. I know he's worth waiting for. I know it."

"You're gonnah get hurt," Debbie carefully warned with a worried frown. "Crushed, even…"

"No, I won't!" Merry Beth argued, rolling her eyes again.

"Yes, *you will!* Your heart is too kind and too trusting, Merry Beth." After a few seconds of silence she added, "But I love you all the same. It's part of your charm and beauty, my friend."

"Hey, watch it! Those are two of my best qualities." She felt better after hearing Debbie swallow a quick giggle.

"What time will you be dropping Lisa home?"

"She wants to spend the night with Bethany."

"Go figure!"

"Is that okay?"

"If you're *sure* you're up to it, if it's not too much on you with a broken arm and mending ribs. I'd bet every cent I own that your right hand isn't wrapped and in its sling?"

Merry Beth smiled, as she glanced at her bare right hand reaching for more fries. "I'm feeling better and better every day. Its fine, I promise." She wiggled her fingers and winced.

"And those aching feet and mending ribs…?"

"I'll soak in a hot bubble bath after they're asleep."

"Okay, then—can I speak to her for a minute?"

"Sure, hold on."

Bethany glanced at her mother and asked, "Mommy, can Lisa and I go ice-skating on White Birch Pond after we leave the Mall? I promise I won't fall. We need to practice our spins!"

Merry Beth smiled as she handed Lisa the cellular. "It's your mommy. She wants to talk to you." She glanced at her daughter. "Maybe tomorrow, baby. It'll be dark soon."

As Lisa spoke with her mother, Bethany asked with a huge ear-to-ear smile. "Can we stop by Mr. Bear'ronn Will'amms house, Mommy? I want to be sure he gets the spe'caall Cris'mass cookie orrna'mints we made'deded for him."

Merry Beth smiled. "I don't see why not, baby. We're supposed to help him decorate his house with all the lights we bought. We'll stop by and see when it'll be a good time. We can't do it tonight—like I said; it will be dark soon. But, maybe we can help do the tree *if* he isn't too busy, baby. It's his tree and his house—it's going to be up to him, okay?"

"*Away in a Manger*" played softly above their heads and Merry Beth smiled. "Oh, I love this song!"

Bethany jumped up and down with excitement. "That's way cool, Mommy! Can we pop'deded some popcorn and make a string like we did for our tree?"

"I guess so. I'm sure Mr. Williams would love it."

"Is he hungry, Mommy? 'Cause I can't eat all my fries. I'm full. I'll save them for him."

Lisa passed Merry Beth back the cellular. "Mommy said she'll call you later. And it's okay if Beth and I stay up late!"

Merry Beth just smiled, knowing better, as she closed the cellular. "Come on you two; get your coats, hats and mittens on. It's time to go. It's getting dark and it just started to snow again."

Her thoughts remained on Baron's black eyes as they headed for his home. Two emotions turned them to gray—anger and passion. Was this what he felt for her, passion? Did he want her as much as she wanted him? Was there a future for them? A new life, a new love—with Baron...?

She smiled as she led the girls to the old Toyota, thankful when it actually started this time. Maybe today would be the day Baron would kiss her, *really* kiss her.

Oh, yeah!
Her heart wanted this.
Her heart wanted Baron.
To have and hold…
…for always.

* * * * *

Baron heard the ringing of his doorbell, but chose to ignore it and covered his still throbbing head with the sheet and blankets and pillow. He silently screamed, *Go away! Whoever you are—just go away!* The constant, nagging ringing continued and he unburied his head enough to glance at his bedside clock radio.

5:12 p.m.—great, just great—the first time I get some sleep in days and someone wants to torture me—endlessly! He jumped up angrily from his crumpled bed and reached for his sweat pants and flannel shirt, just barely opening his eyes. He dressed as he walked slowly down the stairs towards his front door. The constant ringing of his bell made him wince.

"Yeah, yeah, yeah…*stop ringing the bell! I'm coming!*" Visions of the last time someone rang his doorbell this way popped suddenly into his foggy brain, and from somewhere called nothing short of another miracle—he smiled as he reached for the doorknob, knowing who was on the other side before he even opened the door.

Bethany smiled up at him with her huge, trusting and smiling emerald eyes and her yellow mittened finger pressed on his doorbell and shouted, "*Merry almost Cris'mass!*"

Lisa sneezed before she shouted, "*It's snowing again! Isn't it pretty?* This house is so big and so pretty! Can we come in? We want to see your tree and decorations and stuff."

Baron thought, *Lord, give me strength!*

His sleepy eyes switched to the tallest of the three. Her pretty smile knocked the breath from his lungs. He glanced down at his bare feet and swallowed his desire to kiss her right there and then to say, "My, my, my—who might this be on my front doorstep? Is it Snow White and two of the Dwarfs? Let me guess—*Happy* and *Sneezy*?"

Bethany giggled. "Lisa and I think you're sooooo funny!"

"We come with tidings of great joy and bearing gifts!" Merry Beth exclaimed brightly and happily, as she gave him a bag of goodies. "There are enough lights in there to light up your entire home like mine. *And,* when you left last night you forgot your special Christmas cookie ornaments Bethany and I made for you. I put them in the bag as well. We put them in a small basket so they wouldn't get crushed or broken."

As Bethany passed him a green-and-red wicker basket filled with decorated homemade ornaments for his tree, Merry Beth couldn't stop herself and kissed him lightly on his left cheek. It wasn't until she slowly pulled away and glanced into his eyes before she knew something was still wrong, terribly wrong. His eyes were still wolf-gray and filled with sadness and pain again. They were—*he* was cold, distant, faraway, reserved and aloof…dark.

She smiled anyway, making up her mind to help him no matter what. "That was to say thanks for being you."

Baron sucked in his breath, and her soft perfume went right in along with it. He fell in love all over again. How could he not—Merry Beth was the most stunning woman he'd ever met. *She* was the hope he needed to go on living. How could he have not seen it?

Bethany stared up at him with a happy, innocent smile and asked, "Aren't you gon'naaah invite us in, Mr. Bear'ronn Will'amms? It's cold out here!"

Baron's dark eyes switched to Lisa. "And who might you be, young lady?"

Lisa shyly glanced up and whispered, "Bethany's best friend, Lisa. How come you don't got any pretty lights on or pine wreath on your door, Mr. Williams?"

Merry Beth winced when she noticed Baron's state. His eyes were dark and bloodshot, and his hair stood straight up on the top of his head like he'd just crawled out of bed. His green-and-white flannel shirt was unbuttoned and wrinkled, and he had just stifled a huge yawn. And that chest! Have mercy; was she drooling for goodness sakes? Look at all that dark hair…

"Oh, my—I think we woke him up from sleep. Maybe we just better go…" She reached for Bethany's hand and turned to leave, but he quickly reached for her right arm and practically shoved the three of them inside at the same time. Merry Beth, Bethany and Lisa stumbled over each other as he reached for the door to slam it shut.

"No!" He lowered his tone. "I mean…come on in."

"My goodness," Merry Beth mumbled with a killer smile.

Bethany and Lisa giggled and stomped snow off their boots. Bethany wasn't shy and asked, "Why's it so dark in here?"

Merry Beth met his eyes and whispered, close, "I hope you find the way to let the light back into your life, Baron."

He looked out the foyer window, all around his yard nervously, for any suspicious looking strangers that might be lurking around. "Just get in here, would you? It's freezing out there! Merry Beth, what are you *doing* out driving that old piece of scrap metal in this ice, wind and snow? Didn't you get my Christmas gift yet? They were supposed to deliver it around two this afternoon."

She smiled from ear-to-ear and helped the girls with their coats. "What gift? I haven't been home since early this morning. As you can see by the bag you're holding with that tight, death grip—I've been shopping, *all day!*"

He winced. "All day...?" He looked down into the bag he held and repeated, "*All day?*"

He watched her shake her head with another brilliant earth-shattering smile. "Merry Beth, that's frightening." He loved the dancing light in her pretty eyes, so much for staying away—dangerous. That's what this was, stupid and dangerous!

"What surprise?" she asked again as she tried hard not to laugh. "Baron—is it true? Did we wake you from your sleep?"

He met her eyes, leaned real close and whispered, "More than you'll ever know, my pretty flour snowbird."

"Hurry up, Mr. Bear'ronn Will'amms! We just *have to* deck'oorate your tree!" Bethany said, as she hugged him tightly around his knees. She passed him a little white bag and said, "Here, these are some fries for you—I couldn't eat 'em all."

He glanced down, took the little bag and said, "Guess you missed me, eh?"

"Why did you wait so long to put up your tree?" Lisa asked curiously. Both girls took off their coat, scarf, hat, mittens and boots and turned to rush off into the dark living room where the bare tree awaited to be decorated.

"What surprise, Baron? Come on, spill the beans; tell me! Tell me, tell me, tell me! I *love* surprises!" Merry Beth asked as he tickled both girls and laughed as they rushed off down his long darkened hallway. He reached over and turned on the lights. The brightness made him wince and he shielded his eyes with his right hand.

"I can't tell. It'll ruin the surprise. Come on in. It looks like you have enough lights to light up my tree like the one in Time Square in Manhattan." Baron helped her with her coat and asked her, "Where's your gloves, Merry Beth? Your hands are freezing! Come into the kitchen—are you hungry? Have you three eaten dinner yet?" As he turned towards where she assumed was the kitchen, he called over his shoulder, "Why isn't your wrist in that bandage and sling?"

"I misplaced them and my gloves again, besides—*cold hands, warm heart?*" She smiled and followed him to the kitchen. "We just ate at McDonald's. If this is a bad time to do your tree we could come back and help decorate another day. Baron, what's wrong? Are you all right? We did wake you from sleep, didn't we?" She searched his dark eyes and frowned at the dark smudges under his beautiful eyes.

"You look...you look tired and sad. Why are you sad, Baron? Is there anything I can do to help?" Her heart filled-to-the-brim with love and compassion for the man she knew God had brought into her life. So much so, that she wanted to weep. She reached out and touched his left sleeve. "Please...tell me..."

He winced, his jaw twitched as he thought, *Just love me...*

Both girls came running into the kitchen with shouts of excitement. "Mommy, look at this pree'tieee house! Isn't it way cool?" Bethany exclaimed with huge, excited eyes.

"You should see the *huge, tall* tree, Mrs. Waters!" Lisa's soft blue eyes sparkled with fun and laughter. "It goes way to the top!" Bethany and Lisa giggled close together and took off running towards the living room once more.

"Bethany! Lisa! You two know better than to run in the house!" Merry Beth scolded after them.

"It's really okay, Merry Beth. Sorry I'm such a mess. But I was catching up on some shut-eye. Sit and I'll put on a pot of coffee." He turned away and reached for his filters and coffee after washing his hands in the kitchen sink. He glanced at the kitchen clock. "Looks like I slept the entire day away. I hope I have milk. I need to make a grocery-store stop soon. I fear my cupboards and fridge are pretty bare again."

Something was wrong.

She could feel it, sense it...but what?

She stepped closer to him and touched him lightly on his arm, stilling his every movement. "What's wrong? Talk to me—I'm your friend and I care about you...very much."

Everything! Go away, Merry Beth. You shouldn't be here. It's too dangerous! He jerked away from her caring touch, and regretted it instantly from the hurt look in her pretty eyes.

"You don't have to pity me with concern and compassion, my pretty flour snowbird. I'll be all right."

"Know that whatever is wrong—I'm here for you. We're friends...for life, okay? My daughter and I owe you our very lives. We'd both be dead right now, if not for your bravery." She smiled and reached out to give him a bear hug around his waist. As she drew closer Baron thought he'd surely pass out from that smell of soft roses again. She fit into his arms like melted silk. Was this a dream? If it was, he prayed he'd never awaken. Were they a perfect match, a perfect pair? He knew, somehow, deep in his soul they were.

"Believe me, I'm not brave," he huskily confessed.

"It's not pity, you silly man. It's called compassion—you know, warmth and caring and friendship." She lifted her head from his broad chest and met his eyes to add, "Whatever it is—won't you let me help you through it? That's what friends are for. Your very own words, remember?"

He returned her embrace and whispered into her fiery curls, closing his eyes, "I need a miracle."

She lifted her eyes to his. "Your eyes—when you're sad or angry or passionate about something, they turn from black to creamy gray. Did you know that?"

He wanted to kiss her so bad at that moment he thought he'd die if he didn't. He pulled her closer instead. Was that even possible? Lord, help him. She was stuck to him like glue and leaning in, and he liked it, wanted it, needed it; needed *her!*

"You're my miracle, Merry Beth. Thank you for coming into my life," he whispered, as he buried his hands in her curls, "and waking me from my deep and lonely, very cold sleep."

She wrapped both arms tighter around his waist. It was very hard with the cast, but she did it. She snuggled closer and breathed in his spicy male scent and hard-steel strength. She closed her eyes and dreamed of the day he'd truly be hers.

"What's this?" he asked huskily, barely recognizing his own voice. Did she realize how much her softness and pretty scent was driving him over the deep edge into the raging river?

"Don't you know?" she asked quietly, leaning closer. *If you push me away, you'll be taking away a brand new dream...*

He only knew two things at that moment. One, she was in his arms. And two, he loved her and didn't want to let her go.

"Life is too short to live in the past, Baron."

He smiled, letting go...almost. "Yes, I believe you're right."

He lifted his hands and buried them in the thick madness of her fiery curls. This was pure heaven and hell at the same time. If he didn't kiss her soon, he'd surely explode! At the moment all he asked for was one more day with this woman and her delightful daughter. He wanted to say thousands of 'I love you and I need you, please don't let me go', but he couldn't. Not yet. Not until he was one hundred percent sure. Not until he buried his past once and for all.

He dropped his head and lightly kissed her forehead. He grinned, was that disappointment in her unique eyes? "You're a treasure in my lonely life, Merry Beth. You're a special and sweet and tempting treasure." *One I can't keep...not now...*

She smiled. "Well now, that sounds like a really good start to me. Where's that coffee? It's colder than winter itself out there. You have any half-and-half cream?"

He chuckled. "Doubtful."

She flashed that pretty grin again. "There's no doubt in this family, only faith!"

As he searched for clean cups and spoons, sugar bowl and what milk or cream he might have in the fridge, she started to sing "*I'm Dreaming of a White Christmas.*" He sucked in his breath and mumbled to himself, "God help us all."

"What was that?" and she only smiled when he didn't answer.

* * * * *

As the girls played Pac-Man on his computer in his home library/office thirty minutes later, against all odds, Baron opened his heart and told Merry Beth the truth about Becky and his son.

"...so you see, it's much too dangerous for you and the Munchkin to come here again. As much as I want you both in my life, it's just not safe. There are some...things that I need to take care of, Merry Beth. Dangerous and possibly even deadly things over the next few days or weeks, and until I do—you can't come back here. You won't see me again until this is over."

Sadness clouded her pretty eyes. "Oh, Baron...I don't know if my heart can take that—anything but that!"

He swallowed against the sharp pain slashing across his chest as he turned away to hide his eyes from her, knowing she saw way too much. "I don't want you or Bethany hurt because of me or something my late-wife was involved in." He turned back and glanced at the now fading bruises and cuts on her face from the accident. "I don't want you hurt—*ever* again. Becky's betrayal has brought more pain in my heart than I ever thought possible to feel."

"But, I care for you Baron. Let me help you!" Her dark emerald eyes begged and pleaded for him to let her in; she could actually feel him distancing himself from her and closing that door to his heart, and that hurt. They'd come so far, hadn't they? He smiled again, he laughed again; he'd opened his door twice, literally, and invited them in.

Baron shook his head no stubbornly. "No! You have to go back to your life, back to the way it was *before* you met me. Go home, and stay there, Merry Beth. I mean it!"

"What you must be going through—your wife, your precious little son— please let me help you!" She reached for him and turned him around to face her, and lifted her right hand to his left cheek and smiled through her tears.

He jerked back from her kind touch. "Don't…"

"Why must you face this alone? I'm your friend, Baron—friends don't walk out on each other or turn their backs when the other is in trouble. Let me help you!" She stepped even closer and their lips were close, real close; kissable close. She wanted him to take the initiative and kiss her, but he withdrew.

"*No!*" He didn't miss how she flinched back from his harsh, commanding voice and reached for her immediately when she paled and stepped back from him a little. He took another chance of his lifetime, deeper than the one he'd taken when he'd pulled her from that twisted wreckage, and pulled her carefully into his arms nice and close. He thought his chest would explode from having her so warm and close in his arms. Surely, their hearts beat as one at that moment? If he let her go, he'd know the truest meaning to the word lonely.

He hated it that he had the power to make this beautiful and vibrant woman cry. "I'm sorry, Merry Beth, but I care too much for you and the Munchkin to *ever* put you at risk. You have to promise me that you're going to be careful…and stay away from me!"

She lifted her head and met his unique eyes. "I'll be careful, but…please don't shut me out, Baron. You *need* me!"

The muscle under his right eye twitched. He lightly shook her to make her understand. "I don't *need* you or that precious little girl of yours dead!" She winced, as if in pain, and he let her go.

"*Promise me you'll be extra careful and aware of everything and everyone around you at all times!* If I'm being watched, then they know you're connected to me already. I can't let you get hurt by this. I can't!" he carefully warned with a voice that didn't sound like his own.

His wolf-gray eyes looked like thunder clouds on a wet and rainy fall day. He wanted to bury himself inside her joy and happiness and hope. *I could hold you in my arms for a thousand years, Merry Beth. Don't do it—don't let me go!*

Merry Beth swallowed against the tears threatening in her throat and behind her eyes. It was hard because she loved him. She didn't understand it, but she loved him and loved him deeply. She wanted to help him.

"I promise," she softly whispered.

He sighed with relief and leaned his forehead against hers.

"Will you be coming back? Are you going to make it to Bethany's Christmas play and concert on Christmas Eve? She's going to be heartbroken if you're not there and…"

She saw it in his eyes when he lifted his head. She was losing him. *Oh, Baron, I'm losing you. I can feel it. I'm losing you and we never even really had a chance to make this work.* "…you'll be at her birthday party as well—right?"

He shook his head no. "I can't promise you that."

Her heart broke in two again. "Why not…?"

The muscles in his jaw twitched and she jerked back and winced from her painful but mending ribs. "Because I don't know who the enemy is. I have no idea from which direction they're coming, Merry Beth. I can't protect you or your daughter!"

Her eyes snapped to his and he felt lost in their glossy silk. "I think the enemy is within *you*, Baron."

He held his temper back. "What are you saying? You think I'm putting distance between us on purpose?"

She stepped from the warmth and safety of his arms and turned to leave the kitchen. "Revenge doesn't solve anything, Baron. This anger, this hatred; this *desire* you feel for retribution for your wife and son's murders—*this* is your enemy, and it will surely destroy you if you don't let it go. What you need—what you're looking for—the *only* way to find it is inside God's love, mercy and forgiveness."

Matthew 9:35-36 "And Jesus went about all the cities and villages, teaching in their synagogues, and preaching the gospel of the kingdom, and healing every sickness and every disease among the people. But when he saw the multitudes, he was moved with compassion on them, because they fainted, and were scattered abroad, as sheep having no shepherd."

Chapter Seven

Luke 2:9-10 "And, lo, the angel of the Lord came upon them, and the glory of the Lord shone round about them: and they were sore afraid. And the angel said unto them, Fear not: for, behold, I bring you good tidings of great joy, which shall be to all people."

Miracle #6, trust, December 18th, Friday, 7:23 a.m.

WHY CAN'T EVERY day be just like Christmas? she silently wondered. What a wonderful world this would be if every day were like Christmas. Baron was right. The world didn't work that way.

Merry Beth stared out her kitchen window at the fluffy white snowflakes falling down, and closed her eyes while she listened to Elvis sing from her windowsill radio, "*It Won't Seem Like Christmas Without You.*" She'd spent most of the restless, sleepless night praying for Baron and his sad creamy eyes and broken heart. If she received the one thing she now wished for—he'd come back. He'd come back safe, unharmed and to stay—completely healed and free.

Suddenly, lost was how she felt without him, and they hadn't even shared one magical unforgettable kiss.

When she was with him, that feeling ended, and was replaced with joy and happiness. She remembered a time when she felt like this about her late-husband. She knew she'd fallen hard and fast then. And now, those feelings were even stronger. She was deeply and desperately in love with Baron Michael Williams. For her, there'd be no turning back. She needed him—with everything they could be together, some sweet day to come, she needed him. Was he safe, wherever he was at this very moment?

A week to go and there's still so much to do. Oh, Baron, wherever you are, know that I'm praying for you, know that I'm waiting for you to come back, know that I love you! Would it have made a difference in his life if you'd told him the truth? How hard can it be to say, 'I love you'? She jumped from her thoughts and reached for the ringing wall phone.

"Hello…"

"Good morning, love. How's it going over there?"

Silence again. Debbie repeated, "Merry Beth, everything okay over there?"

Oh, the sweet magic of a lifetime and lasting friendship. Why was it that Debbie always knew when she needed to hear her voice? Why was it that Debbie loved her unconditionally—despite her foolish mistakes, despite the truth that she'd been right about Baron hurting her? *Oh, Debbie, I've fallen hard in love with a dark, possibly dangerous, mysterious, but wonderful, strong and handsome man!*

"Good, the girls are up in Bethany's room working diligently to finish their special cards. What's up with that, anyway? Where did they get the idea for these cards?" Merry Beth smiled as she placed her phone under her chin, and reached for her whistling silver teakettle. Her right hand felt better and better as each day passed.

Debbie smiled and answered, "From their teacher at Day Care Tots. They're supposed to make a special Christmas card for the one that they love the most, and tell them why they love them inside it. They have to be made from scratch— you know, with stuff like construction paper, macaroni, glitter, sequins, feathers…"

Merry Beth chuckled, despite missing Baron. "You should see it up there! There's colored construction paper all around, glue, scissors, glitter, magazines all cut up, ribbons, lace, sequins, feathers, macaroni, Indian beads—you name a craft item—they have it scattered all around Bethany's bedroom floor. I opened the door enough to snap a few pictures for us."

"What did you end up buying your new friend for Christmas? Did you get him the yellow Tweety-bird slippers?" Debbie asked with curiosity across the wire.

Merry Beth turned towards the back door window. "Nothing yet, but wait until you see what he bought for my baby and I! You're going to freak out. Try to guess what it is. You'll never guess—not in a million, trillion years!"

"When am I going to get to meet him, anyway? You might as well tell me…what did you get? You know I'll probably never guess. And how come you get to open your gifts early? That's not fair!" Debbie lightly scolded with a teasing laugh.

"Soon, I hope. And, this gift is kind of hard to wrap. Just wait until you see the beautiful, brand-new, shiny, *gorgeous* black Ford Bronco 4X4 truck sitting in my back driveway. It only had fourteen miles on it when they delivered it!

Fourteen! This is the one and only time I'm not complaining about the color black. It's a new truck, Debbie. *Can you believe it? A brand new truck!* And it's all paid for! Should I keep it or should I send it back?" Merry Beth glanced once more at the falling snow out her kitchen window and smiled. It was beautiful—the way the sunshine made it sparkle like crushed jewels across the fields.

"A new truck…? Are you delusional?"

"How much snow are we supposed to get today?"

"Stop trying to change the subject. Are you *crazy*—a *brand new truck?* Keep it, girlfriend. Wow! This guy must like you, Merry Beth. I mean, *really* like you. He must have the bucks. And what do you mean when you say soon, I hope?"

"Just—I hope." *He's lost in a place I'll never understand or be able to reach. He's gone, Debbie. Just gone…*

"Hope for what?" Debbie asked with concern.

"I've invited him to come to church on Christmas Eve, and he's not sure he can make it." *But I'm praying. Oh, how I'm praying. Another miracle, we need another miracle!*

"What does he look like? Tell me everything. Don't leave anything out. It sounds like you've finally got yourself a winner here. I might be inclined to change my mind about cops!"

Merry Beth closed her eyes and could clearly see his features behind her eyelids. "Midnight black eyes that turn gray on every turn, he's tall with broad shoulders, he has thick rich-brown hair that's turning silver around his sideburns, he has this jagged scar on his left temple which I've yet to ask about…" *He kissed my hand, my nose, my forehead, and I think I've lost my chance to catch him under my mistletoe any time soon for that first earth-shattering, lip-lock unforgettable kiss!* "…he's everything wonderful, Debbie! He's very handsome, steel-strength-strong, extremely vibrant, trustworthy, sexy, charming…funny…"

"The scar is probably from when he was in the Navy *or* from being a cop, or maybe he was clobbered on the left temple by a bank robber or drug cartel guy, or something. I know—he stopped a serial killer from hurting his next victim. Or better yet—he stopped a little old lady from being mugged down on Main Street in front of Billy's *Four for a Buck Market!* Life's worth taking chances, it's true, but are you *sure* this man knows how to give the sunshine and sky more than a passing glace?" Debbie asked, all in one breath.

Merry Beth chuckled at her friend's weird humor, and rolled her eyes. "You've watched too many crime dramas and read one too many love stories, and watched way too many *Starsky-and-Hutch* reruns, and listened to one too many country love songs."

Merry Beth leaned her forehead against the wall and closed her eyes, thinking, *He held me in his arms and I felt safe and secure and loved, but he didn't say the words. He's gone, he says it's to keep me and Bethany safe, and I miss him, and I'm worried about him. I'm scared I'll never see him again. I feel like I'm losing him, and I never really had him to begin with!*

"I have this weird, funny feeling that something bad is about to happen. I mean, the truck is nice and all, but I have this terrible feeling that everything is about to fall apart," Debbie warned with a worried brow and husky voice.

Merry Beth shivered and rolled her eyes again. "Not again, with whom this time...? You always did have this sort of sixth sense, or something. I'm trusting in God to keep us safe, and we *are* going to have a snow-white and happy Christmas—just like the ones I used to know when daddy was alive, you just wait and see!"

"Who else...? *You! I am very worried!*" Debbie exclaimed.

"Daddy always told me, and I quote, 'Why worry when you can pray'. Relax, will you? Everything's going to be fine, you'll see." *With sleigh-bells in the snow and merry and bright days ahead, when Baron comes back—I'll never let him go again!*

Debbie sighed. "You always say that."

Merry Beth smiled. "It's going to be fine, trust me."

Debbie's eyes lifted toward her kitchen ceiling when her son yelled her name loud enough to wake the dead. "Oh, Merry Beth—I need to go. Jason is yelling down the stairs. Something about not being able to find his special Redskin tie, clean socks and his ironed light-blue dress shirt. Honestly—my kids...they'd be lost without me or Todd to lead the way. Let me know when you want us to pick Lisa up. Bye, love you!"

"Bye, love you more, see you later." Merry Beth laughed and smiled as she hung up her phone. As she made her hot tea she made a wish out loud.

"May your Christmas become as white as new fallen snow, Baron, and wherever you are; be safe. And whatever you do—please, please come back, because I need you and I love you!"

Suddenly, the quiet made her shiver and she reached for her warm sweater hanging on the hook by the back door, before she reached over to turn up the radio. Trisha Yearwood began to sing, "*Sweet Little Jesus Boy*" and her worry turned to another killer smile. God would bring him back. He'd never, not once in all these years, let her down yet. So, He wouldn't start now. She trusted Him for everything. She'd trust Him to keep this vibrant, strong and powerful yet so hurt man she knew she'd fallen in love with, safe.

* * * * *

One minute there was blessed peace, the next—a living nightmare! Twenty minutes after talking to Debbie on the phone her heart literally stopped in her chest, and the warm blood in her veins turned to frozen ice chips when she opened her front door. The man she feared the most, the same man whom she had a restraining order against, the man who'd tried to destroy her life before and after Bethany was born, stood like a threatening, powerful nightmare on her front porch with his finger glued to her doorbell. He stared at her with his usual hatred and contempt and evil hazel eyes. She smelled the strong-odor of liquor instantly and thorny panic set in quick, hard and fierce across her hammering heart.

In an instant she slammed the door shut in his face, and locked it with shaking fingers. She forcefully rammed the locks and chains in place with a frightened heart and painful right hand. She knew the extent of his anger and hatred and contempt. He'd never once set eyes on Bethany in all these years, and as God was her witness—he never would!

The phone! She needed to dial 9-1-1…now!

"*Go away, Earl! If you don't—you'll be forcing me to call the police!*" Merry Beth didn't waste another second and reached inside her black purse on the table by the front door for Baron's cellular. She dialed 9-1-1 with shaking fingers, thankful that she'd remembered to charge it; knowing Earl would probably cut her phone line, and cringed when her ex-father-in-law banged loudly on her front door.

"*Open this damnable door, Merry Beth. I want to see my grand-daughter, and I want to see her now. You've kept me from her long enough. Open this door or so help me, I'm going to bust it down with my bare hands! You're dead, you hear me—dead! Open…this…door!*"

"9-1-1, state your emergency," Winterville's police dispatcher, Marl Ellen Walter, calmly stated in her right ear.

Merry Beth recognized the voice. "Yes, Mary, hello…this is Merry Beth Waters at 252 West Chestnut Drive, I live in apartment one. Please, send someone quickly!"

Mary Ellen frowned and signaled with a raised hand to the sheriff that there was a serious problem. "What seems to be the problem, Merry Beth?"

"It's my ex-father-in-law, Earl Anthony Waters…he's out of control and banging on my front door. As usual, I smell liquor on him—I don't know if he's drunk, his words are all slurred and he's threatening me. As you all know, I have a restraining order against him. He's not allowed within five-hundred yards of me or my daughter or our apartment..." She ran out of breath and words at the same time, and sucked in all the air she could. Her right fingers throbbed, and trembled as she whisked her bangs out of her eyes.

She quickly raced to her living room and peeked out her white curtains and blind. She winced and flinched back from the terrible sight of her ex-father-in-law lifting a baseball bat to the side windows of her new Ford Bronco.

"Try to stay calm, Merry Beth—a unit is already on the way. Stay on the line, okay?" the Police Dispatcher informed, as her fingers raced like lightning over her computer keys.

Tears burned, like fire, in the corners of her eyes. "Oh, my goodness...he's going to smash the windows of my brand new truck with a baseball bat. You *have* to hurry!"

She cringed away from the terrible sight and dropped the blind and curtain and turned away. "Yep, he just broke the passenger side window with Bethany's baseball bat. He must be drunk—he's way out of control. He's like this when he drinks...please hurry!"

She tried to remember the last time she'd checked on the status of the restraining order and couldn't. Debbie had warned her just a few months back to check, but her ex-father-in-law hadn't spoken to her or bothered her, not once since she'd dropped the sexual harassment charges against him, after Bethany was born. Stupidly, she'd let checking the order slide, thinking he'd gone away for good. Bad idea!

"His name is Earl Anthony Waters—he's the president of the First National Bank on Main Street in downtown Winterville," she whispered through her fear and aloneness to add, "...you have to hurry. There are two children in this house! I have weapons here, Mary, and I am *not* afraid to use them to protect my daughter and her best friend. I'm hanging up now."

"No, Merry Beth, please...stay on the line," the dispatcher carefully warned once more. "A unit is on the way."

Merry Beth cringed inward in fear, as her ex-father-in-law screamed in his drunken state from outside near her front door, *"Come on, Merry Beth. Open this door and let me in. I want to see my granddaughter. If you don't let me in I'm gonnah break every window in this pretty new truck. And then I'm gonnah break every window in your apartment, and then every bone in your body once I finally get in there!"*

Every sense of trepidation imaginable zeroed in close in front of her eyes, like a camera lens; sadly she'd felt them time and time again in the past. She thought this kind of nightmare was over. Evidently it wasn't.

Mary Ellen winced. "I heard what he just said…"

"Please, tell the police to hurry. He's known to be a violent man, Mary. Check your records from over six years back. He's been violent and arrested several times for ignoring the restraining order. I have a gun for protection and I am not afraid to use it if I have to. I know how to shoot in self-defense. My father and late-husband taught me how! Please…*hurry!*"

"The sheriff will be there in ten minutes. Please remain calm and don't hang up," Mary Ellen said calmly.

Merry Beth quickly turned from the living room window and ran to the stairs. "I have two children in my home—my five year old daughter and my pastor's niece, Lisa Marie Thomas. *He's liable to set my apartment on fire. He's tried to do that in the past. Please, call the sheriff on his radio and tell him to hurry!*" Her heart thundered in her ears as she raced up the stairs two at a time. This wasn't happening!

Merry Beth closed the cellular to off and quickly open and on again, and dialed Debbie's home number as she reached the top of her stairs. There was no way either one of the girls would be hurt, she'd see to it. "Bethany! Lisa! Come here to me—*now!*"

"Hello, love," Debbie said. "Merry Beth, I know it's you. Todd installed a brand new caller ID and it's so neat to know who's calling before I pick up the phone. They're so neat and…"

"Debbie, call Todd and you guys get over here—right *now!* It's Earl. He's back!" She didn't waste another second and turned the cellular off by closing it and threw it on Bethany's bed.

"What's the matter, M…mommy?" Bethany asked with frightened eyes, as she glanced up from her and Lisa's creative but well organized mess.

Merry Beth fell to her knees on the thick, fluffy pink carpet, and reached for both girls for a bear hug, ignoring her screaming ribs. She didn't want to frighten them, but knew she already had by the tone of her voice.

"Nothing's wrong, baby. I thought you'd both like to play a *fun* game. I want you both to come with me—we're going to play hide-and-seek. Won't that be fun? I used to play this game when I was a little girl with my daddy and grandfather!"

Bethany fussed. "But, Mommy…we're really busy now!"

In seconds, she led both girls towards her bedroom closet and pushed them gently inside, forcing a smile so they wouldn't be scared. It was a huge walk-in closet and there was plenty of room for both girls to hide without being noticed.

Bethany frowned a little and asked, "Why we hiding in your closet, Mommy? We need to finish our special cards!"

Merry Beth's white wedding gown was hanging against the back wall in a plastic dry-cleaners see-through bag. She helped both girls step behind the long beautiful lacy gown with a smile. "Do you see mommy's pretty wedding dress, babies? I want you two to hide behind this! Later, mommy will let you both try it on. *And* I'll even let you play with my pretty veil. I'll take pictures. Now, stay behind this dress and be *real quiet!*"

She lowered her voice to a soft whisper. "*I think Mr. Williams is here and we don't want him to be able to find you. You both can surprise him when he gets close and yell 'surprise', okay?*"

Lisa's blue eyes lit up with innocent excitement, trusting her words. "Way cool, Mrs. Waters! This is fun!"

"Maybe he wants us to help him deco'radeded his house with our prett'tiee lights today, Mommy," Bethany whispered as both girls stepped quickly behind Merry Beth's lacy white gown.

"I'm sure he does. Now, stay back here, and remember—be *really* quiet!" Merry Beth lightly warned with a soft voice.

Lisa glanced way up at the beautiful gown and looked at Merry Beth in awe and wonder. "Wow, this dress sure is pretty! It sparkles…like real diamonds!"

Bethany touched the gown through the plastic. "It looks like *real* diamonds, Mommy!"

Lisa whispered softly, "My mom's wedding dress is just as pretty, Beth! Next time you come over, I'll show you."

Merry Beth smiled to reassure them that this would be a really fun game and hugged them close once more. "Now, girls, remember to stay hidden. Don't move a muscle, and stay quiet!"

"Can we play with your pretty white wedding shoes Mommy, and can Lisa wear those soft white gloves you keep in the spe'caaall box up there on the top shelf?" Bethany pointed to the top shelf with an innocent smile.

"The ones daddy gave'deded you for a wedding present? 'member…you said they was *really* special?"

Merry Beth kissed both girls on their cheeks before turning away. "You sure can! Now, you both stay in the back of this closet and hide, *I mean it, Bethany. You and Lisa stay here. Mommy's going to go make sure Mr. Williams can't find you!"*

She hugged them both quickly and her heart filled with regret. To see fear in those precious innocent eyes, even for just a moment, it wasn't going to happen. She heard both girls giggling and laughing lightly as she rushed away back down the stairs to the first floor.

She didn't waste another second to run to the kitchen, to the spot where she kept her daddy's old .38 Luger hidden. She ran to the silverware drawer where she kept the key hidden. The gun was hidden in the highest cupboard locked in a small metal box, above the stove, loaded and ready for the day, just like today.

She'd always feared this day would come—he'd been silent and stayed away too long. She'd feared, deep in her heart, that the peace and serenity she'd found for herself and Bethany would one day come to an end. Her heart thundered in her ears as she raced quickly towards the stove. It just had.

Just as she reached for the white stepstool that sat by the stove, her fingers froze in mid-air when she realized her back kitchen door stood wide open. How could she not have noticed? Her ex-father-in-law surprised her by grabbing her roughly by her right wrist in a terrifying, tight and painful grip. She knew there would be bruises there in no time; she bruised very easily. Her mending sprained wrist throbbed unmercifully now. The pain was unbearable. Anger and tears replaced her fear in seconds.

"It's payback time, Merry Beth. I've waited long enough!"

"*Hey*, let me go, you *bully!* Get out of my house! You're not welcome here, Earl. Can't you just leave me alone?"

His hot, liquored breath burned her healing left cheek as he yanked her closer. "*I busted through the back door, Merry Beth! Now, where's my granddaughter?*"

How could her husband have ever come from this man? They were as different as night and day, water and oil, rain and fire. As Merry Beth stared bravely into her ex-father-in-law's evil eyes, she silently prayed for strength and courage to say the right words and do the right things to keep Bethany and Lisa safe and unhurt. She prayed for forgiveness for any anger, hatred or resentment she still felt in her heart for this man. She prayed for Debbie and Todd to get here in time. She prayed that wherever Baron was—he'd somehow know, he'd somehow *feel* that she was in trouble and come and rescue her from the flames again, the flames that burned her skin from Earl's brutal hands and hot, liquored breath.

Tears blurred her vision. Dear God, had he just broken her sprained wrist? She felt dizzy and sick to her stomach and feared she'd pass out from the terrible pain his grip on her wrist inflicted. Where were Todd and Debbie?

* * * * *

Baron cringed when he saw the shattered and broken glass scattered like leaves in the wind all across the white snow on the side of the new Bronco, and also across the front seat. The warm sun made it sparkle like crushed diamonds. The chilly wind blew his hair in his eyes. The broken glass whispered up to him— calling out his name on the brittle northeastern wind, telling him that Merry Beth was in trouble. His heart thundered with fear. He immediately reached for his holstered 9mm Smith & Wesson as he raced quickly towards Merry Beth's apartment.

He felt them all, as he raced across the snow towards the front door—horror, terror, fright, trepidation, alarm, dismay, anxiety, dread, apprehension—fearing in his heart that danger had come calling to her door because of him.

If someone from his world had come here to hurt Merry Beth or her daughter it would be his fault and his fault alone. He'd never be able to forgive himself. He couldn't, *wouldn't* let that happen. Dear Lord, was it already too late?

He quickly tried the door and winced when he found it locked. In seconds he raced around to the back of the apartment, as police sirens wailed behind him. As he raced towards the back door his thoughts made him run faster. *I'm coming, my pretty flour snowbird. I'm coming. Oh, please dear God, let them be all right. Let them be all right!*

In all the years in the Navy and on the police force in Manhattan, he'd never felt such strong, terrifying and gripping fear than he did when he saw Merry Beth's back kitchen door busted open. Parts of the split wood hung loosely, dangling dangerously in mid-air from the busted doorframe. A booted footprint called out to his alert gray eyes, more evidence that the door had been kicked violently in. His eyes, a darker shade of gray now, were blinded to anything but finding the ones he loved safe and sound.

As he stepped into the kitchen he raised his loaded weapon higher. "Merry Beth, are you here? Are you all right?"

Sweat and icy fear dripped down his back, like a cold and melting ice-cube, and he shivered. When his eyes lifted from the busted wood on the floor, he knew he'd never been so angry in his entire life than he was at that second.

Standing in Merry Beth's kitchen was a tall man dressed in black jeans, black-

and-white flannel shirt, unzipped beige suede jacket and brown leather boots; he was a huge and bulging man despite his height, a man who had his massive hand brutally around Merry Beth's right wrist. His wolf-gray eyes quickly switched to the woman he'd fallen in love with. There were tears of pain in her pretty eyes, and ice-cold fear. In seconds Baron's loaded weapon pressed against the intruder's neck.

He'd come by the apartment to say a final good-bye, to pull her close and kiss her; *really* kiss her for the first time. Was it too late? Was God really giving him another chance at love? Had Becky ever loved him to begin with? Had God really put he and Merry Beth together—was her car accident really fate? He wasn't sure of very much at the moment, but knew he wanted to kill the man who held Merry Beth's mending wrist painfully in his brutal grasp.

His feet had moved across the kitchen in seconds. He'd gladly pull the trigger…

* * * * *

"Get out of my house right now, Earl. You know you're not supposed to be here. I've called and the sheriff is on his way!" Merry Beth tried to break her mending right-wrist free from his strong and bruising hold, but couldn't. He'd always been too strong and violent—there was nothing she could do now but pray and wait for the sheriff or Debbie and Todd to come.

"I'm back all right, and I want to see my granddaughter—right *now!*" Earl hissed close to her right ear.

In seconds, her drunken ex-father-in-law pulled hard on her right wrist and yanked her around and slammed her hard against the stove. Flashes of white-light pain sparked in front of her eyes as her healing ribs throbbed from his attack, as her lower back slammed hard against the hard surface.

She swallowed the fear back. It wasn't an option! "Earl—please, don't do this. You're hurting me!"

"*You're gonnah pay for all that you've done to ruin my good name and life in this town!*" He yanked her closer and laughed when her eyes filled with tears. He heard her cry out and liked it. "You think I'm gonnah just stand by and let you get away with it year after year? *You stole my life! And I'll be damned if I let you steal my only granddaughter!*"

She had to fight back. She wasn't a wimp. She raised her right leg and kicked Earl as hard as she could in his left knee. He cried out in pain and fell back a few feet. "*You're hurting me, Earl. Let me go. Get out of my home. You have no right to be here!*"

Merry Beth flinched back as far away from him as she could, yet he grabbed her bruised and throbbing right wrist again, and lifted his right arm to strike her across her face. "*It's been a long time, Merry Beth, a long, long time!*"

An arm came from out of nowhere to stop Earl from hitting her face, thank God, and in seconds her ex-father-in-law had a gun pressed hard on the main artery in his neck.

"*I believe that the lady asked you to get out of her house. Now, drop your hand from her wrist and let her go—now!*" Baron thundered just inches from Earl's flushed and angry but turning pale face. Earl instantly let go and Baron quickly slammed him hard against the refrigerator doors, blooding his nose.

The dainty, antique teacup and saucer that had belonged to Merry Beth's grandmother came crashing down from the top of the refrigerator to the hard vinyl kitchen floor with a loud crash.

Merry Beth cringed and felt so many different emotions in that moment. Relief to see the man she loved come to her rescue, pain—dark and fierce, as it slashed across her ribs and lower back and swollen right wrist, and loss as she bent down to gather the broken china with a trembling right hand.

Baron's gray eyes never left Earl's. "You're going down *by my hand—it doesn't matter who you are!*"

"Oh, look what you've done to my grandmother's antique china. Its b...broken!" Tears glistened across her dark lashes and she winced as she cut her right hand fingers. Dark red blood dripped down her fingers and bruised wrist. It dripped slowly onto her fluffy white slippers and clean white vinyl floor around her feet. The more she cried the more she couldn't see, but kept right on picking the broken pieces up anyway, ignoring the pain. This wasn't happening! How could this be? She wanted to give this china to Bethany one day.

Baron's darkened angry-sky-gray eyes glared close to the strange man who'd hurt Merry Beth. He held his loaded 9mm under his chin with enough force to knock the wind out of him. Bethany's grandfather hissed angrily, "You can go to Hell-fire!"

"*Who are you, and why have you intruded on Mrs. Waters' home this way? State your business here—now, or I'm going to take great pleasure in making...you...talk!*" Baron demanded, jaw twitching, eyes blaring.

Merry Beth sobbed, "Oh, my grandmother's china. It's broken. It can't be f...fixed. *It can't be fixed!*"

Baron quickly glanced at Merry Beth's broken china and bleeding fingers, and anger he'd only felt once before crashed forward in his heart again. He swallowed against the sudden hatred for the old man and closed any space between them and thundered, "*You have three seconds to start talking or I'm going to rip your throat out with my bare hand!*"

Dark memories flashed close from his Navy SEAL days, days he'd done just that to more than one man. Dear Lord, what kind of man had he become? "One…two…"

"*Drop your weapon, now!*" Sheriff David Clemens ordered, as he pointed his loaded .38 directly at Baron's back. "Drop your weapon, sir, and back away!"

Merry Beth lifted her eyes. "No, don't shoot him!"

Love doesn't ever ask why, not once, you just react to protect the ones you love, no matter what the cost, when they're being hurt or threatened. Merry Beth quickly rose to her feet and stepped in front of the sheriff's weapon. "Don't— he's a friend…he's also a State Police officer…"

Baron just chuckled lightly and said boldly, "Not on your life am I dropping this weapon. Merry Beth…get back!" He didn't even flinch or back away from Merry Beth's attacker, and pressed his loaded pistol harder in the old man's throat.

Sheriff Clemens asked, "What's happening here?"

"My name is Sergeant Baron Michael Williams. I'm a State Police officer, and this man has invaded and assaulted my lady—that's B&E and assault…" Baron met hazel eyes head on and held them firmly in a locked stare. He jabbed his weapon   harder   with   each   following   word. "…and…I…want…to…know…why!"

Earl Waters screeched through his own fear, "Get him off me. *He's crazy. Get him off me. He's going to kill me. I have my rights. He's threatening my life—get him off me!*"

Merry Beth realized she was cut and bleeding and cried out. "Make him go away. Please, just make him go away!"

She sobbed quietly, as Sheriff Clemens, an old family friend of her father's, carefully helped her up from the bloody floor.

Police officer, Deputy Hugh Masters backed his new boss and partner with rapid speed. He didn't lower his loaded .38 and demanded, "Lower your weapon, sir. This is your last warning."

Merry Beth turned on wobbly legs that trembled, closer to Baron's side, and he instantly, but gently, moved her out of harm way behind him. "Stand back, honey…"

"No! Don't shoot," she pointed to her drunken ex-father-in-law and added, "...this is my ex-father-in-law. His name is Earl Anthony Waters, and I have a restraining order against him. He broke into my house and threatened me and..." she stammered.

Sheriff Clemens asked, "Well, well—it seems old Earl Waters has risen from the dead. Where've you been, Earl? Long time no see. Looks like you've gone and got yourself in some trouble today."

Merry Beth cringed in shame, knowing the police officers remembered after all these years. "Just make him go away..."

David glanced at Earl. "I'm new in town but I've heard the rumors..." He regretted his outburst when Merry Beth paled and swayed on her feet. He reached out to steady her.

"It'll never be over. It'll always come back to haunt me. Just do what you have to, to make him go and stay away!"

Baron's angry-wolf-gray eyes never left Earl's hazel. He jammed his 9mm tighter under his chin. "I believe you need a lesson in manners. You the student, me the teacher!"

Deputy Masters lowered his weapon immediately but Baron never moved. "I remember now, how many years back?"

Merry Beth covered her face in shame as best she could with one hand and blood dripped slowly down her cheeks from her cut fingers. "Almost six years. Please, just make him go away. It's all I ask, sheriff. Lock him up and please check to see if my restraining order has expired. I should have checked but..."

Baron remembered her story about her sick, twisted boss whom she'd suffered humiliation and sexual harassment from and immediately pressed his weapon harder once more under the old man's throat, realizing for the first time this man was one in the same. He thundered through white anger just inches from his face, "*Enough of this silly little chit-chat, sheriff—I'm placing him under arrest for assault and breaking-and-entering...*"

Suddenly all thoughts of Christmas and snow angels were non-existent. Suddenly all thoughts of candy canes and pine trees disappeared, as shame zoomed in across Merry Beth's lashes.

She whispered, "He grabbed me and shoved me hard against my stove...my ribs—I think I'm going to be sick!" She gave in to her nauseous and rumbling stomach and doubled over in pain, and gave into the dizziness that swarmed all around her, trying hard not to vomit as she leaned over her kitchen sink.

As the deputy and sheriff both reached for her, she said, "Thank God you came, Baron—I was so s…scared." She shook from head to toe in relief and fell backwards, and reached for her kitchen table to steady herself.

"Merry Beth! You're falling…watch out!" the sheriff yelled. The sheriff and deputy both helped her to sit at her kitchen table.

Baron immediately reached behind his back for his handcuffs. "I'm placing you under arrest for assault." He searched Merry Beth's eyes and knew the answer before he even asked. "Merry Beth…?"

"He broke in the back door when I was upstairs hiding the girls in my closet. I must have forgotten to lock the door when I took out the trash and brought in some more wood for the stove earlier…" she answered, as the sheriff reached for a kitchen towel to wrap her burning and bleeding right-hand fingers.

The deputy kindly helped her wrap her bruised wrist and bleeding fingers. "You need medical attention."

"Help is on the way." In seconds the sheriff called for paramedics and an ambulance on his cell phone.

Baron cuffed Earl and started reading him his rights. "I'm placing you under arrest for assault and B&E…you have the right to remain silent…"

Pastor Todd came running through the back kitchen door like a man possessed. "Merry Beth, are you all right?"

Debbie raced quickly to her side. "The girls…?"

Debbie helped her to the kitchen sink to check her bleeding hand. "Oh, my, what in the world is happening here? Come on, let's rinse off your hand to see how bad it is."

Pastor Todd quickly informed Baron, the sheriff and the deputy, "This man is Mrs. Waters' ex-father-in-law. He knows she has a restraining order against him. He's not allowed within five-hundred yards of her or her daughter or this apartment. He knows that!" He noticed the cuffs and added, "Good—you're arresting him. Do something to make him stay away for good!"

Baron had enjoyed snapping his cuffs around Earl's wrists' behind his back. He grabbed Earl's arms and slammed his face in what remained of the back door. It didn't bother him in the least that his nose started to bleed again. "Yeah, well…it seems that he needs reminding!"

Sheriff Clemens instructed his deputy to place Earl in the back of his patrol car. "Finish your report and I'll meet you with the…intruder at the station in twenty."

Merry Beth's eyes filled with tears from the stinging cold water. "Debbie, the girls…they're hiding in my bedroom closet."

Debbie interrupted her brother-in-law and said, "Todd, Lisa and Bethany are upstairs hiding in Merry Beth's closet. Go check on them and make sure they're all right, would you?" She turned back to her best friend. "I'm so glad you called. Sorry it took so long…my truck wouldn't start again."

Debbie dried and wrapped a clean kitchen towel around Merry Beth's right hand. "These cuts aren't too deep…"

Baron stepped close at that moment and reached for her cut, bruised and very swollen right wrist. "Let me see…"

Pastor Todd and Sheriff Clemens raced quickly from the kitchen to check on the girls, and before anyone could attempt to stop her, Debbie raced across the kitchen in seconds, and pounced on Earl like a wild cat in heat, beating on his chest with her clenched fists', digging at his face with her long nails.

Merry Beth cried out, "Debbie—no. I'm all right!"

Baron immediately reached for Debbie to pull her back, as Deputy Masters tried to remove a swearing Earl from the house.

Debbie didn't adhere to her best friends words. "*I can't believe you have the nerve to come here. What's the matter with you? There are children in this house. You're as dark and evil as Satan himself—may God help you!*"

Baron, knowing she was Merry Beth's best friend, pried her angry, clenched fists' from the front of the old man's beige jacket carefully. "Easy, it's over now," he whispered softly and close. "Let him go. Deputy Masters is taking him away now."

Debbie didn't let go and thundered, "*What's the matter with you, Earl? Why can't you just leave them alone?*"

Earl nastily spat, "She stole my life. She has to pay, damn-it!"

"Let go, he's going to jail. *Come on, let go!*" Baron gently set Debbie aside before he turned back to help nurse Merry Beth's cuts and bruised wrist.

He looked at the deputy and said, "Take him away, I'll meet you and the sheriff at the local police station in a few minutes—as soon as I'm sure Mrs. Waters is all right."

In an instant Baron reached for a sobbing Merry Beth and lifted her up into his arms, close to his chest. "Are you all right, Merry Beth?" When she remained silent, except for weeping in his arms against his chest, he quickly walked from the kitchen to her living room couch.

"Merry Beth...? Are you all right?" He gently placed her on her lumpy old couch and covered her with the patched quilt that lay on the back. "Answer me, Merry Beth...please."

Debbie smiled and turned quickly away when she heard the ambulance siren pull up into the yard, and quickly raced up the stairs to check on the children. "I'll just leave you in his capable hands, Merry Beth. I'll check on Todd and the girls."

Merry Beth lifted her tear-filled eyes to Baron's in trust. She didn't waste another second to lift her right arm around his neck and hug him tight and close.

"Oh, Baron...I'm so glad you came when you did. That terrible man—I thought I'd seen the last of him—he's like an unwanted toothache or...s...something. He never learns. I always feared this day would come. Thank God you came back!"

"Your ribs...? Do you need to go to the hospital?"

She shook her head no. "I'll be all right..."

He carefully rubbed his fingers across her bruised wrist before he lightly kissed it. "Your wrist...? Is it broken?"

She shrugged her shoulders. "It hurts...pretty bad."

The muscles in his face twitched in his anger. "It's true—isn't it? *He's* the one who humiliated and hurt you all those years ago on your job? *Your father-in-law...?*"

Merry Beth cringed from the inside out. "Yes. Oh, what you must think of me!" She lost control and sobbed in his arms.

Baron waited until her tears and sobs subsided before whispering close, "My pretty flour snowbird, you have nothing to be ashamed of. Don't cry, honey—everything's going to be all right, you'll see. I promise you."

He pulled her closer to his chest once more and buried his hands in her fiery red curls. "I see you finally received one of your Christmas presents. I'll call and make the arrangements for those broken windows on the Bronco to be replaced before I leave town."

Her tear-filled eyes lifted sadly to his. He leaned down and kissed along the nape of her neck with feather-light kisses. His heart broke when she whispered, "You're leaving...?"

A muscle under his left eye twitched. "Yes..."

Fresh tears glistened across her lashes. "You're *leaving?* Why did you call me honey just now, if you're leaving?"

The anger was gone from his eyes, and they begged her silently to trust him, as two paramedics rushed inside Merry Beth's living room. "Because you are my honey…" Baron whispered close. "…and I must leave, today. Just as soon as I help to get you to a hospital and checked over, to make sure that you're going to be all right. He might have broken those cracked but mending ribs and sprained wrist…"

She shook her head no violently. "No, no hospital! I'm fine, Baron, really. You worry as much as Debbie does."

"I heard that!" Debbie said as she followed her brother-in-law and both girls into the living room.

Sheriff Clemens nodded towards Baron that he was leaving, as Pastor Todd said, "Look who we found hiding upstairs. They said you were playing 'hide and seek'. That's a fun game! Maybe we'll all play later."

"Mommy, you and Mr. Bear'ronn Will'amms didn't come and find'deded us!" Bethany exclaimed as she rushed to be picked up by Baron. "Why is Mommy crying? Is she sad?"

Baron picked up Bethany, enjoying and savoring her sweet innocence and smile and trusting eyes. He sat near her mother and placed her in his lap for a bear hug. "Your mommy just hurt her hand again, Munchkin, but I don't want you to be worried or scared—she's going to be fine." He kissed her softly on her forehead and whispered close, "I missed you, baby."

Debbie stepped closer to her best friend and asked, "Your hand need stitches, Merry Beth? It's bruised and really swollen—is it broken?"

"Hey, that's what my Mommy calls me!" Bethany smiled into Baron's black eyes and giggled. "I guess'deded it's okay if you call me that…*if* you prom'isss to come back again!"

Her little arms went around his neck and Baron knew in his heart that this sweet child and her mother were the missing pieces to the jumbled mixed-up puzzle called his life. He'd only just found them, how in the world could he ever let them go this soon?

Tears burned the back of his dark eyes and he fought hard against them. He could barely whisper, "Your mommy is going to be just fine, I promise."

Debbie watched as the paramedics checked Merry Beth's bleeding fingers and asked again, "Does she need stitches?"

"No…but this wrist is terribly bruised and swollen—it may be broken; it'll need to be X-rayed…are you in pain anywhere else, Mrs. Waters?" His name tag stated EMT, John P. Tilton. He had blonde curly hair and the softest brown eyes she'd ever seen. She liked his caring touch and friendly smile and helpful voice.

Merry Beth tried to smile and answered, "Yes, my ribs on the left side and my lower back…"

Todd stepped closer after sweeping up the broken china, not liking the look of fear in his sister-in-law's best friend's eyes. "Earl is gone, Merry Beth—he won't be back. I'll see to it."

Merry Beth shook her head no and Debbie picked up Lisa into her arms as she said, "Mommy! Can I stay over again? Beth and I aren't finished with our special cards yet, and we get to wear Mrs. Waters' wedding dress and veil. She *promised!*"

"I think it's best if you came home, honey." Debbie glanced at the mysterious, huge but handsome man holding her best friend's daughter close in his arms and asked, as Todd lifted his niece from Debbie's arms into his own, "So, who's the Terminator, Merry Beth? I'll pay whatever he costs so you can keep him, and is he coming back if he decides to leave any time soon? Is *this* the man who bought you your new truck?"

Bethany hugged Baron tighter and said, "You can't have him—he's mine and Mommy's. He found'deded and save'deded us when we smash'deded up grandpa's fancy car!"

Lisa giggled and added, "He's nice—just like you, Uncle Todd. He tickled me and made me laugh…like you always do!"

Todd hugged his niece closer; thankful she wasn't hurt, thankful she was a happy child. "I love you, baby." He started to tickle her again and Lisa laughed outright, over and over.

Baron searched for Merry Beth's emerald eyes. "So, do you need rescuing again, Mrs. Waters? Are you doing this on purpose so I'll keep coming back?" he lightly teased.

Baron turned and smiled at Todd. "Baron Williams—it's nice to meet you both. And yes, I bought her the truck."

Todd had a stricken look to his face. "Hey, that old Toyota might be like the walking dead—but she's trustworthy."

Baron winced, and winked at Todd. "Your eyes—do you need glasses?"

Merry Beth burst out laughing and both girls giggled and asked what was so funny. "Debbie, this is Sergeant Baron Michael Williams—Baron, this is my best friend Debbie, and her brother-in-law—our pastor, Todd Thomas. Debbie's a widow."

Baron placed Bethany on the floor and both girls rushed off towards the stairs to finish their Christmas cards, when Debbie reached out and snagged the collar of Lisa and Bethany's sweaters. Todd chuckled and said as the men shook hands, "My friends call me Pastor Todd."

"Hold it right there you two busy-bees. Lisa—it's time to go home," Debbie said with a firm, husky voice. "Bethany—let's go into the kitchen for a snack while the nice and handsome paramedics fix your mommy's hand and prepare her to go to the hospital for those needed X-rays…"

Debbie glanced at Merry Beth and whispered close, "I like him. He's cute." She knew Baron and Merry Beth needed a few moments alone and took both girls into the kitchen for a drink and Christmas cookies. When Todd didn't follow her she said over her shoulder, "Come on Todd—help me find a snack for the girls. Milk and Christmas cookies sound good…*now!*"

Baron told the paramedics he'd make sure Merry Beth was brought into the E.R., a.s.a.p., and turned back to the woman he loved once they were alone and whispered close, "Please, trust me Merry Beth. I know what I'm doing. I know my job well and I have friends—good friends, to back me up. I won't be facing any dangers alone, I promise you. You trust me, right?" *I can't do this unless I know you trust me and will be waiting for me here when I get back.*

He sat next to her on the lumpy couch and reached for her and pulled her into his arms. "I have to do this. I have to go."

She lifted her sparkling but sad emerald eyes to his and whispered, "I don't want you to go. I like having you here."

Sadness filled the empty places in his heart. "I like being here, too, but I have no other choice."

Sadness engulfed her heart. "When will you be back?"

He shook his head. "No promises, Merry Beth."

Her heart was breaking in two. "It's Christmas! And we still have to decorate your beautiful house with our twinkling lights that the girls and I bought for you at Wal-Mart! And there will be gifts for you to open come Christmas morning under our tree…"

Baron carefully kissed Merry Beth's swollen and bruised right wrist. "I have to go, Merry Beth. If there was any other way to handle things, I would. I've already sold my house to a couple who's been after me to sell for the last six months."

She gasped in surprise. "You have? But…why?"

He winced at her disappointment and hated her tears and continued, "I'll tell you what, why don't you and the Munchkin use all of those fancy lights to decorate the pine trees and bushes out front, and down by the main road and along the fence. Then," he bent really close to whisper, "then, I'll be sure to find my way back to you and the Munchkin when all of this is over."

Their eyes and hearts locked—both silently praying it would be forever. She smiled and he fell in love with her all over again. He stared deep into her dark green eyes so she'd know he was serious when he said, "Be very careful about going out at night alone, okay? I'm going to have a security and alarm system installed first thing Monday morning—whether your landlord likes it or not, and I want you to be very wary of strangers or new acquaintances, Merry Beth. Don't tell anyone you don't know that you live alone. Keep my cellular charged and with you at all times. Don't open the door to anyone you don't know, all right? Do you have a gun in the house?"

She winced. "Yes, a .38," she pointed towards the kitchen to add, "I was going to get it when Earl grabbed me. I also have three of my daddy's old rifles locked in a wood gun cabinet in my bedroom. He, my grandfather and my husband taught me how to clean, to load and shoot…always in self-defense. I also hunted every November with them since I was eighteen. And Todd is my landlord—so there won't be a problem with the system you want to install. You have to let me pay you for it…"

"No way; keep the .38 with you at all times, honey. I want you safe. There's no telling who might come crawling out of the woodwork because of me." He helped her to her feet. "Let's get you to that E.R. for those X-rays."

"I'm all right, really…"

"I'll miss you, Merry Beth…"

"When will you be back?" *Oh, Baron, please, please come back to me. I love you. Bethany and I need you!*

"I don't know." *Oh, Merry Beth, I love you, baby. Please pray for me. I'll come back to you, I promise!*

"Will you call?" *Why does love have to hurt so much?*

"I can't." *You're in my heart and in my dreams and thoughts always!*

"Why not…?" *It's hard to trust you, but I do.*

"Too risky, and I don't want you hurt." *I've already lost Becky and my son. I can't lose you, too. I can't! I live in the real world, Merry Beth—a world that's filled with danger and darkness and uncertainty and flying bullets.*

He hated the fear that snapped back in her eyes as she quietly asked, "Will they keep my ex-father-in-law in jail?" *God will keep us safe. He always does, but I need you!*

"There's no way I can stop it if he gets bail, honey. I'm sorry. I have to go to the police station now. I'm the one who made the arrest. I'll have to fill out my report." *He'll never hurt you again. I swear it on my life—never again!* He made the move towards the kitchen, and she held on to his arms tight so he couldn't leave.

"Thank you, Baron." *I love you.*

He leaned down and whispered close, "You do trust me, right?" *I love you.*

"Yes." *I'm placing your heart and life in God's hands!*

He smiled as he lowered his lips to hers to share their first passionate kiss. His kiss was everything she'd ever dreamed it to be. It was soft—gentle, compassionate, tender, yielding, pliable and serene. It was warm—sincere, cordial, ardent, eager and genuine. It was gentle yet strong, sturdy and potent. It was binding—unconditional, unchangeable and hard and fast. She leaned into him, soaking in his steel strength, wanting more, much more.

She melted, like milk chocolate on a hot summer day in the sunlight; from his touch, his caress, his binding kiss, and leaned in closer, closer, closer…trying to get closer still. She wanted this. Oh, boy—did she ever!

He slowly broke their kiss, trembling as much as Merry Beth was, and searched into the darkness of her emerald eyes before whispering close, "I'm trusting in God to keep you safe until I return to you and the Munchkin, Merry Beth."

He let her go and turned away, but not before Merry Beth whispered, "And I'm trusting in you to keep your word and come back to me and Bethany…in one piece, safe and unhurt."

He met her eyes again and brushed his right hand fingers down her healing left cheek. "You'll both be with me, Merry Beth, in my heart—no matter what happens."

Her tears of good-bye fell from her eyes then. She couldn't hold them back. He touched his lips slowly and softly across hers one more time. The words, 'I love you' wouldn't come. Something held him back. One kiss with her and he knew that his life would never be the same. He wanted more, much more.

Baron was a unique perfectionist. In both his personal and professional life—he left no rock unturned, no file unopened, no witnesses unprotected, no tall grass uncut; so to speak. He was a hard man, like brick or steel. One who loved as hard and fast as he lived, and when he loved, as he now loved Merry Beth and Bethany, it was forever. There'd be no going back.

He'd get to the truth about Becky and his son's murders. He owed it to himself, Mitch, Becky, his son, and now Merry Beth and Bethany as well. He couldn't start a new life with them until the past was set right.

Todd and Debbie promised Baron they'd make sure Merry Beth got to the E.R., and he quickly left and walked away without once looking back; tears blinding his clouded yet steady way. Suddenly, it hurt to breathe again.

Merry Beth smiled and said, as he walked out her busted kitchen door, "And you with us. Be safe, Baron—watch your back. It's dangerous out there. And zip up your coat—it's also very cold!" *I love you—please, be careful!*

* * * * *

Several hours later—Merry Beth, Bethany, Todd, Debbie, Kristi and Lisa spent the rest of that day and early on into the evening decorating the tall pine trees in front of Merry Beth's apartment, the complete driveway along the fences, and also down by the main road on the mail box and fence. By the time they were done the entire yard and two acres surrounding the property lit up like a hundred Christmas trees.

It was a beautiful, festive, merry and colorful sight—one that Merry Beth prayed would call Baron back to her and Bethany, safe and sound, some day, soon. Maybe next time he'd stay forever.

Mark 11:22-24 "And Jesus answering saith unto them, Have faith in God. For verily I say unto you, That whosoever shall say unto this mountain, Be thou removed, and be thou cast into the sea; and shall not doubt in his heart, but shall believe that those things which he saith shall come to pass; he shall have whatsoever he saith. Therefore I say unto you, What things soever ye desire, when ye pray, believe that ye receive *them*, and ye shall have *them*."

Chapter Eight

Luke 2:11-12 "For unto you is born this day in the city of David a Saviour, which is Christ the Lord. And this *shall be* a sign unto you; Ye shall find the babe wrapped in swaddling clothes, lying in a manger."

Miracle #7, wishes and wants, December 19th, Saturday, 7:23 a.m.

"BUT, MOMMY...I thought'deded that if I wish'deded hard enough Santa *always* brought'deded what I want'deded under the tree on Cris'mass morning!" Bethany stated with belief in her little heart, before reaching for another piece of toast smothered with margarine and homemade strawberry jam.

Merry Beth filled her bowl with Cream of Wheat that was warming on the wood stove in a non-stick pan. The snow had stopped a little after three in the morning, and it was a beautiful, bright and sunny morning. The snow glistened across the fields like sparkling stars and shiny, crushed jewels all around the little apartment house.

She knew there had to be at least a foot of snow out there, and looked forward to plans she'd made with the girls to make angels in the snow again. They also had plans to finish making their special Christmas cards after lunch, and attending the Tree Lighting Ceremony at Northgate Mall at seven.

Lisa lifted her head from her hands and asked sincerely, "Why don't Bethany and me have earth-daddies? All our friends in our Sunday-School class at church have earth-daddies?"

Bethany grinned at her mother. "Yeah, Mommy—how come Lisa and me don't have earth-daddies?"

Merry Beth carried her warm bowl of hot cereal to the table, thankful that her right wrist wasn't broken, and swallowed a smile. "Well, let's see—how about if we three make a special wish to Santa right now. Come on—let's hold hands. And if you want to, you can both send Santa a special card asking for a new earth-daddy for you and Bethany."

She placed her bowl on the table and reached for Bethany and Lisa's hands. She smiled when Lisa very carefully placed her tiny hand over her bruised left hand fingers that were cradled near the cast close to her chest.

"Does your broken arm hurt, Mrs. Waters? Mommy said it must be itching like the old dickens. What does that mean? What's an old dickens?" Lisa asked softly.

Bethany glanced up at her mother and said, "I think I rather'deded ask God instead, Mommy. Santa's real'lieee busy right now and this is a *really* import'ant wish!"

Merry Beth shook her head that it was okay and said, "My arm is healing just fine, and that's just an old saying, Lisa. All right, hold on tight—close your eyes—and pray to God for new earth-daddies for you both. Are you sure that this is what you both want?"

Bethany cried out, "Yes—I want Mr. Williams!"

Lisa agreed. "Yes, mommy says she needs all the help she can get. I want my Uncle Todd!"

Merry Beth chuckled, and watched the girls with their eyes closed tightly and smiled, thinking of Baron's magical and special kisses. "All right then—now, who's going to pray first?"

The power of prayer was indeed extraordinary and wonderful, in a world so cold and dangerous. Merry Beth closed her eyes, thinking, *Oh, Baron, I wish you could see and hear this. It's so sweet. I miss you so much already! Please, be safe and come back to us soon, my love. May God keep you safe and warm and heal your wounds and touch your hurting soul. I love you very much...*

Bethany spoke right up. "I do, Mommy!" After a few seconds of complete silence she prayed with all the trust in her young heart. "Dear God—it would be real'lieee neat if I had an earth-dad'dieee, don't yaaah think? Lisa needs an earth-dad'dieee, too, and all my friends at day care have an earth-dad'dieee and all our friends at Sunday-School have earth-dad'dieee's. And if it ain't too much trouble, maybe Mommy could have an earth-dad'dieee, too! 'Cause Grandpa and my real dad'dieee have been in Heaven for a long, long, *long* time and we really, really, *really* miss them. Amen."

Merry Beth's throat choked up with rising tears.

Lisa spoke softly next, "Dear God—maybe if it ain't too much trouble—my best friend in the whole, wide world, Beth, could find a special earth-daddy? She really, and I mean *really* likes Mr. Baron Williams! Maybe *he* could be Bethany's earth-daddy, you think? And mommy, Kristi, Jason and I miss daddy—he's in Heaven with you—like Beth's daddy is, but...could you send a new earth-daddy for us—it would be kind of neat if Uncle Todd could do it. Really, really, *really* neat! Amen."

Merry Beth smiled before she prayed, "Dear God—bless Bethany and Lisa—they're such a treasure in my life. Thank you for Your love and forgiveness and for sending baby Jesus to be born all those many Christmases ago in Bethlehem. Thank you for the bright star that showed the three kings the way. Thank you for our many blessings. And if it is Your will—please bring Mr. Williams back to us safely, and please bring someone into Debbie's life for her to love—so sweet little Lisa can have her new earth-daddy. In Your Name we pray, Amen."

Merry Beth hugged both girls and said, "I love you both very much, do you know that?"

Bethany stared at her mother funny. "Mommy, of course we do. You're so silly sometimes!"

Lisa giggled as she hugged Merry Beth's neck. "Yeah, Mrs. Waters, of course we do! You're way cool, I love you!"

The girls jumped up and down with excitement, already thinking of finishing their special Christmas cards, and Merry Beth smiled. "Come on, girls, sit and finish your breakfast. After we eat I'll clean up the kitchen, then we'll get dressed and make those special angels in the snow that you've been talking non-stop about! And don't forget, girls—tonight is the tree lighting ceremony at Northgate Mall. It's going to be a busy but fun-filled day!"

Bethany and Lisa gulped down their remaining cereal and orange juice. "May we be ex'coosed, Mommy?" Bethany asked while wiping her chin and mouth clean with a napkin.

Merry Beth accepted a quick hug and sloppy kiss from both girls before they rushed off. "Make sure you make your bed and pick up your room, Bethany, after you get dressed, *before* you get to go out and play in the snow!"

She called them back and bent over low enough so she could kiss both girls lightly on the cheek. She glanced at her daughter and said, "Please put all your dirty clothes in the hamper, baby. And no running in the house, I mean it!"

Lisa hugged Merry Beth's waist. "You're the coolest!"

"Okay, Mommy," Bethany said as she giggled with laughter and fun with her best friend as any five-year-old would. "Lisa's gonnaaa help'deded me." Both girls took of on a dead run, forgetting her warning in seconds.

Merry Beth sat to enjoy one more cup of hazelnut coffee and reached for the weekend paper, and immediately winced back from the front headlines on the Winterville section. She read the article out loud as she sipped her creamy coffee...

"Mr. Earl Anthony Waters—ex-President and Bank Manager of First Northern-National Bank on Main Street, was arrested early yesterday evening at the home of his daughter-in-law, Mrs. Merry Beth Waters. The arrest was made by State Police Officer Baron Williams, with Sheriff Clemens and Deputy Masters as back-up. Mr. Waters was charged with several counts, including— breaking-and-entering, assault and breaking his restraining order.

"Mr. Waters had been fired from his job at the bank just six weeks ago, after second sexual harassment charges were brought up against him, by Mrs. Nancy Bellows, a five-year employee at the bank. That case never went to court, with Mrs. Bellows mysteriously dropping her suit and moving away to Boston just three weeks ago."

Merry Beth gasped at the news and covered her mouth with her wrapped right hand. She'd been friends with Nancy and was shocked to hear that she'd left town.

"Mrs. Merry Beth Waters brought sexual harassment charges against her father-in-law over six years ago after the death of her husband, Thomas Earl Waters. She was an employee at the same bank for six-and-a-half years. After the birth of her daughter, Mrs. Waters dropped the charges and the matter was dropped. Mr. Waters was held overnight in the Winterville jail, and his court-appointed lawyer is still waiting to receive the date for Mr. Waters' bail hearing."

Tears filled her eyes. Their safe and quiet life had been invaded once more; she felt violated, again. Her hands shook as she held the paper. She frowned as she stared at her ex-father-in-law's picture. His eyes were the same as his heart— evil and dark, his face now aged and wrinkled, and his hair was now completely white and balding on top, where it had once been thick and brown like her husband's. Thomas had been nothing like his estranged father.

Deep inside Earl's heart and soul, she knew that he hadn't changed. He was still evil, dark, immoral, wicked, blasphemous, malicious, profane, hostile, rancorous and just plain old mean. She threw the paper in the kitchen wood stove and turned away in disgust. Her fingers shook as she reached over her sink to turn on her radio. Elvis' *"Blue Christmas"* made her smile, despite painful past memories. She wasn't the woman she'd once been because of the sexual harassment. She was brave and strong! God was her refuge and strength. He kept her and Bethany safe and happy.

"If you dare to come back here, Earl, I won't hesitate to do whatever I have to do—to protect my child!" As she turned away from the sink the phone rang. The man who was going to fix the broken windows on her new Ford Bronco informed her that her truck would be delivered back to her house around three that afternoon. She thanked him and continued cleaning up her kitchen, while singing along with Bing Crosby's "*We Three Kings*" on the radio.

She filled her wood box and threw two more logs in the wood stove before she hurried upstairs to make her bed, shower and get dressed for the day. Despite missing, loving and worrying about Baron, she remained happy and thankful for all her many blessings, as she helped both girls make their special 'angels' in the snow an hour later. Her right wrist was mending but by that time it throbbed like an unwanted toothache. She took three pain tablets, hoping to ease the pain. The E.R. doctor had given her a lower dose, one that wouldn't make her feel sleepy all the time.

She wasn't aware that dark evil from two different worlds was about to come down on her home and daughter, fierce and hard. One was from her ex-father-in-law's world. He was a man who wasn't about to take no for an answer.

The second was from a hired Assassin's world. He was a dark, mysterious, nameless and faceless, evil and lethal man. A man seeking revenge against Sergeant Baron Williams and Captain Mitchell McMillian, and anyone who ever stood in his way of ever accomplishing their deaths.

She worked on her budget at the kitchen table as several men from the hardware store in town, hired by Baron, whistled as they repaired her busted knotty-pine back door. She sipped hot cinnamon tea and chewed on her pencil's eraser. She rubbed her throbbing forehead and tapped the pencil on the paper pad. She couldn't concentrate on the figures because all thoughts of Baron's creamy yet dark eyes were in the way.

Where was he at this moment, and were his unique eyes black or wolf-gray? Man, oh man—what a kiss! One kiss and her heart was lost to him forever.

* * * * *

In Fort Kent, Maine, at Mac's Coffee Shop around 9:30 a.m., despite the dangers lurking about—the miracles kept on happening. Baron sipped his black coffee while he waited for Mitch to show up. The popular coffee shop was packed to the pine rafters. How many times had he and Mitch met here, for a meal or a secret meeting concerning their work? Mitch was late and he couldn't help but feel worried and anxious about his boss. He knew the dangers that hid in the shadowy places, and knew anything could happen at any time. But thanks to Merry Beth, he was slowly learning how to pray again and trust in not only her, God again.

It was a miracle—trusting again, one that gave him a true sense of hope; a true sense that everything really was going to be all right. He smiled; just about everyone around him in the many booths', lunch counter, table and chair sections had greeted him in one way or another when he'd first walked in. This was a wonderful community where everyone knew everyone else. They'd all been there, at the funeral, when he'd buried his wife and infant son.

It was warm and friendly, welcoming and safe, and The Coffee Shop was decorated for Christmas to the extreme. He hoped that Merry Beth and Bethany would love it here in Fort Kent, and planned to bring them soon to show them the area.

Baron smiled as Mr. Barry Stone, Fort Kent's one and only mailman and the waitress named Polly's husband, as he dropped a few quarters in the old fashioned music box in the far corner, and Patty Loveless began to sing, "*How Can I Help You Say Good-bye.*"

He thought of his *pretty flour snowbird* as the song played, and regretted not telling her he loved her before he'd left. Good-byes were hard for a man like him who loved deeply. He knew his love for Becky had blown away, as if from a bitter and cold, brutal windstorm because of her lies and betrayal. Hurt like this had nothing to do with loving someone.

Now, there was only Merry Beth. Sweet, trusting, happy and cheerful and wonderful Merry Beth, with her pretty emerald eyes and genuine smile, with her caring touch and giving heart.

He already made the arrangements to sell the house he'd shared with Becky and his son, knowing he desperately needed a brand-new start, a new beginning, and a new life. To make a new life with the wonderful miracle God had given him was all he wanted—Merry Beth and Bethany. Every step he took from this moment on had to be carefully thought through and planned.

Even though he'd only lived in northern Maine for four years, Baron loved living here. With her icy, cold and snowy winters to her soft, graceful and breezy springs, and often-chilly summers and fall. And the Fort Kent area of the state, to him was just as breathtakingly beautiful as the rest of the state. The people were friendlier, the winters colder, the grass greener; the sunshine warmer.

He loved the tall, dark pine trees and Chickadees, lakes and endless wilderness, camping out and campfires, hiking and skiing, swimming and boating, whale and seal and eagle watching; the wild animals brought the state to life—deer, elk, bear, raccoon, moose, eagle, loons—they were free to roam the wild, just as God intended them to do in the first place.

Maine was home, yet he missed the lights and glamour of Manhattan. But he'd never move back there, not in a million.

In the back of his mind he had plans to marry Merry Beth, and bring her and the Munchkin to the northern tip of Maine to live. He had sights on a four-bedroom log cabin for sale on the Allagash River, about thirty-five miles southwest from Fort Kent. He hoped to retire from the uniform, badge and gun and become a plain old potato farmer, and prayed Merry Beth would want to become a plain old potato farmer's wife.

Timber attracted the French Acadians this far northeast, up the St. John River Valley to settle northern Aroostook County. While lumbering remained one of the area's main industries, ambitious settlers quickly learned that the plentiful earth was plenty and rich for potato farming. Maine potatoes were highly prized throughout the United States for their size and tasty quality. Even with a recent decline in farming, it still remained an important economic factor in St. John Valley and Maine.

The small manufacturing plant that reproduced infant and children's sleepwear employed over four hundred area residents. And a frozen food plant, many small businesses concentrating on manufacturing and production, and a varied array of craft-persons added to the frugality of the area. A buckwheat farm that produced its own flour and commodity for distribution—combined both farming and manufacturing in the Fort Kent area. Oh, yes. Fort Kent, Maine could easily become *home*.

Baron liked the idea that the region combined two cultures and two countries. He knew that the town's varied economic and social characteristics and constructed businesses attracted new businesses, new residents, and new and repeated tourists all the time. The town was small, yet growing.

He felt at peace about this move and the changes he wanted to make in his life. He'd prayed diligently over the last twenty-four hours for God's guidance and wisdom and strength to do what he had to do, safely. He smiled at his boss and best friend, as Mitch walked quickly towards his booth fully dressed in his impressive uniform. He sucked in his breath thinking, *Here we go...*

Mitch was a good man, an honest and dependable man, but Baron also knew he was a man with many secrets. His eyes were trust-worthy though, and that said a lot for a man's worth.

"What's up, boss? I thought you had today off."

"Sorry I'm late, Bear. It's been a hectic morning." Mitch sat across from Baron with a smile anyway and removed his dark sunglasses, and sat his radio and truck keys on the table. "Have you been waiting long?" He turned the radio down a little and removed his Stetson and placed it in the seat.

"No, only about twenty minutes." Baron signaled for his waitress to bring Mitch a coffee. "What has you so rattled this early in the morning? Is Carolyn all right?"

"Matthew called in sick with the flu so I've been on duty at headquarters since six this morning. I spoke to Carolyn's boss at the manufacturing plant privately at his home first thing this morning, and he's agreed to give her some time off over the next month. He's a good man and cares about every one of his employees at the plant. But, he's also family—he's Carolyn's uncle. She's already on her way south to Bangor where she will catch a Greyhound bus at four p.m. today to go and be with her sister in Long Island, New York." Mitch smiled up at the pretty waitress named Polly as she filled both cups with fresh Maxwell House coffee.

"Polly, tell your hubby over there I have a package in my car I'd like to get in the mail today if I could. I'll give him plenty of money for postage if he takes it off my hands before he leaves." Baron smiled his thanks.

"Sure will, mornin', Captain. How's Carolyn? Tell her the ladies at the church are looking forward to her needlepoint class this Tuesday night. We're hoping to finally finish our quilts in time for Christmas."

Polly smiled before turning to walk away. "Don't know what we'd do without Carolyn and her tips on all those different cross-stitches! I'm almost done a red-white-and-blue patched quilt that I'm making for my youngest sister."

Baron smiled at her, passed her a ten-dollar bill to pay for the package, their coffee and a tip, and said, "Thanks, Polly."

Mitch stopped her by touching her lightly on the arm. "Carolyn's gone, Ms. Polly—family emergency in Florida. She left suddenly to go see her brother so, if you don't mind—could you let the ladies know the needlepoint class for Tuesday night is cancelled? I'll let you know when she's coming home."

"Oh, that's too bad. I didn't know that Carolyn had a brother. I'll let everyone know though," Polly promised with a warm smile as she rushed away to help other customers.

Both men waited until they were alone once more before Baron whispered, "Long Island—is that safe? I know it's been years since the attacks on 9-11. But Long Island is pretty close to Manhattan, Mitch. They're on high alert there on and off, and Polly is right, Carolyn doesn't have a brother."

Mitch grinned and winked at him and Baron thought, *More secrets, Mitch?* "Spill it—what's up?"

"You're right, she doesn't. It's just a little lie to help keep her safe." Mitch added cream and sugar to his coffee. "I should have asked for decaf—I'm already too wired as it is."

Mitch leaned closer and whispered, "Carolyn will be safe in Long Island, Bear. She's not alone. Someone I trust with my life and hers is with her at all times. If things get out of control there again with the terrorists'—well, she has a way to get out, believe me." Mitch reached for his spoon and stirred his coffee.

Baron lifted his eyebrow in question. "Is he another buddy of yours from Vietnam, Mitch? How many of these mysterious buddies do you actually have hiding in the shadows anyway?"

Black eyes met and locked with a tight grip on hazel. Baron lifted his coffee to his lips before he said, "Come on, you old Maine coot—spit it out. Time's a wasting!"

Mitch just laughed lightly but didn't answer his question. Baron sipped his black coffee before saying, "Good. I'm glad she's going to be safe. I have a feeling this is going to get a little messy, Mitch, messy and bloody."

"And Merry Beth and the little girl...?" Mitch signaled for their waitress once more. He knew the menu by heart and didn't need to look to know what he wanted to order. "I'm starving! Have you eaten yet?"

When Baron shook his head no he continued, "Good. Let's order a hardy breakfast. My stomach is growling louder than a northern grizzly, my treat!"

Both men smiled as Polly walked back to their table. "Barry said he'd give you the change from the ten the next time he sees you, Sergeant Williams."

Baron smiled at Polly. "Tell him to give it to you—for the coffee and your tip."

Polly chuckled. "Thanks. You two want grub? The specials are on the board."

Baron and Mitch both ordered the 'Steak and Eggs Special' and talked to several friends who stopped by their booth on their way out, before Mitch asked Baron, "So, tell me, what are your plans now...?"

Baron worried, yet smiled. "To keep Merry Beth and the Munchkin alive and safe, and make them mine...one day soon."

Mitch searched Baron's black eyes with a smile. "You love this woman and her child?"

Baron didn't hesitate to say, "Yes, very much."

Dark eyebrows lined with silver raised. "That was fast."

Baron smiled. "As fast as blinking, yes. Why?"

"You *sure* this woman is legit?"

"She's a kindergarten school teacher and farmer, Mitch."

"And there were babies in Nam who were secret informants hiding weapons and ammo in deep holes in the ground, remember? They liked to play with loaded machine guns and C-4 and grenades, instead of stuffed bunnies and a deck of cards and play dough. You can trust no one in this bloody mess, trust me."

"She knits scarves and mittens to earn extra money..."

Mitch lifted his coffee cup to his lips. "Betty Crocker by day; double agent and informant by night...?"

Baron shook his head no. "No way, she's clean."

Mitch let it drop. "Did you get the medical records you requested from the hospital where B.J. was born?"

Baron reached in the red-leather seat next to him for his black briefcase, and reached for his keys to unlock it. "Yes."

Mitch frowned slightly. "Well, don't sit there like a bump on a pitched-log—what did they say?"

Baron opened his briefcase and passed a dark brown file across the table marked 'Medical File' to his boss. Mitch opened Becky's file and began reading. "There's no way the boy wasn't mine, Mitch. Here, read this."

He passed Mitch another file marked 'Confidential'. "The General's blood type—its type B.—B.J. was my son, Mitch. He was *my* flesh and blood."

Four more customers walked in and by their table and two more quarters were dropped in the music box, and Celine Dion began to sing "*Christmas Eve*" before Mitch spoke.

Mitch's hand shook a little. "I'm not going to ask where you got this medical report from."

Baron chuckled and sipped his coffee. "Good. I'm not going to tell you, even if you get on your knees and beg me."

Mitch lifted his eyebrow and frowned as he read the two stolen photocopied pages from the General's medical file.

Baron glanced out at the falling snow. "I guess you could say that I have—*friends* in high places."

Mitch took a few minutes to look over the two files and smiled. "B.J. was yours…that's good."

"Yes. He was mine. There's no doubt in my mind. Becky, B.J. and my blood type's match perfectly. And according to that file the General was sterile. He couldn't have children, Mitch. Not since he had an irreversible vasectomy in '87. There's no way that…monster could be the father of *my* boy!"

"Good, I'm glad." Mitch glanced across the booth and didn't miss the glistening tears Baron was trying hard to hold back. "What's our next move, mate?"

Baron passed Mitch a small piece of paper. "I've contacted seven men from my old Navy SEAL Team—two are watching over Merry Beth and the Munchkin as we speak. The other five, you and I will meet at this location on the twenty-first, early, around five a.m."

Mitch placed the paper inside his shirt pocket without reading it. "I'll be there with my own friends."

Baron raised his right brown eyebrow. "Your five friends from the war—the 'Redemption Force'…?"

Mitch sipped his creamy coffee. "Yes. What did you do with the file you took with you from Dunkin' Donuts in Winterville?"

"Destroyed…"

"And the disc…?"

"Don't worry. It's safely tucked away. If anything happens to me—well, let's just say it'll be passed on to a major, higher player."

"I have that feeling across my chest and up and down my spine again, like I used to get in Vietnam just seconds before we were hit and ambushed by the enemy, and I don't like it! There are too many unseen and unknown, shadowy players this time."

"We're going to get him, Mitch. There's no way we can lose this battle, I promise you." Baron lifted his coffee cup and enjoyed its rich flavor across his tongue. His stomach grumbled and he glanced towards the kitchen when he heard Polly laughing at something her husband had just said.

"How you figure?" Mitch smiled and signaled that their breakfast was coming as he spotted Polly walking their way.

"We have good and decency and truth on our side, *and* God. He's always watching, or so Merry Beth says."

Mitch passed him a surprised, shocked expression. "You become a praying man again?"

"Since I met Merry Beth, yes…" He knew that under the surface of her sweet smile there were more riches than a hundred mines filled with hidden diamonds. She didn't need money or a big fancy truck or expensive clothes to measure her worth. And he—he felt warmth and sunshine and love in her arms, and that treasure was more valuable than any amount of gold, money or riches he could ever want or wish for. He *trusted* her.

He frowned. He'd only *really* kissed her once. But oh, what a memorable kiss! He could still feel her sweet lips under his in juicy surrender. He could still feel her entire body tremble from his kiss, with need. He smiled, promising himself he'd pull Merry Beth close for another one; and much more…real soon.

"Good, we need all the help we can get," Mitch mumbled as he reached for the ketchup, salt, pepper, margarine and jellies.

Baron reached for his steak knife. "This looks delicious." He smiled as Polly refilled their coffee mugs.

Mitch added steak sauce to his steak. "Yes, it is. Carolyn and I eat in here a lot. Eat up, enjoy…then we have work to do."

Baron added pepper to his steak. "Start talking, my good friend. Christmas is coming soon, and I for one have plans in Winterville on Christmas Eve."

"The General's as good as a cooked Christmas goose."

"Is that so?" Baron asked between bites.

"The thunder is rolling in, toward the east."

"Before the storm…?"

Mitch grinned. "Before and during…"

Baron's eyes lightened gray. "Could be a *little* dangerous…"

Mitch chuckled. "Well, all right…*maybe* just a little."

Both men reached for their coffee and took a sip. Mitch cut his steak and whispered, "You're right, Bear—this one's gonnah be bloody."

Baron agreed by a nod of his head, and finished eating his breakfast in complete silence.

* * * * *

Later that same day, around 6:37 p.m. at the Northgate Mall in Winterville, Merry Beth kept her eyes on Bethany, as she walked by Debbie's side towards the huge group of townsfolk that were gathering around the sixty foot pine tree, about to be lit for the Tree Lighting Ceremony. Something was wrong. She had that nagging feeling across her shoulders for the past twenty minutes or so.

"Debbie…" Merry Beth whispered.

Debbie glanced at her best friend and smiled. "Isn't it going to be just beautiful, Merry Beth? I love this ceremony every year. And look at the sky. There must be at least a billion, zillion stars up there tonight. Look for Todd in the crowd for me, would you? Lord only knows where he is."

Merry Beth glanced towards the heavens and smiled as it started to snow lightly. She tasted the snowflakes on her lips and tongue with pleasure. "Debbie…"

"What is it, love? Is something the matter?" Debbie glanced all around them carefully. "You don't see that nasty man Earl in the crowd, do you? As far as I know he's still in jail…"

"No, but…" Merry Beth nodded to the right not even fifteen feet away. "Look over there—there's that strange man again." Her heart hammered in her chest.

"Where…?" Debbie's brow frowned as she quickly looked all around. "What strange man? What are you talking about?"

Merry Beth nudged Debbie's shoulder. "Over there—leaning on the white-and-blue brick wall of Wal-Mart, near the ice and soda machines…don't you see him?"

Debbie glanced in the right direction and said, "Merry Beth, there's at least a dozen people over there. What are you talking about…what man?"

Merry Beth rolled her eyes. "Can't you see him? *That man!* He's dressed in black from head to toe. *I hate black!*"

Debbie giggled, "Merry Beth, your new Bronco is black!"

Merry Beth giggled right back. "What do you want me to do, Debbie—give it back?" She kept one eye on the dark stranger and one eye ahead on her daughter's back.

"There's a lot of people around I have never seen before."

"But, I've seen him at least four different times today, Debbie. I don't like it. He makes me feel very uncomfortable. It's like he's watching me. Who do you think he is?"

Debbie glanced over at the drink machines and spotted a man wearing all black. "He's the tall one, the one with the sunglasses on? That's really odd—why's he wearing sunglasses? It's snowing and cold, the middle of winter..."

"That's the one. I've seen him four other times today."

"Where have you seen him today?" Debbie pointed to their children and said, "Let's find a spot near the front. You don't see Jason and Kristi anywhere, do you?"

Merry Beth and Debbie walked towards Bethany and Lisa. Merry Beth chuckled. "Are you kidding?"

Merry Beth grabbed for Bethany's yellow winter coat just as she started to disappear in the thick crowd. "Oh, no you don't, young lady! You're staying right here next to me where I can see you and touch you. There are too many people around, baby. Stay close to mommy. I could lose you faster in this crowd, faster than I blink!"

Debbie grabbed for Lisa's pink coat as well. "You, too, young lady—stay close, and stop squirming!"

"*But, Mommy—Lisa and I want to get right up front!*" Bethany glanced up at her mother, and Lisa stared up at hers, both with pouty expressions across their faces. They had rosy cheeks and excited eyes as huge as bowling balls, both standing with their hands on their cute little hips.

Lisa rolled her eyes to the sky. "Yeah, Mom—we want to get right up front!"

Debbie smiled and said, "You two stay with us!" She glanced at her watch. "It's almost seven now. Oh, Merry Beth! Isn't the snow beautiful?"

Merry Beth silently prayed, at that very moment, for Baron—that he was safe and warm wherever he was, that he would come back soon. She closed her eyes for a moment and silently wished secretly for him to whisper the words, "I love you" before capturing her in a close, warm embrace and sweet, binding kiss once more.

Just seconds before seven, the hundreds of community members of the small town of Winterville, Maine began to sing "*Oh, Christmas Tree*," and all clapped and cheered loudly as the beautiful festooned tree lit up the dark night sky with colors of red, green, blue, yellow, silver and gold.

Twenty-five minutes later, as Merry Beth and Bethany, Debbie and Lisa worked their way through the heavy yet joyous crowd towards their vehicles they'd parked side by side, the dark stranger dressed in black followed only a few feet behind, forgotten and unnoticed in the happy crowd.

* * * * *

Inside the empty Fort Kent, White Pine Restaurant lobby, around 8:07 p.m., Baron glanced at his watch for the tenth time and reached for the ringing phone in the phone-booth immediately.

"Hello…"

"Ace here…"

"You're seven minutes late. What's wrong?"

"Sorry, but your lady and the kid just got in."

Baron sighed with relief. "And…?"

"They're fine. Out and about most of the day but now safely tucked away inside the apartment. Hey, BMW…?" All of Baron's buddies from his Navy SEAL Team had always called him BMW, and he smiled. It had been a long time. It felt good to hear it again.

"Yeah…?"

"What's up with the bright lights?" Ace frowned.

"What bright lights?" Baron smiled, knowing what Merry Beth had done.

"Your special lady friend has this whole place lit up with millions of Christmas lights. You can see her house from a mile away! How am I supposed to stay hidden and watchful when the entire house, yard, fences, and every tree and bush in sight is glowing brightly with blinking lights of every make and color?"

Ace frowned once more as his expert black eyes scanned all across the property. "I can hear the music coming from the apartment—it's full blast and someone's singing. I think it's called "*The Twelve Days of Christmas.*" Where'd you find this broad anyway? At a church yard or bake sale?"

Baron chuckled. "She wants to be sure I find my way back home, and she's a *lady*—not a broad. So watch it!"

"Yeah, well—hurry up and do just that, old friend. It's cold out here! How can you stand to live up here in the *Great White North?* My feet are freezing, my eye lashes are covered with ice, my legs are numb, it's snowing *again*, everything you see is covered with snow and ice, *and* I just smoked my last cigarette!" Ace complained as his dark expert eyes scanned his surroundings once more, carefully.

"I see nothing's changed much—you're still a grouch."

"What about you, old friend? You still lethal…?"

"That's me all right. Lethal as a poisonous snake…"

"This place is too cold and too lit up for my taste. You know me—I like to keep hidden. How am I supposed to do that when your lady *loves* these silly blinking *bright* Christmas lights?"

"Where's Mac?" Baron asked, swallowing chuckles rising in his throat. His alert eyes scanned the crowd as a party of eight walked in the restaurant.

"I just sent him to buy some warm blankets, dry socks and warmer coats, cigarettes and something to eat. I'm starving! You missed the tree lighting ceremony. It was—nice…I like Miami better!" Ace grumbled with teeth chattering.

"You owe me—remember?" Baron whispered. "You haven't changed much, old friend. All you ever did was complain, complain, complain…about *everything!*" He chuckled. "Are you still wearing only black? You better watch your back—my lady doesn't like black!"

"The *only* reason I came." Ace shivered before stepping closer inside Merry Beth's shadowy, chilly and ancient barn. The cow and horse and chickens stirred for a moment or two, then settled back down. "There's actually animals in here…they must be frozen!"

Silence slithered across the line as both men thought back to the time Baron had saved Ace's life by pushing him out of the way of that flying bullet that left its permanent scar on Baron's very own left temple. That was a dark day. One neither man wanted to think back on or ever relive again.

"Just remember, the old man will be getting out of jail first thing Monday morning. Keep your eyes open and…" Baron carefully warned in a deep husky voice. There was no way Merry Beth's ex-father-in-law would hurt her again.

"I know, I know! Stop worrying, okay? You just do whatever it is you do best and hurry up about it, will you? I miss my own lady, and the warm sunshine and white sandy beaches I call home! It's warm there—you get my *chilly* drift?"

"Tomorrow, same time," Baron said as he checked his watch. Soft Christmas music, "*Silent Night*" filled the air above his head in the impressive restaurant lobby and he smiled.

"Yeah, yeah, yeah, yeah—later," Ace grumbled as he disconnected the call on his impressive, expensive cell phone.

The line went dead, and Baron frowned as he walked away back to his table to eat his dinner of hot turkey sandwich, fries, gravy and black coffee. He wished, above all things at that precise moment as he ate alone, for mercy and forgiveness, strength and guidance, peace and serenity, and safety for his *pretty flour snowbird* and the *Munchkin*. He wished for answers! He wished for a normal life—the one he thought he'd had with Becky and his son. He wanted that normal life more than anything—the one he was determined to have with Merry Beth and her daughter...some day, real soon.

Psalms 23:1 "The LORD *is* my shepherd; I shall not want."

III John, verse 2, 11 "Beloved, I wish above all things that thou mayest prosper and be in health, even as thy soul prospereth. Beloved, follow not that which is evil, but that which is good. He that doeth good is of God: but he that doeth evil hath not seen God."

Chapter Nine

Luke 2:13-14 "And suddenly there was with the angel a multitude of heavenly host praising God, and saying, Glory to God in the highest and on earth peace, good will toward men."

Miracle #8, a shining star, December 20th, Sunday, 4:22 a.m.

BARON GROANED LOUDLY, the pain in his head intensifying, and grumbled, "Go away, Mitch, and let me sleep—*please!*"

Mitch continued to shake his friend from his deep sleep. "Come on, Bear—*get your sorry butt up and out of that bed, right now!*" He poked and pawed until Baron lifted his head from underneath his borrowed pillow with only one eye open, barely.

"Why, for goodness sakes?" He winced when he reached over to glance at his Rolex on the nightstand and saw what time it was, and saw Mitch was dressed in black from head to toe.

"What's wrong with you anyway? Are you *mental* or something?" He rubbed his eyes awake and sat up and shivered. "Goodness, Mitch. Turn the heat up. It's freezing in here! What did you do—run out of oil?" Baron complained and grumbled.

"Stop complaining and get up! We have work to do," Mitch said before turning away.

"My men won't be here until tomorrow morning, Mitch. Remember? I said five a.m. on the *twenty-first!*" Baron yelled after his boss as he disappeared from sight, the darkness and shadows swallowed him whole in seconds.

"*Hurry up, Bear—we have company!*" Mitch yelled as he rushed down the stairs. "*We have only thirty minutes to get to that church. All my men arrived one day early!*"

In seconds Baron was up and running. He grabbed clean clothes from his black zip-up bag lying on top of the chair where he'd left it the night before.

Adrenaline pumped through his veins as he rushed to the bathroom for a quick hot shower, shampoo and change of clothes. He was dressed and ready in less than ten minutes. As he raced quickly down the stairs he checked his 9mm Smith & Wesson to make sure it was fully loaded, and placed it in his brown leather holster on his left shoulder.

As Baron rushed down the stairs he mumbled, "What'd you do, forget to pay your light bill? It's darker than a tomb in here!"

Mitch waited by the back door and passed him his black leather jacket. "You're slower than an old turtle going uphill. My truck's all warmed, so let's get ready to rumble! We're meeting my men at the church at precisely five a.m. And don't worry—they're bringing the coffee and donuts." Mitch laughed as Baron grumbled, as he walked towards the truck with only the moonlight to light their way. "Man, is it ever cold out here—or what?"

"Who's bringing the bright plan we need to expose and bury the General, Mitch?" Baron asked as he walked towards the passenger side door to Mitch's light-blue Chevy pick-up truck. "Ace is right—it is colder than death out here!"

"Oh, ye of little faith…" Mitch smiled as he turned and locked his back door with his key. "Look up there—see that bright star?"

Baron glanced quickly towards the dark heavens. "Which one, Mitch…? There are at least a million bright stars up there?" *I wish I may, I wish I might, wish upon a star tonight…ah, I mean this morning…Merry Beth's kiss—this is what I wish for. She loves me, she loves me not, she loves me, she loves me not…*

"You're wrong, son—there's only one bright star, and it's going to lead us to the right road. Don't worry, Bear, you'll be home with your Merry Beth and Munchkin before you know it. You just have to have a little…" Mitch grinned at Baron, as he raced around the front of his truck to the driver's side door.

"I know, I know. Merry Beth told me—we all need to have a little bit of faith!" Baron slammed his door shut and leaned his wet head back against the headrest. When his friend opened the door and jumped up behind the wheel he said, "Mitch, promise me, when we confront the General in Washington D.C., promise me that *I* get to throw the first *and* last punch."

Mitch just smiled as he turned on his parking lights, put his truck in reverse and left his driveway quietly so the neighbors wouldn't hear or see.

"This isn't about revenge or punches, Bear…"

"Oh, yeah—says you and whose army?"

"…this is about justice, and making right the terrible wrong that was done to Becky and your son. This is about bringing a powerful, influential yet *dirty and corrupt and evil* man to his knees. And we're gonnah need God and all the angels *and* that bright star to show us the way. We need all the help we can get on this one. You say you're a praying man again—well, guess what...so am I!"

Baron closed his eyes and whispered in the shadows and darkness of the early hour, "Like I said before—this one's going to get messy, messy and bloody."

Mitch heard him and replied, "You know me! I *like* messy and bloody. The General is going down. Just like the Titanic. We're gonnah catch him in his own web of lies, betrayal, murder and greed, and there isn't enough life boats to save his sorry and pitiful, murderous carcass!"

Baron didn't open his eyes and answered, "But whose blood, Mitch? There are too many people close to us that can get hurt. And I for one don't want to see anyone I love, care about or *trust* get in the way of any flying bullets or evil, vindictive and dangerous, highly paid assassins..."

Mitch turned right. "Don't worry, they won't."

Baron chocked on his doubt, as he opened his eyes and glanced over at his boss. "You can't promise that. I thought I'd spend the next sixty or more years with Becky. Where is she now? She's in a cold and black and dark grave, alone!"

Mitch smiled in the morning darkness. "Have a little..."

"Faith...yeah, yeah, yeah—where was faith when my wife and son were butchered, Mitch?" Baron asked huskily.

Mitch had no answer for that and Baron rolled his eyes to the dark sky when it started to snow again. He was cold, cold to the bone. "I must be crazy to love Maine so much. Snow, snow, snow and more snow—it and the cold never stops!"

"Complain, complain, complain..."

"Who's going to stop me...?"

Mitch passed Baron a look that silently stated, 'Who do you think you're dealing with?'

Baron said, "You don't scare me, Mitch."

Mitch chuckled as he turned right. The church was up ahead, about a mile on the left. "I should, my friend, because I scare myself."

* * * * *

Inside the knotty-pine Winterville Baptist Church, at 11:43 a.m., Christmas was a wonderful time for friends to gather in worship. There were twelve glass-stained windows in the old country church, each symbolizing one of the eleven apostles and John the Baptist; each glowed with a lit red candle nestled in green pine, red cranberries and brown pinecones decorated with silver glitter. It was a beautiful sight. The dancing light cast a glow of warmth and safety throughout the church.

Pastor Todd Thomas glanced out over his congregation and smiled. The church was packed and it was a welcoming sight to see God's house filled to capacity with family and friends. He spoke clearly and from the heart, hoping to reach anyone in spiritual need…

"Read with me in Matthew, chapter two, starting with verse one." He smiled at the beautiful lit candles throughout the auditorium—one in every window and several near the open Bible on the shiny oak table at his feet, decorated with green holly and white orchards. His sister-in-law and Merry Beth had decorated and lit the candles before the church service had begun. The church was quiet while they waited for him to continue his sermon on 'The Shining Star.'

"Now when Jesus was born in Bethlehem of Judaea in the days of Herod the king, behold, there came wise men from the east to Jerusalem, Saying, Where is he that is born King of the Jews? For we have seen his star in the east, and are come to worship him. When Herod the king had heard *these things*, he was troubled, and all Jerusalem with him. And when he had gathered all the chief priests and scribes of the people together, he demanded of them where Christ should be born.

"And they said unto him, In Bethlehem of Judaea: for thus it is written by the prophet, And thou Bethlehem, *in* the land of Juda, art not the least among the princes of Juda: for out of thee shall come a Governor, that shall rule my people Israel.

"Then Herod, when he had privily called the wise men, inquired of them diligently what time the star appeared. And he sent them to Bethlehem, and said, Go and search diligently for the young child; and when ye have found *him*, bring me word again, that I may come and worship him also. When they had heard the king, they departed; and, lo, the star, which they saw in the east, went before them, till it came and stood over where the young child was.

"When they saw the star, they rejoiced with exceeding great joy. And when they were come into the house, they saw the young child with Mary his mother, and fell down, and worshipped him: and when they had opened their treasures, they presented unto him gifts; gold, and frankincense, and myrrh. And being warned of God in a dream that they should not return to Herod, they departed into their own country another way."

Pastor Todd glanced up from reading God's Holy Word to smile over his congregation one more time. "Let us all give thanks to God above for our many blessings—not only during this wonderful Christmas season, but also all throughout the year, every day of our lives. We must always search out Jesus diligently—just as the Wise Men sought the Savior on that blessed night Jesus was born so long ago. We must sincerely ask God for forgiveness, strength and guidance every day, to keep our eyes on Him! Let us all bow our heads in prayer, and remember the most important gift of all—*Jesus!*"

Everyone in the little country church shook Pastor Thomas' hand and smiled and greeted him with warmth and affection as they exited the church ten minutes later. It was snowing lightly and every vehicle in the parking lot was covered with a light film of fresh snow. It sparkled like little opals as the warm sunshine caressed the freshly fallen snow.

After picking her up from her Sunday-School classroom, Merry Beth held on to Bethany's tiny hand tightly so she wouldn't run and disappear in the thick crowd like she usually did every Sunday morning. She smiled down at her young daughter as she asked, "Mommy, before we leave can we please go out back and talk to daddy for a minute?"

Bethany pulled a crumpled long white envelope out of her yellow coat pocket. It was simply marked, 'Merry Christmas Daddy', and she searched for her mother's eyes.

"I made'deded him this spe'caall card and I want to read it to him. See! It has a pree'tieee yellow star on the front. And I sprink'eeled some pree'tieee gold and silver glitter on top. It's like the spe'caall star the wise men followed to find the baby Jesus in the stable!" As they walked down the hall leading towards the entrance and exit doors she added, "I wish I had a real *live earth*-daddy, Mommy."

"It's okay, baby…your dad knows you love and miss him." Merry Beth's breath caught in her throat as tears glistened across her lashes, and as they worked their way through the line to exit the church, her thoughts were on missing Baron.

"It's been a while since we visited your dad's grave. We'll come to church tonight early and bring him some pretty flowers, how does that sound?" She wiped her tears away. "I think we have some pretty red, white and yellow silk ones in the garage."

"Okay, Mommy. Daddy's gonna love them!"

Thomas Earl had been a good man—just as sweet, kind and loving as his mother and daughter. She missed him. They hadn't been only husband and wife and family, they'd been best friends. She smiled, knowing the sweetest treasure was to be able to look back and know you were loved. Thomas and his mother had touched her life; she'd never forget them. As they exited the church Merry Beth added, "We'll visit Grandma Waters' and my mom and dad's graves as well. Your grandpa will like that."

Merry Beth wasn't surprised when Bethany whispered, "And I made'deded grandma a card, too Mommy! Hers has a pree'tieee shiny green tree on it—with red-and-blue bows on it. And Lisa help'deded me glue silver glitter all over the angel we taped on the top! Do you think daddy and my grandma's and grandpa will like their cards, Mommy?" She reached inside her yellow coat pocket and pulled out three more envelopes.

"See—this one if for Grandma Waters and these two are for your mommy and daddy. You think they'll like them?" Bethany asked as she searched for her mother's familiar eyes.

"Yes, baby! I know they will." Merry Beth and Bethany stepped towards the door and Pastor Todd smiled at them, as he shook both their hands and leaned down to kiss Bethany's cheek.

Christmas was a wonderful time for friendship and shining stars. Bethany was her star, and Merry Beth thanked God every day for her sweet baby girl.

"Glad to see you and your little one here this morning," Pastor Todd said, as he ruffled Bethany's hair. "I hope you're feeling much better, Merry Beth? Nice set of wheels…?"

"Yes, I am; thank you, Pastor Todd. The truck was a…Christmas present from a dear friend. Come by the house any time for your car, okay? I filled it with gas. Thank you so much for letting us borrow it after the accident."

Merry Beth and Bethany stepped down the church steps and immediately turned left to walk towards the back of the church where the cemetery was. As they turned the corner Merry Beth bumped hard into the same man she'd spotted watching her five times the day before; her heart immediately pounded in her chest with icy fear.

She looked into his black eyes and shivered. He was still dressed in black from head to toe. His face was shadowed, scarred, dark and rugged looking. He was tall, about six feet, with broad shoulders and a jagged looking scar down the right side of his face from temple to chin. He was eerie looking and his entire demeanor spoke volumes of danger. Who was he, and why did she keep *bumping into him*, so to speak? He made her very nervous and on edge.

She shivered and he lowered his black eyes and mumbled his apologies as he turned quickly away. Her eyes followed his back until he was out of sight in the diminishing church crowd.

Merry Beth's heart thundered in her chest and she feared, in her heart, this man was dangerous—possibly even deadly, and was following and watching her and Bethany's every movement. Who was he and what did he want with her or her daughter? If she spotted him again she would call the sheriff and report it.

She whispered a quick prayer for safety as she followed Bethany through the thick snow towards her parent's graves. It was bitter cold and her feet ached from the dampness as snow melted under her toes. But a new pair of boots was an extra extravagance she just couldn't afford right now.

She still had to plan Bethany's sixth birthday party and buy her birthday gift, make out the invitations and send them out, blow up all the balloons and bake the cake. All of that cost money, yet it was such a joy to plan the party every year, every Christmas!

No matter how hard or how tough it all seemed sometimes, God always provided her every need. She had a beautiful daughter, her teaching, her gardens and flowers, good lifetime friends, her faith, her strength, her courage, her honor and word, a warm and safe place to live, a little money saved, a brand new truck; she was truly blessed.

She thought of Baron at that moment and couldn't help but smile, thankful for this second chance at love. Lord, help her—how she missed him already.

One kiss! They'd only shared one magical kiss!

She shivered and buried herself further down in her warm coat. It had been magical, but it had been a good-bye kiss.

Merry Beth watched her daughter place her special Christmas cards on top of the snow in front of her daddy, grandpa, grandma and grandmother's headstones. Bethany smiled and talked to them a mile-a-minute, as if they were right there with her, kneeling in the snow. What she said to her father brought tears to Merry Beth's eyes.

"Daddy...I miss you sooooo much! It's cold today and my feet are tingling but I came to see you anyway. Mommy is here with me and we wish you a Merry Cris'mass! We'll bring you some pretty flowers later today, before church tonight, okay, Daddy? We love you, Daddy... *very, very much!* Mommy said it was okay if I ask'deded God for another *earth*-daddy. Please, Daddy, don't be mad or sad, okay, 'cause I will always love *you*, my Heaven Daddy. *Always!*"

As they walked back to their new truck hand in hand, Bethany asked her mother, "Mommy, you *sure* daddy heard what I just said?"

Merry Beth buckled her daughter safely in her car seat in the back seat. She leaned in and kissed her cheek. "Yes, baby—your daddy heard every word you just said. But more importantly—*God* heard your prayer; sweetie…God knows what's in our heart."

Bethany smiled. "Okay…good then. Mommy…?"

Merry Beth made the move to lock and shut the door. "Yes, baby…"

Green eyes clashed with green. "Now that grandpa got sick and died and is in Heaven—will he be able to find grandma…'cause your mommy's been dead a long, long, *long* time, right?"

Merry Beth held her tears back. "Yes, baby—my mommy and daddy are together in Heaven now…with Jesus."

Bethany smiled. "Okay, Mommy—that's nice."

As Merry Beth carefully jumped up into the driver's seat, Bethany asked, "Mommy—are they happy in Heaven?"

Merry Beth started the truck. "Yes, baby…"

"Are they singing to Jesus in Heaven?"

Merry Beth smiled and turned the heater to defrost. "Yes, baby—they are."

"Do they think the angels are pretty, Mommy?"

Merry Beth turned on her windshield wipers. "Yes, baby—the angels are very beautiful."

Bethany watched out her side window at the snow falling lightly down. It was beautiful. "Will we see daddy, grandma, grandpa and grandmother again, when we get to Heaven?"

Merry Beth turned in her seat and smiled at her daughter. "Yes, baby—we will. What's with all these questions?"

Bethany giggled. "Just curious, Mommy, that's all."

"Okay then, let's get home and cook our burgers!"

Merry Beth and Bethany sang Christmas songs together the entire way home, driving through the fluffy, pretty snowflakes that continued to cover the earth in a warm blanket of white.

The roads were icy and slippery so Merry Beth took her time and drove really slow the whole way home. One accident in a lifetime was enough. She smiled. The cuts and bruises on her face were a thing of the past. Her right wrist felt better every day. She and Bethany were counting down on the calendar when she could get her cast off. Christmas and Bethany's birthday were just around the corner. She was in love again. All seemed happy and well in her world. If only…if only Baron would come back home! God only knew how much she missed him, loved him, *needed* him. Would today be the day?

* * * * *

Later that same afternoon, around 1:20 p.m., Bethany asked her mother, "Mommy…?"

Merry Beth looked up from rinsing a sink full of washed dishes and smiled. It was still hard with only one hand but it was getting easier with practice. "Yes, baby?"

"I love you, Mommy. Will you always love me back?"

"Of course I'll always love you!"

Bethany was diligently working on making her father, grandmother, grandpa and grandma a special bouquet of flowers from an assortment of silk flowers they'd found in a box in the garage marked 'flowers and ribbons'. It had been stuffed with left over items from a summer yard sale they'd had the summer before. Merry Beth had found four white wicker baskets and spray painted two red and two green when they'd first got home from church. They sat near the wood stove to dry.

Merry Beth smiled at her daughter as she asked, "How are your special flower bouquets coming along, baby? You almost finished?" She finished rinsing the remaining clean dishes before turning off the warm tap water to reach for a dishtowel to wipe her right hand.

"How does this look, Mommy? Do you think daddy and grandpa will like these?" Bethany held up two bouquets of silk flowers she'd tied together with white ribbon. "I like'deded the pree'tieee pink and yellow ones the best."

Merry Beth walked towards the kitchen table with a smile and hug for her daughter. "Oh, baby, these are beautiful! Your dad and grandpa will just love them. You did an excellent job. If you want to, you can make Mr. Williams a bouquet later. I'm sure he'd love one as well when he comes back. He's a special friend, and he's all alone and would love your flowers." *Oh, Baron—where are you right at this very moment? Please be safe and come back to us really soon!*

Bethany's eyes lit up with excitement. "Cool, Mommy. What colors? Do you think he'll like the orange-and-purple ones the best? And I could use the light-purple ribbons for his! Mommy…?"

"What?" Merry Beth answered as she glanced at the ribbons.

"I love you, Mommy."

Love didn't ask why, it just was—inside her daughter's soft green eyes, and Merry Beth hugged her daughter close and kissed her softly on her freckled nose. "I love you, too, baby."

Bethany was everything good and safe and happy and joyful in her life. Without her *and* Baron, there was nothing.

"He's going to love the orange-and-purple one, baby."

"Do you think the baskets are dry yet, Mommy?" Bethany asked as she sprinkled gold glitter over the glue drops she'd placed all over the white ribbons.

"Let me check..." Merry Beth jumped a foot when the phone rang. She reached for it with shaking fingers—hoping with everything she was, that it was Baron.

"Hello," she whispered. When she recognized Debbie's voice she sighed lightly.

"It's me, and I heard that sigh. What's that guy look like—the one you said you bumped into after church?"

Instantly Merry Beth's heart began to pound fiercely in her chest. She quickly turned her back on Bethany and whispered so she wouldn't hear the conversation.

"He's tall, dark and mysterious looking. He was wearing nothing but black, with a scar on the side of his face. Why? Why are we whispering?" Merry Beth asked with a thundering heart. There was that feeling of fear across her shoulders again, and she hated it!

"Because Todd just rented the apartment next door to you, that's why! To a tall, dark, stranger *who's wearing all black clothing, that's why, and he has a jagged scar on his face!*" Debbie exclaimed quickly with fear in her own heart.

"This can't be good. Who...who is he?" Merry Beth reached to check and make sure her new back door was locked and chained, and closed the blind and tiny curtain.

Debbie glanced at the lease she held in her hand. "His name is Carter—Michael Alan Carter. He's a teacher from Boston; he teaches high-school, science and math. He's a widower, and has been transferred to this area to teach at the high school and be the new boys' basketball coach.

"Todd double-checked all of his references *and* resume carefully, Merry Beth. Everything checked out. He paid for six months in advance—*with cash!* That's one thousand and eight hundred dollars—Todd just gave it to me for bills, and for the kids—for Christmas! What do you think? You think he's friend or foe? I don't like it—something doesn't feel…quite right."

It was true; her heart was racing. But…"It can't be the same man. I think you're being paranoid, that's what I think! *And* I think you now have yourself a good sum of extra money to catch up on bills and also for Christmas shopping. You said you were praying for another *money miracle!* Well, here's your answer. Ever since Earl busted in here I've been walking on eggshells. It has to stop, Debbie. I can't live like this…and you—when are you going to admit you have feelings for Todd other than his being your late-husband's brother? I know it's true—I've seen it in your eyes…admit it!"

Debbie gasped. "I do not!"

"Yes, you do."

"*Do not!*"

"*Do, too!*"

Merry Beth rubbed her right hand over her tired eyes as she held the phone under her chin. Her knees felt weak suddenly and her stomach churned with frustration. "I'm worried about you, Debbie. You've been alone for far too long…"

"Oh, and you haven't?" Debbie exclaimed.

"I found Baron—or, I should say he found me!"

Debbie rolled her eyes. "Lisa is only a baby! I'm too old to date, too old to start looking again; too old to start over, too old for all that romance stuff, too old to ever marry again!"

"That's bull, and you know it! You're still young—put on a sexy new dress—black lace always looks good on you, fix your hair different at a salon in town, get a manicure, buy new clothes, lose those ten pounds you always complain about, get some new and romantic perfume, buy some new make-up, get your teeth whitened—anything, just do it so Todd will notice you and finally ask you out!"

Tears burned Debbie's dark eyes. "I can't…I wouldn't know what to say—how to act—he's my husband's *brother!*"

Merry Beth shook her head. "*Late*-husband, Debbie. You still talk of your husband like he's still around. It's time to let go."

"I'm sorry. I don't mean to worry you. It's just that…" Debbie began with concern across her heart.

"I'm sorry, too…I'm tired today, my head aches, my arm and wrist are throbbing, my feet are freezing and I feel like I haven't slept in days!" Merry Beth glanced outside at her wood box, rolled her eyes and groaned. "*And* my wood box is almost empty again!" *Dear Lord, forgive me for complaining and being so ungrateful...*

Debbie sat at her cluttered kitchen table, as her tired legs gave way. "Merry Beth, what about this man that rented the apartment next to yours...?"

"I shouldn't complain. There are people out there who don't even have a wood box. And I know I could have very easily been killed in that car crash. I'm thankful my baby didn't get a scratch. I will *not* live my life in fear, Debbie. I was just being paranoid about that guy at the Mall and it has to be coincidence that I bumped into him five times and..."

"All right! I know; I'm probably over-reacting. But you heard what Sergeant Williams said before he left. 'Be wary of strangers and new people lurking around'. That apartment has been empty for over two months. Don't you think it's *really* strange that it's been rented, *now*, in the middle of winter?"

Merry Beth sneezed, three times, and Debbie asked, "Are you getting the flu bug or something? Do you need me to make you some more soup, and take Bethany off your hands so you can get complete rest for a few days? Christmas vacation is hard on us mother's—with you, it's even harder since the accident."

Merry Beth smiled and swallowed back all her fears. "No to all of the above questions! Come on, Debbie—you said he checked out. Now, about Todd and you...?"

"There is no Todd and me. About this strange guy; it's just that..." Debbie began again with worry in her heart.

"*Will you please stop worrying?* How do the angel costumes look that Azelia, Lovina and Janet finished sewing for me?" She reached over and turned on her teakettle for a cup of hot tea.

"They're fabulous! Oh, wait until you see them. Don't forget, tonight at six— the dress rehearsal for the Christmas play and concert at church. The kids will be wearing their outfits. The donkey and lamb costumes are gorgeous!" Debbie laughed lightly. "I'm bringing my camera to take some pictures. Hey, why don't we take the girls to get an ice-cream after practice? Doesn't that sound like fun?"

"I'll be there. I'll be the one wearing the bells and yellow star earrings," Merry Beth promised with a genuine smile.

"Great! See you, bye. And about Todd—he already asked me out and I turned him down." Debbie swallowed her fears and worry as she hung up the phone.

210

"Debbie…you didn't!" Merry Beth closed her eyes at the dial tone in her ear, and sighed heavily as she hung up the phone. She leaned her throbbing forehead against the wall for a second or two, and said a silent prayer. *Lord, please take this headache away. I can't take much more…it hurts and I need sleep! Help my best friend to realize that she has feelings for Pastor Todd and it's really okay to act on them!*

"Mommy, are they dry? I real'lieee want to get these done today! It's real'lieee important 'cause their graves need'deded pretty flowers!" Bethany urged seriously.

Merry Beth smiled, trusting God for safety, as she checked the wicker baskets before making herself a cup of hot tea with honey. As she settled down at the kitchen table to help Bethany finish her special four silk-flowers baskets, she hummed to the tune of "*Away in a Manger*," her headache gone.

"They're beautiful, baby. You're quite the artist!"

Bethany's eyes danced with pride. "Thanks, Mommy."

Merry Beth had lived in fear enough in the past because of the sexual harassment and her ex-father-in-law's threats. She wasn't about to start living that way again, no matter what. She was free from all of that, and each day was a new beginning *and* Baron *would* be back again…soon!

Now, what to do to get Debbie to agree to go out with Pastor Todd on a romantic date? Some candlelight, soft music and slow dancing, a nice dinner, flowers, maybe a movie—a romance one, would be nice for starters. The next time she saw Todd, she'd casually mention these ideas and many more in his ear. It was time she did something to help put her best friend and Pastor on the same *romantic* page…

* * * * *

The Fort Kent, Lonesome Pine Ski-Trail was covered with two feet of packed, frozen snow. His feet were frozen. His fingers tingled; his nose was red. Baron glanced at his Rolex, it was almost 3:30 p.m.—it would be dark within the hour. Merry Beth had been right. Christmas was indeed a wonderful time for dreaming of things to come in the future, a time when the world seemed a little kinder, a little nicer, a little more giving. And he would make it back to Merry Beth and Bethany by Christmas Eve. He would!

Baron glanced at the beauty of the snowy but darkening forest and ski trail all around him in silence, while Mitch's men went over the plan once more. He, on the other hand, remained apart from their tight group, thinking of no one and nothing at that moment but Merry Beth and Bethany coming here to live after all of this was over. He knew he was jumping the gun, so to speak. They'd only just met and she didn't love him. But her eyes—her eyes told him she cared, cared deeply. And when he'd kissed her, she'd kissed him back—passionately. They had connected!

In the past three years there had been no light at the end of the tunnel. There had been no smiles, no laughter, no friendship, no hope, no compassion, no trust or faith left inside him. But from the moment he'd first glanced in Merry Beth's grass-green eyes, there was. He frowned, missing her.

She was the type of woman who believed love could find the way, love could light the way; she believed that love could move every mountain. He knew moving mountains was what they needed to do, to make this plan to snare the General work.

He wanted to believe in that happily ever after, and like Merry Beth, touch the clouds and sky, but his heart was filled with doubt. He'd been alone for so long, alone inside himself for so long that there'd been only darkness and pain to greet him every time he opened his eyes. It was hard to open up that locked door and trust and love again. But, oh, how he wanted to.

To be loved by someone, touched by someone, to mean something to someone, to be cared about by someone—someone special, like Merry Beth; it all seemed like a wonderful, beautiful, yet distant far, far away dream that he couldn't quite reach. A dream that he thought he'd lost forever when his wife and son had died. But now new plans, new dreams, new beginnings and a little bit of hope for the future filled his lonely existence.

Merry Beth had changed his sight of only shades of grays and blacks to blessed reds, blues, yellows and greens. *She* put the bright sun back in his dark sky. *She* put hope back in his lonely eyes. *She* put the gift of faith back in his forgotten prayers. *She* put the colors back in the flowers. *She* came into his life and cared, and now there were once more bright colors everywhere he looked. He chuckled, at the moment the only colors he saw was white snow, brown oak, tall green pine trees and the dancing shadows the chilly wind created all around him.

He'd found his reason to believe again because of *her* smile and laughter. *She'd* become the special someone in his life worth living for. Now, he believed in wishing on that shining star she talked about, and so wanted to kiss her again. His knees still trembled, just thinking about their special kiss!

Yet, he was a man who lived his life by the badge and gun, a man who upheld the law at any price, a man who'd seen the ugly side of both life and death, a man who stood by his principles and worked hard to change the world, one case at a time.

His life had been filled with loss and pain for almost three years—he forgotten any other kind of existence, until he met Merry Beth. Now, there seemed to be an end to his pain, and a reason to believe again in sight. *She* made his life worth living for. *She* put happiness back in his heart, and made him finally see he needed to trust and believe in God again, in *life and living* again. Because she was right—without *God*, there was nothing, in this life or the next.

He knew that, deep in his heart he believed...

"Are you with us?" Mitch asked Baron for the third time.

It started to snow again and Baron felt the cold all the way down to his soul. He shook his head to clear his thoughts and rubbed the toe of his right boot deep in the snow.

It was so cold Baron could see their breaths. "Becky and my son's blood is on *my* hands, Mitch, of course I'm here. Where else would I be, but right here, making the plan to bring their murderer to justice?"

Mitch frowned before turning to glance over the group of six men. "So, we're all agreed? We meet, along with Williams' friends from the Navy, at eleven p.m. sharp, December the twenty-second, in front of the Vietnam Memorial in Arlington?"

Everyone nodded in agreement before turning away. Mitch and Baron watched the five men until they disappeared inside the thick, dark forest from which they'd come just an hour earlier, each man now assigned and ready for action to bring down and bust an authoritative and influential, yet criminal man.

Thomas Tony Trent, better known as *Mr. T.* was placed in charge of weapons and ammo. Adam Bryan Baker, better known as *Adam Bomb* was placed in charge of surveillance equipment. Scotty Taylor Black, better known as *Mr. Spade* was placed in charge of laptop and computer equipment needed to break certain codes. Jack Michael Jasper, better known as *The Joker* was placed in charge of two-way radios, listening devices and taping equipment, and Royce Kenneth Bishop, better known as *Rolls Royce* was placed in charge of the dynamite and C-4, and creating certain...diversions. When the men were out of sight Mitch turned back to Baron.

"This plan is going to work, Bear. Try not to worry."

The muscles in Baron's face twitched. "We're planning on breaking into

C.I.A. Headquarters in Langley, Mitch. Worry is my best friend until this mission is well over with."

Mitch replied, reaching for his cell phone inside his jacket breast pocket. "I need to check in with Carolyn."

Baron and Mitch walked away side by side in silence.

Sometimes the greatest gift anyone could ever give to another human being is the touch of friendship, the touch of compassion, the touch of kindness, the touch of caring, the touch of healing; the touch of this world's most priceless gift...

To look back on your entire life and *know*, without a doubt, that you were loved by someone special. It wasn't Becky's eyes he saw at that moment through the blowing snow and blistering northeastern wind, as Baron walked out of the thick and dark forest; it was Merry Beth's.

Why did loving someone have to hurt so much?

In Baron's thundering heart, her smile was the reason. Her laughter gave him the incentive to live again. Her eyes gave him new meaning and new purpose. Her response to his kiss gave him hope—hope that she'd fall in love with him one day, hope that he'd become *her* husband, *her* everything...

Soon, very soon!

* * * * *

Merry Beth sat in the front row pew, in the Winterville Baptist Church; it was 6:47 p.m. and she watched Debbie work her special magic with the young children. Debbie was gifted with that soft motherly touch needed to comfort, guide, manage, supervise, direct, lead, influence and regulate any group of children in the palm of her hand, including her own. She was a good friend—one Merry Beth had relied upon over the years of her life for everything from friendship to advice to warmth to hugs to laughter to guidance.

Merry Beth knew if she ever lost her way or if the strength inside her seemed gone or if her world seemed dark and gray or it seemed there wasn't any light ahead in sight—she had her faith in *God* to see her through any storm. *And* she had her best friend, Debbie, by her side...no matter what.

So, she didn't worry or fret when everything seemed scary, frightening, black or unsure. She didn't worry when the night seemed lonely and cold. She didn't worry when she cried a little bit once in a while. She didn't worry when she fell twenty steps backwards—God always reached down with *His* loving and merciful arms and picked her up again, and made her smile when she wanted to cry, just as Debbie always did.

Her thoughts had been on Baron all day and she prayed for him constantly. Prayed for his safety, prayed for God's guiding hand on his life, and most important—she prayed for his soul. She knew God was watching and listening, from a distance. She knew God cared and loved her and Bethany, and smiled as she listened to her best friend work her magic.

"All right, all of you need to stand close in a small circle surrounding Mary and baby Jesus, that's it, good! Now, *smile!* You are God's special *angels,* and you are happy and rejoicing. Good, that's just perfect. Hannah—look this way…all right…"

Debbie turned her attention to Steven who played the part of Joseph. "Steven, honey, come stand right here next to Deidre, that's it. Good! You look wonderful in your costume, Steven. Deidre—you make a very pretty *Mary!* All right everyone, smile!"

Yes, it's true, Merry Beth thought, *love doesn't ask why—it just is!* "They look wonderful, Debbie. Those costumes are the best yet. This is so cool—you *all* look fantastic!"

Debbie turned to the young men next, Jason and Shane, and instructed them where to stand. "Jason, Shane, you sure make wonderful Shepherds. Now, hold those sticks straighter—that's right. Shoulders up, head held high—*wonderful!*"

Jason and Shane rolled their eyes to the ceiling; too embarrassed to say they were proud to be in the play even though they felt they were way too old for it.

Merry Beth smiled. "They all look great Debbie. This will be the best play yet, you wait and see."

Merry Beth knew the children's play and concert would be a smashing success. It was every year. The children were wonderful—all so young, so innocent, so sweet, so trusting, and filled with happiness and life, so filled with promise and hope. Yes, even the older boys. She watched Bethany with a smile and pride filled her eyes. If only her father were here to see her now…

Debbie turned to the three young boys who were playing the parts of the three *Wise Men.* "Okay—Patrick, Joshua, Ryan—you three stand right here." She turned to Eric who played the part of a *Shepherd.* "Eric, you'll stand right here next to the sheep—that's good. Hold your staff up high—*perfect!*"

Debbie instructed the three *Wise Men* where to stand to the right of *Joseph* and *Mary.* "You each hold your gifts to baby Jesus in your hands; that's it. Now when the angel, Marie, lifts the bright shining star, you each place your gift to baby Jesus in front of *Mary* in the hay…"

Merry Beth glanced at her watch and interrupted Debbie, who was now talking to Marie—the little ten-year-old girl who held the bright yellow, shining star tightly in her hands. It was decorated with shiny silver glitter and different colored sequins, and when she held it up above her little head it caught the rays from the spotlight Pastor Todd worked in the balcony.

"Debbie, sorry to interrupt but, church starts in fifteen minutes. We better close the practice for now." Merry Beth watched with a smile as all the children went quickly running in different directions after Debbie excused them. She stepped down from the pulpit and sat next to Merry Beth and removed her black heels and rubbed her tired feet.

"Well, what do you think, Merry Beth? You think the children will remember their lines? Doesn't Marie look cute in her little white angel costume? And that star! Lisa and Bethany did a wonderful job making that star. I love it. Todd wants to frame it and hang it in the church lobby so everyone can see it year round that walks through the lobby doors."

Merry Beth glowed with pride. "Remind me to thank Azelia, Lovina and Janet with something special for all the work they did to finish the costumes for me. I think I'll give each woman one of my hat/mitten/scarf sets. I don't feel like I've contributed much for this play this year. With this broken left arm and sprained but mending right wrist—I wasn't able to do much. You've done a marvelous job with the children, Debbie. I'm proud of you!"

The best friends hugged and Merry Beth added, "I love you, thanks for being my best friend...my entire life!"

"I love you too, and are you kidding? You're in charge of the singing. The children sound wonderful singing all those special Christmas hymns. It's going to be great. You'll see. The church members and guests will love it." Debbie's dark eyes glowed with excitement but her friend's seemed sad suddenly.

"You're thinking of *him*—Sergeant Williams?"

Merry Beth rubbed her forehead. "Yes."

Debbie smiled, liking Baron tremendously. Yet, her heart worried. She leaned over really close and whispered, "You're falling in love with him."

Merry Beth's head whirled to search for her best friends eyes. "How did you know?"

Debbie hugged her good friend to her breast, tight. "I know because I know you, silly. I know your smiles, your worried look, your sad look, your anxious look, your happy look, your mournful look, your playful look, your..."

Merry Beth smiled. "Yes, I guess you do at that."

"Don't worry, it'll all work out—you wait and see."

"We have to have hope, Debbie—hope and faith."

Merry Beth and Debbie hugged once more before they went separate ways to find their children for the evening church service. Miracles were still in the making, both here in Winterville, Maine and also in Washington D.C. There was no stopping them.

God's hand was too powerful to ignore. Merry Beth had been right in what she'd told Baron. Satan's time *was* limited here on earth, and his time was almost up.

* * * * *

"Mommy, look! There's a light in the 'partment next to us! Who is it, Mommy? Do we have new nay'boors? Where's their car or truck, Mommy? I don't see one."

Merry Beth stared ahead with a thundering heart. A little bit of uncertainty and fear whispered close, she couldn't help it. "I don't know, baby. I'm sure it's okay, sweetie. Pastor Todd checked the nice man out and he's going to be the new boys' basketball coach at the high school. He's a teacher—he teaches math and science. I don't want you to be afraid."

"What's his name, Mommy?" Bethany tried to lean forward in her seat with curiosity, but the seatbelt held her back.

"I don't know yet, baby." Merry Beth frowned; she didn't want her daughter anywhere near any unknown, mysterious stranger.

"Bethany—you sure looked pretty up there wearing your angel costume in the practice. I was so proud of you, baby. You're a beautiful angel," she said, trying to change the subject.

"Do you think Mr. Bear'ronn Will'amms will make it on time on Chris'mass Eve to see me and Lisa in the play, Mommy?" Bethany asked before saying, "I love this pre'tieee new truck, Mommy. It shines! How come'deded Mr. Bear'ronn Will'amms gave'deded it to us, Mommy?"

Merry Beth smiled. Smiling came easy when you thought of someone you love. "Because he's a really nice man, baby…"

Merry Beth pulled her new Ford Bronco in front of her apartment and placed it in park. She turned off the radio and the ignition and lights before jumping down to carefully walk to the other side to get Bethany out. As she unbuckled her daughter and helped her jump down, she said, "Wait for me, baby, because

217

it's really slippery out here. I need to put down some more rock-salt. Lock your door, thank you, baby."

She reached for her daughter's tiny yellow mitten hand. "Can I tell you a secret?" Mother and daughter walked side by side to their front door through the snow, slush and ice.

Bethany jumped up and down with excitement. "Cool, Mommy! I love secrets! I promis'deded I'll keep it! What is it, Mommy?" She hugged her mother's knees and looked up at her with a smile. "Are we gonna make'deded some more of those neat tree-shaped cookies with red sprinkles on top?"

As Merry Beth closed and locked their front door behind them a few seconds later she whispered with a smile, "I think Mr. Williams is pretty special, baby. I'm sure he'll be back soon."

"I'm glad, Mommy...'cause I really miss'deded him!"

"And I think he'll be here for your special play on Christmas Eve. We better decide what we're going to make for him and wrap it and put it under our tree. It's late, baby—go get in your nightgown and I'll read you a story before bed. You can take your bath in the morning." She blew her daughter a kiss and hung up her keys and placed her purse on the foyer table.

Merry Beth removed her winter coat and smiled as her daughter rushed off to get ready for bed. "I think he's pre'tieee special, too Mommy. I love him, Mommy. Do you think he loves me back? I just *know* that God is gonnah answer my special prayer when I ask'deded for a new *earth*-dad'dieee."

Merry Beth sighed, a little. *I hope so, baby...*

Danger was close but Merry Beth didn't know or feel it at that precise moment, as she turned towards her kitchen to put on the teakettle for a hot cup of cinnamon tea. She was in love, and nothing could stop her now! It was a wonderful feeling, and the memory of that one special kiss gave her confidence.

Yet, even though unseen danger lurked close, they were safe because God kept His protective hand over Merry Beth and Bethany in the little town of Winterville, Maine that night.

And many miles away, in Fort Kent, Baron waited alone for his friends from the Navy to come into town one by one. And while he waited throughout the long sleepless night, he prayed for the second time in years. He prayed for forgiveness, for guidance, for strength and mercy—on his knees, by the single bed Mitch had let him borrow to sleep in. He prayed for another chance to make it past the storm-filled sky in his mending heart.

God answered his prayer with the graceful twinkle of the crystal-clear, bright shining star that looked down upon him from the heavens. The unique star shone with hope for a better tomorrow, and deep in his heart, even though there was still so much to do to set things right in his past, Baron felt true peace for the first time in almost three years as he closed his eyes in restful sleep on his borrowed soft pillow.

Psalms 4:8 "I will both lay me down in peace, and sleep: for thou, LORD, only makest me dwell in safety."

Chapter Ten

Luke 2:15-16 "And it came to pass, as the angels were gone away from them into heaven, the shepherds said one to another, Let us now go even unto Bethlehem, and see this thing which is come to pass, which the LORD hath made known unto us. And they came with haste, and found Mary, and Joseph, and the babe lying in a manger."

Miracle #9, letting go, December 21st, Monday, 5:22 a.m.

BARON'S BLACK EYES scanned the small group of men standing in a circle in the dark balcony of Fort Kent Baptist Church. His friends, one by one, had arrived in town between the hours of one and four a.m. Mitch and his friends were already well on their way to Washington D.C. His heart was beating calm, yet weary, and he knew the plan was dangerous and deadly. One wrong move and it would all be over, and there would be no going back to Merry Beth and Bethany, ever. Any chance for a future with them would be over with one slip up. There couldn't be any mistake.

The man known to the small, tight group as *The Bullet* searched for Baron's black eyes in the dim shadows of the early morning dusk, and frowned with worry and concern as he asked, "What do you think, BMW? You think this plan will work? We need to be as quick and as unseen as moving shadows."

All five pairs of eyes glued to Baron's while waiting for his answer. He glanced at each man carefully. These men were good friends, friends he knew he could trust completely. He had in the past and knew he could again in the immediate future. Their bond was unbreakable, even through distance and time.

Each man here was, at one time or another, responsible for saving the other four lives. Each man staring at him was highly intelligent and extensively trained by the military to find their way in and out of any dangerous and deadly situation thrown their way—alive and un-scratched. But this time, if they got caught they were on their own, they'd be as good as dead with no government—home or foreign, to back them up.

Baron didn't like the thundering *calm* pounding of his heart, and creepy doubts and jagged fears danced the jig up and down his spine. This time, he feared they wouldn't all make it out alive or in one piece, and that fear kept him off balance. He was a man who hated to be off balance and calm at the same time! He hated the jeopardy each man was willing to place himself in on this mission.

The men, his friends—*The Bullet, King of Hearts, Silent, Whisper Wings*, and *Speed* stared at Baron while waiting for his answer. Reunions were great, but there was work to do.

Suddenly, Christmas and all its trimmings were far, far away. All thoughts of a new life with Merry Beth and Bethany seemed out of reach, again. They had a mission to do, and bringing down this General needed to be the *only* thing on his mind. Baron shook his head to clear it; easier said than done when all he saw at the moment were grass-green emerald eyes.

"You *sure* you trust this Mitch and his weird buddies from Vietnam?" The Bullet asked with uneasiness across his tongue.

"You *sure* we ain't walking in on a sticky trap we can't get out of?" King of Hearts asked with the same sense of apprehension.

"You *sure* that this hot-shot General is going to be where he's supposed to be, at *exactly* the right moment?" Silent asked, as he lit a cigarette. "You trust this cop, this Captain Mitch McMillian and his *Redemption Force*, enough to put all our lives and our women and children's lives, on the line?"

The man called Whisper Wings yanked the lit cigarette from Silent's lips and crushed it out under his shiny black military boot. *"You're in God's house, man. What's wrong with you? Put that thing out!"* He turned his coal black eyes to Baron's and said, "Piece of cake. I *always* wanted to snoop inside C.I.A."

"I'm sure of only three things at this very moment. One, I'm breathing. Two, I'm doing this for my butchered infant son. And three, this General is going down by *my* hand," Baron answered huskily. *And I'm doing this for you and the Munchkin, Merry Beth. For us, for our future, for that new life I see for us when this is over!* He closed his eyes, hoping it was true. No matter how many times Mitch said it wasn't—he knew, for him, this was about retribution.

Speed quickly stepped closer to Baron and slapped him affectionately on his left shoulder. "You better go make your call, my friend, and tell Mac and Ace it will be good to see them again when all of this is over."

Ten minutes later, the group of six men left the dark church with no sign they'd ever been there. Even the cigarette butt under Whisper Wings' boot was gone. A small window near the place where the church bell was was left open a tiny crack to omit the smell of the burning cigarette. Baron instructed the men to meet in front of the Fort Kent Post Office at seven a.m. sharp, where they'd drive together to Bangor International Airport, where Ace's private plane would be fueled and ready for takeoff for Washington D.C. at exactly six p.m. sharp.

Baron's hand was steady as he stood in the dark, knee-deep in frozen snow behind the church, and held his new cellular and dialed the number he'd memorized by heart.

"Ace here…"

"It's me."

"Your lady and the kid are safely tucked away inside the apartment, sleeping soundly as we speak. I have the bugs in place and can hear every movement, even their whispers and soft breathing in their sleep! We're close enough that if there's any sign of trouble we'll be there in five seconds."

"It only takes one second to fire a gun."

"Point taken…"

"Good."

"The guys make it in on time?"

"Yeah, Speed said to tell you that he's looking forward to a reunion when this mission is over."

"Yeah, it's been a while."

"Any sign of any strangers hanging around?"

"None…"

"You sure…?"

"Affirmative, why so jumpy…?"

"Good reasons."

"Care to name a few?"

Baron closed his eyes and rubbed his throbbing forehead. "My *dead* wife was involved with some pretty shady, dark, *unknown* and very powerful, greedy players, Ace. I'm positive they're hiding and lurking in the shadows around Winterville. Just keep your eyes open and ears to the wall at all times. I'm not sure who *they* are," he carefully warned.

"Will do—oh, and BMW…?"

"Yeah…?"

"I really, really, really, *really* like your lady friend. She's breathtakingly gorgeous, she's *beyond* beautiful, and she has the prettiest smile and sexiest legs I've seen this side of Vegas in a long, long, *long* time!" Ace whistled softly over the line. "She ain't wearing no ring on her left hand—you *sure* she's yours?"

"I haven't had time to get her that special ring yet." Baron chuckled. "You just keep your hands to yourself, *old* friend...she's mine, all right. Where's Mac?"

Ace rubbed his right hand over the stubble on his face and winced. "He's counting sheep. I gottaah go, I hear movement inside. Good luck, my friend, and God speed."

Baron gripped the small cellular with his right hand and slowly reached to turn it off. As he placed it back in his black leather jacket pocket, he prayed for a miracle. And as he worked his way through the falling snow towards his black truck, he knew he had miles to go before he could go back to Winterville and pull Merry Beth close again for another one of those sexy and earth-shattering, unforgettable, over-the-fence, deep-as-the-ocean kisses.

He wanted to love her and make her his bride and promise things with her in front of God and family and friends and minister. He wanted to glance into her beautiful eyes, knowing he'd get lost inside. He wanted to grow old with her, in trust. He wanted to legally adopt the Munchkin and make more babies with her freckled face, pretty mother.

So close, this dream, yet so far.

He shivered and turned up the heater in his truck.

Loneliness...

He lived the word, until Merry Beth.

He rubbed his hand over his tired eyes and whiskered face.

Man, he was tired.

* * * * *

Merry Beth lifted her head from her restless attempt to sleep, and sat up from her crumpled sheets and blankets to reach for her housecoat she'd left lying across her mother's old white wicker rocking chair by her bed. She winced when she saw how late, or to some people, how early it was. Just past 5:30 a.m.

The room was chilly and her feet were freezing again. She put on thick socks and her fluffy white slippers, and hoped that Santa remembered to bring new ones in her red Christmas stocking. The bloodstains from her cut hand hadn't come out in the wash, and every time she wore the fuzzy and warm slippers she thought about her grandmother's broken antique china cup-and-saucer still lying in that little box on the top shelf in the laundry room. There was no way they could be fixed.

She shivered against the chill. Maybe if she asked nicely, Todd would replace this old wooden floor with a thick new carpet.

She lost her footing and stumbled from a forgotten dirty pair of jeans on the floor, and stubbed her right toes really hard on the oak dresser near her closet. "Ouch, that hurt!"

She waited for the pain to subside before continuing her way through the darkness of the old but familiar apartment to Bethany's room across the hall. She smiled; Bethany was safe and sound asleep in her warm bed. In seconds she was reaching for the banister of the staircase. The only sound she heard, as she floated down the stairs, was the sound of her own heartbeat.

A cup of warm milk will do the trick. Maybe then I can get some sleep! She knew in her heart that she had miles to go before she slept peacefully through the night again. She couldn't get Baron and the sound of his good-bye out of her head, and the memory of that kiss haunted her dreams. Man oh, man—what a kiss! She looked forward to the day she receive another and another and another…

But she also knew the reason she couldn't sleep was from worrying about her new neighbor next door. She'd listened all evening—like a secret spy with her ear and glass against the wall, and laid awake into the early hours of the new day waiting for some kind of movement or noise from next door. There was nothing. All was silent. It was like no one was over there. Maybe he wasn't home.

She shouldn't worry, within arms' reach in seconds if she needed it—her father's old, but cleaned and loaded .38 lay cold and silent in its locked box, reminding her that dangers could possibly be lurking close at any time. Was Earl out of jail yet?

Maybe the man who'd rented the apartment next door had changed his mind and moved elsewhere. There'd been no footprints in the snow and no car or truck parked in the driveway, not even any lights on. It was weird, eerie. It was like whomever it was over there was like a ghostly shadow. She knew she had to be very careful, as she remembered Baron's warning before he'd kissed her and left. It hurt that he'd turned away and walked out of her life without looking back. Why didn't he look back?

Her thoughts rushed quickly through her head as she walked like on thin air to the kitchen. *Is the man next door the same man I bumped into behind the church? Is he the same man I saw watching me six times? Is he the same man that watched me at the Tree*

Lighting Ceremony leaning against the wall by the soda machines in front of Wal-Mart? Is he the same man I saw just outside Shop-'til-you-Drop when I stopped there just before the children's Christmas play practice? Is he the same man I saw three people behind me in the line when Bethany and I went to the bank to pay our light and phone bill? Is he the same man I thought was following me home from church last night?

She shook her head to clear her troubled thoughts away, and filled a small copper pan with milk to heat. She reached for her favorite huge '#1 teacher' mug and opened the drawer near the stove for a spoon. As she dumped three heaping teaspoons of Hershey's chocolate mix into her mug she thought, *No, if that man was the same man each time, he had plenty of chances to get to me or Bethany. He had plenty of chances to grab either one of us, hurt us, kill us—the man next door has to be someone different, someone we can trust. He has to be!*

She had no money, there was nowhere for her to go, and she was on her own. Running wasn't an option. This was her home, and she wouldn't let anyone chase her or Bethany from it in fear.

As she reached for the warm milk her right hand shook lightly as she filled her mug. She knew she'd give anything to see Baron walk through the door right now! She knew she wouldn't get any sleep now that she was up, so she might as well stay up and get a few things done for Bethany's birthday party. In her heart she prayed Baron would make it back in time so he wouldn't be alone anymore, so *she* wouldn't be alone anymore, so Bethany would get her wish for a new *earth-daddy*.

Her thoughts flashed to the jagged looking scar on the dark stranger's face and she shivered. His eyes had been as icy cold, as stone-steel hard, as serrated as the scar.

She spilled milk on the stove and wiped it up. "You're being paranoid, Merry Beth. If we were in any kind of danger, surely, surely you'd know it. You'd feel it. I'd *know* if something was out of place or not right, wouldn't I?" She shook her head to clear away her troubled thoughts again. "Yes, of course I would."

She stirred her hot cocoa and walked to the back door to peek out into nothing but darkness. From the dim streetlight down by the main road she could tell it was snowing again. It was coming down in fluffy but thick flakes and she smiled, telling herself it was God's way of making His earth white and clean again. What would winter or Christmas be without snow?

She leaned her forehead against the cold glass and closed her eyes, thinking, *Oh, Baron, where are you at this exact moment? Are you thinking of us, missing us? Are you somewhere close by or are you far, far away? Are you safe? Healing? Are you finding a way to finally let go of all the hurt and pain from your wife's betrayal? This kind of betrayal—you can't come back from without faith, without hope in your heart. Are you finding the answers you need to find peace in your heart and life again, to let go? Be safe, wherever you are. I love you…we love you!*

She turned away from the window and thought it strange that her new neighbor, if he even existed, didn't have a car or truck. She shivered again and closed the blind and curtain to turn back to her hot cocoa, hating feeling uncertain or uneasy.

"Come on, Merry Beth—you can't sleep, you might as well try to finish writing Bethany's birthday poem."

She settled down at her kitchen table to work on her daughter's special birthday poem with a song in her heart and a prayer on her mind. "*It Came Upon a Midnight Clear*" played softly and low from the windowsill radio as she'd turned it on, and she smiled as she picked up her pen.

Through everything she'd been through over the years with her husband's estranged father, then her husband's cancer, his death and delivering his daughter alone, the humiliation from her name scattered all across the front pages of the paper and in the news, from being threatened and forced to drop the sexual harassment suit, from being literally forced to quit her job, and even now the threat of Earl's existence in her life once more, the accident and injuries—through all of that, Merry Beth remained strong in her faith, and never gave up.

She was a woman who received her strength from within. God was her refuge and her strength. She prayed diligently and talked to God as if He actually stood near her side from time to time. In her heart, He did. She could actually feel Him close because He lived in her heart, through her. She let her heart control her hand—even now, as she wrote her special birthday and Christmas poems to both Bethany and Baron.

The storm picked up its force, and the brittle wind howled with a hurricane's strength, the blistering snow beat against the old apartment roof, walls and windows—making them rattle, the dead of winter prowled like a thief in the middle of the dark night; inside, Merry Beth was safe, happy, in love and warm.

In her mind there was no safer place to be…

She had her faith in God, and His forgiveness.

She had her daughter's smiles, trust and love.

They had a warm, safe and dry place to call home.

She had her teaching, gardens and craftwork she enjoyed.

She also had Baron; in her heart—for now.

Would he come back soon and make it forever?

She had to believe!

* * * * *

That same morning, around 8:30 a.m., Baron and his five friends were traveling to Bangor International Airport together in a rented van that couldn't be traced back to any one of them, in any way. Each man wore leather gloves to omit fingerprints being left behind in the van. Baron was driving and smiled, as Whispering Wings passed him a take-out cup of coffee they'd just purchased at an Irsing Truck Stop, off the connection from Route 1 South to the Interstate 95 Expressway in Houlton.

Whispering Wings, known to the government and Navy Intelligence, as Retired Cpl. Matthew John Wright was Native American, Apache Tribe, thirty-four, residing in Dallas, Texas on his grandfather's horse ranch. He had feral black eyes, shoulder-length black hair tied back with a brown suede string and squint lines at the corners of his eyes whenever he smiled.

He was six feet tall, strong and muscular, and broad-shouldered with tanned native skin. He had perfect white teeth and a knockout smile and creamy charm—generally known to melt the ladies' hearts. He was a jack-of-all-trades and highly intelligent. He had a special gift for languages. He could clearly speak his own native tongue, Italian, Mexican, Chinese, French and German. And like Spade, he was also a computer science genius. He was a man you'd want around in any kind of crisis, computer or otherwise.

Matthew owed no man or woman his allegiance. He was a free man, with no wife or children to call his own. His wife and daughter had both died in a terrible house fire two years back. Now, he only answered to *The Great Spirit*. He wasn't what some would call a *religious* man, but he was strong in his beliefs and faith—both in ancient customs and in his Savior, Jesus. He prayed daily for strength and guidance and now enjoyed the simple life, away from military life and influences—the horses.

Baron glanced in the rearview mirror at the four men sitting quietly in the back of the van sipping coffee and eating their breakfast. Separate—they were so different. Together—as a unit they were one. Between the men there was a considerate amount of credence, confidence, dependence, reliance, faith and trust. He knew these men were men he could rely on, depend on, believe in, and count on to back him up in any situation or crisis. These men were his best friends.

227

Standing together, word on Capital Hill said they were unstoppable. Even though at times lethal, they'd been the best.

They'd traveled the world together—Bosnia, Iraq, Iran, Vietnam, Cambodia, Germany, China, Italy and France. They'd saved each other's lives so many times he'd lost count over the years. He owed each one of them his.

Silent, known to the government and Navy Intelligence as Retired Cpl. Michael Dalton Pierce was Mexican American, thirty-one with golden brown, eerie and unsmiling eyes, light brown hair, a clean-shaven face, well groomed and trimmed as any F.B.I. Agent's hair would be. He had dark tanned skin, was five-feet-and-eight-inches of nothing but pure muscle, very large and intimidating—he didn't look like F.B.I. with his black jeans, black sweatshirt and windbreaker and leather cowboy boots.

He spoke four languages—Spanish, English, French and German. He was married with two infant twin daughters. He and his wife resided in El Paso, Texas where his wife owned and ran a nightclub/restaurant. He was a soldier of fortune, a secret *undercover spy*, a cowboy/rancher, *and* husband and father—what a lethal combination. How he kept it all together was his own guess.

The Bullet, known to the government and Navy Intelligence as Retired Lt. Cpl. Samuel Chase St. James was a southern boy born and breed. He was born and raised in southern Mobile, Alabama, thirty-two, with mystical cryptic hazel eyes tinted with dark orange, dirty blonde shoulder length hair, well built—strong as steel, brawn, tidy with the strength of twenty men, five-feet-and-seven-inches of nothing but pure iron.

He spoke Chinese, Italian, Spanish, French, German and English. Samuel had been, and still was, a weapons and firearm expert. He could make any weapon or bomb by hand, had in fact, faster than a normal housewife washed a load of clothes. He now resided in south-eastern Virginia Beach, Virginia where he owned and operated his own private detective agency. He was married to an elementary school teacher and they had one two-year-old son.

King of Hearts, know to the government and Navy Intelligence, as Retired Cpl. Ricardo Jordon Valentino was true-blue Italian-American. He was born and raised in the Florida Keys, thirty-six, with midnight black eyes as observant as a wild cougar, with ebony, well-trimmed hair with a slight touch of gray around the sideburns. He was vigorous—brisk, energetic, active, blithe, strong and spirited, lively and forceful, vivacious and very powerful. He was nothing but five-feet-and-seven-inches of pure unstoppable power.

He spoke Chinese, Italian, English, Russian and German. He had what some would call a special *gift* for creating bugging devices from scratch. Also an expert at computers, he could build any type bomb or explosive by hand. He now resided in Miami Beach where he worked as an A.T.F. Agent. He was married to a Miami police officer and they had one three-year-old daughter.

And last but not least, Speed—better known to Intelligence as Cpl. Anthony Trent Clements...he was African-American, born and raised in Atlanta, Georgia, thirty-five, with hard sea-breeze blue eyes, coal black hair, five-feet-and-nine-inches of nothing but pure rock-steel energy. He had the strength of ten horses—he was very brave, bold, daring, strong, gallant, valorous, adventurous, magnanimous, chivalrous, audacious, courageous and fearless.

He was known to move silent and faster than a speeding bullet; some called him *Superman.* Some called him *Breath.* Others called him *Mr. C.* But to Baron's Navy SEAL Team Squad, he was known as *friend.* He was an expert at creating any kind of diversion, and also a computer genius. He could put any hacker to shame. He still did *certain secret* jobs for the Navy now and then, and resided in Ocean City, Maryland where he was married to a novelist, with one five-year-old daughter and one infant, three week old son.

Oh, yes! Christmas seemed far, far away.

Baron glanced ahead once more as Matthew asked, "You still drink your coffee black?"

Baron nodded yes, and Matthew removed the lid. As Matthew passed him his coffee he asked, "It's good to see you again, my friend. How are your father and grandfather? Are you three still working with the horses?"

Matthew smiled, "Always. Father and grandfather are both well and said to tell you if they don't see your sorry butt sometime in the near future they'd *find you.*" After a few seconds of silence he continued, "I'm sorry about Becky and your son, my brother. You should have called. I would have come. We *all* would have come."

Regrets, Baron had more than a few. He shook his head. The taste for revenge and retribution made the coffee taste bitter, yet he sipped it anyway. "Can't change it now—it's over and done."

"We all loved Becky and your boy. You know that."

"There was nothing any of you could have done, until now." Baron turned on the radio and searched for a weather report. "I hope we don't get another bad storm. I don't want anything to go wrong to keep us from lifting off." His fingers stilled when *"On a Snowy Christmas Night"* played from the radio station. That had been his wife's favorite Christmas song.

Matthew turned his head to glance over his left shoulder at Michael. "You still legal to fly Ace's plane, Amigo?"

Michael just smiled, "Perhaps."

Baron glanced in his rearview mirror once more and asked Anthony, "You got your laptop handy, Speed?"

Anthony immediately reached inside his well-worn canvas knapsack by his feet and placed his expensive *military issued* wireless laptop in his lap. "What do you need, boss? It's charged and of course I have the right equipment so we can hook up to the Net, in a moving van, no less. Are you impressed?"

Baron sipped his coffee before answering, "Thrilled to the bone. See if there are any messages from Mitch coming through. We should have heard something from him by now."

As Anthony's expert fingers raced like warm velvet over the computer keys, Samuel lifted his hazel eyes to his old friend in the rearview mirror and asked, "You going to kill the General *before* or *after* you visit Ms. Becky's grave at Arlington?"

A hushed silence filled the van like a foreboding thing, as the question sliced through the warm air in the van like a sharp razor blade. Baron didn't waste a second to answer, "I'm not going to kill him—*we* are going to bring him to his knees and make sure he goes to federal prison for the rest of his pathetic, miserable, lying, dishonest, crooked and murderous life!"

Ricardo laughed lightly and replied, "When hell freezes over. I see it in your eyes. You want him dead…by *your* hand."

Samuel agreed with Ricardo and said, "And we all know *that* will never happen."

Baron frowned and sipped his coffee and just listened.

Michael said firmly, "No one's going to kill anyone on this mission. And it's *my* job, literally, to make sure of that fact. I'm an on-line F.B.I. Agent, for goodness sakes, and Ricardo," he glanced quickly at his friend. "…you're an expert A.T.F. Agent!"

He glanced at Baron and continued, "And you, you're a State Police Officer." He quickly glanced at Anthony before finishing, "And you, you still work secretly for the Navy, now and then. *No one's killing anyone. We protect and defend. We don't commit murder!*"

The muscles in Baron's cheeks twitched. His heart raced like a raging river, yet he remained silent.

Samuel disagreed with light laughter across his hazel eyes. "And what was that we *all* did when a SEAL? It sure wasn't babysitting or making homemade Christmas cookies for Santa!"

Michael answered, "It's called war, my friend. War is war. Murder is just that—*murder!*"

Matthew joined in the fun, "Is there a difference?"

Ricardo spoke forcefully, "It doesn't matter who or what we once were, or even what we are now—BMW's family was eliminated like they meant nothing. A five-star-General sells secret information about chemical and illegal weapons and drugs to foreign countries—it's called treason and baby-killing. And for these crimes he must pay. Whether it be right or wrong, whether it be murder or a military elimination—the General will pay in one way or another, either in death or life in prison. It's up to him. It's according to what moves *he* makes whether he goes down for good, or not."

Baron spoke up and said clearly, "No killing, only in self-defense. That's always been our motto, remember?"

Matthew turned back in his front seat and stared straight ahead. "Looks like you're going to get that unwanted snow-storm, my brother. Look," he pointed ahead to add, "…it's snowing again. Explain to me once more why you live in this wilderness some call *The Great White North*?" He reached over and turned the heater to defrost. "It's freezing in this state!"

Baron's grip tightened on the wheel as he replied, "The reason is now a woman. Her name is Merry Beth and I'm doing all of this as much for her, as well as for my son. We all know life as hard, cold, uncaring and filled with unknown dangers lurking around every corner. She knows life to be nothing but softness, warmth, loving and filled with hope, dreams, smiles, laughter, friendship, com-passion, faith and kindness."

Anthony replied, "Sounds like a lethal mix to me, boss."

All the men whistled loudly and Baron winced. "Take it easy, and settle down. We have a lot of work to do!"

Baron glanced in the rearview mirror at Anthony once more. "Is there anything coming through from Mitch and his men by e-mail?"

Anthony nodded yes as he turned his laptop off and closed the lid. "There's just one message, boss."

Baron asked, "Which is?" as he turned the radio down. It was so silent in the van, Baron shivered from its eeriness.

Elvis started to sing softly from the radio, "*I'll Be Home on Christmas Day,*" as Anthony answered, "It's a go."

Matthew smiled and sipped his creamy coffee. "See, there's nothing to worry about."

Baron frowned. "Yeah right, and I'm really one of Santa's elves! There's plenty to worry about, trust me."

His best friends teased him, and wanted to know when they'd be invited to be groomsmen at his and Merry Beth's wedding. He ignored their teasing and concentrated on his driving, his thoughts on a pair of pretty green eyes.

* * * * *

As Michael and Ricardo, both licensed pilots, settled up front in the small but impressive cockpit of Ace's eight-seat aircraft, at Bangor International Airport around 5:45 p.m., Baron and his men settled in the back to find their seats and try to catch some sleep. The snow had stopped and they were just waiting for clearance from the tower to take off.

Michael buckled himself in and glanced across the cockpit at his friend. "Hey, Ricky—you got a bad feeling about this mission, or is it just me feeling the heebie-jeebies? I don't like it—something doesn't feel right."

Ricardo shook his head no. "Your fed-friends, N.S.A. and several A.T.F. officers in several states have been after this General for years, my friend. Receiving BMW's call has ended up being our dream come true. You and I both know we're taking advantage of this mission to get on the inside; can't you hear the bells ringing? *Every time the bell rings—one more traitor goes down!* This mission is the icing on the chocolate cake, my friend. It's the opening of my entire career! We play our cards right—there's stripes and money in it. Sounds like a plan to me…you watch my back, I watch yours?"

Michael shook his head. "I don't hear no bells ringing, and my boss and the *President* wants this General stopped *yesterday!* This special Redemption Force of Captain Mitchell McMillian's must have certain—*connections* to dig up so much dirt and secret information on the General like they have, don't you think? These six men go as far back as Vietnam—if not further, and you and I both know they're connected to only God knows whom. There are so many players in this game I don't know who to trust, *friend!* It makes me feel out of my depth, and you know how I hate to feel uneasy and out-of-sorts. I get antsy."

Ricardo glanced over at him and asked, "We both know McMillian isn't just an ordinary Captain for Maine's State Police Force. You're what—*thirty*? How did *you* end up becoming a Special F.B.I. Agent? Exactly what kind of *strings* did you pull, my good *friend*, to get in on this so-called Redemption Force mission Mitchell and Baron have created...so suddenly out of the clear blue?"

Unspoken accusations zipped between the two men as they stared each other down. For the first time in years the two men stared at each other with doubt and uncertainty in the way.

Michael just frowned as he reached for the headphones to confirm their take off. "I don't know what you're talking about, *friend!* And I'm thirty-one, by the way. And I work for the Federal Government, and *my* orders come from the President; they are to bring this General down...no matter what."

Ricardo just smiled easily and said, "You don't have to get so defensive, *friend!* We *are* still on the same team, right? And the *no matter what*—does that include murder?"

As the small plane exited the runway ten minutes later, silence controlled every heartbeat and doubt on board. The four men in the back had heard the conversation between Michael and Ricardo. Baron didn't like it. He needed to be able to trust these men—*his* men, trust them with his life. If doubts were in the way then someone was going to get hurt, possibly killed.

He didn't want to come out of this mission zipped inside a black body bag. In and out, plain and simple—he winced as he settled back against his seat and closed his tired eyes. There was no such thing as plain or simple about this entire mission. Sure, the General had slept with his wife. Sure, he'd ordered Becky and his son's murders when she'd tried to pull out. But, who did the General answer to?

He or she was the one Baron was after.

It was do or die trying.

* * * * *

Earlier that same morning in Winterville around 8:30 a.m., Christmas was a great season for letting go of old hurts and moving on past the pain they inflicted. Was Baron doing just that? Merry Beth's heart worried—she couldn't help it, she loved him and wanted to help him heal *all* the wounds.

The world was dressed in a blanket of pure white, and a silent glow covered the earth with its white softness. Yet, it was cold and icy underneath, and Merry Beth shivered as she worked her way through the storm towards the post office.

She'd dropped Bethany off at Debbie's house to spend the day with Lisa, and she wanted to take advantage of her time alone, without the girls, to prepare for Bethany's birthday party.

She looked up and smiled as she walked through the door, as Barry Stone greeted her with a warm smile. "Mornin', Mrs. Waters. Cold one, eh...? Nice truck! Is it new?"

Merry Beth stomped snow off her boots and smiled. "It was an early Christmas gift from a...friend. How's Polly? I *love* the candle and green holly pieces she made for the windows at the church. They're lovely!" She dropped her stamped and addressed Christmas cards in the 'out box' with a smile. "I have a special package to mail, Barry. As usual, I need your help."

Barry walked towards the front of the small post office and asked with his strong northern accent, "Anothaaah package for sweet Bethany? Oh, yeaaaah," he turned away suddenly and reached for a medium sized brown package, "...this package came for you! It came in just this morning, from Fort Kent."

She felt reborn and smiled from ear-to-ear as she reached for the package with her right hand. She hoped it was from Baron. There were too many miles and much too much distance between them; this letting go stuff was hard. The package, if it were from him, would make him seem closer.

It seemed like forever since she'd seen him, and as she reached for the package with shaking fingers she smiled. "Thanks, Barry." She reached for her wallet and asked, "What'll it be for seven stamps and to mail this at the two-day rate?" She handed him a small package and winked.

"I want this package to be delivered to Bethany on Christmas Eve—is that possible, Barry, since it's from me? Just like we did the last two years?" The door opened and the brittle wind blew across the back of her shoulders and she couldn't help but shiver and dream about the warmth spring would bring. Someone was there; she could feel it—watching, listening to her every move. She didn't turn.

"It's for Bethany's birthday...you should see her face when she looks in the mail box down by the road and finds a package there. Her face lights up and she runs all the way back to the house!"

"For you—anything's possible, doll. Let's see..." He placed the package on his scale and weighed its content. "It's not too heavy this year—the total, including the two-ninety-four for the seven stamps comes to," he added it on a scrap piece of paper with a pencil and added, "five-twenty-four. You want this package to be put right in your mail box like last year?"

"Yes, please." Merry Beth smiled as she passed Barry six one-dollar bills. "Bethany checks the mail and will love getting a birthday package delivered from me again. You should hear her screams of delight!"

"I'll deliver it myself, I promise." Barry passed her the correct change with a smile. "Nice truck, I wantaaah get the wife and I a new one in the spring."

"Thanks, Barry. Have a good day," Merry Beth said with another smile. "Tell Polly I want to buy three pies from her own batch—order me two apple and one blueberry, would you? I'll stop by the diner to pay for and pick them up Wednesday afternoon. They're gifts for friends at church, and with this broken arm and sprained but mending right wrist it's been hard to do a lot of baking this season."

Barry smiled as she turned away. "I sure will; bye-bye now. Have a great day. Stay warm! I'll make sure I tell Polly about the pies...I won't forget like I did last time—with the package, I promise!"

As she turned to leave the post office she didn't miss the tall, dark and mysterious dressed-in-all-black stranger leaning against the blue post office box outside the front door, reading the newspaper and drinking black coffee from an Irsing's take-out cup. Despite the rugged scar, he was a different man than the one she'd bumped hard into behind the church.

Although she'd spotted him around town on several different occasions since Baron had left, he was a different man from the one she'd spotted close by on several other occasions in the last few days. He was dressed in black from head to toe and smiled at her, and nodded his head in a friendly greeting as she walked quickly by, down the steps towards the walkway that led to the street. She shook her head, something wasn't right. The scar—were there two different men? No, impossible. Yet, something didn't quite fit together in her mind at that moment.

Her heart literally sped up with heated adrenaline and un-certainty from thinking of the man. *Who is he? What does he want? Is he friend or foe, enemy or ally?* As she neared her new truck she stopped dead in her quickened steps when she noticed her ex-father-in-law leaning up against her passenger side door.

He grinned wickedly at her as he tormented her by swishing a sharp switchblade back and forth in mid-air. The morning sun caught its shiny blade and made her shiver. She looked all around for some kind of back up; winced and cringed inside, knowing there was no one to help. She was on her own, when would this man ever go away for good; and facing Earl alone once more brought it all back...

The deep and sharp pain, the humiliation, the unwanted fear, the taste of uncertainty, the breath of anguish, the hint of scandal, the act of mortification, the embarrassing shame; the truth of betrayal in all the papers for everyone to read.

Letting go of her painful past with this man wasn't easy, wasn't over, and as she stepped closer to her truck—it was clear to her it was far from finished, as she reached inside her black leather purse for her father's loaded .38—time stood still, as still and as silent as death between them.

"Get away from my truck, Earl." In seconds, against all odds, she pulled the hammer down and pointed the loaded weapon at his heart with her right hand, as Baron's package fell silent to the snow near her wet boots. "You have less than five seconds to back away, or I *will* shoot!"

Earl's drunken and sickening laughter left goose bumps all up and down her arms. She hated it that she trembled with fear again. She hated it that he still held any power over her.

"My, my, my…it seems the old girl is threatening *me!* Now, I ask you Merry Beth, *why* in the world would you be pointing that gun at me like that? What can you do to me *with only one arm?* I ain't breaking the law. I'm just standing here, as any good citizen has the right to do, waiting to go inside and pick up my mail. Now, I ask you, what's the harm in that?"

He taunted her with sneer and mockery in his quiet yet husky and stern voice. "What's that silly little law that states we still have the right to 'bear arms'? You have your gun and I have my knife. So, now, my sweet daughter-in-law…is there any difference between you and me?"

Merry Beth swallowed her fear and alarm, and didn't back down. "You're breaking my restraining order. Get away from me and get away from my truck. I mean it, Earl. I will shoot. I see the knife, and I know it's a threat. You want me gone so you can get your grimy hands on my daughter and her father's life insurance money. Well, it's never going to happen. Not as long as I am breathing. That money is for Bethany's future education. Now…*back off.*"

Earl laughed wickedly and stepped closer, almost tripping to the snowy ground in his drunken state. "I think not, my pretty but *stupid* daughter-in-law. I think not. Don't you get it—you're going to die! You owe me; remember? You stole my entire life; you *bitch*, and now you're gonnah finally pay!"

Psalms 27:1 "The LORD *is* my light and my salvation; whom shall I fear? The LORD *is* the strength of my life; of whom shall I be afraid?"

Chapter Eleven

Luke 2:17-19 "And when they had seen *it*, they made known abroad the saying which was told them concerning this child. And all they that heard *it* wondered at those things which were told them by the shepherds. But Mary kept all these things, and pondered *them* in her heart."

Miracle #10, love, December 22ⁿᵈ, Tuesday, 9:12 a.m.

"MERRY BETH, TELL me the rest of the story! *What happened after Earl stepped away from your truck closer to you?*" Debbie asked for the second time, as she helped fold Merry Beth's laundry. She stared at the piles and piles of unfolded clean clothes in disbelief.

"Goodness, girlfriend, how long has it been since you folded clothes?" She blew her brown bangs out of her eyes and reached for another crumpled towel.

Merry Beth held up her cast and grinned. "Ages…"

Debbie rolled her eyes and said, dramatically, "All right, let me get this straight. You stood there like a *cold-stone* statue pointing your father's loaded .38 at his heart. The snow fell *silently* from the sky all around you. Your heart *thundered* in your chest as adrenaline pumped through your icy veins. Earl *threatens* you as he steps away from the curb onto the snowy sidewalk. He starts to stagger *slowly* towards you—closer, closer, closer, closer, threatening, powerful, evil, and darkness *loomed* nearer with his raised knife, and *what? What happened next?*"

Debbie placed the folded towel in the huge stack piling up on the kitchen table and reached for another. "Goodness, Merry Beth. I guess you don't need towels for Christmas!"

Merry Beth roared with laughter. "Honestly, you sound like a murder-mystery novelist, or something. Ever thought about writing a book? For you—it would be a natural."

Merry Beth chuckled and reached for her hot cinnamon tea. "What do you suppose Lisa and Bethany are doing up there? That music is loud enough to wake the dead. But, it's okay really—I *love* the Chipmunks!"

Merry Beth and Debbie both glanced up at the ceiling, Debbie covered her ears and Merry Beth laughed and they both said at the same time, "Not!"

"*Merry Beth Waters!*" Debbie threw the towel down she held in her hands and put her hands on her hips.

"You're eluding my questions. *And* you haven't told me what was in Sergeant Williams' package yet." She stopped long enough to sip her creamy coffee before she said, "Come on and please tell me the rest. If you don't right this very moment, that's it. I'm returning your Christmas gift for a full refund!"

"All right, honestly! I'm only teasing you. Let's see, Earl staggered closer and two things happened at once. I'm not really sure which, but the stranger—the dark, scary, mysterious one dressed in black—he's a different man than the one I bumped really hard into behind the church Sunday morning," she shivered and added, "...that jagged scar gives me the willies—*he*, can you believe it, came from out of literally nowhere!" Merry Beth's eyes were as big as saucers as she told her story.

"He did? Wow!" Debbie glanced into Merry Beth's darkened green eyes with worry and confusion. "Is this a good thing or a bad thing? You sure there's *two* different men? I'm confused..."

Merry Beth reached for her blueberry muffin, licking her lips because it was smothered with real butter. "*Good!* Well, he didn't *exactly* come from out of nowhere—I passed him as he was leaning against the blue post office mailbox just outside the doorway, reading the paper and drinking coffee. Anyway, in *seconds*, Earl's knife was lying in the snow. Then the nice man..."

"Nice man? Who are we talking about now, Merry Beth?" Debbie interrupted her story by holding up her left arm. "You're confusing me here...and I bet it's on purpose!"

"The dark stranger is now a *nice* man, Debbie—*aren't you listening?*" Merry Beth laughed lightly and tried her best to fold a stack of underwear and socks with one hand.

"He is?" Debbie looked at her best friend in utter confusion and reached for the crumpled towel stack once more.

"Yes! In *seconds* he disarmed Earl and had him backed hard against my new truck—choking the very life out of him. You should have seen it. Earl actually turned green! His face was the color of summer-grass when it hasn't gotten enough rain. It was absolutely fabulous. The man in black is now my friend, my hero, my very own Rambo come to my rescue!"

Merry Beth shook her head and blew out her breath. "Whew, I think I've been watching too many movies!"

"He is?" Debbie swallowed a sinful giggle. "Oh, I wish I could have seen that old nasty Earl turning green like that! It must have been…"

A loud thumping on the ceiling above them caused Debbie to yell, "*Quiet down you two! It sounds like you're tearing down the house up there!*" Quiet reigned after that.

Merry Beth glanced at the ceiling and yelled, "Anything gets broken; you're both in trouble, Bethany! I mean it!"

Debbie and Merry Beth resumed their folding. "The mystery man with the jagged scar on the left side of his face saved me from Earl's attack. Anyway, just as he bent to pick up the shiny switchblade, Deputy Hugh Masters drove by and immediately, upon observing the situation and seeing Earl so close to me and seeing me pointing a gun at him, stopped to assist." Merry Beth sighed heavily in frustration.

"Oh, Debbie, it's just next to impossible to fold clothes with one hand. I can't wait to get this cast off my left arm!"

Debbie moved the huge stack of folded towels to the sideboard, out of their way. "It's only been twelve days, Merry Beth. You have six weeks to go."

Merry Beth enjoyed chewing another bite of her blue-berry muffin. She loved it every time Debbie brought her some. "Oh, thanks a lot! I'm going to need your help with Bethany's birthday party big time! How can I blow up balloons and make the cake and wrap gifts and make goodie-bags with one hand?"

Debbie sipped her creamy coffee once more. "No problem. Now, Earl *was* arrested again and thrown in jail?"

"Well…no," Merry Beth whispered and didn't dare meet Debbie's shocked eyes for the first time ever.

"No! What do you mean—no! Why not…?"

She already feared she'd made another mistake. "It's *Christmas!* You know, the season of hope and forgiveness?"

"Merry Beth, what did you do?" Debbie asked with hands on her hips. She wore jeans and white sweater and black boots. Her hair was curly but braided in a French-braid to her scalp.

"I told the deputy to let him go," Merry Beth confessed.

Debbie's heart pounded. "Oh, Merry Beth—are you *crazy?* That man is a lunatic, a nut-case, a psychopath!"

"I can't explain it Debbie, but I don't feel fear or frightened of Earl anymore. I did at first—but then something inside me just snapped when I pointed that gun at him. It's like I've been released from any power he once held over me. I have finally let go of all of it—the past is just that, *the past! He can't hurt me anymore. No matter how much he threatens or bullies me.* And that man," Merry Beth sighed and reached for her hot tea.

"The *nice* one…?" Debbie asked, as she finally finished folding another huge stack of towels.

Merry Beth smiled. "Yes, he's a friend, Debbie. I don't know how I know it—I just do."

Debbie started folding cords and jeans next. "You think Sergeant Williams brought him here to keep an eye on you?"

"Yes." Merry Beth smiled. "He's here to help me, I just know it. He saved me from another one of Earl's attacks. For that I'll be forever grateful. If it came down to his life or mine, I would have hated it but would have pulled the trigger."

Debbie met grass-green eyes to ask, "You think *he* is the same man who's now living next door?" She rolled her eyes at the large stack of blue jeans and dark flannel shirts that needed folding. "You sure all of this got dirty in *one* week?"

Merry Beth giggled. "Yes. You said so—the man Todd rented the apartment to had a scar on his face. Well, the man who rescued me from Earl this morning definitely has a scar on his face. It has to be the same man…right?"

Debbie frowned. "I don't know—what *is* the truth?"

Merry Beth shivered. "Without the truth—aren't we power-less to stop whatever *it* is from happening…*if* this guy with the scar is indeed my enemy…I mean, my friend…I mean…?"

"Merry Beth, you're talking in riddles again!"

The loud thumping started up again and Debbie yelled towards the ceiling, *"Knock it off up there! No quiet—no Mall, no ice-skating, no eating out and no Christmas shopping…I mean it!"*

Quiet ruled after that and both women laughed. Merry Beth pointed to the huge stack of unfolded clothes and said, "Pass me that stack of washcloths. I *can* fold those with one hand. Anyway, I came home, and as Baron promised, men came to install my new security alarm system. And to answer your question a moment ago, I haven't opened the package yet."

All fear and attempted attacks forgotten, Debbie searched for Merry Beth's eyes. "Merry Beth…?" She grinned; telling Merry Beth she was up to mischief again.

"Can we open the package now?" Debbie playfully got down on her knees, bent in front of Merry Beth on the cold vinyl floor and begged her over and over.

"Please, please, please, please—can we *please* open it? We could just take a quick peek to see what's inside. Then, we could be good little girls and wrap it back up again and stick it under the tree. No one would *ever* know. It'll be our very own tiny-teeny, little, tiny-weenie, itty-bitty secret." She crossed her heart with a huge X. "Come on, girlfriend...*please?*"

"God would know, and shame on you. You're terrible." Merry Beth pushed playfully on Debbie's shoulders. "Get up. You're making *my* knees hurt!"

Debbie stood and resumed her folding. "When I was a little girl—our girl's age—I used to sneak and peek and shake just about every gift under the tree in curiosity. Remember? Mama used to hide three-fourth of the presents until after I had gone to bed on Christmas Eve." She laughed, as she told her treasured secret. "Come on, girlfriend. Let's do it—let's be wild and adventurous and daring. Let's peek and then not tell!"

"No! Like me, you'll have to wait until Christmas, Debbie. Honestly, you're as bad as Lisa and Bethany. Speaking of which, I better get up there and see what the little munchkin's are up to. They're banging loud on the ceiling again."

Debbie chuckled. "Our girls—we *have* to love 'em!"

Merry Beth hugged her dear friend. "They're exactly like we were when we were little. Scary, eh...?"

Debbie pretended to shiver, and smiled as she followed her best friend from the kitchen. "Come on, Merry Beth—let's open Baron's package!"

"No!"

"Yes!"

"*No!*"

"*Spoil sport!*"

The lifetime best friends rushed upstairs to check on their daughter's to see what kind of mischief they were into this time. In minutes the four were laughing and giggling up a storm. It had been years since Debbie and Merry Beth had joined in on a feather pillow-fight. There were white feathers everywhere in Bethany's bedroom! There were feathers in their hair, in their eyes, all over the carpet and bed. It'd probably take weeks to clean up the mess, but who cared!

* * * * *

At Arlington National Cemetery, in Washington, D.C., at 9:12 a.m., Baron stood like a stone—unmoving, cold, frozen, as if hardened into ice, and chilled to the bone as he stood in front of Becky's white marble headstone. Blue snowflakes fell all around him, silently. Blue memories sifted inside his head and his heart literally shattered one more time. How was that possible? Hot tears glistened across his dark lashes as he...let go.

Almost three years were past since he'd stood in this very spot. And he was surprised to feel nothing but release. He was relieved to feel that heavy weight lift off his shoulders. He was happy to feel a serene and gentle peace wash over him. It was over—the lies and deceit and betrayal called his marriage.

And now, as he stood in the cold and brittle wind, alone, staring down at his wife's dark grave covered with ice and snow, he dreamed of the white Christmases to come. Just like the ones he used to know from his childhood, and in the first years of his marriage—before death and destruction and betrayal had come knocking at his front door, unheard and unseen invited in.

The past Christmases where the treetop always glistened with that bright shining star or angel, where he always listened to hear Santa's magical sleigh bells in the snow on the roof-top, where the days were always merry and bright, where the mistletoe hung silently waiting to capture two people in love underneath—his parents or him and Becky, where presents waited impatiently under the tree for Christmas morning, where pretty lights twinkled in house windows, shops and stores—*and* in his heart, where candles' dancing light lit the way back home through a blinding snowstorm in the darkened cold window; where the world was safe and happy. The kind of world Merry Beth believed in. The world he doubted existed.

He'd be home for Christmas in Merry Beth's arms—after, after he accomplished this one last mission. Then, he could go back to Merry Beth and her sweet little daughter; then, and only then would the future be merry and bright again. He'd turn in his badge and gun and live a normal life.

He laughed bitterly. What was a normal life for an ex-cop, an ex-Navy SEAL, an ex-lawyer, an ex-State Police Officer, an ex-husband and grieving father?

Where would he go from here?

Hell-fire if he knew.

As he turned away from Becky and his son's grave, he felt free. Well, almost. He felt like he was caught between two worlds at that moment. One world was safe and secure and the other was unsure and unsteady. He felt like he was balancing on the edge of a tall rocky cliff, with one foot calling him back to Winterville, Maine, and the other leading him towards death and destruction in the rough and course waters below.

* * * * *

In Winterville, on the same day around 11:30 a.m., Debbie and Merry Beth prepared a home-cooked meal together.

"Come on, Merry Beth—spill all! This curiosity about Sergeant Williams is just killing me. He must be rich—*look at the beautiful truck he bought for you!* I'll have you know that a man doesn't buy a *friend* a Christmas present like that. He likes you, *a lot!*"

Merry Beth thought back to the one and only kiss they'd shared before he'd left to go on some secret mission to find his dead wife and son's murderer, and knew in her heart of hearts that it was true. Baron had feelings for her all right. She'd seen them in the depths of his wolf-gray eyes. But, were these feelings *love*? Did he *love* her…*need* her…*desire* her…*want* her?

"Can I tell you a secret, Debbie?" Daring to hope…

Debbie stood at the gas stove stirring a new pot of homemade beef and vegetable soup and smiled, "Oh, I just *love* secrets. What is it? Tell me, tell me, tell me; tell me!"

Merry Beth rolled her eyes towards the ceiling and stood to refill her teacup with hot water from her whistling teakettle. "Honestly! You're such a romantic at heart."

Debbie placed the lid back on the huge pot and whirled to search for her best friend's eyes. "Come on, Merry Beth—spill the beans! What's your deep, dark secret? I can't take it any more…you have to tell me before I burst!"

Merry Beth stepped closer to her lifetime best friend and whispered with a warm smile, "I love him. And, he's coming back—he *will* be here for Bethany's Christmas concert and play on Christmas Eve. He'll be here for Bethany's birthday party—*I just know it!* And I just know Bethany will get her special wish for a new *earth*-daddy. I feel it in my heart."

Miracles were still in the making in Winterville, Maine.

Debbie reached for her best friend and hugged her tight. "Oh, honey, I hope you know what you're doing, for your sake and Bethany's. I hope you're right about him. Despite the happiness I see in your eyes—I'm still uneasy about him."

In Merry Beth's safe world, life was filled with wonderful surprises, warm happy sunshine, graceful colorful rainbows and flowers in a spring garden with no weeds, smiles and friendship, compassion and giving, hope and trust, shining stars and glowing angels—*she* knew where to look to find all these things.

God's love, mercy and forgiveness were the key.

Without *Him*, life wasn't worth living. What would anyone have to live for?

* * * * *

In Washington, D.C., in the White Pine Restaurant on New York Avenue Northeast, Baron glanced at his gold watch, 6:21 p.m., then across the dining booth table at his boss. Was he a friend he could trust? Mitch looked tired, worn and just plain old worried. He could feel something was wrong and asked quietly, "Are you all right? You don't look so good…"

Mitch reached for his coffee and answered, "I'm fine."

"Have you heard from Carolyn in Long Island?" Baron took another bite of his medium-rare Prime-rib steak.

"Yes. She's fine." Mitch pushed away his baked haddock dinner, half eaten, quickly turning cold.

"What's wrong?" Baron signaled for his coffee to be refilled as their waitress whisked quickly by near their table.

"Nothing, why do you keep asking me that…?" Mitch rubbed his tired eyes. "It's getting on my last nerve!" He grinded his teeth, anxious and a whole lot nervous.

"Because I know you, and something's wrong." Baron smiled as their waitress filled both cups with fresh black coffee. He waited until she'd walked away before continuing, "Come on, Mitch—talk to me. Is this about the sudden change of plans? Because I tell you honestly, I was a little skeptical and nervous about trying to bust into C.I.A. Headquarters in Langley. It's doable, but next to impossible. You're absolutely *sure* that the General will be at that condominium on K-Street Northwest tonight? What if he doesn't show? What if we're all in place and he doesn't come home when he usually does?"

"I'm sure. Don't mind me, I'm just tired. I can't wait for this mess to be over with." Mitch avoided looking into Baron's eyes, and stared at the blinking white lights in the restaurant windows that faced the cold, dampened, foggy and rainy street.

"You *do* know that once Michael and Ricardo arrest the General, in reality— it will only be the beginning, Mitch. There will be inquiries, court dates set, trial dates set, testimonies, motives revealed, opportunities questioned, alibi's researched, depositions…" Baron paused to take in a long breath. He rubbed his temples where a threatening headache thundered.

Mitch shook his head and asked, "Have you ever heard of a man by the name of Daniel Anthony Turner?"

At that moment Vince Gill sang from the music box near the kitchen double-swinging doors, *"Breath of Heaven,"* and Baron smiled, liking the song tremendously.

Their waitress waltzed by and he waited to ask, "No. Who is he?" Baron asked as he sipped his black coffee.

Mitch added sugar and cream to his coffee. "He was an undercover F.B.I. Agent, based in Chicago; it seems he once was buddies with your friends Michael Pierce and Ricardo Valentino. *And* there seems to be another major player in this little game to indict members of this mysterious so-called deadly, militia *Alliance* that moves across our land." He lit a cigarette and Baron frowned and suddenly lost his appetite, pushing his plate away.

"Who's the player? And since when have you joined the idiot-class and started smoking again?" Baron asked with a frown, hating it that getting information out of Mitch was like pulling teeth. "You said *was* an agent, does this mean he's dead?"

Mitch's hand trembled as he lifted the cigarette to his lips.

"Put that thing out—you'll draw attention our way. There's no smoking in here—you know that!" Baron thundered.

Mitch crushed out the lit cigarette on his dirty dinner plate. "She's ex-D.E.A., and her name is Sarah Annette Mitchell—ever heard of her?"

"No. Why? What do these people have to do with the General, and what's all this have to do with what we're working on? What's the connection?" Baron asked as he pushed his half-eaten steak dinner plate away, losing his appetite.

Mitch remained silent, distant, as if his thoughts were a million miles away. "Why do I suddenly get this nagging suspicion in the pit of my gut that you're about to tell me things I don't want to hear... *again?* What is it, for goodness sakes? Just spit it out!" Baron demanded, frustrated to no end. Something was wrong; he could feel it in his soul. Why was Mitch holding things back?

Baron's hands started to itch, and that meant one thing—trouble with a capital T. "You're making me nervous and uncertain, Mitch. And I *hate* feeling that way. Are you in some kind of trouble you can't seem to get out of?"

Two waitresses rushed by their table before Mitch met Baron's eyes to answer quietly, "Ms. Mitchell worked deep... real deep undercover for almost an entire year to bust a man by the name of Steven Matthew-Charles Kelly—his... businesses were home-based in Chicago. In the drug cartel world he was known as *Smack.* Kelly ordered the hit for her twin brother's murder—he was also D.E.A. The top man Kelly worked for was none other than..."

"Ah, let me guess... General Madison. You said *was*—is this Kelly character dead or in prison?" Baron asked quietly.

Mitch didn't lower his eyes. "Dead, shot in the forehead by an Assassin—*Queen*, his very own brother, a little over seven months ago on May seventh at St. Paul's Church in downtown Chicago. F.B.I. Agent, Daniel Turner was also shot, as well as D.E.A. Agent, Sarah Mitchell that night…"

Baron winced and sipped his coffee before asking, "And? Come on, Mitch…you're holding stuff back. I can see it in your eyes—just talk. I'll do my best to help you."

"Agent Turner was shot three times—twice in the chest and once in the head. He's dead, I'm afraid, and Ms. Mitchell was shot in the back trying to save her father from being shot—who is now a retired Lieutenant for the Drug Enforcement Agency, home-based in Chicago. Ms. Mitchell went through months of rehabilitation at Walter Reed and then just…disappeared."

Baron's eyebrow lifted. "Disappeared or…murdered?"

Mitch sipped his fresh coffee. "Contacts that your men have, Michael and Ricardo, said Ms. Mitchell is now a truck driver. She bought a new rig and is on the road most of the time with her partner and friend, a woman named *Cat*. They haul fruit."

Several men walked by their table and Mitch and Baron sat in silence until they were alone once more. "What's all this got to do with us, Mitch?" Anger boiled inside Baron; knowing his boss was keeping important secrets from him, and his eyes turned to a dark shade of gray. He hated secrets. He hated mistrust!

"Turner and Mitchell worked for my boss—D.D.O. for the F.B.I., Senior Agent Samuel Nelson. I'm F.B.I., Baron. Nelson and I have worked for months—*years* to bring this man Kelly to an arrest and trial, and now…" Mitch didn't back down and his eyes remained locked on Baron's across the table.

"Now…?" Baron was an intelligent man, and it didn't take much to figure out what Mitch wanted. He glared into his hazel eyes filled with deception and lies. "You've lied to me. From where I come from—*friends* don't lie to each other."

Mitch stared at Baron, straight in his creamy-gray eyes; regret clouding his vision. "Now that Kelly is dead…"

Baron never even flinched and didn't look away or back down from his questioning. "Now you have a chance to bring the top notch in—the General. Why the lies and secrecy…?"

Mitch had the grace to flinch. "I followed your friends today, Baron. You'll never guess where I ended up."

Baron sat back against the black leather booth and crossed his arms over his broad chest. "Oh, do tell—you're sure filled with pleasant little surprises tonight, Mitch. Your name *is* Mitchell McMillian, isn't it? And why are you posing as a Maine State Police Officer in *Fort Kent, Maine* of all places? What's really going on here?"

Baron wished for a cigarette for the first time in years, but chose to send up a silent prayer instead. *Oh, dear God in Heaven—please take away my anger and help me to understand what's really going down here tonight. Merry Beth says it's easier to believe. As usual, I'm doubting again...*

Life was filled with millions of little silent secrets just waiting to be revealed. This one made Baron's stomach nauseous.

"Yes, my name is Mitchell McMillian, and I've been working in Fort Kent to bust major players in the General and Kelly's organization. There are men and women who have been transporting both illegal drugs and stolen weapons over the Fort Kent/St. John River border, Baron. They're major players in the games we call drug-running, and the illegal sale and distribution of stolen weapons, worldwide. Kelly has brothers still out there, brothers who are known assassins and evil terrorists'..."

"You know who they are—just find them and bring them in. You have names, photographs, fingerprints on them?" Baron asked.

Mitch shook his silver head. "It's not that simple..."

"Nothing in life is. Come on, Mitch. Talk to me!"

Mitch's eyes finally dropped to the red-and-white checkered cloth tablecloth. "I was sent to Fort Kent to keep an eye on you..."

Busted! Baron's anger boiled and he hissed, "You brought me into this private little hell-war when you showed me that file at Dunkin' Donuts in Winterville, Mitch. You *knew* I wouldn't be able to back down and look the other way once I read it. *These men you and Nelson are after—the General, Kelly's unknown brothers...they killed my wife and son—didn't they? This General—tell me—tell me who signs his paycheck, Mitch? Who...?* Spill it all, *friend...* we aren't leaving here until you do!"

Mitch leaned over the table closer. "Keep your voice down. Your wife ended up being caught right in the middle of all this un-stoppable hell-drug-blood-war madness!"

Mitch looked away from his friend to glance outside at the pouring rain hitting the window and icy pavement. He knew that the terrible truth wouldn't set Baron free. The truth would only destroy what was left of his shattered heart and life. Suddenly he wished he were anywhere but here sitting across from Baron's black-turned-gray, angry, tell-me-or-I'll-strangle-you eyes.

"It's all an unstoppable game, you know—all of it."

"Where did you end up today, Mitch?" Baron's jaw twitched in his anger. "Tell me the truth, I deserve that much."

"I followed Special F.B.I. Agent Michael Pierce and A.T.F. officer Sergeant Ricardo Valentino—*your* Navy SEAL Team buddies, In-House." Mitch turned back and searched Baron's gray eyes, begging for forgiveness for keeping the truth from his good friend for so long.

Baron sat back in his seat and rubbed his pounding temples. "You were inside the White House? You know we're all tied to Capital Hill in one way or another—what's your point? We all have…or did have In-House clearance."

"I, too, have certain—*friends*," Mitch whispered as he reached for his cooling creamy coffee. "Who do you think Nelson and I work for—we answer to the *President*, Baron? We answer to him and him alone. We take our orders from him and him alone."

Baron shook his head, yet didn't lower his eyes. His chest hurt. Too many people he'd trusted had lied to him. He hated lies!

"I can see that you do. And this mess isn't unstoppable, Mitch. *I* am going to bring it down. I've had enough of all your silly games—*Washington's silly games! And where I come from—friends don't lie to one another!* I'm out of here…and you can go jump off the nearest bridge!"

Mitch reached across the table and grabbed Baron's right arm when he stood abruptly to leave. "Keep your voice down! One person can't stop the madness, Baron. It's going to take a thousand men and women, just like you and me *and* your dead wife, to stop the hatred, the violence, the crime, the drug and weapons smuggling, the terrorists' that maim and kill and destroy lives! Terrorists' that will and do try to destroy the very foundations this nation was built upon—what is it that they all want—with their C-4, their own blood, our planes that turn into murderous weapons—to take away our freedoms, Baron! Don't you see?"

Baron yanked his arm free from Mitch's grip. "All I *see* is that someone else I trusted…*lied to me!*"

Both men sat still in silence until Baron added, "And the murder—let's not forgot to mention the murder. What do you think it was that happened when those four planes went down on 9-11? It was murder, plain and simple. I've killed men, Mitch—while in the SEALS. You killed men when in Korea and

Nam. So, tell me, what makes us any different from the General or any of Kelly's assassin or terrorists' brothers?"

The muscle under Mitch's right eyes twitched. "The color of our hats…"

"What's going on, Mitch? Talk to me," Baron demanded once more. "Tell me the truth or I'm going to strangle it out of you bit by miserable pathetic bit!"

"I *am* talking to you—now—tonight! *Before* we go in there and bring this animal to his knees. I have a life, I have a wife, children, grandchildren, a family; I do not want to be taken out of there in a black body bag. Ex-D.E.A. Agent, Sarah Annette Mitchell was shot because of information she'd stored on a disc once. Don't you see? It's all about the bloody information. What did you do with the disc I gave you, Baron? Where is it?" Mitch demanded with thundering hazel eyes as he rubbed his own throbbing temples like he was in severe pain.

"I, too, had a wife, a son, a family! And they are dead because of men like this General and Steven Kelly and his nameless, faceless brothers! I don't want to be walking in on some kind of ambush tonight, *and* I'd like to know all *our* men are clean, and *all* working for the same goal, and on the same team. I know my men are clean as bleach—*are yours?"* Baron demanded just inches from Mitch's flushed-red and angry face.

"You won't, and they are," Mitch whispered confidently. "You can trust me and my men, Baron—I give you my word."

"Why don't I believe you?" Doubts sailed quickly across Baron's thundering and bitter creamy eyes. He felt betrayed, left in the dark; he didn't work that way, ever! It was time to go.

"I can't really help what you believe." Mitch reached for his suede jacket and gray Stetson, preparing to leave. He glanced at his silver watch. "It's late…it's time to move."

And life moved on. The music box blared with Celine Dion's *"That's the Way It Is,"* and despite the cold, hard facts about the cruelty and darkness and evil in the world, laughter erupted from the next booth. Its joyful sound and the lethal glare Baron passed his way made Mitch flinch in his seat, as if he'd been slapped hard across his face. Baron stared across the table in disbelief. "Who *are* you?"

Mitch reached inside his vest pocket for his wallet to pay for his meal. As he opened it and removed a twenty he answered, "Nelson and friends inside the White House call me *The Shadow.* Carolyn calls me sweetheart. My men and you call me friend. We are, aren't we? Still friends?"

Creamy eyes clashed with ebony across the booth table. "I don't know,

Mitch. You tell me. *You* opened all this up in my face, Mitch. *You!*" Certain facts started to click in Baron's clever mind and the anger he felt across his chest buried him.

Mitch—being F.B.I. and working undercover to keep an eye on him because of his ties to Becky. Mitch—working directly with the D.D.O. of the F.B.I.— who worked directly with the President. Horror, as gray and as fierce as his eyes, thundered through his heart like the thousand wild stallions running wild and free on Whispering Wings grandfather's ranch in Texas.

It all seemed unreal suddenly; forlorn, desolate, wretched. He wanted out so bad it tasted like crushed diamonds on his tongue. Baron let his anger control his emotions and actions as he reached across the table in a quick flash, and grabbed the front of Mitch's suede jacket and pulled him forward across the table. Their faces were but a few inches apart, and as the last of Baron's control snapped their coffee spilled all over the table. Their dirty dinner dishes fell to the floor in a broken crash.

"Who ordered my wife to sleep with this General Madison? *Who...?*" Baron thundered with clenched teeth. "You have five seconds to answer me truthfully, Mitch, or I swear there won't be nothing left of this restaurant when I'm done taking out my sweet revenge for Becky and our son's death on your lying hide. Now talk, and I want the truth—*who?* Tell me, or so help me God—I'll slit your lying throat!"

Mitch paled and hissed, "Get your hand off me, now!"

When Baron calmed down a little and realized they were drawing attention from several restaurant customers and employees, he let go of Mitch's jacket and sat back in the booth once more.

"The President's National Security Adviser, against the President's orders, secretly ordered Becky to do what she had to do—to get information on the General and..." Mitch's soft whisper of truth echoed loudly inside Baron's skull like liquid fire, causing him to feel sick to his stomach and nauseous, lightheaded and violently alone. He swallowed the vomit back down.

In seconds Baron was up out of the booth reaching for his black leather jacket, and out the front doors of the restaurant and running. He completely ignored Mitch yelling after him, "*Baron! Come back! Please—where are you going? Baron!*"

Even though the damp and cold and rain hit him square in the face, as he rushed through the restaurant doors outside, Baron didn't feel cold. There was no way out, he felt trapped.

Baron was trapped between Becky's betrayal and the love he once felt for his *wife*, and the love he always felt for his country while wearing the uniform. And now, as a police officer sworn to serve and protect the general public, he was torn.

Was it all just a game, his life? Was it real, Becky's painful betrayal? Was his past an illusion, had he and Becky ever truly been in love? Was it all lies, every time she'd touched him? What was the purpose for every oath he'd ever taken? The beating rain froze his face and hands, as frozen as his very soul, as he whistled for a yellow taxi to stop on the busy rain-soaked and slick curb.

He was torn in two—one half loving his country and his past military life with Becky, the second half hating the very mention of her name. Hating the very country he'd once fought for. No, it just wasn't possible!

Unlike Becky, there was no way he could ever turn his back on his own. He would never do that, not in a million years. He would never do that, whether his own be his family or his country, he couldn't do it. *He* was a man of honor. *He* was a man who always kept his word. *He* was a man who honored his commitments and vows. *He* hadn't been the one to lie, to cheat, to betray; to keep lethal secrets that killed the ones you loved the most.

At that moment, as the yellow taxi left the restaurant parking lot wet curb, headed where he didn't know or care, Baron was a man who truly stood alone.

There was nowhere to turn.

His heart raced with pain and doubts.

Merry Beth—she'd help calm his rapid pulse.

Sweet, sweet, loveable and caring Merry Beth…

Was she safe on this wet and cold night?

Tears burned his eyes.

He couldn't go back to her.

Not now, not ever.

It was over.

* * * * *

At that exact moment, in Winterville, Maine, Bethany asked her mother, "Are you all right, Mommy? It's too quiet in here—can'deded we turn on the radio and listen to some pretty Christmas music?"

Bethany walked quickly into the living room wearing her pink slippers and fluffy pink housecoat, and carrying another one of her favorite stories for her mother to read.

"I brought us Sleeping Beauty for us to read tonight, Mommy. Can I sleep with you tonight? It's cold in my room. Have you seen Mittens, Mommy? I can't find'deded her."

Merry Beth loved this time of the day. She loved reading to Bethany before she closed her eyes in sleep. She smiled; there would never be any skipping parts or skipping words. Oh, no! Not for Bethany! She was too smart, and knew every line and every word in *every* book by heart.

Merry Beth shook her shoulders and head, to clear away the nagging feeling in her heart that she'd carried all day; that something was terribly wrong with Baron. She smiled as she turned away from staring out her living room window at the hundreds of different colored Christmas lights blinking in the trees and bushes, all across her lawn and down the driveway and fences and mail box.

"Your kitten is asleep on the mat by the back kitchen door, and you can listen to music any time you like, baby. What shall I put on? And yes, I'd love to snuggle close with you tonight. You can help keep Mommy's cold feet warm. I love it when you do that."

Bethany giggled. "Okay, Mommy! You're silly!"

Merry Beth put three more logs on the fire in the hearth before turning towards their stereo. It had been her father's. He'd found it four years ago on a yard sale, it was old fashioned—the oak wood was chipped in places. It was an old table-turn stereo, the kind where the top opened up to expose a radio, eight-track player, table-turn, CD player and slots to store old records and new CD's. She wouldn't trade it for anything.

"Let's make this a slumber party—for just you and me!"

Bethany sat in front of their lit and blinking Christmas tree and glanced way up to the top at the star. "Let's listen to Tweety-bird's Christmas. Mommy…?"

Christmas was a wonderful season for music and trust and snuggling close, a wonderful time for sharing dreams and God's grace and gift. As Merry Beth searched for the right CD she smiled, "Yes, baby?"

Bethany stared straight up, way up, to the top of their tree. "Do you think that Mr. Bear'ronn Will'aamms can see our bright star on top of our tree from where he is? Do you think we have enough lights outside, bright enough so he can find us again, because I really, really, really, *really* love and miss him, Mommy?"

Merry Beth chuckled as she turned on the stereo to CD and pushed the right buttons to play Bethany's Christmas 'Tweety-bird' CD, starting at song one. "Oh, yes baby. I know he can. He'll be back as soon as he can—he has an important job to do and as soon as it's over he said he was coming back." As Merry Beth turned away from the stereo she thought, *I can feel that something's not right in your world, Baron. Please be safe wherever you are, whatever you're doing, be careful. I love you—we love you! We just want you to come back, safe and at peace.*

Merry Beth settled on the old couch once more, and snuggled her feet and legs under her cherished patched quilt.

"Do you think he'll make it for my play and see me in my pretty angel costume on Christmas Eve?" Bethany stared at the blinking lights on the tree and smiled over at her mother.

"Can we light'deded some more red-and-green candles, Mommy, and pop'deded some popcorn again, and watch 'One Magic Christmas' again?" Bethany asked, her bright eyes twinkling as bright as the lights outside and on their tree.

Merry Beth smiled as she rose to her feet and turned towards her kitchen. "Come on, baby. You get our drinks. I bought us some apple cider at Shop-'til-you-Drop today, and I'll pop the popcorn. This slumber party for just you and me is going to be so much fun—what do you say about that, baby? We'll sleep in our sleeping bags in front of the warm fire, we'll tell stories and stay up past midnight, we'll cuddle close and try to guess what we're giving each other for Christmas, we'll sleep late and make homemade blueberry pancakes for breakfast."

Bethany giggled. "Way cool, Mommy!"

Yes, Christmas was all about healing and giving special homemade gifts. These special moments with her daughter were moments she'd always cherish. She'd found all she needed in God's grace, her daughter's eyes and trust, and in Baron's kiss.

When they settled in the living room with a blazing fire crackling, sleeping bags, pillows and blankets side by side on the floor, cider and buttery popcorn in their laps, dressed in their nightgowns and housecoats, Bethany asked, "Can I put'deded Mr. Bear'ronn Willaamms special Christmas card on the tree now, Mommy? It's finally finished."

Bethany reached under the couch's cushion where she'd hidden the card earlier in the day. "See," she held the card up for her mother to read and added, "...it has his name on it, and a bright gold star with shiny silver glitter on it, like the one Lisa and I made for Marie for the play at church."

Loving someone as sweet and as innocent as Bethany was oh, so easy. It came natural, like breathing. She was her very own flesh and blood, her very own miracle. Thoughts of Bethany's grandfather slithered near but Merry Beth pushed them way, way back. Earl would never be a grandfather to Bethany, not as long as he drank and threatened. Thoughts of her own father made her smile. Thoughts of Baron made her sad, but she smiled anyway.

"I don't see why not, baby."

"Okay, Mommy." After Bethany placed the card on the tree and settled on top of her blanket and sleeping bag once more, she said, "I love my favorite pink-and-white blanket that grandpa gave me last Christmas. I miss him, Mommy."

Tears burned the corners of Merry Beth's eyes, but she held them back. "And I love my patched quilt that your Grandmother Waters gave me when you were first born. It's warm, and it looks like it's never going to stop snowing out there! Maybe tomorrow you can go sledding, how's that sound? Maybe we could pick up Lisa and see if she'd like to go sledding, too. It's getting late, baby—we should get some shut-eye. Before we know it—it will be Christmas. Remember, first thing—we sing *Happy Birthday* to Jesus *and* you."

Bethany's eyes glowed. "Way cool, Mommy!"

Mother and daughter kissed and hugged good-night, before Merry Beth turned out all the lights and snuggled inside her father's old sleeping bag next to her daughter on the floor.

Loving someone who was hurting and in pain—like Baron was...was hard. Especially when that special someone was far away in body, out of her physical reach. Especially when that special someone had only kissed her once, and never said the words before he'd turned and walked away.

* * * * *

Mitch and his old friends from Vietnam—Thomas, Adam, Scotty, Jack and Royce stood in a small circle, in the dark shadows of the thousands of whispering white headstones, in Arlington National Cemetery. It was 11:47 p.m. Many had been their comrades, all of which would forever be their friend. They'd waited for Baron and his SEAL Team to show in complete silence for the last hour, until now.

"They ain't coming. It's over," Thomas whispered as he lit a cigarette, his right hand shielding the lighter light.

Mitch flinched, and shivered against the chilly wind and belting, cold rain. "It seems that way."

"It's not over! Stop saying that," Jack thundered through clenched teeth. "They're coming and they'll be here. Just give them a little more time..."

"Look around you, my friends. All I see is the six of us idiots standing here in the darkness and damp rain, with our hands in our empty pockets. It's a no-show," Adam whispered huskily, angry.

"We can do this—the six of us—how hard can it be? The General's shacked up with his latest lady-lover friend in her condo on K-Street, Northwest. There's only going to be the one security guard on duty where he lives, and you *know* that I can break through *any* security code. I can even break the security code's code! Busting in the General's condo will be like pouring hot gravy over creamy homemade mashed potatoes, compared to breaking in C.I.A. in Langley," Scotty whispered close to Mitch's ear in the darkness of the midnight hour. "It's only 3.8 miles from here—we could be there in exactly 6.3 minutes and…"

Royce reached for Thomas' cigarette and yanked it out of his mouth and stomped it out under his black Army boot. "Put that thing out, Thomas. You want everyone on the Hill to see *and* smell where we are? We're not even *in* D.C. We get caught—our butt's are in a thorny sling…*alone*, if you get my drift."

Thomas snickered. "Calm down, will you!"

Royce passed Thomas a heated glare. "*You* calm down!"

Mitch roared, "All of you calm down…right now!"

Mitch turned to his left at the sound of movement near the Lincoln Memorial. "They're here." He turned his expert hazel eyes to search through the shadows and darkness.

Baron, Matthew, Michael, Samuel, Ricardo, and Anthony walked side by side silently through the night towards Mitch and his friends, slowly up the hill. The only sound at that moment was the crickets in the night, the light rain, the flapping of well-lit American and P.O.W. flags in the wind nearby, and the sound of silent footsteps on the wind of death across the wet melting snow. Fog was settling in, over the graves, around the men.

In seconds, twelve men stood eye-to-eye in the mystic, murky, dusky rain and fog and glared at one another in silence. Twelve good men—honest, loyal to family, friend and country, sharp, intelligent, extensively educated both home and abroad, trustworthy, forthright and honorable, devoted and patriotic, dependable and true, and all trained by the military—at one time or another in past or present—to kill.

Special F.B.I. Agent, Michael Dalton Pierce broke the deadly silence between the men with a whispered question, "It's a go?"

Baron let out his breath and sighed. "It's a go."

The rain beat upon the men harder, the tension in the air just as thick as the fog. Baron broke the tension that zoomed through the chilly air like a lightning bolt from the dark heavens.

"Mitch—you better be one-hundred-percent sure that the General *isn't* home. My men and I don't want any surprises sneaking upon our backs *after* we go in, and I don't want to see any man here being sent back to their family in a black body bag." His dark gray eyes searched for Mitch's hazel in the darkness, fog and rain. It was a damp and chilly night, and Baron shivered inside his warm black leather jacket.

Mitch answered, "He won't be there. I'm sure."

"No mistakes, gentlemen. In and out, as easy as whipped cream over homemade strawberry pie," Baron added quietly. His eyes lightened to gray in the misty, rainy shadows.

The men remained rigid and silent as they waited for Mitch to speak. He turned slightly and stared at the Vietnam Wall Memorial and let the glistening tears fall from his tired but alert eyes, tears that were hidden in the beating rain.

"I think we've *all* seen enough death to last us twenty life-time's—don't you?" Mitch asked quietly through the rain.

At that moment, Baron's only thought was why he hadn't told Merry Beth that he loved her *before* he'd left her. It was another regret to add to his belt. "You talking Nam or you talking the evil terrorists' disburse in *this* decade?"

Mitch lightly touched Baron's right shoulder. "Is there a difference? Murder is murder, death is death and war is war."

All twelve men turned in unison—all standing in a straight line in front of the *Wall*. And one by one they each said a silent prayer for their fallen comrades, before Mitch placed a single white rose on the cold, wet stone in front of the *Wall*. A rose that reminded the men, as Americans, that freedom didn't...*doesn't* come without a sacrifice from blood, sweat, tears and death.

Was it true what Merry Beth had said? Did love *always* direct your path home, or in her case, hundreds of different colored blinking Christmas lights? Baron hoped so, as his dark eyes scanned the thousands of names across the wet *Wall*. He couldn't help but wonder where it had all gone wrong. So many lives and families broken, so many dreams crushed; so many questions unanswered.

Every name on the *Wall* was a hero. How did it come to this?

The twelve men thought of home and loved ones at that moment, not unlike the names on the *Wall* of the men and women who'd fought and died in that hell called Vietnam, men and women who'd *never* come home again, alive and free.

I Timothy 6:7-11 "For we brought nothing into *this* world, *and it is* certain we can carry nothing out. And having food and raiment let us be therewith content. But they that will be rich fall into temptation and a snare, and *into* many foolish and hurtful lusts, which drown men in destruction and perdition. For the love of money is the root of all evil: which while some coveted after, they have erred from the faith, and pierced themselves through with many sorrows. But thou, O man of God, flee these things; and follow after righteousness, godliness, faith, love, patience, meekness."

Chapter Twelve

Luke 2:20-22 "And the shepherds returned, glorifying and praising God for all the things that they had heard and seen, as it was told unto them. And when eight days were accomplished for the circumcising of the child, his name was called JESUS, which was so named of the angel before he was conceived in the womb. And when the days of her purification according to the law of Moses were accomplished, they brought him to Jerusalem, to present *him* to the LORD."

Miracle #11, giving, December 23rd, Wednesday, 2:21 a.m.

MERRY BETH LAY motionless in her sleeping bag surrounded by the silent, moving shadows and darkness of the early hour, with only the warm moonlight shining through the living-room window to light up the dark room. The howling wind begged for entrance against the old apartment building roof and windows, the fire in the hearth long gone cold.

She turned and watched her daughter sleep; who'd had no trouble at all falling asleep and staying that way, as every creak and tiny little sound the old apartment building made kept her awake. She tried telling herself over and over that the sounds in the night were the reasons for her lack of sleep, but knew in her heart that her thoughts of Baron were solely responsible for her restlessness and troubled spirit.

So, she lay awake, and spent most of the long, quiet hours praying for another miracle. Oh, the power of Christmas and prayer. It often helped the miracles to come true!

Dear Father in Heaven—well, it's almost Christmas, another year almost gone, and still the world seems dark and lost. I thank You for everything You give me and my baby, and the power of prayer is evident in both our lives. I pray for Baron, Lord. You know? The man I was telling you about. He's in trouble, Lord. I don't know how I know it, I just do. He's hurting and trying so hard to get past the barriers that hold him back in a past that's painful, dark and lonely. He's learning how to smile again, laugh again, make friends again, find hope in his broken heart again, and he's filled with compassion and goodness and kindness.

He's learning how to trust again. Of all the wants and wishes I could ever ask for this Christmas, of all the bright shining stars You give me to wish upon—oh, and thank You for helping me let go of my fears and uncertainties because of Earl, Lord. I wish for Baron to find a way to get past his wife's betrayal, to find his way back to Winterville, Maine, to find his way back so he can trust again, love again. You have given me this chance to find love again. Help me, Lord, and show me the way so I can help Baron find the gift of living in his heart again. In Your Name I pray, Amen.

Before Merry Beth snuggled under her patched quilt and sleeping bag one more time to try and sleep, she placed four more logs on the fire. Two guardian angels, dressed in glittery white, lingered around her and one reached down and touched the tears across her cheeks as she drifted off into a peaceful and restful sleep a few minutes after her prayer. Both whispered...

"Miracles, in this world, are so hard to find..."

"Some people make themselves see what they want to see."

In another world, in Washington, D.C., twelve men were determined to make the cold and dark world a better and safer place for the children; all the children, even the lost and misplaced ones that couldn't find their way back home. What would dawn hold, for so many different people?

* * * * *

"Speed, Joker, acknowledge."

Outside the Restful Recreation Center Condominium Apartments, at 1:57 a.m., Mitch searched all around him in one huge but very careful sweep, to make sure everyone was in place, before he whispered close to the tiny microphone attached to the inside of his old Army jacket collar.

Anthony and Scotty, both experts in computers, radio equipment, surveillance and breaking through security codes, had been assigned to stay behind in one of the black vans hiding safely amongst tall maple trees, five-hundred feet away near the Anacostia River, which faced the south side of the huge and very expensive condominium complex.

Both men were dressed in their own chosen military camouflage, and both men answered Mitch's call at the same time. "Go ahead."

"Speed, exactly two minutes after Spade's go, do your magic with that laptop of yours and get us inside that sky-rise. We're all counting on you, 10-4?" Baron whispered close to his own device inside his old Navy jacket collar, as his ebony eyes scanned the beautiful and expansive quiet complex. Getting inside the building was easy; he knew Anthony's work.

Thinking about getting inside the main gate sent creepy shivers up and down his spine; he didn't know Scotty's work. "I don't want to accidentally set off any silent alarms—if you get my drift. I just want to go in, deliver the package, and get the heck out of Dodge as fast as we can."

Anthony chuckled lightly. "Take a major chill pill, BMW, and stop worrying. You're getting old, my friend, or are you just out of practice? What you want for Christmas this year, *world peace*? Ain't we working on that part, here, tonight?"

Mitch grumbled, frustrated and anxious, "Can we cut the stupid, useless chit-chat and just get on with it?"

Baron whispered, "We're waiting on you, M & M."

"Spade, on my mark, do what you do best and eliminate the silent alarm to the main gate's computer lock and I'll open the gate," Mitch ordered while glancing to his right and giving Baron the thumbs up that everything was a go in seconds.

Baron placed his fingers between his lips and gave the birdcall to the men scattered about, hiding close to the entrance of the front gate, and waited for Mitch's signal to inform them it was time to move. *Here I go, Merry Beth. Please be praying for me tonight, and remember me when I am gone away, remember me until I find my way back to your arms and sweet responding kiss...try to love me, if only for a little.*

Mitch glanced at his watch through the tiny holes in his black ski mask, and counted the seconds in his head before racing across the wet grass in the darkness and shadows the moonlight above them created through the tall trees. In seconds he covered the security guard's mouth, disarmed him and pointed his loaded, silenced military-issued .22 on his right temple.

"You blink or even dare to breathe and you're dead, understand?" Mitch's lie burned on his tongue, like fire and ice mixed together. The guard immediately shook his head yes.

Mitch lifted his left hand and quickly inserted the needle in the guard's neck. In seconds the guard fell unconscious to the floor colder than a native hard-stone. He whispered softly in his tiny microphone, "It's a go, Spade, on my mark—five, four, three, two—now...go!"

Spade did what he did best on his top-of-the-line military-issued laptop inside the van. He smiled as he watched his friends on the little screen above his head, as they raced like thieves in the dead of night, quickly through the front gate towards the front of the huge and beautiful gray-marble sky-rise. In seconds, Thomas stood guard in the security guard shack—dressed in the correct uniform to fool anyone who might pass through.

So far so good yet, each man knew at any given moment anything could go wrong. Baron's expert eyes scanned the area.

Scotty glanced quickly at Anthony's sweaty brow and smiled. "Bingo! I still got it." His fingers were steady as a rock as he reached for his black coffee.

Anthony quickly wiped the sweat from his brow and Scotty demanded, "Come on, man—get those fingers of yours moving over those keys and do your stuff. You have less than two minutes!" The game these men played this dark night was dangerous and deadly, beyond lethal, but for them it was indeed a piece of creamy chocolate-moose cake, smothered with crushed walnuts and smooth-as-butter white whipped topping.

The seconds ticked by too quickly for Baron's taste.

Revenge, vengeance, repayment and retribution lay solely in their hands—not God's, on this cold and rainy night. Oh, what a wicked web these men knew how to quickly weave. The adrenaline in each of their heart's burned hot, yet slow. They knew how to do what they had to do, to survive.

Anthony's fingers raced like light-speed across his black laptop keys and in one minute, twenty-two seconds he sighed with relief and wiped his brow again. "I can't believe how smooth this is—it's like a butterfly's wings. A few buttons here; a few buttons there…and what do you know, we're in!"

In less than the two minutes that Anthony had needed to prepare to silence the security alarm inside the front doors to the condo, the men moved forward, silently through the dark night. Mitch, Baron and the remaining seven men expertly and as smooth as Anthony's butterfly wings, worked their way unnoticed through the main gate towards the front of the tall gray-marble sky-rise.

As all nine men lined their backs against the expensive gray stone of the building, Mitch searched for Baron in the shadows and once more gave him the finger signals that everything was a go in five, four, three, two and one.

Anthony whispered, "Security cameras out, it's a go."

Before Casper could whisper 'Boo', all nine men were inside the building unnoticed. In less than the time it took to take a breath, the men scattered throughout the lobby and ground floor like fallen fall leaves in a bitter windstorm. The darkness and the shadows of the early hour swallowed them whole. Because of the hour there was no one in sight, the lights in the lobby and hallways to lead their way were dim, and the entire building was deadly quiet in sleep.

Four of the nine men stayed below on the ground level—Adam on the north wing, Mitch on the south wing, Jack on the east wing, and Royce on the west wing. Two took the north side elevator—Matthew and Samuel. Two took the south side elevator—Michael and Ricardo. And Baron, who always worked best solo, took the one and only stairway.

His feet were silent as he floated through the darkness and shadows, his mind alert. His heart remained calm as he rushed silently across the expensive gray-and-white marble shiny floor towards the stairway—reminding himself he'd done this very thing a hundred times in his career as a Navy SEAL. It was what his team did the best. In and out, just like air in an open window-screen, with a snap of the fingers, with no casualties except their *mark*, or sign they'd ever been there.

As Baron's hurried, silent footsteps finally reached the seventeenth floor less than four minutes later, he whispered into the tiny microphone, his only link to the outside world, "Silent, WW, Bullet, KOH—what's your twenty?"

Baron smiled when the four men answered that all was clear, and they were in place. But his smile instantly turned to a worried frown when he heard Thomas speak low but clearly in his left ear, "You're not going to believe this, but we got ourselves a *little* problem out here."

His fingers on his right hand lifted to his ear. "How little…?" Baron whispered, as his feet moved as quiet as a silent prayer across the red carpeted hallway, leading to the General's empty condo on the south-wing. Everything depended on getting the disc buried inside the General's condo *tonight, inside* his safe—as in yesterday!

It was too quiet. When there was no answer Baron repeated, "*How little, damn-it?*"

He knew there was enough information on the disc to bury the General and at least twenty-eight of his secret *Alliance* militia army men and women across the states. He knew they had to get the disc inside *before* N.S.A., A.T.F. and F.B.I. swarmed the condo at precisely nine a.m.—the exact time when the General was always at the condo every morning before going in to work at his office at the White House on Capital Hill. Every second counted. They didn't need any distractions.

When Thomas didn't respond Baron asked the third time, "Mr. T., how little?"

Mitch spoke clearly in his tiny microphone, "What's the problem, Mr. T.?"

Baron whispered to Anthony inside the van, "What's going down, Speed?"

Scotty answered, "We got company coming to our little private party boys! Looks like the G and his latest lady-lover friend decided to come home for a little unexpected visit after all, earlier than planned."

All the men answered to inform they knew what to do, "Affirmative."

God and angels and Christmas seemed a million miles away, as the original plan crumbled into dust. Yet, Baron just smiled; he'd learned a long time ago it was always best to have more than one way out, and more than one back up plan.

As Michael and Ricardo moved quickly and silently through the darkness and shadows to his side at the far end of the south-wing, Baron signaled with sign language they were moving on to plan B. They were putting their trust and lives completely in Mitch and his men's hands, on the ground floor to immediately cut the power to the entire building; cutting off all elevators and electricity. They knew they had to hurry, time was against them now. The white sand was running out of the glass hourglass, too fast.

Baron quickly inserted the key and whispered quietly, "Let's hope we paid for and bought the right key, gentlemen."

In seconds, the three men were inside the General's condo. Baron placed the key back in his black cords pocket and stood guard just inside the doorway to the extravagant condo, as Michael moved quickly across the spacious living room immediately to the library where the General's secret safe lay hidden under the Persian carpet in front of the fireplace hearth. Ricardo moved quickly towards the right corner of the living room towards the General's personal, extremely expensive home computer.

The amount of money Deputy Director for the F.B.I. in Washington, D.C., Samuel Nelson had paid for the information stored on the disc was more than Baron would ever see in thirty lifetimes. He doubted he could count that high.

The condo was very spacious, rich-lush and breathtakingly beautiful with expensive red, blue and green Persian rugs and carpets covering shiny hardwood pine floors. The shiny and as-smooth-as-glass baby-grand-white-piano sitting quietly in the left corner of the large living room sat still and soundless. The very expensive black leather sofas and chairs sitting in the middle of the room facing the wall made of glass sat empty and noiseless; this wall of glass completely took up the back of the condo living room, overlooking the Anacostia River on the south side.

Baron wasn't impressed with the expensive carpets and antique tables and crystal lamps, nor the chandeliers of crystal, glass and diamonds—all sparkling, and beautiful, and glistening silently in the moonlight hanging above his head in the room.

He had learned from Merry Beth that material things weren't what mattered in this life. Just thinking of her calmed his thundering heart, as he stood in tranquility in the shadows thinking, *Oh, my pretty flour snowbird, there are so many things I want to give you—starting with pulling you into my arms for another one of those warm hugs and tender, tempting and binding, sexy kisses…*

His swarthy eyes scanned the room. The expensive silver coffee-and-tea-set sitting on a silver tray near the sofa sat empty and cold. The floor to ceiling bookcases, lined with every novel imaginable, surrounded the entire living room. The antique priceless coffee table in front of the huge black leather sofa was as smooth and as shiny as a newborn baby's bottom. The painted art hanging from every wall he knew to be priceless. The impressive sixty-inch television and very expensive top-of-the line stereo and speakers sat mute and silent. Everything inside the huge condo smelled of laundered or stolen, embezzled money, and Baron felt a tight knot in the bottom of his empty stomach.

It was blood money.

It was illegal drugs and stolen weapons blood money!

It was dirty and laundered money stolen by a traitor!

He wanted no part of this kind of life. The life he wanted was back in Winterville, Maine inside Merry Beth and Bethany's eyes. They were two people he *knew* he could trust to never lie to him or betray his trust.

Baron prayed, at that very moment, for another miracle to make it out of here alive. He knew it was up to himself, Michael and Ricardo to complete this mission. Planting the incriminating disc would put a stop to General Madison's reign of terror and power and nationwide *Alliance*—hopefully forever. Maybe, just maybe, ex-D.E.A. Agent Sarah Mitchell's murdered twin-brother and murdered F.B.I. partner could now rest in complete peace.

Merry Beth and Bethany's stunning smiles flashed across his alert ebony eyes, as he scanned the expensive living room. At that moment he again regretted not telling her that he loved her before he'd left her, and promised himself if he made it out of here in one piece, it would be the first thing he told her when he looked into her emerald eyes again.

This would be his last mission. His plans to turn in the badge and gun tickled his spine and made him shiver. He wanted to end it—now, tonight. He glanced at his Military issued Rolex. Too much time, they were wasting too much time!

His somber eyes turned to his friend across the living room secretly stealing important, vital information from the General's personal computer files, and as he counted the seconds silently inside his head he knew they needed to hurry faster. Time was up. Sweat dripped down his left temple down his chin. He quickly wiped it away before it dropped to the carpet.

Baron glanced at his expensive gold watch again, and frowned, before whispering in the tiny device attached to his Navy jacket collar once more, "Silent, is it a go? Are you in?"

Michael immediately answered, "Negative. This could take a few minutes…"

Baron glanced across the dark and shadowy living room once more at Ricardo working his magic, as his fingers flew across the General's home computer. "KOH, are you in?"

Ricardo's fingers didn't stop moving across the computer keys as he answered, "I'm in."

"Silent, company's coming in the next few minutes. What's taking so long, damn-this-entire-mission-to-Satan's-hell?" Baron's heart pounded wildly in his chest, as lava adrenaline pumped quickly through his veins. He would not rest easy until they were all out of here…alive and in one, healthy piece. They were moving too slow. He feared the mission was going to be a bust, any second now.

At that moment on the ground floor, Mitch held his silenced Army issued .22 from the war tightly in his right hand, and lifted his left, gloved hand to his tiny microphone and softly whispered to the five men on the seventeenth floor. "You got company on the way up, stairway, three to five minutes." He didn't smile when his five men acknowledged his warning.

Baron swallowed his panic; knowing they were out of time, and whispered, "WW, what's your twenty, need your help in deferring the enemy."

Matthew smiled as he answered, "I'm right behind Bullet, in fifteen seconds."

Baron frowned as he stepped quickly into the library. "Make it two."

Sometimes, even a perfect plan B has a few little glitches.

Baron quickly stepped to Michael's side. "What's taking so long? We need to move and move now." He could barely hear his whisper above the pounding in his ears and heart, as he reached for his holstered, silenced 9mm Smith & Wesson. "This plan B is all shot to hell. Get a move on, would you? I'm starting to sweat here, and you all know what that means. I don't like to sweat…ever!"

Baron spoke quietly in his microphone. "We're about to get caught up here with our shoes untied, boys. The General and his lady-lover friend are on their way up the staircase. Let's pray they move really slow, 10-4?"

Every second counted…

Every breath counted…

When a plan went sour…

Michael grinned and passed Baron a thumb up sign, silently stating that he was finally inside the safe. In seconds he hid the disc inside the General's floor safe, locked it shut again, and reset both silent alarms.

"There are two separate codes to break on this mother—sorry boss—it's been a while." Michael quickly gathered his special equipment he'd used to break into the safe and break the silent codes, and stuffed them back in his black backpack. He doubled checked to make sure he didn't leave anything behind before whispering, "It's a wrap, let's move."

In seconds, Baron and Michael raced from the library to the living room where Ricardo was still floating his fingers across the General's personal home computer.

"Close up shop, it's time to move." Before Baron or Michael could blink Ricardo smiled.

The clock was ticking and they each knew if they were caught—they were as good as dead.

Michael began to pace nervously. "Come on! We're losing it! We gotta move, *now!* Acknowledge?"

"I need…five…more…seconds…" Ricardo stood while waiting for certain information to transfer to the disc he's inserted minutes before. "Got it!" He put the shiny silver CD disc back in its case, back in his pocket and immediately logged off and turned off the computer. "Let's move."

There was no soothing Christmas music, only silence at that moment. Silver bells, fluffy snowflakes on Christmas Eve, and city sidewalks dressed in holiday style were far away as the three men raced quickly towards the condo's front door.

Festooned silver and gold trees, glittery angels dressed in white lace and bright stars, and peace were non-existent. Holly leaves, hot cranberry pie, stuffed turkey and ham dinner, pretty wrapped gifts under the pine or fur tree, red and green stockings hung by the chimney's fire, lights a glow and pine mistletoe all seemed like a forgotten dream. It was all a wonderful dream, but it was beyond Baron's reach as he reached for the doorknob—it seemed in…slow…motion…

A key sounded in the lock and the doorknob moved in the dead and silence of the dark night. In a flash the three men separated in three different directions. As Baron's steps silently carried him to the hallway where he chose the first door on his right to hide, he whispered in his tiny microphone, "Abort! I say again, abort!"

Mitch frowned from below on the ground level when both Scotty and Anthony asked softly in his left ear from the van outside, "Has the package been delivered?"

Mitch didn't waste another breath to signal for Jack to restore the electrical power to the lights and elevators in sign language. Mitch, Adam and Royce waited in the dark shadows until Jack returned before the four men disappeared back outside in the darkness and beating, cold rain.

Baron closed his eyes in the blackness of the General's walk-in bedroom closet, and softly whispered, "Affirmative, package has been delivered. Mitch, get the men the hell-fire out of here!"

The incriminating disc had been planted; the trap for General Madison had been set, the President and D.D.O. of the F.B.I.—Senior Agent Samuel Nelson, slowly paced the blue-carpeted floors of the Oval Office, nervously waiting for news. And everyone made it out of the condominium building alive, safely and unnoticed.

Everyone except Baron...

It was every mission's worst nightmare come true.

A man had been left behind. Baron—a man who now stood alone again; alone to face the lethal enemy—the very man who'd slept with his wife and probably gave the order to murder her as well.

His heart pounded.

The blood in his veins pumped fast.

If he was caught, he knew he'd die from a bullet to his skull.

As Baron hid inside the huge walk-in closet, he prayed silently for yet another sweet miracle to make it out alive so he could start that brand new life he desperately craved with Merry Beth and the Munchkin, far away in Winterville, Maine.

It was pitch dark inside the closet. It was hot and his heart pounded in his ears. It was time to end it. It was time to let go. Sweat broke out on his brow as he closed his eyes and very slowly removed his wedding ring...

* * * * *

Oh, the joys of living in Maine in the winter!

"Mommy…?" Bethany asked her mother, as Merry Beth placed a warm, yellow, wool, thick sweater over Bethany's fiery red curls near 6:30 a.m. The radio announced it was just five above zero and more snow was on the way, and she didn't want Bethany to catch a cold again.

"Yes, baby?" Merry Beth smiled as she reached across the bed for Bethany's Beauty-and-the-Beast pink-and-white hairbrush to brush out her daughter's long curls. "You want your hair braided today as usual? It's hard for mommy to do it with only one hand."

"No, I think I want it in a ponytail like yours, Mommy. How many more days until Christmas…?" Bethany held her cherished Mr. Lefty close to her young heart and smiled.

Merry Beth grinned, knowing what was coming next. "Today is Wednesday, and Christmas is Friday, two more days until…"

"My birthday—how many more days until you go back to school…?" Bethany asked as the hairbrush worked magic on her waist-length red curls, leaving static in its wake. "Mommy—that feels really good…"

"I have to be back on January the fifth. I feel like it's been ages since I saw all my students. Have you missed day care?"

Merry Beth loved being a kindergarten teacher. She loved the challenges a classroom filled with twenty-one five and six-year-olds always brought into her life. She called her students her 'adopted babies' and treated every one of them like she did her own flesh and blood. With love, care, concern, warm touches, smiles and a gentle voice of learning.

"Just think, Bethany—next year I'll be your teacher. Won't that be neat?" Merry Beth tickled her daughter's ribs.

Bethany giggled and answered, "Way cool, Mommy!"

Merry Beth finished brushing. "I love you, baby."

"I love you, too—Mommy…?" Bethany asked, as she turned to smile up at her mother. She passed her mother the red- and-green barrettes and ribbons for her hair to match her special Christmas outfit of red sweater, green cords and white socks.

"What, baby?" Merry Beth set the hairbrush aside and kissed her daughter's cheek before she clasped the barrettes and ribbons Bethany had picked out for her to put in her hair. With only one hand it was hard, but she managed somehow.

"There—you look very pretty!" She began straightening Bethany's bedroom and passed her daughter several forgotten dirty socks that lay near the foot of her single bed. "Put these in the dirty clothes pile in the hallway, baby. Are you *sure* you haven't been changing clothes more than one time a day again?"

"What do you want for Christmas?" Bethany took the dirty socks and threw them in the hallway with the huge pile of dirty clothes lying in the middle of the floor. "I made'deded you a special card, Mommy, and I don't have much money—so it will have'deded to be something I can make'deded you by hand."

Bethany began picking up all her cherished storybooks and placed them in a not-so-neat pile on her little pink-and-white worktable. After she finished straightening all her books she started picking up her toys and stuffed animals and placed them one by one in her knotty-pine toy chest that her grandpa had made for her last Christmas. "I don't know how to knit or sew yet, but I could try, Mommy…I could try to make you some mittens! What color yarn do you have, Mommy?"

Merry Beth smiled and kissed her daughter's cheek. "The best gift that you can ever give someone is something you give from your heart, Bethany. Not something you can buy with money. It could be a smile, a bear hug, laughter, friendship, a kiss, or even a kind word. Or, you could give something like a pretty flower you see in the meadow, a basket of vegetables you grow yourself in the garden, or…" Merry Beth leaned over to straighten the unmade single bed, its sheets clean and its cherished yellow quilt puffy.

Bethany's eyes danced with excitement. "I know, Mommy—a basket of pears! Like the ones we gave'deded to Mr. Will'amms for his thank you gift!"

"Yes, baby. Like the gift we gave to Mr. Williams." Merry Beth stepped to her daughter and pulled her close for a warm hug. "All I want or need is you, baby—just you." She hugged her daughter close to her breast and silently added, *and Baron. I need Baron. Dear Lord, bring him home…soon!*

"Help Mommy straighten your bed and then we'll throw these dirty clothes in the hamper and after breakfast…"

"Can I go outside and play, Mommy?" Bethany asked as she placed her beloved Mr. Lefty on her pillow. "Can Lisa come over today? We still have stuff to do to be ready for Christmas."

"It's too cold to play outside today, baby. How about if you and I make some special Christmas cupcakes, and I'll call Mrs. Thomas to see what Lisa's plans for the day are, okay?"

Merry Beth smiled as she watched Bethany try to pick up most of their dirty clothes in her little arms at once. As she carried them, Merry Beth picked the fallen dirty clothes up behind her as she followed her down the hall. "You sure are helping Mommy this morning, baby. Thanks! What would we do without Mrs. Thomas' help folding all our clean clothes?"

"Mommy, do you think Mr. Bear'ronn Will'amms will come back today? Tomorrow is Christmas Eve, and I can't wait to give him his special card!" Bethany dumped the dirty clothes on the bathroom floor in one huge flop.

"We don't have all our pretty lights on during the day—how's he gonnaah see his way back here without the lights, Mommy? What can I give'deded him for Christmas besides the card I made?" Bethany stuffed the dirty clothes inside the hamper with a worried frown and little helpful hands.

Merry Beth smiled. "A kiss! Give him a big kiss when you see him again. I'm sure he'll love that. And you could give him the biggest hug around his neck...that would be *really* special."

Bethany's little arms struggled with the dirty clothes. "Oh, and don't forget, Mommy—the poems! We need to finish them today, just in case he comes back a day early. I know how I'm going to finish mine!"

"He knows the way, baby. Don't worry; if he doesn't make it by Christmas, we'll just give him his presents when he gets here. The gift of giving should be in your heart every day of the year, Bethany. Not just on Christmas. And don't ever forget what the real meaning of Christmas is. It's about God's special gift to the world and..."

"I know...baby Jesus." Bethany smiled at her mother before following her back down the hallway towards the stairs.

"That's right." Merry Beth glanced back at her daughter and asked, "You didn't answer my question before. Have you been changing your clothes more than once a day, baby? There seems to be an awful lot of dirty clothes again. Although, every time you go out and play in the snow I have to change you into dry clothes when you come back inside, but still..."

The little girl shook her head no as she passed her mother on the stairs. "Mommy, can you help'deded me finish my poem now? I'm stuck'deded on line three."

After her husband had died Merry Beth had sought the break that would make it all, all right again, in Bethany's eyes. It worked every time. When she felt alone, lonely or scared—she glanced into her daughter's eyes, she prayed, she relied on her faith to see her through by reading the Bible, God's Holy Word.

"After breakfast, okay? Do you still want homemade, blue-berry pancakes for breakfast, baby?" Merry Beth smiled, as she followed her chattering daughter down the stairs towards the kitchen. Bethany took off in a dead run and she yelled after her, "And no running in the house, Hope Bethany—I mean it!"

"I won't, Mommy. I promise'deded!"

Merry Beth chuckled as she opened her fridge for the pan-cake ingredients. "Oh, yeah, I can really tell. One of these days you're going to fall and really hurt yourself."

"Will I have a broken arm, like you, Mommy?"

Merry Beth winced. "If you stop running through the house, you won't."

Bethany gulped down her orange juice as her mother passed it to her in her favorite Sleeping Beauty glass. "I'll try, Mommy. I promise'deded!"

Merry Beth measured out the ingredients needed for the homemade blueberry pancakes by memory, in a huge blue-and-white mixing bowl. "What mommy could ever ask for a more helpful and beautiful daughter? I love you!"

Bethany giggled as she quickly put the syrup and butter on the kitchen table. "And I love you more, Mommy!"

Merry Beth turned on the radio and smiled. "Oh, it's *Silent Night* again!"

* * * * *

In Washington, D.C., inside the Northeast Pine Inn, on New York Avenue Northeast, room 317, at 7:20 a.m., Mitch stared at the group of ten men around his motel room with worry across his sweaty brow and fear in his thundering heart. "We should have never left him!"

All the men seemed to speak at once after that, leaving his temples pounding and his heart filled with regret and contrition.

Anthony walked towards the window and glanced down at the large crowded parking lot and hissed, as he watched the beating icy rain, "Baron ordered to abort. In the Navy SEAL's when ordered to abort—you abort."

Sometimes a well-thought out plan seemed simple and easy on paper, written in black and white. But in the real world, like the one they'd all faced the night before; it was deadly if compromised in any way. Every man in the motel room knew Baron's chances were slim to none, if he wasn't already dead.

Samuel stepped real close to Anthony and frowned with worry. "We ain't in the Navy anymore, and I agree with Mitch—we shouldn't have left him." He checked his firearm to make sure it was loaded and placed it under his brown leather jacket in the holster on his left shoulder. "It's the SEAL's code, after all, to never leave a man behind, dead or alive...or have you forgotten?"

Samuel quickly glanced at all the men and shook his head. "Technically, none of us are even *in* Washington. We all need to abort, if you get my drift—out of this city, as fast as we can, separately, as planned. You all know it's what Baron would want us to do. It was part of the plan, remember?" He frowned before continuing, "You know it's the right move—we can't stay here! It's time to get out…*hours ago!*"

Lighters flickered as several of the men lit cigarettes while doing their own fair share of nervous pacing across the thick brown hotel carpet.

Matthew began pacing nervously back and forth in front of the two queen-sized motel beds. "Baron can and will take care of himself, but I don't like it. Why hasn't there been any news on the radio or on the television about the raid and bust yet. Something's gone wrong. You know the press—they're like vultures. Once word spread through the Hill about busting the General…"

Michael quickly turned off his cellular and faced the ten men. "I just spoke with my boss who just finished talking with his boss on Capital Hill, Senior Agent Samuel Nelson—he said that he received a call from Baron at exactly six-forty-eight this morning. He said that the raid on General Madison's condo was a go as of six-fifty. He's still waiting for word; only God above knows where Baron is. When the three of us separated when the General turned his key in that lock, I don't know where Baron went—all I know is; he never came out!" He threw his cellular on the bed. "Damn-it all to hell-fire!"

Michael turned towards the bed and reached for his dark blue duffel bag. "I agree with Samuel, I think it's best if we all leave the city, *now*—before anyone recognizes any one of us. Word travels fast in this city; we know Baron got out and…" He reached inside the duffel bag for his airplane ticket and wallet.

Mitch frowned. "We don't know that. He had his cellular on him—he could have very easily called the D.D.O. of the F.B.I. from his cell phone from inside that condo!"

Ricardo lit a cigarette and frowned. "I got this funny feeling across my shoulders," he glared at Matthew in frustration and spat, "…will you stop that constant pacing. You're getting on my nerves!"

Mitch rubbed his throbbing temples. "I can't think with all of you rambling on and on about nothing. Will you all shut up for a minute, and let me think!"

Scotty reached for his black coffee and whispered, "How long are we going to wait? This mission's been compromised!"

The seconds ticked by in slow motion for every man in the room. Mitch spoke up and answered sternly, "You men do as you see fit. As of this moment you're on your own. But, I'm not going anywhere until I'm one-hundred percent sure that Baron is out of there—alive, safe and in one piece, and on his way back to Fort Kent, Maine!"

Mitch turned away from the men and walked to the window and watched as the belting rain turned to snow and ice-chips right in front of his tired eyes. His thoughts flashed quickly to the way Baron's dark eyes always filled with dancing light every time he mentioned Merry Beth and Bethany back in Maine. What he wouldn't give to see those eyes again right now!

Ricardo stepped close to Mitch, close enough to feel his warm breath on his face and hissed through clenched teeth, "For the safety of every man in this room, and every man's family and children—I say we abort Washington. Now! *All of us—including you!* How do any of us know it wasn't *you* who set Baron up for this fall?"

Scotty added, "I agree. Who are you *really* working for?"

Mitch turned on Ricardo and Scotty with built up anger and frustration and yelled, "*I don't know how you SEAL's do things in the Navy, but in the Marines in Vietnam we didn't abort—ever! It was shoot or die! And if we ever did abort a mission—we didn't leave one of our own behind—dead or alive!*" He angrily pushed at Ricardo's broad chest and warned, "Now, get out of my face or pay the price!"

All of Baron's men came to Ricardo's defense and stepped quickly close to Mitch. Michael and Matthew both said at once, "Back off!"

Jack stepped close to Mitch and said, "Take it easy. From what I saw, this Sergeant Williams is the kind of guy who can take care of himself. He called Senior Agent Nelson didn't he? That must mean he got out. He would want us to stick to the plan and split up. If the Sergeant stayed behind in that condo for some kind of *personal* vendetta then…"

Anthony grabbed the front of Jack's Army jacket and pulled him close to his face and slammed his back up against the wall, hard enough to knock his breath from his lungs, and thundered inches from his face, "You watch your mouth. You say one more word against Baron and I'll rip your throat out. Sure, he has plenty of reasons to make this bust happen. His wife and son were murdered by the command of this slimy bastard, but he would *never* jeopardize this mission or any other, for any kind of personal vendetta!"

Michael stepped close and pried Anthony's fingers from the front of Jack's Army jacket. "Take it easy, we're all on the same team here." Anthony let Jack go and Michael shook his head. "Watch your back—all of you. Speed here can and he will rip your throat out if you cross him just once. It's not a pretty sight—I've seen him do it in the past…more than once."

Matthew whispered, as his ebony eyes searched each and every man's eyes standing in the motel room. "Are we? Are we really all on the same team?"

Mitch spat in frustration and anger through clenched teeth, "Don't be stupid man, of course we are. We all want the same thing—to bring Kelly's brothers and the General and their ties to the *Alliance* to a screeching halt, once and for all. And I'll face any man down who ever accuses me of treason against one of our own!"

Adam answered earnestly, huskily, with a two-pack-a-day voice, "Different wars, different times, different tactics, different plans, strategies, approaches, maneuvers, and courses of action, but we all—*every* man in this room—has blood on their hands!"

Royce finished his black coffee in one huge gulp before he said, "If only we could have done something to stop the General and his lady or slowed them down, at least…" He glared at Thomas with an angry and frustrated heart.

Thomas said with anger and defeat, "Oh, and just what is it I could have done, Royce? Come on, you got something to say—spit it out! Don't hold anything back! We all broke the law—it's called breaking and entering. And planting that disc in that safe like that—it's called tampering with evidence! Except for me, who stuck *my* face out in the wind uncovered for anyone to see passing through that guard shack, you were all wearing black ski masks. We were all armed and ready, but for what? This has all been for nothing if Sergeant Williams got caught inside with his personal vendetta. Sure, he called Nelson—it doesn't mean he's out of there—then or now!"

Adam spoke up, "What we did was *not* for nothing! The disc was planted as planned. If the raid and bust went down as planned, they'll find the incriminating disc, arrest the General and be out of there in minutes. There's enough evidence on that disc to bury the General alive. It will put a stop to this deadly *Alliance* once and for all, the President will be happy, and we can all just go home, back to our normal, happy and safe, boring lives!"

Mitch frowned. "If only it were that simple. For men like us—there is no normal life…not ever."

Ricardo reached for his ringing cellular. "It *is* simple. Let's hope this is from Baron."

Mitch worried as each man prepared to leave the hotel room. He knew the odds were all for Baron being trapped on the inside of that condo. What worried him the most was that Baron hadn't contacted him or any of the men in almost five hours, if he'd gotten out safe and unseen; unhurt.

Mitch knew that the right thing to do was to get out of Washington D.C. as soon as they could. His head and extensive training told him it was the right thing to do, but his heart told him something entirely different. He couldn't turn his back on Baron and walk away. He couldn't. Baron was his friend.

His heart feared for his good friend's life, and told him to stay put until he heard from him. Mitch knew that in Baron's heart this mission was an end of an era in his life. And he knew that Baron couldn't walk away from his troubled past until he was sure the General was well on his way to being locked in federal prison for the rest of his miserable life, with no chance of parole or escape.

Why couldn't every day be like Christmas? The eleven men in that motel room knew first hand that the world didn't work that way—no matter how many evil men they stopped or put away in prison.

Mitch stared out the window at the beating ice chips. "You men do what you must—I'm not leaving Washington until I see Baron face to face."

In minutes the motel room was empty, with no sign that anyone had ever been there. The beds were made, the furniture was left shiny with no fingerprints left behind, the lights were off, the television was off, the carpet didn't look like anyone had stepped on it; the bathroom hadn't been touched. The only thing that lingered in the chilly air was cigarette smoke.

Mitch closed his weary eyes, tired to the bone, missing Carolyn. Where was Baron? Had he been hurt, shot or left for dead in some back alley somewhere?

Why hadn't he called?

* * * * *

Merry Beth and Bethany spent the morning and most of the afternoon finishing their homemade Christmas gifts for Baron—each reliving the true meaning of giving gifts from the heart and not the wallet. It was now after 4 p.m. and Merry Beth was bone tired. Her broken arm throbbed and she'd just taken another pain pill.

Merry Beth made Baron, with her sweet daughter's help because of her broken left arm and still tender right wrist, a stunning red, green, silver and gold cloth wreath for his door—symbolizing friendship and welcoming entrance, just as Joseph and Mary welcomed the shepherds and animals into the stable of straw, where baby Jesus was born so many years ago in Bethlehem.

Bethany made from scratch a pretty gold bow covered with dozens of tiny, shiny gold sequins for the wreath—symbolizing the gift of gold that one of the three wise men gave to baby Jesus the night He was born.

Merry Beth chose a black hat, scarf and glove set she'd knitted months ago. In her heart she wanted to give him the red or green set, but knew he wasn't the red or green kind of man. And black would match the leather jacket he always wore.

She also chose her very best hand stitched patched quilt. It was queen-sized and every square was cut from material from old clothes her and Bethany had discarded over the years—symbolizing something old, yet something new, filled with warmth and care and love. Just like the story of Jesus' birth and old prophecy fulfilled with new hope for a sinful, dying world.

Bethany searched through her toy chest and thoughtfully chose several 'forgotten' toys at the bottom of the wood box in her bedroom. First, there was *Mr. Gray*—a stuffed donkey Bethany's grandpa had bought for her on her second birthday—symbolizing the donkey Mary rode on to Bethlehem the night Jesus was born. And second, *Mrs. Cotton*—a stuffed lamb that was old and ragged and worn; it had belonged to Merry Beth when she was a little girl. It symbolized the little lamb that watched as the baby Jesus came into the world thousands of years before in a lowly stable manger.

To give something cherished that was your very own, symbolized unselfishness and lack of greed. Merry Beth held the wrapping paper in place as Bethany secured the gifts with tape. Together, they wrapped the special gifts for Baron with love in their hearts and hope that he'd make it back in time for Christmas to open them together with their own gifts from Santa.

Psalm 84:11-12 "For the LORD God is a sun and shield: the LORD will give grace and glory: no good thing will he withhold from them that walk uprightly. O LORD of hosts, blessed is the man that trusteth in thee."

Chapter Thirteen

What is the Good?
John Boyle O'Reilly

"What is the real good?"
I ask in musing mood.

"Order," said the law court;
"Knowledge," said the school;
"Truth," said the wise man;
"Pleasure," said the fool;
"Love," said the maiden;
"Beauty," said the page;
"Freedom," said the dreamer;
"Home," said the sage;
"Fame," said the soldier;
"Equity," said the seer.
Spake my heart fully sad:
"The answer is not here."

Then within my bosom
Softly this I heard:
"Each heart holds the secret:
'Kindness' is the word."

It was a cold Christmas Eve morning, December the 24th, Thursday—just past 7 a.m. Merry Beth finished reading her favorite poem out loud, and placed the antique book that had belonged to her mother on the kitchen table, as Bethany jumped down from her booster chair and ran across the kitchen floor in a hurried flash.

"Mommy, look outside! It's snowing again! I love the snow, Mommy—its sooooooo pretty. Maybe later we can go out and build a snowman? Wouldn't that be fun?"

Before Merry Beth could reach out to stop her, she opened the back kitchen door and immediately bumped hard into their new neighbors' arms.

Merry Beth's frightened heart thundered in her chest with uncertainty and quickened fear. She jumped up from the table so fast she knocked over and spilled her hot tea. "*Bethany! Watch out!*"

Too late, her daughter was trapped in the strange arms of the tall, dark and mysterious man who'd saved her from the clutches of her ex-father-in-law in front of the post office on Monday morning. The jagged scar on the left side of his face seemed white against his cold and red face. Christmas was a wonderful time for trusting God for strength and serenity, yet she shivered. Not from the cold and chilly wind, but from fear.

Feeling slightly unsettled and unsure, Merry Beth immediately reached out for Bethany and pulled her back inside the warm apartment, safely behind her back.

"Bethany, I've told you and told you to not run in the house!" She lifted her dark green eyes to the coal black eyes of her neighbor and smiled nervously. *Was* he her neighbor? "I'm sorry. My daughter wasn't watching where she was going. Are you all right?"

His ebony eyes were as dark as the midnight sky, with no moon or stars shining down, and she couldn't help but wince and flinch back from the beastly, powerful huge man as he towered over her. She reminded herself how he'd saved her from Earl's clutches on Monday, and scolded her ungratefulness, and swallowed her rising fear enough to say, "Bethany, say you're sorry to the nice man. You bumped him really hard."

Bethany peeked her curly red head from around her mother's legs and mumbled, "Sorry…"

Merry Beth couldn't help but stare at the ragged looking scar that ran from his left temple down the side of his face to his chin. The black Stetson he wore did little to hide or shade the jagged looking scar, and she silently scolded her bad manners and rudeness once more, and lifted her eyes to his in apology. There was no telling what Earl might have done if he hadn't stopped him on Monday.

"I never got the chance to thank you for helping me on Monday in front of the post office…" In an instant the dark and potent stare he sent her way turned warmer and friendlier, and she sighed with ease. "But I had the situation under control. I would have shot him, if he hadn't dropped that knife. He's a mean drunk, you see. I'm used to his binges and rages. My ex-father-in-law is…"

He spoke for the first time and his deep, scratchy voice sent shivers up and down her spine. "Your little girl should be more careful, ma'am. You never know who might be lurking in the dark, shadowy places just waiting to snatch their prey when busy Mommy's aren't looking or paying attention carefully."

The man stood at least six feet tall, with broad shoulders and huge black leather gloves covered his massive hands. He was dressed in black from head to toe, and didn't smile when he mumbled, "Good day." In seconds, he turned away and quickly walked off the back porch through the snow and ice storm, towards the front of the apartment building, to the driveway that led to the main road.

Merry Beth frowned down at her daughter as she quickly closed her kitchen door and locked it. "Bethany! Don't you *ever* do that again, I mean it. You wait and let mommy check the yard or porch or doorstep before you rush out!"

"But, Mommy," Bethany started, as she looked up at her mother to add, "…you said that he was a nice man! I only wanted to see the pretty snowflakes. I'm sorry, Mommy."

"Don't *but Mommy* me, young lady. You can go out and play in the snow after you eat your breakfast, after you get dressed, *after* you make your bed and pick up that room of yours again. Just because there is no school or day-care doesn't mean we neglect our regular chores, chores that we do *every* morning!"

She watched her daughter's bottom lip tremble slightly, and Bethany mumbled as she slowly walked back to finish eating her breakfast. "All right, Mommy…I'm sorry…I didn't mean to be bad…honest. I won't do it again."

"Bethany, Mommy just wants to make sure that you're safe, honey—always. Mommy is doing the best I can with only one arm and mending sprained wrist…" Merry Beth swallowed a giggle as she turned away. Whenever she had to be extra stern or cross with Bethany, she always made the cutest little pouty faces. She rarely complained or misbehaved; it was hard to remain firm. But this was an important lesson for her to learn.

"All right, Mommy, I'm s…sorry," Bethany whispered softly as she reached for her orange juice.

Merry Beth reached for her best non-stick frying pan and placed it over the fire before breaking two eggs in melted butter.

"The snow is very pretty, baby. I love it when it snows on Christmas Eve."

She reached over and turned up the little radio that sat in the kitchen windowsill as *"The Wonderful World of Christmas"* began to play from their favorite station.

"I love this song, baby, don't you?" Merry Beth sprinkled her fried eggs with salt and pepper and glanced over her left shoulder at her unusually quiet daughter eating her hot oatmeal sprinkled with sugar and cinnamon in silence. "What's the matter, baby? Are you mad at Mommy for scolding you?"

"Nope," Bethany said as she shrugged her shoulders.

"Then why so quiet all of a sudden?"

"It's Christmas *Eve*, Mommy, don't you remember, and Mr. Bear'onn Will'amms isn't here yet!" Her innocent emerald eyes clouded over with unshed tears.

"I know, sweetie. I'm sorry." Merry Beth plopped two pieces of wheat bread in the toaster with a troubled heart. It seemed like her baby girl had really taken to Baron, hard. Did she dare hope he'd ever come back? And how in the world could she know, or hope, how much he cared for her by only one kiss—one sweet, magical, special, wonderful and unforgettable, earth-shattering kiss?

"Are you excited about being an angel in the play at church tonight? Do you want to call and see if Lisa can come with us to Wal-Mart this afternoon when we go to buy Mr. Williams his Tweety-bird slippers?" Merry Beth asked, as she placed her two fried eggs on a plate. The toast popped up and she covered them with butter and homemade strawberry jam.

Bethany glanced up at her mother with an anxious, excited smile. "Can we, Mommy? That'll be way cool!"

Merry Beth walked to the table and gave Bethany one of the pieces of toast. "Sure, baby. I'll call Debbie after I eat my breakfast. Here, I put strawberry jam on your toast for you. I know how much you love it."

After Bethany finished her breakfast she jumped down from her little booster chair and hugged her mother tight around her neck. Her little eyes sparkled as she said, "I love you, Mommy."

Merry Beth smiled. "And I love you, baby."

As Bethany took off on a dead run to her bedroom on the second floor, Merry Beth yelled after her, "No running in the house!"

As she cleaned her kitchen her thoughts remained on her mysterious new neighbor. Who was he, and why would she be scared of him one moment and not the next? What was his true story, and what did he want with her? Why had he been on her back porch?

He had to be a friend, right? He'd saved her from Earl in seconds flat. His dark eyes had turned warmer and friendlier, right in front of her own, hadn't they? Maybe she needed to call the sheriff and make *sure* this man was safe and who he said he was. Yet, hadn't he just blown his chance if he was here to harm them?

* * * * *

"What are we gonna do now, Mommy?" Bethany and Lisa stared up at Merry Beth with troubled faces and worried frowns, yet excited anxious eyes. They were shopping inside the Northgate Mall, in Wal-Mart, and it was just past 1:30 p.m. Time was running out if they wanted to buy Baron a pair of yellow Tweety-bird slippers for Christmas.

"The nice lady is checking out back to see if there's any more slippers, baby. It's the best that I can do."

Merry Beth glanced at the dozens and dozens of beautiful new sneakers and reached for a white pair that had a red *sale* price tag on it. She glanced at the tag and frowned a little—they were now twelve dollars. She winced; she still had a dozen things to buy on her list to finally complete Bethany's Christmas and birthday list. The sneakers went back on the shelf. They'd have to wait for another Christmas.

"Mommy, can Lisa and I go and check to see if Santa is here?" Bethany asked, as the girls giggled back and forth and whispered to each other. "He's 'posed to be near the back of the store where all the Christmas stuff is? Can we go look, *please?*"

"No, not alone; we'll go check as soon as..." Merry Beth frowned as Bethany and Lisa took off on a dead run down the slipper and sneaker aisle where they were waiting for the shoe clerk to come back. "*Bethany! Lisa! You girls get back here—right now! Come back—this isn't funny, not one little bit!*"

At that moment she wondered where all the miracles were. They seemed few and far between lately. In the blink of an eye—as the girls disappeared around the corner out of sight, her entire life changed. Just like that, with no way to ever make it right again. The background music in the store began to play Trisha Yearwood's "*The Sweetest Gift*," yet she frowned as they didn't heed her word and come back. She made the move to run after them in two seconds...

Just as Bethany and Lisa disappeared around the corner the shoe clerk came walking towards Merry Beth with a huge smile. "I found a pair out back, ma'am. And it's even a size extra-large. I hope it's what you need?" Vera smiled her warm friendly smile, as she passed the box to Merry Beth.

"Thank you." Merry Beth quickly ran to the end of the shoe and slipper aisle. "*Bethany, Lisa—where are you?*" Her thundering heart dropped to her shaky knees and then quickly to the floor around her ragged white sneakers, when the girls were nowhere in sight.

"*Bethany! Lisa! Where are you? Bethany—come to mommy, honey—where are you? If you're playing a trick on mommy—it's not very funny! Bethany! Lisa!*" Her frantic eyes searched down every shoe aisle and when Bethany and Lisa didn't answer her call, she panicked, literally. Adrenaline pumped through her thundering heart quick and fierce, leaving her knees weaker and her stomach nauseous.

"Bethany, Lisa! Where are you?" *Dear Lord, please tell me this isn't happening? Help me find them, Lord—please!*

In seconds Merry Beth alerted the shoe clerk—Sally, that there were two missing children in the store and in less than fifteen seconds she heard a store clerk say loudly over the intercom, "Code Adam, Code Adam!" along with Bethany and Lisa's descriptions.

Merry Beth was impressed; that was fast. She quickly gave the clerk a description of both girls and what they were wearing, and in seconds it was over the intercom.

Merry Beth knew the code meant the front and back and side doors would be shut and locked down, but would they be locked down in time? Had someone grabbed the girls and taken them away against their will? Or were they just being innocent and curious and adventurous as any five-year-old would inside a huge department store—especially at Christmas time?

As Merry Beth and several store clerks and the manager quickly searched through the entire store—the Christmas department first, tears of fear burned her eyes. They were gone. The girls were nowhere in sight. It was like they'd vanished off the face of the earth, with no trace that they'd ever been there. How could this have happened so fast? Dear God, where were the girls?

This wasn't happening. It wasn't!

As the store manager called the sheriff, and the sheriff called the State Police twenty minutes later...Merry Beth's knees crumbled and she fell in her exhausted and fearful state, in the same booth she'd shared with Baron right after she'd bought them lunch, when he'd gone back to retrieve her fallen purse and their carry-out baskets, when she'd been hit in her cast by that woman with her cart.

What she wouldn't give to have him sitting across from her right this moment! He'd know what to do to find the girls!

Panic seized her heart. Bethany and Lisa were missing! Dear God, no! This *wasn't* happening! She started to hyperventilate…

* * * * *

It seemed like years.

Had it only been an hour?

Merry Beth glanced up through a wall of glistening tears as she heard Debbie call out her name. *"Merry Beth…"*

She'd been sitting with the store managers and two security guards at a table in McDonald's in the front of the store for the past ten minutes. Deputy Hugh Masters and police detective, Linwood Patterson stood nearby after asking Lisa several important questions.

"Did you see what the strange man was wearing?"

"Did you notice his height, his hair color, his eye color, any noticeable scars or tattoo's?"

"What did he look like?"

"Was he tall, short, stout, skinny; bald?"

"Was he wearing a hat or coat?"

"Was Bethany crying when he took her away?"

Even though the questions were very important, there was nothing they could do. Bethany had literally vanished into thin air, like a vapor or lifting thick fog after a rain storm.

Just as Debbie reached Merry Beth's side and noticed her daughter, sitting close by her side crying her little heart out, an officer from the Missing and Exploited Children's office in Fort Kent stepped near the table to ask Lisa more questions.

The entire store had been searched from top to bottom at least a dozen times. The local sheriff and State Police—men from Baron's Headquarters in Fort Kent, had been called, and now, the F.B.I. as well. They were in the process of interviewing every man, woman and child that had been locked inside the store, just after Sally had phoned in the Code Adam. No one saw anything. Merry Beth knew the statistics. Her daughter was gone. As every second ticked slowly by, chances of getting her back grew darker and darker.

Bethany's name had been called over the intercom over and over, to no avail. She never answered or came back to her mother. Bethany was gone, vanished, taken away, and all Merry Beth felt in her heart was fear. It consumed her heart, controlled her senses, and rocked her solid world.

This wasn't happening.

Tomorrow was Bethany's birthday.

Tomorrow was Christmas.

Baron was coming home.

He'd make everything all right again!

Her eyes filled with burning tears…for the hundredth time. Her head throbbed unmercifully. Her broken arm was painfully hurting her—evident on her ashen, pale face. She'd been violently ill inside the Ladies Restroom just twenty minutes before. Merry Beth was exhausted, both physically and mentally. She was terribly shaken and sickly pale. Her sweet baby was gone. What kind of mother was she? How could she have let this happen?

When she heard Debbie's voice she tried to smile, but couldn't because of the pain. When brown eyes met and clashed with green, their entire *safe* world crumbled. Debbie *knew* without asking, Bethany was still missing!

"Lisa!" Debbie opened her arms as her daughter rushed from the booth and ran to her mother, crying her little heart out.

Merry Beth sobbed like a little baby and could barely get the words past her dry lips. "A very…tall and…dark man…grabbed…my baby! Debbie…he…was…dressed in all black. *Oh, Debbie—Bethany is gone!*"

Debbie's eyes glistened with burning tears as she hugged her daughter close. "Mommy, Beth and I were just going to see if Santa was here, and a *stranger* grabbed her and took her away!"

Debbie bent down on both knees and searched into her daughter's blue eyes as she placed her little feet back on the floor. "And what did the strange man do, honey?"

Lisa's bottom lip trembled and fresh tears fell from her frightened eyes. "He took her away. I yelled *stranger*—like you and Uncle Todd taught me to, but no one helped me!"

Debbie pulled her frightened daughter close once more; grateful she was here and safe and alive and unhurt. She lifted her eyes to her best friend and whispered, "Oh, Merry Beth. I'm so sorry, but who? Who in the world would want to take Bethany away like that? Things like this don't happen in Winterville!"

Lisa wiped her tears with the back of her hand. "We saw the *nice* man, Mommy. A few minutes before that *mean* man took her away she said, 'Look Lisa, there's that nice man I bumped into on our back porch this morning. He's near the Christmas paper—see him?'"

Debbie met her daughter's eyes and asked, "The man she bumped into on her back porch—*he's* the one who grabbed Bethany and took her away?"

Lisa shook her head no. "No, Mommy. It was another man—*honest!* And he had a funny looking scar on his face. It's ugly, Mommy. I don't like him!"

Lisa's bottom lip trembled as she burst into tears in her mother's arms. Debbie held on to her daughter closer and whispered, "Don't be scared honey. I'm s…sure Beth is all r…right." Her voice trembled and her eyes said different as she glanced at her best friend.

Merry Beth cringed. "Oh, Debbie…what does it mean?"

"Who do you think it was, Merry Beth? Are there two different men—both with scars on their faces? How can that be? Something doesn't sound right to me…"

Merry Beth frowned when a tall man with blonde hair and sea-glass-blue eyes, dressed in blue-jeans and red-and-white flannel shirt and brown cowboy boots asked her quickly, "Have you contacted your husband, ma'am?"

He didn't miss her stunning gold wedding and diamond engagement rings she wore on her left hand again, and just assumed she was married. When she just stared up at him numb-founded, he continued as he bent down to eye level and reached for her right hand, "My name is Detective Longwood, ma'am. I work for the 'Missing and Exploited Children's Department' based in the Fort Kent area. Deputy Hugh Masters called me and I drove right down, is there someone I can call for you?"

Debbie said with conviction, "They'll find her, Merry Beth. I know they will. We have to believe that. We have to!"

Merry Beth swallowed back her tears and fought against the huge lump in her scratchy throat. Her eyes sought her best friend's as she answered, "Debbie, we have to find her…" *Dear Lord, without Your sweet grace I'd be lost. Help me, dear Lord. Give me strength and courage. Please give me my sweet innocent daughter back. I beg You, dear Lord. I gave her to You when she was born—please, don't take her from me now!*

"She must be so scared…" Merry Beth whispered.

"Mrs. Waters…?" Detective Longwood knew deep in his heart that too much time had already passed; the chances of finding the young girl were slim. And as every second ticked away into another minute, and every minute into another hour, the chances grew darker and more hopeless of ever finding her again. Yes, even on Christmas Eve in Winterville, Maine, the dangers can reach out and snag the young children away.

"Ma'am—is there someone you'd like for us to call?"

Merry Beth lowered her pulsating eyes and mumbled, "No, it's just me and Bethany. There's no one to call. I'm a widow." *Oh, Baron—I wish you were here. Where are you? Are you coming back? I need you—someone took my baby!*

"Have you noticed any strangers lurking around in the past few days, ma'am?" Detective Longwood tried to give her a reassuring smile, but it was hard. He'd seen too many of these cases—hundreds of them over the years, and seventy-five percent of the missing children were never found and returned safely to their parents and loved ones.

Debbie sat with Lisa in her lap. "Tell him, Merry Beth."

Merry Beth's heart took a double flop and her eyes searched for Debbie's. "We do have a new neighbor. I've only seen him twice…I think. He helped me on Monday in front of the post office—at least I think he's my new neighbor."

She glanced over at Deputy Masters and continued, "The deputy was there; he can fill you in on the details. Anyway, he helped me when my ex-father-in-law broke his restraining order *again!*" Panic set in, hard and lethal.

Oh, no! No, no, no, no, no, no, no! Please, dear God in Heaven—don't let it be true! In an instant Merry Beth was up from the booth and running towards the front of the store in icy panic that tried to yank her under like thick quicksand.

"Dear Lord—please; don't let it be true. Don't let it be true!" Merry Beth said in fear over her shoulder as she rushed towards the front doors. "If he's hurt one hair on her head I'll…"

Debbie stood and raced after her with Lisa tightly against her breast, and stopped her quickly by grabbing her right arm hard. Detective Longwood reached for Merry Beth at the same time to help her back inside the store.

"Where are you going in such a hurry, ma'am? If you think you know who's taken your daughter…please, talk to me."

Merry Beth lifted frightened eyes to her best friend and asked through her fear, *"What if it's Earl, Debbie? What if he's taken my baby? What if he's taken Bethany to get back at me?"*

Debbie quickly explained to the officer, "It's her ex-father-in-law…he's known to everyone in Winterville to be quite the psycho. He's deranged, mental and extremely violent—the whole nine yards. You name it—he has done it, to hurt Merry Beth over the years. He's a mean bully, he's a drunk…"

Detective Longwood helped Merry Beth back to the table. "Please let the police officers do their job, ma'am."

His hardened blue eyes searched for the deputy and he quickly stated, "Check her ex-father-in-law out, Hugh. See if you can find his whereabouts in the last few hours." He signaled for one of the McDonald clerks to bring Merry Beth a glass of water after she gave the deputy Earl's latest known address.

"He's a crazy man, and he hates me. He'd do anything to get back at me. He blames me for losing his job at the bank—I know he does. But, *would he hurt an innocent child?*" Merry Beth wiped her tears away with a napkin. She stared at her best friend and couldn't control the tremors rushing through her pounding temples. "His own granddaughter...? Would he hurt his own flesh and blood like this? Is he really that far gone?"

Lisa sobbed in her mother's arms. "I'm scared, Mommy. I want Beth back. We didn't mean to run off, Mommy. I'm sorry. We won't do it again—*ever!* I promise, Mommy. Can't we just have Beth back? It's Christmas Eve, Mommy...make Beth come back!"

Debbie tried to smile but it was lost in her concern for her best friend and her worry for Bethany. She watched her and knew Merry Beth was beginning to hyperventilate, and calmly advised, "Take it easy, take deep breaths, that's it...you have to remain calm, Merry Beth. Getting sick isn't going to help you or help get her back...okay?"

Merry Beth placed her head down between her knees and took calming breaths in and out slowly. "If he touches my baby in any way I don't know what I'll do. He's sick, you know. Oh, I should have taken my baby and moved far, far away years ago. And to think I let him go on Monday because it's the Christmas season! How could I have been so stupid?"

Debbie spoke up and said, "His name is Earl Anthony Waters, officer, and I think everyone in this town knows the history between Merry Beth and that monster. You have to *do* something—if he's taken Bethany there's no telling what he'll do. He's a crazy madman, I tell you! He's drunk all the time!"

Merry Beth swallowed against the bitter bile taste in her mouth and whispered, as she lifted her swimming head, "She must be so scared, Debbie. She doesn't have any idea whatsoever about Earl. She doesn't even know he exists. What if—what if he's taking her out of state! *Please, help me find my baby!*"

Debbie reached for her and Merry Beth sobbed in her arms. "Shhh, you're going to make yourself sick. You have to calm down, love. I know it's hard, but please try."

Deputy Hugh Masters walked closer to the detective and Merry Beth, and

Debbie frowned when the sheriff came into view. "I checked him out—he has an air-tight alibi. Seems he spent the whole morning and is still in the emergency room at Winterville General as we speak. He hit a car broadside—OUI, I'm afraid. He's clean—of *this* crime anyway."

Merry Beth and Debbie both sighed with relief. But fear still lingered between the two women, like a slippery serpent.

"But, what if Earl hired this new neighbor of mine? Maybe he's not really a friend. Maybe he's not really the new boys' basketball coach at the high school. Maybe he's been watching me to find just the right moment to grab her and take her away—*away to Earl! Oh Debbie, that's it! Earl hired my new neighbor to act like a friend when all along he's not!*" Merry Beth lowered her throbbing head in her right hand.

"I think you're reaching, Merry Beth," Debbie said, as she sat in a nearby chair holding Lisa in her lap. "I told you, Todd carefully checked him out—his references, his resume…"

Detective Longwood searched Merry Beth's dark green, tear-filled eyes once more, as he quietly stated the truthful words they didn't want to hear, "References and resumes can be forged, ma'am."

He spoke softly as he asked Merry Beth, "You said you saw who you think is your new neighbor…twice? Can you tell me about it?" He didn't miss how she was shaking from head to toe and took off his warm leather jacket and placed it over her shoulders. As he carefully enclosed it around her broken arm and bent shoulders, he asked, "Are you all right, ma'am? Do you need a doctor?" He knew she was in shock. She was trembling and much too pale.

"No, I'll be okay. I saw him just this morning. Bethany bumped into him on our back porch. But, he has to be a *friend!* He helped me when Earl came at me with a switchblade in front of the post office on Monday. It can't be him!" She searched for Debbie's eyes once more and whispered through her pain, "What's his name, Debbie—do you remember his name?"

Detective Longwood glanced at Debbie and asked, "How do you know Mrs. Waters' new neighbor, ma'am? And men who snatch children away usually make themselves to appear to be a friend. That's usually how they manage to get close enough to grab them. If you think he's a friend, you let your guard down, and when you're not looking…"

He stood and rubbed the beginning of what seemed to be a migraine pounding in the back of his skull. "…before you know it's happened—your child is gone."

Debbie frowned with worry. "My brother-in-law—Pastor Todd Thomas, owns the apartment building where Merry Beth and Bethany live." She rubbed her own throbbing forehead and temples and searched her frantic mind and couldn't come up with a name. "Oh, I can't remember his name…"

Merry Beth pleaded, "Think, Debbie…try really hard!"

Detective Longwood said, "Is there someone you can call to find out—your brother-in-law, maybe? We can run a background check on this new neighbor through the F.B.I. data base, see if he has a record, see if he has any priers in the distant past, see if he's wanted, see if he's ever spent time in jail or prison…"

Debbie rose from the table holding Lisa tightly in her arms. "I'll be right back, Merry Beth. Try not to worry. I'm sure Bethany is fine. The detectives will find her. I know they will!"

Merry Beth swallowed her panic and said with a terrified heart, after taking another sip of cold water, "I've noticed another man several times over the last few days—six times, at least. It's like he's watching me, or something, but always from a distance. He's never made one move towards my daughter or me, to harm us in any way. And the man with the scar on the left side of his face—after he helped me Monday morning, I no longer felt frightened or scared of him anymore. A little wary, maybe—but not cold-fear…

"He's big and strong and powerful. He had Earl pinned up against my truck faster than I could blink. He is eerie though, he has this jagged looking scar that runs from his left temple all the way down to his cheek…" she shivered and buried herself deeper inside the detectives warm jacket.

Tears burned her eyes. "I'm sorry—I just don't know…"

"Appearances can be deceiving, ma'am. Someone we think might be a friend…isn't," Detective Longwood informed huskily. "Can you give a complete description of the two men's faces to a police sketch artist, Mrs. Waters? We could get their pictures statewide—even nationwide, on the net media outlets within the hour. Can you do that for us, ma'am? It'll be done by computer, we can leave right now."

Merry Beth shook her head yes and wiped her eyes and asked, "You think Lisa is right? You think that there are *two* different men; but are they working together? I have no money for ransom—why would they take her away?"

A few minutes later, Detective Longwood passed Merry Beth another glass of water and watched as Debbie raced quickly towards the McDonald's lobby with a crying Lisa in her arms. "Merry Beth, the news isn't good."

Everyone in the little group stopped talking and turned to look at Debbie at once, as she whispered through her fear, "His name is Michael Alan Carter and Merry Beth…"

Merry Beth looked up at her friend and wiped the tears from her flushed cheeks. "What…what is it? What'd Todd say?"

The entire group of store employee's and law officials stopped talking at once; waiting to hear what Debbie had to say.

"What is it, Mrs. Thomas? What's wrong?" Detective Longwood asked as he rubbed his throbbing temples and neck once more. "Just spit it out, every second is critical."

"Your neighbor has a scar on his face all right, but…" Debbie's chocolate brown eyes stared into Merry Beth's dark green eyes with worry, concern, anxiety and fear.

Merry Beth felt them all: horror, terror, fright, alarm, dismay, panic, anxiety, dread, scared, apprehension in the last hour of her life, but when she heard her best friend's next words everything in her whole world shifted and then just stopped.

"Todd said that the scar that Mr. Carter has *is* on the *left* side of his face, Merry Beth. I just talked to three witnesses, three store clerks who all say that the man who took Bethany away had a scar on the *right* side of his face."

Debbie searched for the detective's sharp sea-blue eyes and whispered, "Lisa is right, there *are* two different men. Remember what Lisa said Bethany said, just before that man took her away. She pointed to and identified to Lisa the man by the wrapping paper as the *nice* man she'd bumped into on the porch, Merry Beth, but…"

Merry Beth buried her tears behind her right hand. "I'm so confused—what's going on?"

Hot, burning tears glistened in Merry Beth's eyes as she cringed, knowing what it meant. The man who took Bethany was probably a terrible and dangerous, deadly enemy—one who preyed on innocent children, one who kidnapped innocent children to take them away to be sold into 'white slavery' or 'prostitution' or the 'black market.'

"Oh, no," Debbie whispered through her fear.

Merry Beth reached for Lisa and pulled her close for a hug. "You're *sure* honey? You're *sure* that the man who took Bethany away had a scar on the *right* side of his face?" Lisa's eyes filled with tears and she shook her head yes.

Lisa lifted her little hand and lightly touched the right side of Merry Beth's face. "I'm sure, Mrs. Waters, I promise."

Merry Beth turned towards the detectives. "I want to talk to these three store clerks—*right now!*"

"Which man is friend, and which one is foe?" Detective Longwood said as he reached for his cellular. "Try not to worry, Mrs. Waters, we'll find your daughter. I promise you that. We'll leave here and go to headquarters and get those sketches of these two men out, a.s.a.p.! The store clerks are already working with a sketch artist from our office." He cringed inwardly, knowing the chances of doing just that were slim to none. If these two men worked together, and their baby-smuggling operation was bi-coastal—Bethany could be long gone, and probably already was.

The smiles and laughter had disappeared from the depths of Merry Beth's eyes over an hour ago. All hope of finding her daughter in her thundering and fearful heart had disintegrated and dwindled quickly away from her heart, as the cold truth continued to set in; as each minute, each hour passed. Bethany was gone, and the chances of ever finding her were weak. She knew that deep in her heart. Bethany was taken against her will, and she might never see her precious baby girl again.

There were a lot of dangerous and evil, lethal predators out there—who loved to prey on young children.

Two men's faces came into view, as Merry Beth rose to her unsteady feet with the help of the nice detectives—both were tall, dark, black-dressed mysterious strangers, both rugged looking with jagged scars on their faces—one on the left and one on the right.

Which was friend and which was enemy?

Who could she trust besides her pastor and Debbie, and where was Baron?

When was he coming back, if ever?

She needed his help to find her baby.

Now!

* * * * *

It was Christmas Eve, just past 4:30 p.m. It was cold, the deadly kind of cold. They were back in the Mall parking lot, close to where Wal-Mart was…just in case.

"Merry Beth, sweetie, you need to go home," Debbie softly whispered, as she reached for her right hand and held it tight in the warm cab of the new Bronco. "You can't stay here."

Merry Beth wiped away her endless stream of tears and whispered, "I can't leave, Debbie. What if…what if she's just wandered off and she comes back? I need to be here if…"

Debbie shook her head no and answered, "She was taken, honey. She didn't wander off. You need to accept that. You need to go home, love, just in case someone from the sheriff or State Police or Detective Longwood's office calls. Those two men's sketches are already out there on the wire—you have to have faith that someone will see them or the television announcement, or someone will call the State Police…"

Sobs, earth-shattering and fierce, raked Merry Beth's entire body and Debbie reached for her and hugged her tight until they subsided. Lisa lay asleep, exhausted from crying and worrying about her best friend, in the back seat covered with Merry Beth's coat. Debbie spotted her brother-in-law's light-blue Chevy pickup truck coming slowly their way through the busy parking lot and she said, "Todd's here." She moved to open her passenger side door.

Merry Beth held on to her best friend's fleece-lined jean-coat left-sleeve in a tight grip, wincing as pain slashed through her right wrist in seconds. "Don't go. I need you. I can't go back to that apartment without her, Debbie. *I just can't!* I can't face walking in there alone…without her…"

"All right, I'll stay with you. I just need to go and speak to Todd for a minute, okay? I need to make the arrangements to cancel the Christmas Eve play and concert at church and…"

"Oh, Debbie—I can't ask you to do that. All those wonderful children— everything's all set!" Merry Beth thought about her sweet daughter dressed in her pretty angel costume and broke out in heart-wrenching sobs again.

"She must be…so scared…without me, or…you, or Lisa or any of her…friends from Day Care Tots or…church around. Oh, I don't think…I can bear it, Debbie, if I lose her forever. *I don't…think I could…bear it!*" Merry Beth cried and reached for another tissue to wipe her endless stream of tears. Her eyes were burning from crying so much, and her chest hurt where her mending ribs throbbed.

"It's being cancelled, Merry Beth—until Bethany comes back. We can't have our play and concert without her and that's final. I'll be right back." Debbie smiled and kissed her best friend lightly on her right cheek before jumping down from the Bronco to the wet and snowy parking lot pavement.

Merry Beth tried to smile but couldn't. It hurt to smile. It hurt to breathe. It hurt to think. It would kill her if she had to live without her baby. Someone had taken her sweet daughter, and there wasn't a blessed thing under the heavens she could do but—pray…

In the midst of pain and trouble, her father had often told her over the years that prayer was a great solution to solve any kind of problem. She knew his words were true; she'd witnessed the blessings prayer could bring a hundred times over the years.

She closed her eyes against the thundering pain across her broken heart and whispered, "Dear God, please, please—if it is Your will, help me find my baby. Someone's taken her, Lord. I don't know whom, and I don't know why. All I know is I can't live without her. Help me find her, Lord. I'm placing her life in Your hands again, Lord—like I did when she was born. Keep her safe until she finds her way home, in Your Name I pray, Amen."

As she opened her eyes from her prayer she remembered the forgotten mail on her dash and reached for it with shaking fingers; wondering by some slim chance that there might be a letter from the man who'd snatched Bethany away. God forbid, like a ransom note…or…something. Her hands trembled.

A little bit of joy waltzed back in her broken heart when she realized one of the letters in the pile was from Baron. She glanced at the postal stamp and whispered, "Monday, December the twenty-first…"

In an instant she ripped the tiny yellow package open, and tears fell anew as she noticed the pretty angel pin in the bottom of the envelope. It shimmered and sparkled as she held it tightly in the palm of her right hand. She cried fresh tears as she read his words out loud. Suddenly, a little bit of her fear died in her heart, replaced with a renewed sense of hope. Baron was gone from her but his words drew him closer…

"Merry Beth, my sweetheart, my pretty flower-snowbird; because of *you* I remember, how could I have ever turned my back on my faith—without God's gift to the lost and dying world, Jesus…without God's grace, love, mercy and forgiveness—there is no hope, none. *You* are my dearest pretty flour-snowbird. I love you, Merry Beth. I regret not telling you before I had to go away. I'll come back to you and the Munchkin as soon as I can. If everything goes well with my plans, I'll be back for the Christmas Eve play and concert at your church. And I don't want to miss that birthday party…"

Merry Beth sobbed and the tears blinded her eyes so bad she couldn't see, until she wiped them away with the back of her hand.

"Look inside the envelope and you'll find a special guardian angel I'm sending to you to watch over you and keep you safe until I can return. It's not just any angel; she's a *special* angel. Some people come into our lives, they smile then quickly go, some become friends and stay for a while, leaving beautiful touches and memories on our hearts, and we are *never* quite the same because we have made that good friend. Are you crying because I said that I love you?"

Merry Beth sobbed, "Yes!" He loved her! Another sweet miracle! "...Please don't cry, darling—*you* are that special friend to me, Merry Beth. *You and the Munchkin!*

"Yesterday is history; Merry Beth Waters—it's gone from our grasp forever. Tomorrow is a mystery only God knows. And today—today is a gift from God. That's why it's called the 'present'! I think life is fragile yet special; we must take what God gives us and grasp it in our hands and savor every single moment—even when we don't understand pain and loss. Take the little angel and keep her close. She is your guardian angel sent by me to watch over you!

"I love (and miss) your laughter and warm, soothing smile and beautiful emerald eyes, darling. I can't wait to kiss you again.

"And when you are fearful, lonely, sad, frightened or blue, remember two things. First, God above is watching over us and He loves us, and you are right—He has never left us alone down here on earth to face the many evils and dangers in this world alone. Thank you for making me see these things again. I will love you forever and a day. You bring sunshine into my dark world.

"And second, I—Baron Michael Williams love *you!* I see you when I close my eyes, whether in rest or my dreams. I hear you whispering from a distance, and I will see you again soon, face to face, I promise you that. I want to be that somebody special in your heart and life, my pretty flour-snowbird. I want to give you a ring and make you my bride. I *trust* you, Merry Beth.

"I am that somebody who is very proud of you and all you have accomplished on raising your daughter alone, who is thinking of you always, who cares for you deeply, who misses you when we're apart, who wants to talk with you for hours, and who wants to be with you until death we do part. And I pray the Lord is keeping you and the Munchkin safe until I can make these things happen by the power of my own hands.

"I am that somebody who is thankful for the smiles and laughter and friendship you have given me, in the short time I've known you. I want to hold your hand. I want to make you happy. I want to celebrate in all of your successes.

I want to give you a gift—my heart, because '*you*' are my gift, Merry Beth. I want to reach for you and hug you close, and kiss you under that mistletoe I know you have hanging in your living room. (I can't wait. By the way, the memory of our first kiss lingers near still).

"I admire your strength and courage. I think of you and I smile. I want to be that shoulder you rely on and depend on when in doubt or trouble. I want to protect you from the dangers in this world and keep you and the Munchkin safe. I want to laugh with you. I value your advice and kind words. Do you know how much I love and care for you and your daughter—more than my own life? Yes. I want to share your dreams and make them ours. I treasure your sweet spirit. I don't think I've ever met a woman quite like you, my pretty flour-snowbird.

"I don't understand how I feel all of these things and more for you so quickly. I just accept that it's true.

"I have been praising God for bringing you and the Munchkin into my lonely world. I praise God for your friendship. Do you love me back, Merry Beth? Somehow I know you do, without hearing the words.

"I feel like I am alive again since I've met you. I have faith in you and trust you completely, and even if you don't love me back—that's okay. Maybe you will one day soon. Yet, your response to my kiss told me you really care.

"I want you to know you've given me my faith in not only God back, but faith in myself back. I'm a stronger, better man since I pulled you from that crumpled wreckage in front of that McDonald's sign, on the night of December the tenth. I'll be looking for those bright and blinking Christmas lights, as I walk around the bend, Merry Beth. They will lead me home.

"I'll love you forever, Baron."

Merry Beth lifted his precious letter to her face and sobbed uncontrollably. After several minutes she quickly opened her truck door and jumped down into the snow, slush and ice. With a thundering heart she rushed towards Todd's truck through the thick snowfall and brittle, northeastern wind.

Merry Beth quickly opened the passenger side door and exclaimed, "Pastor Todd! Debbie! I have to get home—now! Baron's coming, he's coming home. If anyone can help me find my baby—*he can!* Let's go…we'll follow each other back, okay?"

Merry Beth searched for her best friend's eyes, pleading for help, for answers, for anything, anything she could hold on to at that moment for a tiny piece of hope. She glanced down at the letter and tiny angle pin she held tightly in her right hand, and smiled.

Snowflakes fell on her face, lips and tongue, trying to still her beating and fearful heart. Was it God's way of telling her it was going to be okay? She knew it was. "We're going to find her, Debbie—I know we are. Come on, we need to get home…she might be there!"

Debbie smiled, despite her tears and worry. "Todd and I will come with you, okay? The detectives are right; you shouldn't be in that apartment alone. You follow us, okay? Are you all right to drive—you want me to drive your truck home?"

Merry Beth swiped at her tears with the back of her right hand. "Bethany is coming home, Debbie. I just know it! *She's coming home!*" She turned quickly away. "Come on, you two—let's get home! Baron might be walking around the bend any second!"

Debbie jumped down from the warm cab and raced around to the driver's side door of the new Bronco. The best friends hugged once more. Debbie held on to Merry Beth's right hand and squeezed it gently. "Bethany *will* come home, love. And when she does, we'll throw the biggest and happiest welcome home and birthday party you've *ever* seen! We'll blow up a thousand balloons. We'll make the biggest and yummiest cake ever. We'll invite the entire town of Winterville to celebrate with us!"

Worry and fear tried to snag at Merry Beth's heart, but she refused to give in. "Another miracle. We need a miracle! God is going to give us one—we have to have faith."

Pastor Todd was standing just behind his sister-in-law—the woman he'd fallen in love with a year ago. He'd just told her that he loved her in his truck. He'd held her, comforted her tears and fears, kissed her passionately for the first time—she'd said it was too soon. He said he'd wait for her forever.

Pastor Todd smiled and agreed with what Debbie had just said to her best friend. He softly whispered, "Let's pray…together, right here, right now." The three held hands and bowed their heads; they prayed together, as the snowflakes fell from the star-filled heavens—like soft white feathers floating through the air after a fun pillow fight.

* * * * *

Earlier that day, around 11:30 a.m., at the Arlington National Cemetery, Baron stood like a cold, hard and unbending stone statue in the pouring icy rain, staring down at his wife and son's grave and silently whispered his final good-bye. Becky and Baron Jr. were buried together in the same coffin. And he knew they were both in heaven together for all eternity.

His slain wife and son were safe where they were now; there was no longer any darkness, danger, or fear to ever scare or frighten or hurt them again. It was time to let go.

The mission was over. The incriminating disc had been planted and found. Go figure! The General had been arrested, and was at this very moment sitting in a cold, locked, federal, jail cell in downtown D.C., demanding bail; demanding his right, his release—which the federal judge refused.

He'd hid deep in the shadows of the General's closet until the raid and arrest were over. It happened really fast—a matter of minutes really, before they'd cuffed the General and dragged him away like the sick dog with rabid that he was. Luckily, Baron hadn't been discovered during the long hours the condo had been searched, through every nick and cranny but one, the N.S.A., F.B.I., D.E.A. and A.T.F. had looked. And he had calmly walked out of the condo eight hours later around ten-thirty—just an hour before now, unnoticed and finally free—with no evidence left behind that he'd ever been there.

"I figured you might be here," Mitch said to his friend.

Baron never moved to acknowledge Mitch's statement from somewhere to his right nearby. He just continued to stare down at the wet earth and melting snow that covered his lost family in the coldness and blackness of God's earth.

"When you didn't call, the men and I got worried. Are you all right?" Mitch asked, as he stepped closer. His Stetson shielded his face from the pouring rain, but the chilly wind made him shiver inside his wet coat.

A muscle in Baron's left cheek flinched. "I will be…"

"How long have you been standing here in the rain?"

"About thirty minutes, why?"

"Why didn't you call and let us know you were all right?"

"I couldn't. I was trapped in the General's walk-in closet for almost eight hours. And *all* of you should have aborted Washington *hours* ago. Why are you still here?" The muscles in Baron's face twitched in anger, but he still didn't turn to look at Mitch, his creamy gray eyes still glued to the headstone that stated in cold white marble stone '*Becky and Baron Williams, Jr.*'

"The men and I got the call that the raid and arrest had gone down as planned, at seven. You must have called Senior Agent Samuel Nelson from your cellular *inside* that closet."

"You're a smart man, Mitch. Glad I got a signal?"

"The General is in jail, and that's all you have to say?" Mitch's eyes flashed like fire. "*You scared me half to death!*"

Baron had yet to lift his eyes. Through all his rapid emotions at the moment, he tried not to chuckle. "Only half...?"

Mitch gritted his teeth. "That's not funny—not one little bit!"

Baron lifted his tired eyes for the first time in over thirty minutes and glared at his friend and boss with anguish, sorrow, misery, pain, suffering, distress, woe, torment and grief in his ebony eyes. Mitch flinched from the way his eyes glared into his.

"What do you want me to say, Mitch? *Everything we did was wrong. It was illegal. If any one of our friends talk...to anyone—it's over. The evidence we planted was tampered evidence, Mitch?*"

Mitch's stubborn chin lifted. He took in a huge chilly breath. It was over. The *Alliance* had crumbled, once and for all. "It doesn't matter. Our plan worked. He's going down...for good."

Baron's wolf-gray eyes were tormented. "*It does matter!* You and your men must have pretty influential *friends!* The incriminating information Nelson stored on that disc I helped plant in the General's safe—and the disc you gave me at Dunkin Donuts...I don't want to *ever know* where you or he got the information stored on them. I don't want to *know* how many laws were broken to make all of this happen. All I *know* is it should be enough to bury General Madison and twenty-eight of his top people—hopefully Kelly's brothers included, and stop the *Alliance* forever."

"I got the disc I gave you from a close friend in Limestone Village, Maine. His name was Jackson Graham and..." Mitch began to explain sadly, missing his good friend to this very day.

Baron winced, his head pounded. "Was...?"

Regret filled Mitch's eyes. "He's dead."

"Why doesn't that surprise me, or make me feel better?"

"He was murdered, like Becky and your son and..."

"I don't want to *know*, so stop right there. Two of the General's top men—Steven Kelly shot dead on May seventh in Chicago, and Marcus Steeves—the ex-D.D.O. of the C.I.A., Kelly's own brother, in a padded federal cell—who's next, Mitch? How many more men in high-up power and government positions that run this country—this *world*, are left to dig out of their slimy holes and dirty fox-hole ditches? *How many*, Mitch? Or do you even know?" Baron thundered with anger and bitterness in his heart. "How many—ten, fifty, a hundred, *a thousand...?*"

"Take it easy, Bear. Everything went according to plan. This mission is over. It's time to go home…" Mitch began, and flinched when Baron exploded with anger. His eyes, as usual when he was angry, turned from black to wolf-gray.

Baron pointed to the ground at his wife and son's headstone. "Because, you see—this is what I *know! It is never over! This arrest of General Madison will not stop the illegal sale of drugs or weapons to kids on the streets, Mitch!* If you ever think any of this madness will ever be truly over, then you're a fool, Mitch. Look where I'm standing."

"No one's going to talk, Bear. There's no need to worry." Mitch stepped closer to Baron and frowned as he stared at Becky and Baron Jr. names on the white marble headstone. "What we did was good. It might not put an end to the violence, but it sure will make a big difference. The *Alliance* has finally crumbled to dust. Surely, you believe that?" Mitch searched for his friend's dark eyes through the pouring rain.

"I know it, and all the men know it, so you might as well say it. I did this for personal reasons, Mitch. That man is responsible for only God knows how many murders and crimes. I just want to be sure he *knows* that I know."

Mitch flinched. "What does that mean? What have you done? Please tell me you haven't done anything to jeopardize…"

Baron reached inside his black cords right pocket and lifted a golden wedding ring so Mitch could see it.

"See this ring. It's Becky's wedding ring. I almost left it inside that condo so the General would *know* who set him up. It has our names and wedding date engraved on the inside…" Baron stared at the ring in the palm of his hand like it was poison ivy.

"You will never know the truth about Becky, son. Why she chose to do what she did—it's buried six feet under with her and your boy. Some things are better left buried, Baron."

"Have you ever wondered why it's six feet, and not seven or eight? What's the difference? Is there a difference, Mitch?"

Mitch shook his head and pointed towards the ground. "No matter how many times you come here, no matter how long you stare down at her…*their* grave—it's done. It's finished. We accomplished what we all came to Washington for, and you have to completely let go—now, today. If you don't, you can't move on with Mrs. Waters and her sweet little daughter back in Winterville, Maine. It wouldn't be fair to you and it certainly wouldn't be fair to them."

Mitch stepped closer to Baron and touched him lightly on his black leather jacket sleeve. "Just let the past go, son. You can't change what happened to Becky and your son. No matter what you do or say…you're right—they're still dead."

The beating rain forced him to blink and Baron shook his head no. "Easier said than done; my friend." He turned and met Mitch's eyes. "You are my friend, right…?"

"You can't look the General in the eye and tell him you *know*, son. If you do— any of the *Alliance's* evil powers that be that are still out there will come after you. And they won't stop until you're as dead as your wife and son. You have to walk away, and leave it in the federal courts hands."

Mitch pointed to the headstone and said, "Leave it in the past. Turn away now, and walk away *now*, and whatever you do—don't look back."

Baron remained silent and unmoving, and Mitch said, "What we did has put an end to this *Alliance* and…"

"If you want to destroy and knock down a man like the General or Kelly or his assassin brothers, you have to do it so they can't get back up, Mitch—*please* tell me we fixed it so they can't get back up…ever."

Baron's tired eyes scanned the thousands of tiny white stones across the hills and valleys of the national cemetery, and his heart was heavily burdened. "Please tell me these men and women didn't die in vain, Mitch. Tell me their deaths stand for something, *anything?* Please tell me, Mitch, least I go quietly and completely insane while I'm standing here in heart-wrenching pain over the grave of my wife and little son."

Mitch quickly glanced over the hills of melting snow and wet mucky-brown grass and white stones and frowned, "These men and women didn't die for nothing, Baron. You *have* to believe that, son. If you don't, you will literally go crazy, trust me. To preserve freedom, and goodness, and right and kindness and decency—some must die. Now, it might not be fair, but it's the way life is. The General and twenty-eight of his men will be locked up in federal prison for the rest of their natural lives, *that* I *can* promise you—with no chance of ever getting parole. Come on, son—let's go home."

Still, Baron refused to budge. "Merry Beth believes that there is still hope. Why can't I see it, *feel* it? I believe it—I just can't seem to grasp it, not at this very moment."

"You will, in time." Mitch shivered in the cold, beating rain and whispered, "Let's go home. It's cold out here."

"And so now what…? We turn and walk away like you say, we never look back and just hope and pray that our legal system works, right? You know as well as I do that nothing in this life is ever secure!" Baron glanced back down at the wet earth where his wife and son lay in silence and blackness in the same white coffin.

Baron sucked in the cold air and closed his tired eyes for a moment. "Becky and my son are a testimony to that."

Mitch touched Baron's wet sleeve lightly. "You have to let go of the past, and trust God for any kind of hopeful future."

"I'm trying, Mitch. That's why I'm here in Washington, but it's easier said than done, my friend. God has no part in all the evil and injustice and bad things that happen in this world. It's up to us, as individuals, to try and make a difference. But every time one bad guy goes down—it seems like twenty more follow in his footsteps. It's like a useless, endless, never-ending cycle that never stops. And I can't help but wonder if planting that disc in the General's safe like we did will really make a difference." Baron's heart thundered with doubt and uncertainty.

"It will—you'll see. You just have to pray and have faith! Come on, son; let's go home. All our men have left Washington. You need to contact your men, Baron. You need to let them know you're all right. They're all worried sick about you." Mitch turned to walk away, but at the last second turned back and pointed towards Becky and Baron Jr.'s grave.

"This Merry Beth and her young daughter—maybe they are in your life now to help you walk away from *this* painful past. Maybe they can help you move past it," Mitch suggested quietly, "and learn to trust and some day love again."

"And where will you and Carolyn go now? It's obvious your real home isn't Maine but someplace else. You're F.B.I. You were sent to Fort Kent in undercover. What are your plans now that the truth is out—now that the General is in jail, where exactly is your home?"

"I'm going to go get my sweet Carolyn and go home—to *Maine!* I've quit the Bureau, just this morning in fact. We're staying in Maine. Carolyn and I love it there, its home to us now. We have plans to," Mitch laughed suddenly and looked into Baron's ebony eyes to add, "…you're never going to believe this, but we have plans to *grow and sell potatoes!* What do you think? You think Carolyn and I will make good potato *farmers?*"

Baron smiled and took in a long cold breath. *Oh, Merry Beth—I'm coming home to you and the Munchkin. Mitch is right, it's over—it's really over. I can let go now. I can move on. Becky and our son's murders will be accounted for. I'm coming, darling. I'm on my way home!*

301

As Baron slowly turned away from his past he whispered through the beating cold rain, "That sounds really interesting, Mitch." He glanced down at the wet ground once more before turning away. "It sounds good to me, my friend. It's time for me to go home, as well—back to Maine. I hope Ace's plane is still at Dulles?"

Just as Baron turned away he carefully placed two rings—Becky's gold wedding ring and his own, on the top of the white marble headstone. Deep in his healing heart, it was his way of finally letting her go—forever.

"It is," Mitch answered with a smile.

"Well then, friend...what are we waiting for? Let's go."

Suddenly—in Baron's dark eyes...pine Christmas wreath, decorated tree, wrapped presents, pretty blinking lights, apple cider, homemade pie, garland and ice-cycles, hymns and candlelight aglow—all in and around a certain apartment in Winterville, Maine sounded really good right about now. He couldn't wait to see the festive sight. He couldn't wait to look into Merry Beth's eyes again, and pull her close for another earth-moving, unforgettable, binding and deep kiss!

"There's a Christmas Eve concert and children's play I don't want to miss tonight, at seven in Winterville Baptist Church. You and Carolyn want to come?" Baron's heart was free as he walked slowly away from his slain wife and son's grave through the pouring, bitter cold rain.

Mitch smiled. "Love to, my friend. Come on, I'm hungry. Let's get something to eat before we split this town...for good."

Psalm 63:1-4 "O God, thou *art* my God; early will I seek thee: my soul thirsteth for thee, my flesh longeth for thee in a dry and thirsty land, where no water is; To see thy power and thy glory, so *as* I have seen thee in the sanctuary. Because thy loving kindness *is* better than life, my lips shall praise thee. Thus will I bless thee while I live: I will lift up my hands in thy name."

Chapter Fourteen

Gifts
James Thompson

Give a man a horse he can ride,
Give a man a boat he can sail;
And his rank and wealth, his strength and health,
On sea nor shore shall fail.

Give a man a pipe he can smoke,
Give a man a book he can read;
And his home is bright with a calm delight,
Though the room be poor indeed.

Give a man a girl he can love,
As I, O my love, love thee;
And in his heart is great with the pulse of Fate,
At home, on land, or sea.

And life moved on. It was Christmas Eve, December the 24th, Thursday, around 5:30 p.m. He'd let go, and he felt free! For the first time in three years he breathed easy. He felt lighter and the heavy burden across his shoulders was gone.

Baron, stretched out resting with his eyes closed in the back of Ace's small eight-seater plane, reached for his ringing cellular without opening his eyes. He lifted the small phone to his ear, opened his right eye for a second—long enough to glance at his watch, and whispered, "Baron here."

He snuggled deeper under the warm blanket Mitch had given him and grumbled, "This better be good. I'm catching some shut-eye for the first time in days." *And I'm coming home to you, Merry Beth and my sweet Munchkin. I want to tell you I love you face to face! I want to kiss you again and again and…*

"Bear, Mac here. We got…" Mac rolled his dark eyes when Baron interrupted him.

"How are Merry Beth and Bethany? Everything okay there? I'm on my way there, by the way. We should be clearing through Fort Kent's skies any minute. Mitch and Carolyn are with me and…"

"We got trouble," Mac whispered with regret in his heart.

Everything just stopped.

Once more, the world wanted too much.

In an instant Baron opened his rested ebony eyes and sat up. "Why? What's wrong?" His peaceful and calm heart slammed hard against the wall of his chest with quickened fear.

"Merry Beth…? Bethany—are they all right?"

"Someone grabbed the kid from a department store—Wal-Mart, inside Northgate Mall, around one forty-five this afternoon." Mac desperately wanted a cigarette but knew that to light one now would give his position away. "Sorry, boss. I was so close; it happened so fast…why in hell-fire was your cell turned off?"

Baron's thundering heart silenced as everything just stopped, and his world shifted once more. "Details, *please*—where is Ace?" He immediately stood and walked hurriedly towards the front of the plane; the warm blanket and desired sleep fell forgotten to the floor.

"Ace stayed behind in the next-door apartment to keep an eye on things there, while I followed your lady to Wal-Mart. It happened so fast. The girl and her little friend ran off and left your lady in quite the frenzy in the shoe department. The man grabbed Bethany before even *I* could stop him. I'm sorry, my friend. I know that we're here to stop this very thing from happening. He came from out of nowhere—*literally!* The store was mobbed, you know—typical holiday shoppers. There were people everywhere. Anyway, I followed him and…"

Lost was how Baron felt at that moment, lost and alone again, tired and worn down. He reminded himself to take deep breaths against the pain slashing at his heart. He just wanted to be in Merry Beth's loving embrace, but now, if the Munchkin was lost forever, he'd never forgive himself if this happened because of something he was tied to. Never!

This is my fault! "Where did he take her? Do you know the man?" Baron asked, before signaling to Mitch there was a problem. He whispered to Mitch, "We got trouble."

"He's a dead man," Mac whispered over the wire.

Baron rubbed his right hand over his eyes and whiskered jaw. "A dead man...? You talking in riddles again?"

"He's the man who cut me from left temple to chin. He's alive, my friend. I'm watching the house where he took her as we speak. How soon can you and your friend, Mitch, be here? Do you want me to wait for you before I go in and get the kid out?"

Mac's eyes scanned the shabby, worn-down, rat-infested, two-story house and surrounding area. The house stood in a small clearing and it was completely surrounded with tall pine trees on all four sides. The abandoned house couldn't be noticed or seen from the road. Blackness—there was only blackness, and sounds the dark forest made in the dead of night. Despite his excessive training he shivered.

"I thought I'd killed him, tell me this isn't happening," Baron said, as Mitch stepped closer.

"It's dark as unburned coal out here, boss, and so quiet. It's eerie really, and the only sounds I'm hearing are noises from the animals in the forest and the noises from the wind. The darkness and wind remind me of those few hours we spent inside Iraq, just over the border, years back..."

Mac's heart trembled in his chest as he continued, "I got this terrible feeling across my shoulders about this one, boss, something's different. Something's not quite—right...it's like that time I sensed that someone was behind me and you shot him before I could turn—before he could kill me by shooting me in the back. I've always trusted your instinct and your judgment and your word; as you've always trusted mine—what's yours telling you now?"

"I remember you saying the same thing about Iraq. We made it out of there alive and unscratched, didn't we?" Baron whispered. "Where are you—give me the address?"

He signaled to Mitch that he needed some paper and a pen. In seconds he quickly wrote down the information.

"Hold on..." The pen in Baron's hand hurried over the paper, like light-speed. "...I got it."

Baron asked the pilot, another *friend* Mitch had from the war, "How long before we land?"

The pilot, *Magic Fingers* glanced over his right shoulder and answered quickly, "Ten minutes. I'm waiting for clearance now. Why? What's wrong?"

Mitch searched Baron's dark gray eyes and asked, "What's wrong? What's happening?" He reached for his old Army duffel bag and loaded his .22 with steady fingers. He glanced at his wife who was asleep lying down near the back of the plane and closed his eyes in a quick prayer. He prayed for strength and guidance to do whatever needed to be done. From the looks of his friend's eyes—he knew he was angry, *very angry!*

"Something's happened to Merry Beth?" Mitch asked.

Baron whispered in the tiny cell phone, "Ten minutes until we land. We'll be there soon Mac. Don't make any move until we get there, unless he makes a move to take the Munchkin elsewhere. Are you sure it's only him? There's no one else inside that house?"

"Affirmative, I checked in every window, he's alone. The house is abandoned, boss. Empty. And the girl. . ." Mac shivered from the bitter cold and rolled his eyes towards the dark heavens as it started to snow again.

Baron closed his eyes against the fear in his throat. He tried to swallow against it, but couldn't. *Just when I think I'm out, they pull me back in!* "Tell me she's. . ."

"She's fine. She's asleep on a tiny cot, unharmed as far as I can tell," Mac informed quietly.

"And Merry Beth. . .?" *Oh, Merry Beth. I'm so sorry!*

"Ace said she's back at the apartment with her friends from the church. The place is swarming with cops and F.B.I., and is lit up like the Fourth of July, *again!* I don't know what it is with this woman and kid and the bright lights, BMW. Anyway, I was talking to Ace on my cellular when the feds busted in. They're inside the next-door apartment questioning him as we speak. . ."

Baron swore a few choice words that made his guardian angel flinch. "You're gonna have to get him out of there. He's been caught inside with all of that listening equipment, laptop, tapes, surveillance equipment and cameras. You and I both know he won't talk, no matter what they do to him. He won't crack under pressure. But you must do what you have to—to get him cleared *before* the feds take him away!" Mac pleaded over the wire. "You owe him—we all do, in one way or another."

"Mitch will make the call to D.C., In-House; a.s.a.p. Ace will be free from their hold within the half-hour. Is our switchblade happy friend one of the General's friends from the *Alliance?*" Baron asked as he reached for his black leather jacket. "My instinct is telling me he is, Mac. This one will get bloody, mark my word." *I'm going to kill him with my bare hands if he's hurt Bethany!*

Mac shivered against the bitter northeastern wind. "It's hard to say." His expert eyes searched the dirt road leading to the front of the house, when he thought he heard a car approaching.

Baron held the cell phone under his chin as he put his leather jacket on, and reached for his 9mm and ammo. "He must have been watching my movements during that last week before the men and I left for Washington D.C., Mac. How else would he be able to tie me to Merry Beth and Bethany?"

The sound of your heart beating next to mine, Merry Beth, it seems light-years away at this moment. If you love me, will you still love me tomorrow if something goes wrong, and we lose Hope Bethany forever? Baron closed his eyes for a few seconds, trying to still the fear that pounded through his veins.

"I can't rightly say; we all have enemies *all over the world!* Are you *sure* you didn't leave any proof or prints behind in that condo? Because if you did, if the General knows any one of us had a part in that set-up, raid and bust—all our wives, children, girlfriends, parents' lives—anyone we're tied to, are in danger!"

Baron answered, "Negative. No prints, I'm sure. We all wore gloves from start to finish—even when I rented the van, even inside the van and that condo—we never took our gloves off, not once."

Mitch asked once more, "Tell me what's happening."

Baron said, "Hold on Mac..." He glanced at Mitch and answered, "An old *friend* of Mac, Ace and I from our Navy days took Bethany. He has her in an abandoned house not far from the Fort Kent/Cair, Canadian border, just off of Route 161. The feds are questioning Ace in the apartment next door to Merry Beth as we speak. We have to get him out of there, *now*, and if our switchblade happy friend is tied to the General and the *Alliance*, then I'm right—it's far from over!"

Baron passed the address to Mitch. "Give this to the pilot—see if he can find a place to land this plane nearby."

Mitch immediately shook his head no. "There's no way General Madison can tie the raid and bust to any of us. We made sure of that. No, this man from your past—he wants *you*, Baron. That's why he's taken Bethany." He grabbed the paper and turned back to the cockpit.

Baron turned back to the phone call. "I can name at least thirty different enemies I have all over the world. I should have known something like this would happen. What about Bethany's grandfather? Earl? What's his twenty?" Baron asked Mac.

"Winterville Emergency most of the morning and afternoon, car accident, OUI, arrested, he's in jail as we speak, why? Ace did some checking on his laptop, and Earl Anthony Waters is nothing but a walking time-bomb! He's a walking disaster just itching to detonate and go off. He's dangerous and deadly. I don't understand why he's out walking the streets. You think he has something to do with this? You think he'd snatch his own granddaughter? Is it possible he's tied to *Ice Man?*"

"With everything we've seen while a SEAL, we both know that anything's possible, my friend, and you and I both know how deadly *Ice Man* is." Baron rubbed his throbbing forehead, and silently prayed for God to show him the way.

"Yeah, well...just hurry up and get here, would you?"

"Anyone else that you noticed hanging around?" Baron couldn't help but wince and jerk back from Mac's next words, and had to swallow against the fear in his throat and thundering heart. "Someone who might be the Ice's accomplice...?"

"Not a single soul, sorry..." Mac's skillful eyes scanned the surrounding perimeter of the house as a black Chevy pick-up pulled into the long driveway leading to the house.

"I gotta go, *now*, boss—someone's coming to join the party. Black Chevy pick-up, two door...hold on and I'll give you the plate number so you can run a trace."

Mac set his cell phone down on the icy snow and reached for his expensive, military-issued, nighttime binoculars. In seconds he reached for his cell phone and whispered the plate number over the wire. "I gotta go, God speed, my friend."

Baron closed his eyes against the swelling fear and raging panic in his heart and throat, as he wrote down the plate number a few seconds later. "Got it..."

"See you soon, watch your back," Mac whispered.

"You, too, God speed," Baron said huskily.

As Baron placed his cell phone in his leather jacket pocket he filled Mitch in. "I know the man who took Bethany—if you can call him a man. He's an old...acquaintance of mine. Someone I once knew in Cambodia while a SEAL. He's a dead man, literally. I killed him, or at least I thought I did. He knows no difference between good and evil, right or wrong; he's pure evil. He has the devil's own lethal and dark eyes and black heart. Right after he sliced Mac's face from his left temple to his chin, I shot him four times point blank in his chest with my silenced 9mm Smith & Wesson..."

Mitch buckled himself in, as the plane started to descend. "He must have been wearing a vest. Tell me all you know about him. Ice Man...the name doesn't ring any bells."

Baron buckled himself in as well, and watched as *Magic Fingers* prepared to land the small aircraft. His thoughts flashed to Merry Beth, knowing how scared and worried she had to be. So close, so close to grabbing that new life. *I won't let anything happen to your baby, Merry Beth. I promise I'll bring her back to you. I love you, my pretty flour-snowbird! I love you. I'm going to fix this, I promise!*

Mitch frowned with worry after hearing Baron's story about the deadly killer. "What's the plan now?"

Baron handed the piece of paper to Mitch and said, "Make the call, will you, and trace this plate number. And call Senior Agent Samuel Nelson to get Ace out from underneath the feds clutches in the apartment next door to Merry Beth!"

Baron placed his throbbing head in his hands and prayed for yet another miracle. Mitch unbuckled, rose and sat in the co-pilots chair, and reached for the headphones and controls to make the call, after he strapped in.

"The man who took Bethany from her mother—*he'd kill the Munchkin for fun, and laugh just to spite me and watch my heart bleed!* I should have slit his throat before walking away. I should have made *sure* he was dead. How could I have been so stupid?"

Regret buzzed inside Baron's throbbing head and he tried to ignore the terrible truth. Bethany was in danger and at risk because of him. He did this. *He* was responsible for Merry Beth's agony and pain, worry, fear and tears.

Mitch reached for his cell phone and dialed Adam's number. He didn't waste a second to ask, "This man who took Bethany, is he a traitor against our own government?"

Sometimes it's hard to forget the sound of the crying of the rain, the sound of good-bye. Baron knew, in his heart, it was over. Any chance, as long as he was alive, for him and Merry Beth and Bethany to create a new life together was over.

"Yes. My men and I crossed his path only once when we went in on a secret mission to rescue four Naval officers who'd been trapped inside a dungeon-type prison in Cambodia. The four men were scheduled for death in front of a firing squad at sunrise. He's a killer, Mitch, a hit man, a hired Assassin..."

"You think he works for The General?" Mitch asked.

"He's part Chinese, part German and part Russian. He's deadly and dangerous. You're right; he's taken the Munchkin to get to me. I thought he was dead, I guess I didn't wait around long enough to make sure. He must have been wearing a bulletproof vest. He was sent in, by God only knows who, to eliminate the four officers before my team could get to them, but my team and I made it in there just in time to save their lives. We got them out before anyone ever knew we were there."

"Why now? Why is he coming out in the open for you? What did you do to him to make him so angry, angry enough to risk everything by coming after you like this...all these years later?" Mitch frowned, unbuckled, stood and quickly followed Baron as he walked towards the back of the plane.

"For starters, I cut his face from his right temple to his chin. Guess he should have never cut Mac like that, eh? I told you this one would get messy and bloody, Mitch. I was right; it's *not* over. It will *never* be over!" As Baron walked to the back of the plane he felt four things...

Regret, fear, pain and a deep sense of apprehension because he knew there was no kind of future for him without freedom. Freedom from his past, freedom from anything in his past that could crawl out of the woodwork at any moment in time to hurt Merry Beth or her daughter, as long as he was alive.

He knew, as he sat at the back of the plane and watched their swift decent to earth it was over. He couldn't stay and commit and love a woman like Merry Beth. They lived in two different kinds of worlds. He so craved hers, and knew she wouldn't be able to survive in his. His life was filled with uncertainty and risks, dangers, plots and schemes, war and death, pain and loneliness, lies, weapons and flying bullets. For a man like him, there was no such thing as Christmas or hope. What had he been thinking to ever think there was?

The dream he'd created inside his heart—the one where he could return to Winterville, Maine and claim Merry Beth and Bethany as his own family, was over.

* * * * *

Merry Beth paced back and forth, back and forth across the cold vinyl floor in her kitchen and prayed silently for a miracle. So many things had gone wrong in the past two weeks.

...the car accident

...losing her father's old classic '69 Chevy

...her broken arm and sprained wrist and other injuries

…falling in love and losing Baron in almost one breath

…love disappearing before it had a chance to blossom

…Baron lost to her in a place she didn't know

…Bethany being snatched by some unknown madman

…the children's Christmas Eve concert and play cancelled

…Bethany not being home to receive and then open her Christmas Eve's package and birthday presents. It was too much. She couldn't take much more!

Now, her home had been invaded by the sheriff and his deputies, the State Police and F.B.I.—men who were at this very moment, next door questioning her mysterious neighbor. Todd had taken Lisa and gone home minutes before, leaving Merry Beth and Debbie alone in the apartment.

…Alone to face the fear.

…Alone to face the panic and anxiety from not knowing.

…Alone to face the uncertainty.

…Alone with unimaginable thoughts.

…Alone to face the truth, and wait.

There was still so much to learn, so much to try, so much to do. Bethany was only five years old! There were dreams to strive and work for, dreams to make come true. There were dozens of more birthdays and Christmases to celebrate, and no matter what life threw her way, Merry Beth knew there was hope. She knew that God was listening and watching, every second. She knew that everything in her life happened for a purpose, in God's will and timing.

There were moments, while they waited for word—any word, that Merry Beth felt a tiny glimpse of hope. Those were the moments while she prayed and asked God for His guiding hand in the nightmare called fear. Other than during those silent moments—all seemed bleak, dreary, barren, bare, cold, dismal, desolate, raw and chilly. Would spring ever come?

And the terrible truth—the truth that the chance of ever finding Bethany again was slim to none, it called out to the two women, whispering mockingly close to their thundering, fearful hearts in the deadly quiet apartment, after the State Police, F.B.I., sheriff and deputies, Todd and Lisa had left.

Debbie glanced quickly at her best friend with glistening tears across her lashes. She didn't know what to say to ease her pain.

"Merry Beth, please—won't you sit down, before you fall down? Let me make you a cup of tea or get you something to eat. You have to keep your strength up, for when she comes home. You're beyond exhaustion, and I'm very worried about you. Todd and I don't want you to end up in the hospital!"

"I c…can't," Merry Beth quietly mumbled, as she fought hard for breath. Tears burned the back of her eyes again, and she swallowed the huge lump in her throat.

Debbie's pleas disappeared with the bitter northeastern chilly wind. "You can't go on like this, love. You'll pass out from pure exhaustion. You'll end up in the E.R. again."

Merry Beth wondered how she could ever eat or drink or smile or be happy, or live any kind of normal life, or sleep again, without her baby safe at home, here under the same roof. Sobs choked her and she swayed to fall into one of her kitchen chairs. She glanced at her friend sitting across the kitchen table and tried to smile but couldn't, not for the very life of her.

"Who do you think h…he is, D…Debbie?" She winced and her breath caught in her dry throat, as pain shattered through her throbbing arm like lightning striking in a powerful hailstorm. There was no sunshine smiling down upon her shoulders with warm promises of a happy Christmas tomorrow at that moment. She wanted her baby back!

"Are there *three* men? The man next door doesn't have a scar on his f…face?" Merry Beth asked for the hundredth time.

"I don't know, love. I'm sure the F.B.I. and State Police and the sheriff and his deputies will figure it all out. We can't lose our faith through all of this. God is with Bethany. He's watching over her. I know it. Can't you feel it? You placed your daughter in God's hands when she was first born. I don't believe that God will turn His back on one of His own children!"

"I need to take something for the pain, Debbie. My arm hurts like you wouldn't believe!" Merry Beth wiped away her constant stream of tears and reached for her black purse that sat on her cluttered kitchen table.

Debbie wiped her own tears away. "Merry Beth…?"

"I hear what you're saying. It's just hard when you don't *know!* When you love someone more than you do your own life, someone who's in danger and lost to you—the pain suffocates."

As Merry Beth searched for the little bottle of Tylenol hidden inside her purse she rambled, "Do you think Bethany has had anything to eat? She must be hungry. Do you think she's warm wherever he's taken her? It's snowing again and it's cold outside, Debbie. Do you think he's hurt her or touched her in any w…way? If he has, I don't think I can b…bear it; do you think Bethany is c…crying w…wherever she is?"

312

Debbie winced. "Don't do this to yourself, please…"

Merry Beth gulped down three tablets after Debbie passed her a glass of cold water. "She's never been far away from me, or our home—unless she's at church, day-care or your house. *Her birthday is tomorrow, Debbie. She's only six years old. A child! A baby!* Do you think he's going to call? Does he know they have all that trace equipment hooked up to my phone? Do you think he has her tied up with r…ropes or…duct tape?"

Merry Beth gave in to the rising panic and stood and swayed from the dizziness the horror inflicted. Her words failed her and she fell to the floor in her fear and isolation and pain.

Debbie reached for her. "Merry Beth, *please…*"

Merry Beth's frightened green eyes were glazed-over with tormenting pain. "Where's Baron, Debbie? He'd know what to do to find her. I…can't…do…this alone anymore!"

Debbie instantly reached for her and pulled her close. She held on to her best friend tight and rocked her back and forth. "Take it easy, Merry Beth. You're going to collapse!"

"I can't…go on…without…my baby!"

Every ounce of strength Merry Beth had left snapped in two, like a broken tree branch covered with heavy wet snow. "Where's Baron? Why isn't he here? Why hasn't he called? I have the Christmas lights on so he can find his way back home. Why isn't he here yet? I can't bear it, Debbie…if my…baby…never comes b…back. I'll die!"

Merry Beth lowered her throbbing head on her best friend's breast and wept like a little baby.

Debbie wiped her own tears away and hugged her best friend tight, comforting her by rubbing her back softly. "They'll find her. Whatever we do—we can never give up searching, *never!*"

"If I lose her…forever, I'll die!" Merry Beth sobbed. "I can't imagine my life without…her…here…with me."

Debbie held on nice and tight and whispered, "God will keep Bethany safe, Merry Beth. I just know it. We have to have faith and believe that the police officers and F.B.I. will find a clue as to where he's taken her."

"I'm trying, but…I'm a mother without her child!"

Dark chocolate eyes clashed with dark grass-green. Both women knew too much time had already passed by.

Debbie shook her head no; refusing to believe Bethany would never come home again. She lightly shook Merry Beth's shoulders. "You can't give up. *You hear me? You can't give up! I won't let you—I won't let you. I'm here for you, please, try not to worry. I know it's hard, but we have to believe!*" She soothed her best friend as best she could. "You need to get some sleep, Merry Beth...before you collapse. Let me make you something to eat, before you try to lie down to rest...?"

Debbie and Merry Beth sat in the middle of the cold kitchen floor holding each other, comforting each other—in whispering doubt that everything was going to be all right. It was several minutes before Merry Beth asked through her constant battle between faith and fear, "Do you think he's tied to that other man? The one next door...?"

The apartment lights flickered off from the raging snowstorm battling against the apartment house, leaving the apartment in complete darkness. Both women jumped apart like frightened children being caught in a lie, as Detective Longwood walked in the back door.

The bitter cold and strong wind and blistering snow blew in the door behind him, as the house went completely black and he said, "Got any candles, Mrs. Waters? It looks like it's going to be a long, cold and dark night."

As both women stood he continued, "The man that's next door as we speak—he's not tied to the man who took your daughter. A call just came in from the Deputy Director of the F.B.I. in Washington D.C., Senior Agent Samuel Nelson—your neighbor is squeaky bleach-clean. We were ordered to let him go."

"Who ordered it?" Debbie swallowed against the shivers tiptoeing up and down her spine and arms as she helped Merry Beth stand on her feet. "Merry Beth, where's your candles?"

Detective Longwood frowned with worry, "You're not going to believe this, but the order came from the President, Mrs. Waters, Mrs. Thomas, and your other neighbor...the one with the jagged scar on the *left* side of his face, is one of the good guys as well...he and the man next door are the good guys. They are not responsible for taking your daughter away."

Merry Beth rubbed her throbbing temples. "So, I was right, Debbie. There are *three* different men."

Merry Beth stood, not too steady, and reached for her kitchen counter to hold herself upright. "You're absolutely sure about this, Detective Longwood?"

Detective Longwood smiled and shut the door against the bitter northeastern wind on his back. "Pink-positive...I talked with the President myself, ma'am."

Debbie asked once more, "Merry Beth, the candles? It's darker than a forgotten closet in here."

"They're in the drawer next to the fridge. Here," Merry Beth reached under her kitchen sink for her flashlight to add, "...use this so you can see." She passed Debbie the flashlight before turning back to the detective once more with her thundering heart, constant fear and questions.

"So...just who are these two men who've been next door? What's all that equipment over there for, if they're not working with the man who stole my baby away like that?" Merry Beth turned towards the sink and poured herself another glass of cold water, and quickly swallowed the entire glass, before continuing with her nervous pacing. "Come on, detective—talk to me. Tell me the truth, *please!* My daughter's life is at stake here!"

Debbie stepped closer to Merry Beth and hugged her to her side, after lighting five candles already in glass vases that sat in the back of the kitchen towel drawer. She placed them around the kitchen counters and after Merry Beth assured her she was all right, she reached for four more that sat on top of the washer in the laundry room off the kitchen. She lit them and set them on the table.

Detective Longwood waited until Debbie had lit four more candles before replying, "The man who rented the apartment next door *is* Michael Alan Carter, and according to the D.D.O. of the F.B.I. and the President, he's a friend, Mrs. Waters. His friends' name, the one we found next door with all the equipment— well, I'll just say he's also one of the...good guys. It seems that they were sent here by a Sergeant Baron Michael Williams to keep an eye on you and your daughter...to keep you both safe."

Merry Beth gasped in shock, but relief. "I knew it!"

Debbie paled and swayed slightly. "Oh, my...Merry Beth...Baron sent them to watch over you to keep you safe."

"These two men served with Sergeant Williams on the same Navy SEAL Team, several years' back. Seems like Sergeant Williams and these two men have pretty...well, I'll just call them *substantial and influential friends* in Washington D.C. Do either of you know anything about that?"

Hope blossomed inside her heart once more, as Merry Beth whispered softly, "*Baron? These men know Baron?*" Her eyes closed in a quick prayer. *Thank you dear God in Heaven, thank You! Forgive me for my doubts and fear. Please keep my baby and Baron both safe until they both come home—together!*

Sometimes the heart has to learn how to let go of the fear and trust, in faith. It's the hardest lesson in life. Merry Beth smiled as she thought of the words her father had told her a hundred times over the years. Oh, how she wished he were right here with her, right now. What she wouldn't give to see his wonderful face, one more time!

"Yes. Your entire apartment is bugged. They have been listening, watching—but what I can't figure out is *how* the D.D.O. of the F.B.I. in Washington D.C. knew this man was being questioned by us at *this* very precise moment in time. How did…" He shook his head and poured himself another cup of black coffee, before he finished his question, "…Senior Agent Samuel Nelson know to call here, now, *tonight?* Unless…?"

Debbie began to pace, uncertain. "Unless…?"

The lights flickered back on and Merry Beth reached for Debbie's hands and held on tight. "Unless Mr. Carter's friend called Baron…"

Detective Longwood shook his head. "It's possible, he was talking on his cellular when we busted in." He began to pace. "Those two men—your new neighbors, they're the good guys, Mrs. Waters. Now all we have to do is figure out whom it was who took your daughter. We know the where, the when…if we only knew the why and who…"

Debbie shook her head no, and winced when the lights went out again. "Baron doesn't even know about Bethany being taken yet," she searched for the detective's hard sea-blue eyes in the moving shadows from the dancing light of the candles across the walls and ceiling and finished, "…does he?"

"How is that possible? I don't understand." Merry Beth reminded herself that Bethany's fate was in God's hands. Love *was* on the way back to her, on the wings of angels. Time was turning the pages, not that terrible man who'd snatched Bethany away. Love would bring Bethany *and* Baron home again—if she believed. Well, she believed!

The detective sipped his warm black coffee as he paced. "It's highly unlikely that…"

Merry Beth smiled for the second time since Bethany's disappearance. "Yes, it *is* possible and Baron *does* know. I don't know how I know it, I just do. Call Todd, Debbie, Bethany's coming home—*my baby is coming home!* Baron has his hand in all of this somehow, and I trust him. He won't let anything bad happen to Bethany, I know it. He knows she's been taken and is going to bring her home!"

Debbie watched her best friend as she lit two, old, red, oil-lanterns that sat on a shelf above the washer and dryer, for Lord only knew how long. Her heart raced with doubt. Bethany had been gone too long. She could very well be over the Maine borders by now—taken anywhere in this country or Canada to never be seen again.

Tears burned Debbie's dark brown eyes.

Her best friend was in love with a ghost—what did they really know about Baron? And Todd—he said that he loved her. What was she going to do about that? Her heart raced with doubts and questions. She could, if she let herself, love him back. Maybe…

Had God given both she and Merry Beth a second chance at love? Was this the miracle they both needed to see them through this dark and fearful, stormy night?

Debbie glanced out Merry Beth's kitchen sink window and gasped. "Merry Beth—look…on your outside windowsill—it's a white dove. Oh, my goodness! Isn't he beautiful? Merry Beth—this is it…this is the sign from God that we need to tell us that everything's going to be all right! Can you feel it?"

Merry Beth hugged her best friend very close. "Yes, I feel it. Everything is all right…you'll see."

* * * * *

The men were off Route 161, just eight miles north of Ouelette, Maine. It was just past seven p.m. Baron wanted to tell Merry Beth, face to face, that the sun and moon arose in her deep ocean-green eyes. He wanted to reach for her with gentleness and caring and pull her close for the rest of his days. He could see her smile, even now, and hear her laughter. He could feel her soft and caring touch on his face. He wanted to hold her close and feel her heartbeat next to his own and kiss her again and again and again. He wanted his renewed faith in his Lord to lead him where he needed to go—back where goodness and kindness and honesty and laughter and hope lived…in Winterville, Maine—in her arms.

Love could open any closed door, Merry Beth had said. Love could heal all the broken wings and shattered hearts, his mother had once told him. Love takes a hold of your heart and never lets go; Bethany's eyes told him it was true. Love grows from everything that matters: kindness, caring, friendship, truth, loyalty, sincerity and honesty, unselfishness, smiles, laughter, compassion, and yes, even Christmas Eve wants and wishes.

"What do you think?" Mac whispered to Baron, as the four men watched the house in the darkness of the late hour.

"There are three men inside, we only outnumber them by one; because I don't want to make any mistakes and put that precious little girl's life at risk." Mac frowned as he checked his loaded and silenced .22 with steady fingers.

Mac frowned before he added quietly in the night, "It's a different game when there's a child inside. Maybe we should just wait until they come out and take them out then?"

"There won't be any mistakes, they don't know we're here," Mitch whispered through the bitter, howling wind and blistering blowing snow. "We have the element of surprise on our side. Still, I'm breaking every federal rule I've ever been taught or taken here tonight."

Baron winced. "It won't be the first time for any of us."

Johnny said, with a two-pack-a-day deep and husky voice, "New game; new rules, and I always play to win."

Baron frowned and shook his head no as he put on his black leather gloves. "On the street and in the jungle there are no rules, you all know that. And Bethany is already at risk—from the moment *Ice Man* snatched her away from her mother, she's been at risk. And this time we don't have listening devices, laptops, surveillance equipment, extra ammo, or a back-up plan to fall back on. This time we go in by surprise, and shoot to kill gentlemen, or that young girl is going to die. And I for one don't want to be the one to have to tell Merry Beth her daughter will *never* be coming home again."

Magic Fingers smiled and checked his weapon, like Baron's it was an impressive, silver 9mm Smith & Wesson. "Lock and load." He took in a long cold breath, calming his beating heart.

Baron searched the surrounding perimeter with Mac's night-time binoculars once more and whispered, "All right, Johnny—you take the back door. Mac—you do what you do best and climb up on that roof again and get into that upstairs bedroom window…"

Baron threw each man a black ski mask and said, "Here, put these on. If *Ice Man* sees my face—he will not hesitate to kill the Munchkin in front of me. He'll want me to watch as he does it, believe me—*I know! He's ruthless!* I remember his black eyes as I cut him from his right temple to his chin, just minutes before I shot him four times.

"We're dealing with a man who can't be killed, gentlemen. He considers *me* his enemy. He wants *my* blood spilled here tonight. And taking the Munchkin is his way of calling me out into the open to face him. Killing her will be his way of revenge for the scar I gladly gave him. It's his redemption—now, by *my* hand, his fate."

Johnny holstered his lethal 9mm Beretta and whispered, "Affirmative. Let's kill the bastard, and leave the world a much better and safer place because we did."

Mitch frowned and asked Baron, "No federal backup?"

Mac shook his head no. "Negative. We don't want to be anywhere near this place when they find the dead bodies. BMW is right—shoot to kill, gentlemen. If you don't, you'll die. Trust me. I'm a believing and praying man, but I also live in the real world. It's a fine line I walk. Remember, we've all tasted death. Everyone on our SEAL Team knows how lethal *Ice Man* is. He kills for pleasure."

Baron met Mitch's hazel eyes in the shadows of the night, both remembering the past. Mitch frowned. "I don't like it, but I'm in. I don't want to see Mrs. Waters' eyes, if anything bad happens to that little girl tonight. Watch each other's backs, gentlemen, heads up and eyes open. No screw ups!"

Baron glanced over the area once more before he quietly instructed the three men, "Wait for my bird call and we'll all go in at once. Mitch is right—heads up, no-holds-barred, there's the element of surprise we have in our favor, and that's about all we have on our side tonight. And Mac, they won't be expecting you to come charging through the back door *literally* from the second floor. I'm counting on you, man."

Mac grinned and gave his friend the thumbs up sign. Baron searched for Mitch's eyes in the thick falling snow. "Mitch, you and I will go in the front. All right, everyone check your watches. We go in at exactly seven-fifteen on the dot."

They did and Mitch whispered, "Let's move."

The black of night swallowed them whole, the spot where they'd been already covered with new falling snow in moments. The night was cold, deadly. The game they played risky, perilous. The life they lived unbalanced, eccentric.

Psalms 140:1-4 "DELIVER me, O LORD, from the evil man: preserve me from the violent man; Which imagine mischiefs in *their* heart; continually are they gathered together *for* war. They have sharpened their tongues like a serpent; adders' poison *is* under their lips. Selah. Keep me, O LORD, from the hands of the wicked; preserve me from the violent man; who have purposed to overthrow my goings."

Chapter Fifteen

"How Do I Love Thee?"
Elizabeth Barrett Browning

How do I love thee? Let me count the ways,
I love thee to the depth and breadth and height
My soul can reach, when feeling out of sight
For the end of Being and ideal Grace.

I love thee to the level of every day's
Most quiet need, by sun and candle-light.
I love thee freely, as men strive for Right,
I love thee purely, as men turn from Praise.

I love thee with the passion put to use
In my old grief's, and with my childhood's faith.
I love thee with a love I seemed to lose
With my lost saints,—I love thee with the breath.

Smiles, tears, of all my life!—and, if God choose,
I shall but love thee better after death.

It was Christmas Eve, 7:21 p.m., and two men lay dead on the bare, dirty rotten and rat infested floor in their own sweat and blood. Bethany lay unharmed and sleeping, safe in Johnny's strong arms far from the abandoned house, inside Mitch's warming truck. Mitch, Mac and Baron stood their ground as they pointed their weapons at the man some called *Ice Man*—their enemy, inside the old and decrepit abandoned house.

"Drop your weapon—it's over!" Baron demanded. He knew the moment he said the words the dark, evil Assassin with black eyes standing less than ten feet away wouldn't do it. He knew it was do or die and thought, *Oh, Merry Beth, I'm so sorry. I love you. I have a bad feeling this time. I'm not going to make it out of here alive. I'm not going to make it back to you! Forgive me? Never stop loving me, if you do. I will always be with you. I will always love you! I'm so sorry...*

Evil, dark, sickening laughter rang throughout the empty and barren and cobweb infested room and left Mitch, Mac and Baron feeling cold, the dead of winter kind of cold.

"Wrong," *Ice Man* whispered. "It's over when *I* say it's over. You tell your men to back off Williams, or I won't hesitate to kill you where you stand. I have exactly two bullets left in this weapon—you, on the other hand, only have five seconds to live. Are you prepared to die this night?"

Ice Man's dark eyes switched to Mac's. "You remember the feel of my switchblade cutting open your face, old man?"

The men removed their black masks, and Baron immediately whispered to his friends, "Back off. I can handle this."

Mac answered with a twitching jaw, "Negative."

Mitch didn't even flinch, as he answered, "No way."

Baron demanded loudly, "*Back off! This is between him and me! Go—now!* Make sure Bethany gets back to her mother safe and sound. Do it. *Now! Back off!*"

Mac shook his head no. "I ain't leaving you here to face this evil black devil alone. This is one abort call I'm ignoring—so you can just forget it. I ain't leaving!"

Baron didn't take his gray eyes away from his enemy as he said, "*Go—now! I know what I'm doing, trust me, now go!*"

Ice Man counted slowly, "Five...four...three...two..."

Baron yelled with very little hope inside him, "*Go, now!*"

Mac ignored his thundering heart. "Godspeed, Baron."

Just as Mac and Mitch turned away Baron whispered, "Tell Merry Beth I'm sorry, and that I love her." In seconds he was alone to face his enemy from his past, and his fate.

"It's been a long time." *Ice Man's* crooked smile and jagged, scarred face was injurious and wicked, cold and hard, as cold and as hard as his very soul, if he even had one.

This was it. This was the final end game.

"I should have known that this day would come," Baron answered, calmly. "Men like you don't die easily. What's wrong, you just a little testy for that scar I put on the right side of your already ugly, betraying, lying, murderous face?"

"You had your chance with me, now it's mine." *Ice Man*'s sickening evil laughter didn't scare or frighten Baron. It only made him stronger.

"I should have slit your slimy throat."

"Yes, I guess you should have."

"Why now…?" Baron asked calmly.

"Why not…?" *Ice Man* answered freshly.

"Why take the kid? You could have come after me without taking the kid," Baron stated, his dark-gray eyes never leaving his adversary. One blink and he'd be dead.

"You're here aren't you?" *Ice Man* just grinned his crooked nasty grin and laughed once more. "I've been watching you for weeks, *years* actually—you're getting old, old man, you're slipping. The love you have for the woman and child—it blinded you and made you unbearably weak, made you make stupid mistakes, made you unaware!"

Laughter erupted from deep within his evil heart before *Ice Man* whispered, "Almost as blind and as stupid and weak as your dead wife. Becky—wasn't that her name? Now *she* was a…"

What was that saying Baron had always heard—the truth shall set you free? At that precise moment the truth only made him bitter, bitter and icy cold, cold and alone; so alone. His face twitched from it, as the truth registered in his alert brain and thundering heart.

This evil man's hand was responsible for what happened to Becky. Baron's weapon lifted a little higher and he fought hard against the black spots dancing wildly in front of his eyes, as the truth sank in. He knew he only had one more bullet—he needed to make this one count if he was to make it back to Merry Beth and the Munchkin to start that new life.

"You're the one. You're the one who threatened my wife and son," Baron simply stated, hatred clouding his thoughts and heart. Only God could forgive a terrible monster such as this, he couldn't, and never would.

"I did more than threaten your wife. I had sex with her *before* I killed her." *Ice Man* truly lived up to his name as he laughed in Baron's shocked, pale face.

Baron wanted to vomit; yet he never faltered as he continued pointing his weapon at his enemy's massive chest with a steady hand. "General Madison…?"

"Word travels fast. He'll never make it to trial."

"You're going to kill him," Baron stated without fear or surprise across his tongue that seemed to want to choke him.

"Yes." *Ice Man*'s cold, unfeeling, empty black eyes deepened with barren, hollow void. "Right after I kill you."

"Ah, but my soul will live on…with my Savior in Heaven—yours…I'm sure, on the other hand, will face hell's fire and brimstone and damnation for all eternity. Are you ready to die?"

Baron smiled before raising his silenced 9mm a few notches higher. "*You* have five seconds. Because there's no way I can allow you to walk away, not this time. This time I'm going to stay and make *sure* you're dead. And when I do, I'm going to bury you six feet under myself, one shovel of dirt at a time."

"Definitely; give me your best shot." *Ice Man* never even flinched, his eyes locked with Baron's, taunting him.

"With pleasure," Baron answered without fear across his tongue. If he was going to die, he was dying *his own way!*

"This is going to be fun," *Ice Man* promised; his eyes as cold as his dead and lost heart.

A muscle under Baron's left eye twitched. "Come on, *old man*, what are you waiting for!"

Ice Man snickered. "It's been a long time coming, prepare to die!" He fired his weapon once at Baron's chest.

Two shots rang through the dark of night at the same time. Listening just outside the broken front door, Mitch and Mac turned back inside, each fearing the worse.

George, the Death Angel, stepped closer and lightly touched Baron's blood-spattered pale face. A light surrounded both he and Baron, but Mitch and Mac didn't see.

Two men had fallen to the barren, decrepit floor in blood and death. Mac reached Baron's bloody body first and yelled as he started compressions to save his life, "*Mitch—get on your cell and get some medical help in here, right now! To hell with the consequences—he wasn't wearing a vest!*"

He leaned down and added, "And he isn't breathing!"

George took Baron's hand and together they walked towards the bright light…

* * * * *

Merry Beth jumped like a caged animal, when the phone rang. For a moment or two she was scared to pick it up. She glanced at the clock. It was 7:46 p.m. It didn't seem like Christmas Eve. She had a creepy feeling across her shoulders that something was terribly wrong. Her insides began to tremble, again, and she felt sick to her stomach and dizzy. What would this call reveal? Was Bethany okay? Was Baron coming home?

Merry Beth paled and looked at Debbie. "Who do you think that is? I'm scared…"

Debbie glanced quickly at her best friend and asked, "You want me to get it?"

Merry Beth raced quickly to her kitchen phone and picked up the receiver with shaking fingers. "Hello…" Her whisper made even Detective Longwood flinch.

"Mrs. Waters, this is Mitch McMillian—Baron's boss from the State Police Headquarters in Fort Kent…" Mitch closed his eyes against the frustration, not knowing if he could do this.

Merry Beth closed her tired eyes and leaned her forehead against the wall, holding her breath in. "Yes…"

"Your daughter is safe. She's at the Winterville Regional Hospital Emergency," Mitch began to explain.

Merry Beth let out a huge held in breath. "Was she hurt…in any way?" *Oh, baby—hold on. Mommy's coming!*

"No, but she is being checked by the pediatrician on call."

Merry Beth's knees trembled and she reached for the stove to steady herself. "And Baron…? *Where's Baron? Please…*"

"I'm sorry Mrs. Waters, the news isn't good. Can you make it to the hospital through the storm?" Mitch asked huskily.

"Yes. I'll be there as soon as I can. Thank you," Merry Beth whispered before hanging up the phone. She turned and raced into Debbie's arms sobbing.

"What is it, *tell us!*" Debbie hugged her best friend tightly.

Detective Longwood asked, "Who was that on the phone? Your daughter…?"

Merry Beth dried her tears with a napkin before answering, "That was Baron's boss from the State Police Department where he works in Fort Kent; he said Bethany is fine, unhurt and we need to get to Winterville Emergency, as soon as we can."

Debbie sucked in all the cool air she could into her relieved lungs and jumped when the lights snapped back on. She started blowing out candles. "And Baron…?"

"I'm not sure." No matter how hard Merry Beth tried she couldn't swallow the hysteria rising in her throat.

"What do you mean you're not sure, not sure about what? *What?*" Debbie demanded as she quickly reached for her winter coat that hung on a peg by the back door.

Merry Beth shook her head to clear away the nausea and asked the detective softly, "Can you take us to the hospital? It's not far from here—between five and six miles. The storm…?"

He shook his head yes, and as Debbie and Merry Beth rushed to blow out all the candles and put on their winter coats and boots, Debbie whispered a quick prayer, "Dear Lord, please, for Merry Beth's sake—if it is Your will, let Baron be all right. Thank You, Lord, for keeping Bethany safe. Guide our steps, Lord, and help us to keep our eyes on You for strength. In your name I pray, Amen."

Detective Longwood placed a fake smile across his face, trying to reassure Merry Beth everything would be all right. "I'll go warm up the car and inform the feds and sheriff's department Bethany's been found. Come on out when you're ready."

As Merry Beth rushed to dress her feet and grab her keys and purse, she prayed silently and thanked God for Bethany's safe return. She prayed for another miracle…for Baron. She wiped away her tears and fears and told herself everything would be just fine, that Baron was also safe, that Baron would be back. He had to. It was Christmas Eve! She loved him, and couldn't wait to tell him face to face.

As Detective Longwood drove Debbie and Merry Beth to the hospital through the raging storm, silence ruled inside the car. No one spoke a single word, each lost in thoughts of their own. Detective Longwood feared the worst. Debbie prayed for her best friend's heart, fearing it was about to get crushed and broken again. Merry Beth prayed for another Christmas miracle.

The snow came down lighter now, as they neared the hospital where Bethany had been born. The wind blew softly through the darkness and bare trees as the storm blew out to sea. The angels were close; yet still unseen. The Christmas Eve bells chimed in the Baptist church steeple as they passed by, Pastor Todd's way of celebrating the safe return of such a sweet child.

Indeed, there was hope in the world.

Merry Beth and Debbie knew where to look…

Upward and…

Inward.

* * * * *

Merry Beth, Debbie, Detective Longwood, Deputy Hugh Masters and two F.B.I. Agents all hurried through the sliding doors to the emergency room at the same time, and rushed towards the registration desk. They all started to speak at once and the pretty nurse held up her hand to quiet the anxious crowd.

Just as Detective Longwood moved closer to ask the young nurse behind the station for information, Mitch walked slowly towards them carrying a sleeping and safe and unhurt Bethany in his arms. She was wrapped in a warm white blanket.

Merry Beth held her breath in and let her tears of relief fall, as he placed Bethany safely in her arms. "She's safe; she wasn't touched or hurt in any way, Mrs. Waters. She's okay."

Mitch wasn't smiling and he wiped his own tears away, as he turned to walk away with a heavy heart and bent shoulders.

Merry Beth reached for his suede jacket sleeve in desperation, noticing for the first time it was splattered with blood. "But, what about Baron...? *Where's Baron? Why isn't he here with you? Did he help rescue my baby?*"

Debbie reached for her emotionally distraught friend and hugged both her and Bethany close. "I'm not sure if you want to hear this, Merry Beth. I can tell by the look in his eyes that the news isn't good. Please, wait until you're stronger...okay?"

"*No, tell us—please...*" Merry Beth barely heard her own whisper through her fear, as she buried her right hand in her daughter's curls. She could barely hold her with just one arm and Debbie lifted Bethany into her arms. It was so silent at that moment in the E.R. lobby that Merry Beth shivered, and hugged her own trembling body with both arms. Her broken left arm throbbed with pain, the pills she'd taken hours ago long worn off.

Merry Beth met Mitch's red-rimmed eyes to quietly beg, "Just tell us he's alive...please..."

Mitch turned back long enough to whisper without looking in her eyes, "He's dead. He didn't make it, I'm sorry."

Suddenly, there didn't seem to be enough air to breathe in. There didn't seem to be any answers why. There didn't seem to be any reason to smile, except for the love and forgiveness of her Savior, and the precious little girl Debbie held tightly yet safely in her shaking arms. Everyone around Merry Beth turned gray as the light went out, like they were standing inside a thick fog. Merry Beth's knees buckled and four men reached for her at the same time so she wouldn't fall to the vinyl floor and hurt herself in any way.

Baron was dead.

How could this be?

Debbie began to sob quietly in Bethany's hair.

Merry Beth let the darkness carry her away, as she fell inside the creamy world called unconsciousness.

The dream of the three of them being a family was over.

The dream of Baron ever kissing her again was over.

Baron loved her, yet it was still over.

Mitch shook his head in regret and walked away.

Detective Longwood's legs gave way as two nurses and two paramedics lifted Merry Beth up onto a stretcher, and he fell in a flop in one of the chairs near the registration desk in shock. There were no words at that moment.

The sheriff rushed inside the lobby, as his deputy and the F.B.I. Agents reached for their ringing cell phones at the same time—turning away in different directions.

The snow continued to fall softly outside, dreams died in.

Hope withered away, for now. Guardian angels wept.

Mitch disappeared inside his own grief and pain.

Pastor Todd rushed inside; his sister-in-law wept in his arms in seconds, still holding a sleeping and safe Bethany in her trembling arms. Baron was gone, and the little town of Winterville, Maine stood silent and still with grief, never again to be the same.

Chapter Sixteen

Winterville, Christmas Eve, Merry Beth's apartment, 4:22 p.m.

LIFE MOVED ON. Merry Beth couldn't believe it had been two years already. Two years of healing. Two years of letting go. Two years of searching for answers. Two years of new beginnings. Two years of constant prayer and soul-searching. Through all the pain, grief, healing and growing—her faith had been strengthened. She trusted in her Lord for everything.

Christmas was a season of hope and miracles, peace and forgiveness, family unity and smiles, mistletoe and garland, blinking lights and pine trees, gifts from the heart and love. Yes, it was true. Christmas was the other side of sadness and loss. Because Christmas was all about the birth of the Savior, so long ago in Bethlehem's manger; Jesus—God's only Son.

It was hard to believe that it had already been two years since that fateful night; the night when Merry Beth had gained so much yet lost the man she still loved with her whole heart.

"Mommy—tell me one more time why the *President* was there at Mr. Williams funeral," Bethany asked, as she lifted the butter knife from the thick and delicious white frosting bowl.

Merry Beth smiled at her daughter's question, as they finished icing thirty cupcakes with white icing and red-and-green sprinkles. She'd only asked the very same question a thousand times in the last two years, and every time Merry Beth answered it, a little bit of sadness lingered near.

After all, she and Baron had only shared one kiss—one magical, special, earth-shattering and unforgettable kiss. A kiss she remembered as if it had happened just yesterday. Sometimes, she could swear she could still feel Baron's lips on hers, so warm and giving and binding. The letter he'd written to her was tucked away safely in her heart, as well as in her jewelry box upstairs. She wore the stunning angel pin he'd sent her every day since his death, Christmas Eve…a happy yet sad time in her heart—for she still loved him. She still saw his smile in her dreams.

Christmas was once more, in their house, a blessed time filled with fun and surprises, pretty blinking lights, pine wreaths, jingle bells, decorated pine tree, glittery angels, dancing lit candles, wrapped presents, birthday's—Jesus' and Bethany's both.

"The President was there because Baron was a true hero, honey. He not only helped to save your life, but he helped a lot of very bad people go to prison."

Merry Beth began placing the cupcakes in the long pink box Debbie had given her earlier that day. "You want to sprinkle the next batch? It's the last one—twenty-four more, and then that's it. They smell and look delicious, don't they?"

"I guess so. Mommy, tell me one more time why they put a United States American flag over his coffin?" Bethany asked, as she turned to the kitchen table and inspected the rows of salads, breads, cakes, brownies, chips, dips, pickles, olives, celery sticks, carrot sticks, cheeses, ham, turkey, salami and roast beef.

"There's enough food here to feed an entire Army!" Bethany giggled and said, "Oh, I mean *Navy*," she plopped three green olives in her mouth with a smile to add, "...and Pastor Todd and Mrs. Thomas hasn't even brought over all her goodies yet!"

"Baron was a military man, honey—and yes, *Navy!* He was a hero to so many, and he was brave and strong and very courageous to us. Men like that are buried with honor and dignity and pride in our nation's Capital cemetery, always with a flag covered coffin."

Merry Beth no longer cried when she thought or spoke of Baron. She only smiled, even though it still hurt a lot to remember his beautiful, creamy black-turned-gray eyes. It had taken months after his death before hope had been reborn in her shattered heart. Trusting in God had led her back to the foot of the cross, where she'd found the peace she needed to go on without the man she'd fallen so hard and so fast and so deeply in love with.

"Why did they have to bury him so far away, Mommy? We can't ever put pretty flowers on his grave like we can daddy, Grandma and Grandpa, and Grandmother Waters' graves."

Bethany jumped down from the kitchen table where she'd been working on finishing her 'shining star' earlier, the homemade star she was going to hold up during the Christmas play at the church in less than three hours. She and Marie had picked straws to decide which one would this year; she had won.

"I miss him, Mommy...when can we go and visit his grave?"

Merry Beth licked her sticky fingers. "He's buried there because military heroes, men and women who've died that served our country in any war or any way, are buried at Arlington National Cemetery, honey. He was buried next to his wife and son. Just as I'm sure he wanted." She smiled as she glanced in her oven at the third batch of cooking cupcakes.

"They smell good, Mommy."

"They're almost done. I love the smell of baked goodies on the holidays." Merry Beth buried her hands in the hot sudsy water and started the long chore of cleaning up her kitchen.

"And, how old am I gonnaah be tomorrow, Mom?" Bethany asked with a teasing grin. She walked to the sinks and offered, "You wash; I'll rinse." Mother and daughter worked side-by-side washing and rinsing their dirty dishes.

Bethany asked, grinning, "Come on, Mom—how old?"

"Let me see—I think you'll be," Merry Beth rolled her eyes towards the ceiling like she was counting the years in her head. "*...eight! I can't believe it. My baby's going to be eight!* Wow, how is this possible? And you're so pretty and smart and sweet—except for when I want you to clean up your messy room. I love you, baby, so much—through the good and the bad times—you can always count on me, honey. I'll always be here for you."

Bethany laughed and nudged her mother's left rib cage playfully. "I love you, too, Mom. But, I'm *not* a baby!"

Merry Beth placed clean silverware in the sink for Bethany to rinse. "I love you forever and..."

As always Bethany finished, "...always."

Minutes later, as mother and daughter iced the third and last batch of cupcakes Bethany whispered, "I miss him, Mom."

Merry Beth smiled, despite the way her heart saddened a little. "I do too, baby. I do, too."

Bethany, young yet growing up, often called her mother *mom* instead of *mommy* lately. For months after her kidnapping she'd had terrible nightmares, every night. Now, they were a thing of the past. She remembered little of the brave man who'd helped rescue and save her from that *bad man*, the hero who'd saved both her and her mother from her grandpa's wrecked car, the nice man who'd called her Munchkin, the man her mother cried about often because she missed and loved him. And, with all of her young heart she missed and loved him as much. She saw him in her dream last night; he'd been smiling, and couldn't help but wonder what that meant.

"Mom, can I have a cupcake?"

"No; not yet…"

"Ah, but Mom…"

"Don't *but Mom* me, young lady!"

Bethany giggled as her mother splashed sudsy water all over her. "You're getting me all wet!"

Merry Beth laughed when her daughter sprayed her with water from the running faucet. "I know—isn't it fun?"

"Yes, Mom—loads and loads of fun!"

In seconds they were both drenched from head to toe with sudsy water, laughing and hugging each other close. Their guardian angels smiled as they watched; each knowing it was time for another Christmas Eve miracle…

* * * * *

Debbie walked up to Merry Beth with a warm smile and gave her a bear hug. The church was filling fast and it was only twenty-to-seven. "How you doing, love? Are you okay?" She searched her best friend's eyes with concern.

"Oh, Debbie, you look wonderful."

Debbie smiled. "You do, too. I *love* these dresses you made for us. They're very beautiful. Thank you, Merry Beth. I thought that tonight, being the night of the shooting, you'd be sad, but just look at you—you're glowing!"

"I am not! You're so silly." Merry Beth smiled back at her best friend. "I'm fine, so you can stop worrying." She glanced at Debbie's green-velvet floor-length gown with a smile. Her eyes sparkled with hope and new beginnings. Every day to Merry Beth was a new beginning, and she knew she was loved. Mitch told her it was the last thing Baron had ever said to him—that he'd loved her. It meant everything to her to know that.

"Everything looks *fabulous!* The angel costumes are fantastic, as usual—I love how you sewed those silver sequins on the skirts and wings, that star that Bethany and Lisa made is beautiful, and everyone's here except Jason, Steven and Shane," Debbie informed, a little nervous yet happy.

Her chocolate brown eyes danced as she added, "I can't believe that Steven and Shane are seniors in high school now. When they graduate, we'll have to replace them in the play. They'll be off to college before we know it, just like Jason. It's hard to believe that my boy is a sophomore in college, and Shane might join the Army!"

"They'll be here—stop worrying. You do this every year just before the children come out to line up to sing their songs. And every year this Christmas play and concert is a smashing success! Besides, we're not here to please anyone. We're doing all of this to worship God and thank Him for sending Jesus to earth so He could be our Savior—when we put all our trust and faith in Him," Merry Beth said in one breath. She took in a huge gulp of air and smiled at her best friend. What would she ever do without her? She couldn't help it and tears filled her eyes.

They hugged, each remembering this night two years ago.

Debbie and Merry Beth turned in unison to glance over the stage that was set to look like a barn across the pulpit. This year they tempted tradition and decided to use real animals.

Merry Beth stared at the beauty of the scene throughout the knotty-pine church—the red, green-and-white candles in every church windowpane were lit. The lights had been turned down low. The church's pews were filling fast. The donkey and lamb and cow were in place. Pastor Todd, now Debbie's fiancé, stood in the balcony ready to run the spotlights. The graceful Christmas hymns were playing softly in the background by the church's organist, Lovina Cochran. The pine and straw in the stable setting filled the air all around them with their heavenly strong scent, and both women smiled from within.

"Do you still miss him?" Debbie asked softly, as she hugged her best friend to her right side.

"Very much," Merry Beth whispered, returning the hug.

"Do you still love him?" Debbie asked next.

"Very much," Merry Beth turned away to hide her tears.

Debbie held hers back and tried hard to smile. "We better get moving. It's almost time to start. You go give the welcoming speech to the congregation and I'll line the children up to take their places." The women hugged close once more before they turned away in different directions.

"Everything will be okay, you'll see," Debbie promised.

"Thanks, Debbie. Love you," Merry Beth whispered.

Debbie blew her best friend a kiss, her dark eyes clouded with sad tears. "I love you, too!"

* * * * *

He glanced at his gold Rolex and smiled as he walked in the back of the crowded church. He was right on time, 6:58 p.m. Well almost, for he was—actually—two years late.

He sighed with relief of finally being here, and excused himself as he worked his way through the crowded back pew on the right. There was one empty seat on the far end and he smiled once more as he sat. He searched the crowd for her and frowned when she was nowhere in sight. He spotted several old friends—eleven in all, with their wives sitting throughout the auditorium and smiled. It'd be good to see his old SEAL Team buddies again.

Today was the day he'd been waiting for.

Today it was all so clear to see.

The sacrifices he'd made.

The lies he'd told to keep them safe.

The part he'd played in the deceit to keep them alive.

The love he felt in his heart for her and her daughter.

Would soon be all revealed, on Christmas Eve.

It was like the moment he'd been truly born again—when he'd trusted in the Savior; a year ago on this night, another miracle come true. He glanced up front of the little country church as the lights went dark. A spotlight shone above his head and he watched and listened in silence with hope in his heart...

"Welcome, ladies, gentlemen, children, members and visitors alike. My name is Mrs. Debbie Thomas and my fiancé, Pastor Todd, and I want to welcome you to God's house on this special night.

"Without the miracle of Christmas, none of us would have hope for eternal life in heaven. Mrs. Merry Beth Waters has a few words to say before we start. Merry Beth..." Debbie smiled at her best friend as Merry Beth quietly stepped from the darkened shadows to walk towards the podium and microphone to the far left of the quiet-as-a-mouse church.

Merry Beth wore a floor-length red-velvet gown that sparkled with silver sequins on the sleeves and collar. She wore silver high heels and her fiery hair was tied on top of her head with a silver ribbon. Her silver-star earrings sparkled in the spotlight, and she smiled as she walked slowly towards the microphone on confident legs. She was beautiful, inside and out. The entire town of Winterville loved her to pieces.

This was the moment he'd dreamed about. For two years he'd waited for this...

He watched her from the back pew and held his breath on every movement she made, drinking in her beauty and radiance and sparkle. Soon, soon he'd look into those warm emerald eyes again and pull her close. Close enough so she'd be in his life for the rest of his days. God only knew how much he loved her. God only knew how much he'd waited for this exact moment. He'd sacrificed all…everything for this moment, even his own name.

"Good evening family and friends, members and visitors. I just wanted to take a moment before the children come out to welcome you to their program tonight. As we did the last two years, my daughter, Hope Bethany, and I want to invite you all to come to our apartment after the service is over for fellowship and good food, music and laughter, and gift swapping…"

The crowd went wild with cheers, claps and whistles. When they quieted she continued, "Now, most of you remember what happened two years ago on this night, when my daughter was snatched away by that terrible stranger inside Wal-Mart. To this day, we thank God for the wonderful miracle of bringing her home safely…"

She paused for a moment, remembering Baron's last words. Tears burned the back of her eyes. "And for the third time we—Bethany, her friends and I dedicate this entire evening, not only to God above for His wonderful mercies and love and forgiveness, but to the man who helped save my daughter's life— the late Lieutenant Corporal, Baron Michael Williams.

"The children also want to dedicate this service to the thousands of missing children worldwide. After the service a special offering will be taken, and the money will be given to different programs throughout our state of Maine for the *missing and exploited children's network*. Thank you all very much for coming. Enjoy and, Merry Christmas."

Baron let out his breath as the spotlight went off of Merry Beth towards the back of the church behind him. His heart over-flowed with love for her at that moment. He couldn't believe he was actually here, seeing her and hearing her voice in person. He'd dreamt about this moment for two years! Without Mitch and Mac's help, he'd still be dead. Every head turned in unison to watch the beginning of the play. His heart beat so fast he was sure the people around him could hear it.

In seconds, six young girls and six young boys walked into the auditorium, all wearing soft white cotton robes with red collars. They each wore black shoes that shined in the spotlight. Merry Beth smiled as they took their places in front of the church, in front of the staged hay-filled stable. He sucked in his breath again. She was so beautiful. He knew he'd never get enough…

Merry Beth took her place and signaled for Pastor Todd to start the tape. Soft music filled the air as Debbie read from the Bible, "Now the birth of Jesus Christ was on the wise: When as his mother Mary was espoused to Joseph, before they came together, she was found with child of the Holy Ghost. Then Joseph her husband, being a just *man*, and not willing to make her a public example, was minded to put her away privily. But while he thought on these things, behold, the angel of the Lord appeared unto him in a dream, saying…"

The spotlight immediately moved to the far right where the young girl named Marie, who was dressed in her angel costume of white, gold and silver wings, stepped quietly to another microphone to say her piece.

"Joseph, thou son of David, fear not to take unto thee Mary thy wife: for that which is conceived in her is of the Holy Ghost. And she shall bring forth a son, and thou shalt call his name JESUS: for he shall save his people from their sins."

The spotlight moved once more on Debbie. "Now all this was done, that it might be fulfilled which was spoken of the LORD by the prophet saying, Behold, a virgin shall be with child, and shall bring forth a son, and they shall call his name Emmanuel, which being interpreted is, God with us."

The spotlight moved over to Merry Beth and the twelve children. Merry Beth smiled as she led the twelve children through their songs of "Silent Night," "O Little Town of Bethlehem," and "We Three Kings."

Baron smiled. So, his pretty flour-snowbird could sing! After the children finished their hymns the spotlight went out. The dancing light from the twelve candles in the twelve window-panes filled the darkness with promise and hope for a better tomorrow and brighter future, and Baron felt at peace.

When the spotlight came on once more the children had taken their places around the staged stable. Joseph, played by Shane—a young man who'd already enlisted in the Army, stood close to Mary, played by a sixteen-year-old young woman named Kristi—Debbie's daughter. Joseph helped Mary up the stairs and she lay down in the hay near the cow, dressed to look as if heavy with child.

Debbie began reading once more. "And Joseph also went up from Galilee, out of the city of Nazareth, into Judea, unto the city of David, which is called Bethlehem; (because he was of the house and lineage of David:) To be taxed with Mary his espoused wife, being great with child. And so it was, that, while they were there, the days were accomplished that she should be delivered."

The spotlight went out for a moment and when it came back on Mary was holding the baby Jesus in her arms, a make believe baby-doll, and Joseph was scooting down on one knee over her shoulder. Debbie began reading once more.

"And she brought forth her firstborn son, and wrapped him in swaddling clothes, and laid him in a manger; because there was no room for them in the inn." As she said the next verses three young boys, all ages twelve, Patrick, Joshua and Ryan, walked down the center aisle of the church towards the front. They were dressed in black-and-white cloth and all carried shepherd's staffs.

"And there were in the same country shepherds abiding in the field, keeping watch over their flock by night. And, lo, the angel of the Lord came upon them, and the glory of the Lord shone round about them: and they were sore afraid. And the angel said unto them…"

Once more the spotlight moved to the little girl named Marie. "Fear not: for, behold, I bring you good tidings of great joy, which shall be to all people. For unto you is born this day in the city of David a Savior, which is Christ the Lord. And this shall be a sign unto you; Ye shall find the babe wrapped in swaddling clothes, lying in a manger."

Baron watched in wonder, his heart filled with awe.

As Debbie read the next Bible verse twenty children came from the right and left and center aisles of the back of the church and walked towards the front. They were all dressed in soft white cotton angel costumes with sparkling silver wings. "And suddenly there was with the angel a multitude of the heavenly host praising God, and saying…"

All twenty children said at once as they joined Marie at the front of the church, "Glory to God in the highest and on earth peace, good will toward men."

The spotlight shined on the three shepherds and Patrick said, "Let us now go even unto Bethlehem."

The second shepherd, Ryan, added his part. "And see this thing which is come to pass."

The third shepherd, Joshua, said, "Which the Lord has made known unto us."

Baron's eyes searched the angels. Where was the Munchkin?

The three shepherds turned towards the staged stable and walked up the steps to where Joseph and Mary looked down on baby Jesus.

Baron had prayed a thousand prayers in the last two years. He was at peace with himself and at peace with God. Tears rolled down his cheeks. He knew he would rather be right here in this little country church than anywhere else on earth on this night.

The spotlight shined on Debbie once more as she continued to read the Bible. "When Herod the king had heard *these things*, he was troubled, and all Jerusalem with him. And when he had gathered all the chief priests and scribes of the people together, he demanded of them where Christ should be born. And they said unto him, In Bethlehem of Judea: for thus it is written by the prophet, And thou Bethlehem *in* the land of Juda, art not the least among the princes of Juda: for out of thee shall come a Governor, that shall rule my people Israel. Then Herod, when he had privily called the wise men, inquired of them diligently what time the star appeared. And he sent them to Bethlehem, and said..."

The spotlight moved to the far left of the church where a young man by the name of Jason—Debbie's son who was home for Christmas break from college, dressed like a king with a golden crown, said to three boys dressed in fancy cloth of gold, silver and purple, "Go and search diligently for the young child; and when ye have found *him,* bring me word again, that I may come and worship him also."

The three boys playing the parts of the three wise men walked quickly towards the back of the church in the darkness where Bethany waited quietly holding her bright yellow star.

The spotlight moved to Debbie once more. "When they had heard the king, they departed; and, lo, the star, which they saw in the east, went before them, till it came and stood over where the young child was."

Bethany held up her shiny and sparkling, sequined star above her head as she proudly walked down the center aisle. The three wise men followed her down and up onto the pulpit where the shepherds, Joseph, Mary and baby Jesus were.

Debbie continued her reading. "When they saw the star, they rejoiced with exceeding great joy. And when they were come into the house, they saw the young child with Mary his mother, and fell down, and worshipped him..."

Baron couldn't take his eyes off Bethany, holding his breath least she disappear. She'd grown up a lot over the last two years. She was taller and he counted the seconds until he could lift her up into his arms and life, for the rest of his days. She was beautiful, as beautiful as her mother. She was alive, and safe!

The three boys playing the parts of the three wise men bowed down on their knees and held up their hands in prayer and worship near the baby Jesus. A camera—Baron wished he had a camera! Parents were snapping pictures left and right.

Debbie continued her reading, "...and when they had opened their treasures, they presented unto him gifts; gold, and frankincense, and myrrh."

The three young boys placed their certain gifts in front of the baby Jesus in the hay.

Baron wiped away his tears as he watched the young girl he'd given his life for, literally, to keep both her and her mother safe. She was so young and so innocent and so pretty, as he knew she would be. And Merry Beth—well, she'd stolen his heart over two years before. Did she still hold it in her hands? Now was the time to get his life back. Tonight, on Christmas Eve!

Bethany, Marie and the twenty other angels', Lisa included, all moved behind Joseph, Mary, baby Jesus, the shepherds and wise men and stood in an open circle. Bethany stood in the middle holding up her bright star. The spotlight shined from the silver sequins and the crowd throughout the church rose to their feet, clapped, whistled and cheered, Baron included.

As the crowd quieted and sat, the spotlight moved on Debbie once more as she read from the Bible. "And being warned of God in a dream that they should not return to Herod, they departed into their own country another way."

All the children came out and stood together on the pulpit. Merry Beth took her place down front and guided all the children in singing "Away in a Manger."

After the hymn was finished, Merry Beth and Debbie stood side by side in the front of the church, and there wasn't one person left sitting as the congregation exploded in praise, shouts, claps and whistles and praise.

The children's play and concert had been a smashing success. Soon, another year would be a thing of the past. Soon, another Christmas day would be over. It was time to move on, time to let go of old memories and start making new ones. Baron smiled as he exited the church unnoticed; to everyone but God. His steps were hurried as he rushed to his truck. As he sat in his warming truck in the shadows the night created, watching and waiting through the falling snow for Merry Beth and Bethany to come out…he prayed, thanking God for his new life.

* * * * *

It was just past ten p.m., and Christmas Eve was a perfect time for a new beginning. Would they open their door and hearts and let him in, or would they send him quickly on his away—hurt because he'd deceived them? He'd waited until the last guest had left. He'd waited until all was quiet once more around the apartment building. He now stood on their slippery and snow-packed front porch with the light snowflakes falling gracefully all around him.

He stood there and stared at the dozens of beautiful red, green, yellow, blue-and-white Christmas lights blinking on and off in all the trees and bushes all over the yard and up and down the long driveway, all the way to the street, on fences and past her mail box. He'd never seen anything like it in his life.

Were the lights a sure sign that Merry Beth and Bethany were still waiting for his return? He frowned slightly, knowing they thought he was dead. Would they forgive him once they knew his motive; the truth that kept them safe and alive?

Snowflakes fell on his black leather jacket shoulders and black Stetson, the light and fluffy kind, the kind that melted the second they landed, and his right hand shook as he slowly lifted it to ring the golden doorbell.

Would Merry Beth welcome him in her home, in her arms, in her heart and life again? Or would she slam the door in his face and send him packing? He knew he deserved that. He prayed she'd be able to forgive him and welcome him home with open arms instead. He needed her—like needing the air to breathe. He loved her.

"Mom, someone's at the door!" Bethany yelled, as she raced quickly towards the front door from the kitchen where she helped her mother wash pans and dishes. "Maybe Ms. Debbie changed her mind about Lisa spending the night!"

"Wait until you see who it is before you open the door, Bethany! *I mean it, and no running in the house!*" Merry Beth warned, as she buried her hands in hot sudsy dishwater to finish off the remaining dirty dishes.

Somewhere there was a gentle stream looking for a raging river—in Maine there were plenty of those. Somewhere there was a quiet dreamer looking for a new and stronger dream—in Baron's thundering heart there was only one. Somewhere there was a drifter looking for his way back home—in Baron's heart he'd finally found that in Merry Beth's emerald *trusting* eyes.

Was Merry Beth waiting to hear Baron say…'I believe in you and me, Merry Beth—please, don't turn me away. I love you. I want to come home.'?

Bethany screamed when she opened the front door and stared up into Baron's black eyes. In seconds Merry Beth came quickly running from the kitchen. "*Bethany! What is it? What's wrong, honey? I told you not to open the door until you…*"

When Merry Beth saw who was standing on her front porch holding two-dozen roses in his arms, her steps froze and she paled to a ghostly white, swaying on her feet. She knew she would have fallen to the bare yet shiny floor if strong hands hadn't quickly reached out for her.

Baron immediately reached out, steadying her weakening knees. "Hello, my pretty flour-snowbird. How I've missed you…" he quietly whispered, huskily, as he stepped inside her warm and cozy, welcoming home. He placed a dozen red roses in Merry Beth's arms and a yellow dozen in Bethany's.

"...and for you, my Munchkin—happy eighth birthday."

It was warm now, safe now. He was home. He knew it was true, he saw it in Merry Beth's tear-filled, grass-green eyes. There was no anger. But there was hurt and questions and shock. He hoped she'd give him the chance to say the words before she sent him packing, back out into the bitter wind and fluffy snow.

Bethany clapped her hands, threw herself at him and hugged him tight around his waist, crushing the flowers. "You're alive! Oh, man—*this is so...way...cool!* Lisa's gonna *freak!*"

"No...it can't be. You're...you're...you're *dead,*" Merry Beth whispered as she stepped slowly closer to look into his eyes.

Bethany hugged him around his waist with enough force to knock him several steps backwards. He hugged the young girl tight with both his strong arms and bent down to kiss the top of her carrot-top, red head. "Actually, it's true. I am dead."

Bethany passed him a weird look and shouted, eyes dancing with excitement, "I *told* you, Mom...that he would come back!"

Tears clouded Merry Beth's vision and he winced, hating that he'd hurt her this way. "Merry Beth—are you all right? Am I welcome here? I've waited to come home, for over two years..."

Christmas Eve was indeed a wonderful time for coming home, his ebony eyes silently begged for it, as he waited for her answer. His heart pounded in his ears, like native drums.

Bethany glanced up through her own happy tears and shouted, "It's a *true* Christmas miracle, Mom. Mr. Baron Williams has found his way home. I told you and *told* you a hundred times he would. You just didn't have enough faith, Mom!" She stared up at him through smiles and tears and asked, "Can I call you dad? I've always wanted a real live *earth* daddy?"

Baron lifted Bethany up into his strong and massive arms and whispered in her fiery curls, "I'd love that, Munchkin—if it's all right with your beautiful, yet much too pale mother."

Merry Beth stepped closer, real close, and stared into Baron's midnight black eyes. She was so close she felt his breath on her cheek, she smelled his rich aftershave; she saw the sweat on his brow. His eyes had turned gray and were now filled with tears. She slowly reached up and touched his left cheek and asked, "How is this possible?"

"Mom—I told you! It's a true Christmas miracle!" Bethany exclaimed, as she rolled her eyes and hugged Baron's neck tight when he picked her up in his massive arms.

"I told you I'd make it back for Christmas Eve. Well, my pretty flour-snowbird, here I am. Alive and breathing and…" He lowered Bethany to the shiny floor and bravely reached for Merry Beth, and pulled her close to his chest.

There wasn't even a breath of air between them as he whispered close, "I love you, Merry Beth. Will you marry me?"

He reached inside his black leather jacket vest pocket and opened a little black jeweler's box, and slowly placed a stunning Champagne colored, one-carat, diamond engagement ring on her left hand when he saw the answer in her emerald eyes.

He smiled. "Say something, Merry Beth…"

"How…? Why…?" Her eyes darkened and she swallowed against her hurt. "You lied to me and Bethany, why?"

Bethany stared at her mother in shock. Then she rolled her eyes to the ceiling and yelled, *"Mooooom!"*

Merry Beth's heart beat so fast she felt dizzy.

The muscles in his face twitched yet his smile never wavered. "Everything I've done is to keep you both safe, and alive. The only regret I have is hurting either one of you when they told you I died."

Bethany glanced at her mother and rolled her glassy eyes again. *"Moooom,* it's okay—*he's back!* Don't you get it? We're a *real* family now! *This* is my Christmas wish come true!"

"I d…don't u…understand," Merry Beth whispered, not quite believing he was alive and here, yet she didn't step away. She lifted her left hand to his face; her fingers trembled. Her tear-filled eyes weren't on the beautiful ring. They were glued to his black-turned-gray tear-filled eyes.

"I had to die, Merry Beth." He glanced down at Bethany hanging on to his waist for dear life. "I had to fake my death so I could come back to you both and *never* worry about any dangers coming out of the shadows of my past to *ever* hurt either one of you, in any way again. Washington thinks I'm dead, legally I am. I can never use my real name again. You are now engaged to Chance Edward Mellows…aren't you?"

He leaned in, enjoying the smells of honey and pine, and softly whispered, "Tell me we're engaged, sweetheart. Tell me you love me. Your eyes say you do. Please, say something…"

Merry Beth searched for the truth in his dark ebony eyes and saw wanting, needing, pleading; love. His eyes were now a wolf-gray and filled with passion and love. Yes! Baron was alive; Baron was back! He still loved her!

Bethany rolled her eyes again. "*Moooom!* This is the part where you're supposed to say *yes!* What cha waiting for?" She grabbed her mother's left hand and screamed, "*Wow, what a rock!*"

Merry Beth lifted both of her arms and hugged Baron around his neck. "I don't understand it or even want to try, but *yes! I'll marry you! I love you!* I have for over two years!"

"Well, it's about time! Oh, this is way cool. I gottaah go call Lisa!" Bethany yelled over her shoulder, as she quickly rushed off towards the kitchen phone to call her best friend.

Merry Beth glanced at her daughter's receding back and smiled. "*We* love you, Baron, so much. Welcome home, darling. I've kept the lights on for you."

Baron pulled her close and they hugged each other for several earth-shattering quiet minutes. When Merry Beth lifted her head from his chest she smiled and whispered, "I love you."

"And I love you." Baron glanced down at Merry Beth's feet and smiled when he noticed she was wearing the new black leather boots he'd sent to her over two years ago. "I see that they fit; that's great. You look wonderful, honey."

He lifted his right hand and lightly touched her rosy left cheek, and whispered, "You're so soft, so pretty, so alive…" He lightly kissed her left temple.

She trembled in his arms. "I can't believe you're alive, you're real, and you're really here…oh, my…"

He whispered, as he buried his face in her curly masses, "The cuts and bruises from that accident are long gone now. Only God knows how good it feels to hold you in my arms like this."

Bethany rushed back to the foyer. "They're not home yet. Man, on man—this is the coolest miracle yet, Mom!"

Merry Beth glanced at her pretty ring for the first time. "Yes, I'm sure." Her eyes lifted to Baron's. "This ring…it's very beautiful. I love it, but I love *you* more."

Baron glanced at Bethany and smiled when he saw she was wearing the golden heart locket he'd sent to her in the same package with the black boots. She lifted her yellow roses to her face and breathed in their rich, silky scent. "Thank you for these roses. They're way cool. I love them, and *you!*"

Merry Beth enjoyed the sight and smell of her red roses. "Flowers in the dead of winter, a miracle…is this a dream?"

Merry Beth cried out when her daughter pinched her hard on her right hand. "Ouch—hey…that hurt!"

Bethany laughed. "Nope, it's for real, Mom."

Baron pulled Merry Beth and Bethany close in a group hug and whispered in Merry Beth's red curls, teasing her, "I see you both couldn't wait until I got home before you opened your gifts. Got any left for me under your tree?"

Merry Beth and Bethany smiled as they led Baron into the living room where his gifts waited under their Christmas tree for him to come home, from two years before. There truly was no place like home, even though Maine was far from Kansas. Baron was at peace with his past, home at last. Merry Beth was a happy newly engaged woman, in love. Bethany loved her new *earth* daddy, as no other.

Psalms 1:1-6 "BLESSED *is* the man that walketh not in the counsel of the ungodly, nor standeth in the way of sinners, nor sitteth in the seat of the scornful. But his delight *is* in the law of the LORD; and in his law doth he meditate day and night. And he shall be like a tree planted by the rivers of water, that bringeth forth his fruit in his season; his leaf also shall not wither; and whatsoever he doeth shall prosper. The ungodly *are* not so: but *are* like the chaff which the wind driveth away. Therefore the ungodly shall not stand in the judgement, nor sinners in the congregation of the righteous. For the LORD knoweth the way of the righteous: but the way of the ungodly shall perish."

Epilogue

July 22nd, present day, Fort Kent, Maine…

BARON STOOD AT the edge of the north field and glanced out over the potato fields with overwhelming pride. All together there were four fields of rich whisky-brown earth, around twenty acres in all, bearing forth row after row of growing *Maine* potatoes.

What a conformation from Navy SEAL to Assistant D.A. to State Police Officer to potato farmer, and he chuckled; wondering what his *friends* from his Navy SEAL Team would say if they could see him now. He hadn't seen any of them since after Christmas, and missed them very much. The happy reunion with them on New Year's Day, after his resurrection on Christmas Eve had been bittersweet. They, Mitch and his wife were the only ones, besides Merry Beth and Bethany of course, who now knew he was alive.

Chance and Merry Beth Mellows; he still couldn't get used to their new names. They were married on February the fourteenth, Valentine's Day.

Baron, Merry Beth and Bethany had moved to the Fort Kent area and bought and moved in to their new four-bedroom log cabin on the banks of the sparkling St. John River. Their next-door neighbors' were Mitch and Carolyn. Mitch and Baron were business partners in the potato industry, growing and selling potatoes statewide. It was exciting—this new life God had granted Baron and Merry Beth, Mitch and Carolyn.

It was a new life each one thanked God for daily. New beginnings came hard in this cold and uncaring world, miracles few and far between. When they come it's important to grab hold, and never let go. He knew that first hand.

There had been no signs of trouble—but then again, there wouldn't be for a dead man. Merry Beth and Bethany had conveyed back and forth from Fort Kent and Winterville five days a week to continue teaching and schooling from February until the beginning of June. When school started up again in September,

Merry Beth would continue her teaching in the Fort Kent Elementary School District where both she and Bethany had been transferred.

Life was good, safe. Trusting in God came easy when you relied on your faith to see you through each day. Baron didn't miss his past life, and savored every moment of his new. His heart stopped pumping at the sound of his daughter's tone as she rushed to his side across the fields at lightning speed.

Something was wrong. His daughter was running towards him like the devil himself chased her.

"*Dad, come quick! It's Mom!*" Bethany screamed, as she ran over the north pasture hill about a hundred yards away from where he stood glancing at the earth's whisky-brown dirt. The tone of her frightened voice made the warm blood in Baron's veins turn to ice chips. His heart literally stopped. His breathing became shallow and he paled to a ghostly white, fearful something terrible from his past had finally caught up with them again. For some reason his legs wouldn't move.

Baron turned quickly and watched as his daughter ran full force across the field as fast as her little legs would carry her, fear screaming forth from her little legs with every step.

He took off on a dead run towards her in a quick panic of uncertainty and trepidation. "*What is it? What's wrong?*"

Merry Beth was almost five months pregnant and the thought that she was losing or had lost the baby made him feel nauseous—he silently prayed at that very moment for God to place His hand on their unborn child and keep him or her and his wife safe, and alive!

Father and daughter met as Bethany ran frantically in his out-stretched arms. "*Dad, you have to come home right now! It's Mom! She's crying! There's a bad man in our house...*"

If you have love and faith and trust that are strong enough on your side, can you still hold on to the hope that every day, in some small way, you can make the world a better place? Both Merry Beth and Baron believed this with all their hearts.

Bethany didn't even get to finish her sentence before Baron took off on a dead run towards home, calling over his shoulder, "Run to Uncle Mitch and tell him there's trouble, honey! Don't come near the house again until I come to you and say it's safe, face to face!"

"*Okay, Dad!*" Bethany started running behind her *earth* father with tear-filled eyes and a frightened heart. Her little legs couldn't keep up with him but she never stopped to catch her breath until she cleared the hill that overlooked the beautiful log cabin down by the riverbank. She watched her father running at a rapid rate towards their house and screamed for him over and over but he just kept on running.

"Dad, wait! That man, he has a rifle! Dad—be careful!"

"Go to Uncle Mitch, Bethany! Now!

Bethany swallowed her rapid panic and frightened tears and started to run as fast as she could down the steep hill. She ran towards the big red barn and hopped on her new ten-speed bike, and peddled as fast as her little legs would go to Mitch's farm less than a quarter of a mile away…

* * * * *

Down in the lovely, very modern and luscious log cabin Merry Beth was trying her best to keep the situation calm and under her control. Yet, it was next to impossible not to be scared spit-less when a man you once loathed and feared with all your heart was pointing a rifle at you, not fifteen feet away. She placed her left hand protectively over her bulging stomach, silently praying for a miracle that Bethany would find Baron in time.

"Come on, Earl—put down the rifle. This is no way to settle anything and…" Merry Beth winced when the rifle came up higher a few notches. "Don't you think it's time to get some help for yourself, Earl? There are so many different programs you could check yourself into to get help. There's Alcoholics Anonymous, therapy for sex offenders, special clinics or rehab…" She watched his eyes glare at her with hatred and contempt.

"You have ruined my life! I lost my job at the bank because of you!" Earl thundered angrily. He staggered closer in his drunken state and swore violently when he almost tripped on the black-and-white Native American style rug, in front of the huge fireplace hearth in the spacious and stylish living room.

"I've lost everything—everything. I've lost my wife, my job, my reputation—my son. You took him from me. You took him from me and filled his head with lies and deceit and turned him against me." He staggered closer and thundered, *"I've spent countless hours in jail because of you!"*

"How's it *my* fault, Earl? Don't you know that you have to account for and answer for your own actions in this life? It's not *my* fault you're a sick, twisted alcoholic who can't keep his grimy hands off women! You need help and…"

The rifle in his hand shook harder, by his trembling and unsteady hand. "Shut up! *I'm sick of your constant ramblings and lies!"*

Merry Beth took a few more steps closer to the open front-screened door. She sighed with relief when she saw Baron running down the steep hill from the north pasture, and prayed for another miracle. She didn't want anyone to get hurt, to *die* in her new home, not even Earl. Not now, not today, not ever! There'd been enough danger and violence in the past. She didn't want any of it here.

Earl took a few more steps closer to her and her bare feet froze to the beautiful shiny pine floor. "*Where do you think you're going? There's no escaping me!*"

Merry Beth now held both hands protectively in front of her unborn child and whispered through her quickening fear, "Just put the rifle down, Earl, and we'll get you into some kind of program. We'll get you the help you need. Don't you want to get well? Don't you want to try and salvage some kind of normalcy and peace in your life? Until you do—until you're completely healed and sober—*I will not allow you to come within five hundred miles of my daughter!*"

"You can't keep me from *my* one and only granddaughter any longer!" Earl thundered as he staggered closer, eyes of fire.

"I will and I can—as long as you are in this state you're in. With the sexual harassment charges and the drinking—*I will not allow you to touch or even breathe near Bethany!* Now, put that rifle down and get out of my house, Earl. Go home. Go home and sober up and get yourself some *professional help!*"

Merry Beth's knees began to shake violently and she felt sick to her stomach. But she would not back down from her ex-father-in-law. Not now, and not ever again!

"*Who's gonna ah pay for everything I've lost, Merry Beth—who?*" Earl demanded with hatred. "*I'm still a reputable man! But because of your lies no one in Winterville believes it!*"

Baron came charging through the front door like a man possessed. He immediately stepped in front of his wife to shield her from any flying bullets and slowly, gently eased her back and away towards the screened door. "Merry Beth…"

She'd immediately thrown her arms around his waist, leaned into his back and sighed with relief. "Be careful, honey—the rifle. Where's Bethany?"

"She's safe, now go outside honey. I'll take care of this."

Baron moved his hands behind him and swiftly but carefully pulled his wife's arms away from his waist and stepped closer to the door. "Go outside, Merry Beth…I'll handle this. It's okay…"

Earl snickered and stumbled a little in his drunken state. "You come to save the day? *I don't think so!*"

Baron lifted his left hand towards Earl. The gold in his wide wedding ring reflected off the lights above his head. "Take it easy, Earl. There's no need for violence. Hasn't there been enough? You're Bethany's grandfather—don't let her see you this way."

Merry Beth slowly eased towards the front door, step by slow step. "He needs help, Baron. He doesn't realize what he's doing, what he's saying!" she pleaded with a thundering heart.

"Earl—don't do this. This is my family—it could be yours, if you'd only sober up long enough to get some help!"

Baron glared across his warm and welcoming, spacious and knotty-pine living room at the man who'd threatened his family for the last time. "*Go outside, honey—now!*"

Merry Beth didn't argue and went. She wiped away tears as she rushed down the front knotty-pine porch and steps to run towards the barn. She glanced up and sighed with relief when she spotted Mitch driving quickly down their long driveway in his new Bronco pickup truck. Dirt and dust from the road clouded the air all around her as he screeched to a quickened stop ten feet away from the front of the log cabin.

She shivered with renewed fear when she saw he held a rifle firmly in his hands as he jumped down from his truck. She hurried her steps towards him and begged, "Mitch! You have to go in there and help Baron. It's my ex-father-in-law. He's been drinking again and is armed. Hurry, help Baron! Help him before he manages to get himself shot again. I can't lose him. *Bethany, my unborn baby and I can't lose him!* Not now!"

Mitch pulled her gently into his strong arms for a reassuring quick hug. "Don't you worry, honey—everything's going to be just fine, you'll see." He searched for her dark green eyes and whispered close, "Have I ever lied to you?" He swallowed back his chuckle at the expression across her face.

"Go and sit by the water. It'll be all right…I promise."

Merry Beth frowned. "Well, actually you did lie—just that one time when you told me Baron was dead. But, I've forgiven you for that; now *go, help Baron—please!*"

"You stay out here!" He passed her his cellular and quickly said, "Dial 9-1-1, just in case." He kissed her softly on her left cheek before turning away to run towards the front door. Time seemed to stand still for her after that. She couldn't stop trembling, no matter how hard she tried.

Her entire world was inside that cabin.

She couldn't lose him. Not now, not ever!

Merry Beth ran past her own Bronco, Mitch's new truck and Baron's light-blue BMW to the edge of the riverbank, and sat in one of the three red-and-white lawn-chairs that sat by the water, as her trembling legs gave way. She immediately closed her eyes in prayer after dialing 9-1-1.

"Dear Heavenly Father—please keep my husband safe and unhurt from my drunken ex father-in-law. As always I'm placing him in your hands, Lord. I'm trusting in You to keep my family safe. In your name I pray, Amen."

* * * * *

She jumped out of her skin when a hand touched her shoulder not even five minutes later, disrupting another prayer.

"Merry Beth, honey—are you all right?" Baron asked softly, as he bent down on both jeans knees in front of her and pulled her close to his rapid beating chest.

"The baby, are you both all right? You're so pale, did he hurt you?" Baron asked with concern across his tongue. He leaned real close and kissed his wife's forehead and freckled nose.

Because of this woman there were soft words and genuine touches in his life again. Because of this woman there were smiles and laughter, cheer and glee in his heart again. Because of this woman the loneliness, pain and darkness from Becky's betrayal and murder were no more lingering in his heart. The pain from losing his son eased with every breath he took.

Merry Beth opened her eyes and immediately they were clouded with glistening tears. *"Oh, Baron—honey! You're all right—you're all right!* I was so scared. What happened?" She glanced back towards their log cabin with a worried frown.

Baron sighed with relief; knowing his wife, daughter and unborn baby were safe. Together, Baron and Merry Beth watched as Mitch led a sobbing Earl Waters down the front steps of their home, as two brown sheriff cruisers came crashing to a halt near Mitch's truck with blue lights flashing.

Merry Beth added, "Looks like the Calvary is here."

Merry Beth turned away from the terrible sight and buried her face in the front of her husband's white T-shirt. It was sweaty and covered with perspiration from his work in the fields, but she didn't care. In his arms she felt safe and protected, needed and loved. He was her and Bethany's everything.

"What will they do to him? He needs help, Baron…"

349

One of the reasons he'd fallen so hard and fast in love with his wife was because she tried to help anyone in trouble—even someone who'd hurt her and humiliated her for years; someone who'd threatened her time and time again.

"I'll see to it that Earl is taken to a hospital or clinic where he can get himself checked into a rehab program to sober up. Then hopefully he'll get some counseling and therapy for his sexual harassment and drug related problems," Baron promised, as he held his weeping yet relieved wife in his arms. He breathed in her soft scent of roses and honey, sunshine and earth, savoring the feel of her close to his heart. She was safe. Bethany was safe. Their unborn baby was safe. Everything was going to be fine.

"You sure you're all right? Do you need to go to the doctor and get checked over?" Baron asked her as he searched for her eyes. He couldn't see them; there were too many tears in the way. He hated that, hated it that she cried for any reason.

Merry Beth lifted shocked eyes to her wonderful and strong husband. "*Drugs*...Earl is on drugs?"

"Yes." Baron nodded to his friend that Merry Beth was all right when Mitch started his truck and pulled away, as the two sheriffs placed Earl in the back of one of the shiny cruisers.

"Are you sure you're all right—the baby?" He searched his wife's pretty grass-green eyes for an answer and touched her bulging stomach where his baby kicked with full force.

Merry Beth smiled as she covered her husband's hand with her own. "We're fine, really."

A muscle under Baron's left eye twitched. "If he touched you in any way, I'll see to it that..."

"I'm fine. He didn't get close enough." She glanced quickly over his shoulder. "They're gone."

When she smiled at him, lifted both arms around his neck, and pulled him closer he knew everything was all right once more in his world. His family was safe and that's all that mattered to him.

"I'm fine, honey. I promise. Where's Bethany?"

"I sent her to Mitch's farm. I told her not to come back until I told her it was safe face to face. She's one brave little girl—I better go get her. I'm sure she's scared to death." He made the move to stand and walk to his new Ford truck, but Merry Beth stopped him by touching his bare right arm.

"Thank you, Baron."

He smiled. "For what, honey…?"

"Thank you for loving me, for loving our babies, for being such a wonderful friend, father and husband. I don't know what I'd do if anything ever happened to you." Tears glistened across her pretty emerald eyes as Baron pulled her closer for another reassuring hug. "You're our world, do you know that?"

He smiled. "As you three are mine."

It was a beautiful, bright sunny day, despite Earl's latest attempted attack. The Chickadees were singing happily from the many birdhouses and bird feeders in the tall pine trees scattered all around the log cabin. The flowers in Merry Beth's flower garden were in full bloom with bright colors of reds, yellows, pinks, oranges, whites and purples. The red, pink and yellow roses from her many rose bushes in front of the log cabin swayed easily in the light breeze coming across the river. The green grass under their feet was darker than the bravest emerald. The diamonds in his wedding rings caught the rays from the sun as Baron touched her face and met her lips with a soft kiss.

Before their lips touched Baron whispered close, "*You* have brought so much into my life, honey. Smiles, laughter, friendship, hope; compassion—you have taught me how to let go of my painful past, to love again, to trust again, *you* and the Munchkin. And because of you I have found my trust and faith in God; my life is now complete."

"I love you."

"And I love you."

As their lips met in another earth-shattering, over-the-fence, mind-blowing kiss, the guardian angels that had been watching over Baron, Merry Beth and Bethany for years turned and walked quietly away, down the dusty road, smiling, for now. They'd return eventually, as they always did, when danger lingered near. And it would because…

The world was, indeed, a cold and dangerous, lost place. Yet, God's love, mercy and forgiveness were stronger and much brighter.